D0438551

CURIODDITY

PAUL JENKINS

ST. MARTIN'S PRESS NEW YORK

CURIODDITY. Copyright © 2016 by Paul Jenkins. All rights reserved. Printed in the United States of America. For information, address St. Martin's Press, 175 Fifth Avenue, New York, N.Y. 10010.

www.stmartins.com

Designed by Greg Collins

Library of Congress Cataloging-in-Publication Data

Names: Jenkins, Paul, 1965– author.
Title: Curioddity / Paul Jenkins.
Description: First edition. | New York : St. Martin's Press, 2016.
Identifiers: LCCN 2016010639 | ISBN 978-1-250-02615-6 (hardcover) |
    ISBN 978-1-250-02616-3 (e-book)
Subjects: LCSH: Museums—Fiction. | Imaginary places—Fiction. | BISAC:
    FICTION / Science Fiction / General. | GSAFD: Science fiction. |
    Fantasy fiction.
Classification: LCC PS3610.E5463 C87 2016 | DDC 813/.6—dc23
LC record available at https://lccn.loc.gov/2016010639

Our books may be purchased in bulk for promotional, educational, or business use. Please contact your local bookseller or the Macmillan Corporate and Premium Sales Department at 1-800-221-7945, extension 5442, or by e-mail at MacmillanSpecialMarkets@macmillan.com.

First Edition: August 2016

10 9 8 7 6 5 4 3 2 1

For my magical wife, the "real" Melinda

Thank you for giving our two little guys the gifts of creativity and compassion.

ACKNOWLEDGMENTS

Special thanks to my friend Bill Russell, without whose support and generosity this work would never have seen completion.

Thanks also to Frank Karic for your dedication, selflessness, and sheer honesty

To Marianne de Pierres for your amazing advice.

And to Mike Homler for your belief in me.

CHAPTER ONE

WIL MORGAN awoke from his regular anxiety dream, in which he had just finished second in a World's Biggest Failure competition.

Outside the window of his one-bedroom apartment, another overcast morning grudgingly announced the start of yet another overcast week. Wil closed his eyes and considered going back to sleep. He briefly flirted with the notion that he hadn't woken up at all, and that his lumpy old bed was just a part of his dream. But it was no use—he'd long since forgotten how to escape reality by use of his imagination. This was going to be much like any other miserable Monday in his life. It would lead to a tiresome Tuesday, a woeful Wednesday, a thankless Thursday, and a forgettable Friday. Wil didn't even want to think about how dreadful the next weekend was already shaping up to be.

He groaned as he rolled out of bed. His left arm had gone back to sleep, and he silently cursed it for its good fortune. The various murmurs and screeches of the city began to filter upward through the damp fog. Wil cursed those as well, just for good measure. As always, a faint smell of mushrooms lingered throughout the apartment but Wil chose to ignore this; partly because the smell of mushrooms made him nauseous but mostly because he had neither purchased nor cooked mushrooms at any time during his entire life. Stepping over a discarded travel magazine, he trudged over to the bathroom mirror, rubbed his eyes, and stuck out his tongue. Not a good time to make eye contact with his reflection, he decided, and he hastily backed away. This particular Monday was already shaping up to set a new record for something, and whatever that something was it was probably going to be something bad. Feeling slightly empty, Wil pulled on his least rumpled set of clothing, grabbed his coat and keys, and headed for the door as a knocking sound coming from beneath his sink leveled up in intensity from mildly annoying to ever-so-slightly obnoxious.

As Wil shuffled past his apartment building's broken elevator and began to trudge down the stairs (he was good at trudging), he wondered for a moment if his devotion to endless repetition wasn't nudging him ever closer to permanent and irreversible madness. No doubt Mrs. Chappell, his landlady, would be waiting for him in the lobby of his apartment building. She would utter any one of four variations of the same pleasantry she had greeted him with since the day he'd moved in, and he would smile and issue one of his three standard responses, and be on his way before she could rally enough of her brain cells to attempt further conversation.

Wil paused on the flight of stairs before the lobby and stared at a deluded old calico cat that was attempting to sun itself on a windowsill. In the middle of the landing, a second, scruffy ginger thing was licking itself in an unmentionable place. It eyed Wil with a slightly annoyed expression that suggested it would have preferred if Wil had tripped over it and gone clattering down the final thirty steps headfirst. From below came the sound of Mrs. Chappell's rusty old voice, cooing to another of her thousand-and-one furry reprobates.

Wil steeled himself and rounded the corner. The old lady was nowhere to be seen. So far so good.

He turned his trudge into a kind of shuffle-cum-sneak, hoping Mrs. Chappell had walked back into her office or—better yet—had suddenly been rendered invisible. It was the use of this particular tactic that allowed him to make it within five feet of the front door before a voice like a sheet of forty-grit sandpaper wrapped around a kitchen knife put paid to his false sense of security.

"*Guten Morgen*, Mr. Morgan!" came the cry from behind him. "Wakey, wakey, rise and shine! The weather's fine!"

Wil gritted his teeth. Involuntarily, he dug in his pocket for his lucky English penny that he always carried with him—gripping it so hard, in fact, that he felt it digging into his skin. Might as well get it over with, he thought, as he turned to face his landlady. By now, his pained expression was morphing into a fake grin.

Mrs. Chappell stood at the far end of the lobby holding something scraggly and brownish wrapped around a pair of accusing green eyes. She had an expectant look upon her face.

"Hello, Mrs. Chappell," said Wil. "Looks like it's going to be another nice day."

He thought about adding a "don't you think?" to the end of his sentence but decided he'd stand a better chance of eliciting a response from the scraggly brown cat. The old lady was already beginning to look vacuous, and the silence was rapidly becoming awkward. With a quick wave of his hand, and not wishing to push his luck, Wil turned tail and hustled out of the front door before any further damage could be done.

❧

OUTSIDE, THE city streets were gray and sodden. Indeed, Wil often fancied this was the city where they had invented the color gray. He settled quickly into the same routine he had practiced since the day he'd arrived, which involved a large amount of trudging and a general avoidance of eye contact with anyone passing by. As he headed off to work, Wil slowly rolled his old English penny in and out of his fingers, feeling its smoothed-down edges and thinking of days long gone. And as he trudged, he allowed his mind to wander. Though not too far, just to be on the safe side.

He thought about his oh-so-predictable life and—not for the first time—he considered the meaning of his recurring dream. If the World's Biggest Failure competition had any significance at all, then why second place? Lately on his morning trudge, he'd come to the conclusion that such was the depth of his inadequacy he couldn't even finish first at finishing last. Somewhere out there was a proper failure, a memorable loser of epic proportions—someone you could look at and say, "Now there goes a real idiot!" Someone who—at the very least—possessed a spark.

Wil settled into a medium-paced trudge, which soon took him across an old stone bridge in the center of town: a decrepit former railway crossing that no local government official had ever seen fit to condemn, and that was fed by a confusing one-way system. Each passing vehicle rattled the bridge in such a way that Wil was reintroduced to every single one of his silver fillings as he crossed. Up ahead, an old brown edifice loomed on the skyline like a fungal growth of brick and mortar: the Castle Towers. Wil's office on the nineteenth floor was the only place in town where he could afford the rent, and from which he was under constant threat of eviction. He glowered at the Towers, and they glowered back at him.

It was Wil who blinked first. He sighed, feeling inadequate. If his life had a soundtrack, he imagined, it probably sounded something like this:

Trudge, trudge, trudge . . . *KLONNG.*

❦

Having successfully navigated the bridge—as he had done for innumerable consecutive weeks, rain or shine, with no days off for either sickness or vacation—Wil headed for the temporary sanctuary of his local coffee shop. The morning fog was thickening directly over his head, and the cold moisture felt like little needles on his skin. Maybe the weather was singling him out, he thought. No one else looked as cold as he did.

Lately, Wil had become more philosophical about life in general and his mediocre contribution to it in particular: So what if he was a damp squib in a world of fireworks? It may well be, he thought, that people always remember bottle rockets that accidentally explode and no one remembers the cheap ones that are left out in the rain. But at least a man living a soggy and boring life would get to the end of it relatively intact. No, he decided, he wasn't going mad. Insane people were those who made the same mistakes with the expectation of a different result. Wil had lowered his expectations to the point where he could comfortably go about his daily routine and anticipate only minimal success.

He paused at the front entrance of the aptly and unimaginatively named Mug O' Joe's, letting the bitter aromas and the whoosh of the latte machines wash around him. If there was an isolated pool of happiness in his world, it was at Mug O' Joe's, where he could be found dipping his toes on a daily—and sometimes hourly—basis.

Exactly the same people seemed to be scurrying in and out of Mug O' Joe's as had been scurrying in and out of it since it had been named Koffee Korner and before that, the short-lived Ye Olde Towne Café. (Like most of the patrons, Wil had felt no purveyor of the simple coffee bean deserved a name with an e on the end of all four of its descriptors, and he had avoided the place like the plague until sanity had been restored. Those painful three weeks without caffeine had been a test of endurance and mental resolve but one had to make a stand somewhere.) Wil closed his eyes for a moment, losing himself in the bustle of energy coming from within, and wishing for all the world that some of this energy might somehow rub off on his day. Here was his Garden of Eden, a place where Chocolate Vanilla Lattes fought a never-ending battle across the elaborate chalk menu with Mocha Pumpkin Spiced Thingamajigs, and other such earthly delights.

Wil resolved to order his usual, a large regular coffee with space for extra cream. This was not the time to try anything that might interfere with his Monday-morning routine. Opening his eyes, he sent up a quick prayer to Saint Joe, the Patron Saint of False Hope, and headed inside.

Behind the counter stood an indifferent teenager of indeterminate background. Wil could never remember one day to the next if this was the same indifferent teenager he'd ordered from the day before; they seemed to come and go with alarming regularity. Yet while the faces changed, the attitude remained the same: namely, one of bored confusion. Not for the first time in his life, Wil felt he had been here before.

"I'd like a large regular coffee with space for extra cream, please," said Wil.

"One Hefty with extra space," replied the teenager. "Would that be a latte?"

"No, a large regular coffee. And I don't want a 'Hefty.'"

"But you just said—"

"I said large. I'm not going to fall victim to Mug O' Joe's' corporate vernacular. I just want a large coffee."

The teenager blinked, confused. This was beginning to go in the exact same direction it normally went whenever Wil stood up for himself: namely, south.

"Hefty means big. So does Bulky. And so does Outsized. We've had this conversation before."

"No we haven't. This is my first day."

"Well, I've had it with all thirty-five of your predecessors. I'm not using your terminology because it doesn't make any sense." Wil pointed at the overly indulgent chalk-drawn menu just to make it clear he and the teenager were discussing the same issue. "Just because someone in marketing happens to own a thesaurus, and just because your shareholders insist all of your drink sizes must appear bigger than they are, and just because you are in between liberal arts colleges and wish to bring your artistic talents to bear on today's menu, it doesn't mean I have to join in. I would like a large coffee with space for extra cream. Please."

"One Heft—"

"Don't say it."

"One large coffee. Regular. What flavor?" The teenager was beginning to get the hang of this argument. He wasn't about to go down without a fight.

Wil looked at the ridiculous array of exotic coffees from around the world piled inside rack after rack around the entire store. True to form, he resolved to ignore each and every one of these exotic flavors individually.

"What's the flavor of the day?" he asked, thrusting out his jaw and widening his stance.

"French Roast," replied the teenager, who at this point was beginning to realize a concession of defeat would probably maximize his chances of receiving an adequate tip.

⌒◇⌒

ROUGHLY FORTY-NINE seconds later, Wil found himself glowering in the general direction of the Castle Towers, this time armed with a large cup of French Roast. The daily dose of caffeine confrontation he endured at Mug O' Joe's was beginning to grate. He consoled himself with the thought that while his job was marginally less enjoyable than working in a coffee shop, at least he'd left behind the acne of his teenage years, if not the angst.

Trudge, trudge, trudge . . . *KLONNG*.

Monday was getting longer and louder by the minute.

∽◌∾

THE WALK to Castle Towers would take another ten minutes or so—time enough for Wil to harden his heart and appropriately lower his expectations for the day. He trudged past an oversized billboard upon which was an oversized poster of a man with oversized hair, a spray tan, and teeth so white you could have skied on them. This was the ubiquitous Marcus James: a national TV personality of no apparent talent who nevertheless possessed the ability to persuade millions of people to part with something useful in exchange for something useless, usually in three or four easy payments. "Do you want teeth as brilliant white as mine?" asked the ad copy below Marcus James. "Then you want the Gleemodent toothpaste system." Further ad copy suggested three easy payments of $19.99 for what appeared to be a double order of ordinary toothpaste and the second (and most vital) part of the Gleemodent system: a toothbrush. Wil quickly decided that no, he did not want teeth as brilliant white as Marcus James for the simple reason that he preferred people not to stare at him and point. Besides, he had no desire to be held responsible for snow blindness or traffic delays.

Wil moved past the billboard and settled back into his reluctant trudge, subconsciously conforming to the flow of the city's one-way system. The warmth of the coffee near his lungs was now putting up a barrier against the freezing mist. While Wil maintained his steady course toward the Castle Towers, he allowed his thoughts to wander, as he always did at this point of the walk. He began to think of better days, all of which lay in the opposite direction from the one he was facing. He thought of those long, lazy afternoons when the future seemed less full of freezing mist. He thought of swimming holes and summer days. And, naturally, he thought of his mom.

∽◌∾

MELINDA MORGAN possessed a healthy sense of mischief and a love of life unparalleled by any other adult Wil had ever met. It was she who encouraged Wil to learn, to embrace knowledge as if it were a glittering prize. It was Mom who taught Wil about the value of imagination, and the acceptance of magic. Wil's dad, Barry, was an accountant at a large firm in town. He generously tolerated his wife and son's bond of adoration, and though he barely understood the first thing about science and magic, he always knew when to get out of the way and let the magic happen anyway. Barry Morgan was a good man: a good, solid, unimaginative man. Together, he and his wife made an effective and unorthodox team.

True to her off-the-wall nature, Melinda was a scientist who worked at a jet propulsion laboratory built into the side of a small mountain on the outskirts of town, where she performed exotic experiments understood by no more than twenty people on the entire planet. Young Wil understood the very basics: these experiments involved something called "electromagnetism," which was a fancy term that Mom used to describe big magnets powered by ten squazillion volts of electricity. On the rare occasions Wil had been inside Mom's lab, he'd been struck by the generous amounts of fizzling material and the fact that everyone's hair stood up on end. Mom's laboratory carried the distinctive smell of fresh ozone formed by any one of the fifty electrical experiments that littered the various test stations, and legend had it that her building could often be seen at night from space.

At home, Wil and his Mom spent countless hours designing exotic inventions and creating elaborate experiments. She bought him his first chemistry set at the age of five, and his first fire extinguisher a couple of weeks after that. Together they had tested the combustibility of virtually every substance in the neighborhood. Using a mixture of soluble starch and baking soda, Wil had once set fire to a local waterfall, which event had made the nightly news. Unbeknownst to him at the time, word of his alarming pyromaniacal tendencies would spread as far as the North Pole. That same Christmas, he received the most stupendous gift of all time: the Nikola Tesla Junior Genius Mega-Volt Test Kit.

Santa was a big fan of Mr. Tesla; and by sheer coincidence, so was

Melinda Morgan. Wil had never met the man but he had it on good authority that Tesla was a mad genius who liked to give pretty much anything a good jolt of electricity just to see what would happen. He was Mom's hero, and—by default—he became Wil's. At the urging of his mom—and with his trusty Nikola Tesla Junior Genius Mega-Volt Test Kit always on hand—Wil pushed the limits of creativity to their maximum levels of stretchiness. At the age of six, he designed the ill-fated five-dimensional multicube out of an old cardboard box. It would have worked, too, if he had remembered to take it in out of the rain. A year later, he created the ill-conceived Magnesium Volcano experiment, which garnered him an impressive last place at his school science fair after it covered the gym floor with a noxious substance that lingered long after the gym floor was eventually replaced. And then there was the ill-advised Unsinkable Electro-Concrete Troop Carrier, which had transported Dad's model soldier collection on its maiden voyage across a local lake. The less said about that, the better. Suffice it to say, Wil learned that day that cement is less buoyant than, say, the engine block of a Ford Crown Victoria, and that certain tin soldiers are worth more of one's allowance than they have any right to be.

❧

WARMED SLIGHTLY by these memories of past conflagrations, Wil's pace quickened as he passed Gretchen's Flower Shop some two hundred yards from his office building. Being of Dutch descent, Gretchen liked to present ornate tulip displays in her storefront. The closer Wil got to his oh-so-forgettable job, the more he would try to remember things that would connect him to his mom, just to give him the strength to wade into his day. Tulips were Melinda's favorite flower, though she wasn't allowed to bring them in the house on account of Barry's allergies. Wil liked the smell of tulips, and Gretchen was the one person he'd always wave to on his way to work if she was outside by her flowers.

Outside the Castle Towers stood a naked statue of Pan, which seemed to shiver ever so slightly in the frozen fog. Mom would have approved of it for the simple fact that Pan's oversized naughty parts tended to make passersby cover their children's eyes or look the other way. Certainly, the statue engendered two opposite reactions: upon seeing Pan for the first time, drivers would either avert their gaze or gawk like crazy people and run the risk of possible death or dismemberment at the hands of the too-complicated one-way system they were supposed to be navigating. Mom always liked stuff that challenged people to think differently. And Pan was certainly a challenge to the safe driving record of the local municipality.

By the time Wil made his way through the revolving door that led inside Castle Towers, the memories of his childhood were winning the battle against his reluctance to show up at work; they always seemed to invite escape from his current predicament. He surprised even himself with a sudden and alarming notion that today might be different after all. Perhaps this would be the Monday when the first day of the rest of his life wouldn't be like all the hideous days that had preceded it. Perhaps this would be the Monday when something finally happened. Perhaps this would be the Monday when—Heaven forbid—someone actually gave him something interesting to do.

Wil moved quickly past the two denizens of the Castle Towers lobby: a pair of identical twin brothers who could be found playing chess by the front window come rain, shine, or Martin Luther King Day. Wil had never learned the brothers' names; they appeared to be in their mid-fifties, and each had chosen a last line of defense against encroaching baldness by reverting to a disconcerting comb-over that could only be considered an act of desperation. The twins always gave Wil the creeps, though he could never put a finger on what exactly was the problem. It was probably the fact that they never spoke. Once, he'd made eye contact with the one nearest the window. It wasn't so much that the twin had scowled at him on that occasion; it was more that the guy had looked right through him. Wil often wondered if one or both of the twins were blind.

Trudge, trudge, trudge . . . *KLONNG!*

Certainly, chances were high that the brothers were both deaf; they had every right to be.

∝⤸

THE ELEVATOR was dank and possessed its own peculiar brand of pungency. No matter how many times Mr. Whatley, the superintendent of Castle Towers, had replaced the single light on the elevator's ceiling, it always flickered on and off and made a sound like an electric horsefly. As Wil ascended toward the nineteenth floor, he found himself being jolted out of his optimistic reverie and back toward reality. The elevator usually had the effect of bringing him down to Earth the farther upward it went.

Wil exited the traveling coffin trying (and failing) to suppress his gag reflex. Mr. Whatley had cleaned the walls of the elevator with bleach on numerous occasions yet the place still always managed to smell like a mixture of curry powder and rat vomit. Curiously, Wil had never seen an actual rat inside the entire building. No doubt they were repelled by the smell of the elevator.

Wil stood for a moment before the door of his office and fumbled inside his pocket for the smooth edges of his trusty English penny, trying to summon the courage to select his keys instead. He knew exactly what awaited him inside his office: an emptiness to match the one inside his heart, the emptiness that had followed him ever since the 207th day of his tenth year of existence. That was the day his mother, Melinda Morgan, had died.

ON THAT particular morning, Wil and his mom had been hard at work on an old and favored experiment: the Perpetual Penny. It was Melinda's contention that somewhere in the world existed a penny that—if spun properly and with the right amount of inverted friction— would continue to spin forever and never fall to the ground. She and

Wil had collected empirical data on the spinning of every American cent they could find, so much so that young Wil had the habit of asking people for spare pennies in the event they were unknowingly carrying with them the Holy Grail of all coins. Wil and his mom had collated the results of every penny spin since he was two years of age but had come no closer to finding the Perpetual Penny. They had so far achieved a 0 percent success rate but, as Mom pointed out, the experiment called for a 2 percent margin for error. This meant that conceivably, 2 percent of their spins had been successful—they just hadn't known it. Despite his lack of success, Mom had encouraged Wil to always keep trying. For a good experiment, she said, could never be rushed.

Lately, Wil had been resistant to his mom's optimism. He had begun to exhibit the typical frustration of a ten-year-old coming to terms with stubborn reality. Something was going to crack, Mom had said, and her money was on reality cracking first. Even though young Wil was not so sure, he'd decided to play along.

That morning, Mom had had an epiphany. She'd given Wil an old penny she'd brought back from a trip to England, where she and Barry had visited for their honeymoon some years before. This penny had a picture of the Queen of England on it, and she appeared to be floating on the sea in some kind of chariot. Like most of Mom's notions, the idea of an English penny being any better than an American one seemed to make little sense at first blush. Wil's dad, as usual, was skeptical about the potential for success. He'd given the pair his customary haughty sniff and had gone off to the upstairs toilet to read about something called the Dow Jones index. So while Mom busied herself with some scientific paperwork, Wil got to work trying to impart just the right amount of inverted friction upon this new candidate. It wasn't long before frustration took hold of the process.

"I can't do it," Wil complained. "It doesn't matter if it's English or American. It's just a penny. Just like all the other ones."

His mother gave him her most patient and understanding sigh. "Everyone knows the Perpetual Penny looks just like any other penny,

Wil," she replied. "It's all in how you spin it. Maybe every penny is the Perpetual Penny, or maybe none of them at all. You have to believe you're going to get it just right. But you're never going to get it right if you give up halfway through."

This was a variation on a familiar theme, and it was one that to Wil's ten-year-old mind was becoming painfully transparent.

"That's not fair!" he whined, doing his best impression of a nine-year-old. "You said I had to believe in the Easter Bunny and the Candy Goblin and then when I asked Santa about it at the mall he said he didn't know who the Candy Goblin was!"

"Fine. Then what do you believe?"

Wil realized he was probably going to have to be careful with his next statement, just in case. Maybe he was getting a little old for the Candy Goblin but there was no sense in ticking off Santa just to prove a point. "Maybe he just forgot," he replied, sheepishly.

Melinda seemed wistful, perhaps realizing this was a pivotal moment for her son. Wil was going to go one way or the other, she probably thought. Either he'd make the conscious choice to retain his childhood innocence and bring his wonderful imagination to bear, or he'd reject the notion of belief entirely and move through life in an entirely different direction altogether. She kissed her little boy and hugged him tightly. "Never forget," she told him. "Your eyes only see what your mind lets you believe." And for some strange reason, she had a small tear in the corner of her eye when she said it.

With that, Dad came down from upstairs to take Wil off to school. He and Mom kissed each other goodbye, and Dad told her to be careful at work, just like he always did.

Wil watched through the back window of his dad's sensible car that morning, and as Mom receded in the distance, he somehow knew with absolute certainty that this would be the last time he'd ever see her. He carried a sense of dread with him the entire day at school, and for some unknown reason he fiddled with the English penny and spun it on his desk innumerable times until the school bus came. Only later that evening did Wil realize that instinctively, he'd known his heart was emptying of all its joy. It became clear the moment the school bus turned the corner on his street and he saw the cop cars outside on his driveway.

❧

WIL ENTERED his office in much the same mood as he'd left it. Thoughts of that terrible day long ago always sent him back to a dark and empty place, and this morning was no exception. The police had come to inform his dad that Melinda Morgan was tragically atomized during an experiment involving 17 trillion megawatts that had reversed the Earth's polarity for a period of almost two nanoseconds. No trace of a body was ever found, such was the intensity of the explosion at the laboratory. Since that fateful day, Dad had never forgiven himself. Neither had he forgiven Mom for leaving him alone, nor the entire universe for taking away the one person he had ever truly loved, and whom he now needed more than ever before.

Wil's junky old answering machine blinked an insistent red. The contents of his desk and most of his shelves had been disturbed over the course of the weekend. His stapler had vibrated all the way across his desk until it was touching the pencil sharpener, and three of his pencils had fallen on the floor altogether. Wil's little air freshener had left a trail in the dust as it had magically wandered from one side of a shelf to the other since the last time he'd seen it on the previous Friday. Wil growled; he knew this was the work of no ghostly agency. Far from it: this constant shifting of his office contents had a very simple, terrestrial explanation. Sighing heavily, he picked up the stack of letters that Mr. Whatley had thrust through his mail slot over the weekend, and he jettisoned the entire pile into the trash. He knew he'd fetch them out a little later in the day but for the moment it felt good to toss all of his overdue bills and pretend he had the power to do so.

Propped up against the wall stood a moth-eaten package—roughly fifty inches long—that represented an ongoing battle of wills between

Wil Morgan, the universe in general, and corporate America in particular. It contained an unwanted item that Wil had neither ordered nor even considered ordering, but that had been shipped to his work address on multiple occasions nonetheless: the Marcus James Air-Max 2000 golf club. On the first occasion it had arrived, Wil had duly shipped the driver back to its manufacturer and thought little more of it. The package had subsequently been reshipped to Wil's office a total of seventeen times before he'd succumbed to the stress and made a phone call to the Air-Max 2000's corporate office. Arrangements had been made with the help of yet another indifferent sales associate—presumably, an ex-employee of Mug O' Joe's—and the item had been returned for the eighteenth time. However, this had the effect of generating an alarming number of increasingly threatening bills, statements, and notices from collection agencies seeking the total cost of the driver, plus shipping, handling, interest, and apparently a subscription to the entire Marcus James Gleemodent toothpaste and clothing catalogue. Within days, the package had mysteriously reappeared just inside his door, thanks no doubt to the ever-diligent Mr. Whatley. And so for the last two years, Wil had held on to the item, still inside its crumbling packaging. In the meantime, the product had been redesigned and reintroduced as the "new and improved" (and slightly more expensive) Air-Max 3000. These days, Wil tended to add the occasional demand letters for the club's purchase price to his regular discard pile. The only loser in this situation was the poor Air-Max 2000, well past its prime and sadly lagging behind the times, destined never to hit the fairways of the professional tour.

Wil looked at the frosted-glass door to his office. From his vantage point, the lettering on the glass read, ROTAGITSEVNI ETAVIRP—NAGROM LIW. Underneath this, in smaller letters and clearly legible from his side of the room, was written the legend DIVORCE AND INSURANCE CASES OUR SPECIALTY. This odd mix of betwixt and between presented an obvious problem, for no matter which side of the door a person stood on, at least one of the lines read completely backward. Wil sighed heavily again, as he always did whenever he considered how much he'd paid a local glass etcher for that particular piece of promotional genius. He wondered for the thousandth time how many potential clients had been put off by his obvious lack of organizational prowess, and settled on "not very many" since they'd have to be crazy to come all the way up to the nineteenth floor of the Castle Towers.

BEING A private investigator, especially one specializing in divorce and insurance fraud, was a far cry from the splendiferous blueprint Wil had originally drawn up for his life. As a child, Wil had planned to follow a unique and spectacular career path, narrowing down his options to one of few possibilities: (1) a hedgehog doctor, (2) developer of the world's first fruit-flavored wallpaper, (3) designer of the personal matter transmitter, or (4) quite possibly all of the above. He'd later settled upon just plain "inventor of stuff." That was, of course, until he reached the 207th day of his tenth year of existence.

After Mom died, the house was a very quiet place for a very long time. Then one day without warning, Wil's father had decided to sit him down and explain How Things Were Going To Be From Now On. Things were going to be very different.

As far as Barry Morgan was concerned, Melinda's fertile imagination and her penchant for electrocuting things were the cause of her demise. While the second of these things was quite possibly true, the logic of the first part escaped Wil entirely. For all of his life, he'd been encouraged to use his imagination, to grow as a person, to see the magic hidden in plain sight all around the world. Well, his dad told him, this was going to change. For one thing, there was no such thing as magic. For another, looking for answers in difficult places had proven to be a dangerous fool's errand that could only end in atomization and subsequent tears.

"You can't live your life like a firework," Barry had explained to his son. "Fireworks explode, and they usually take a few fingers and eyeballs with them. You're better off staying rooted to the ground and watching other people flame out."

After that nugget of wisdom, Dad had made Wil listen for three hours as he explained about the difference between imagination and reality. He'd told Wil the shocking truth about Santa, explained the economics of safety, and drilled into Wil that magic was always a trick. Always.

Young Wil had been resistant to his dad's new world order at first. He would secretly build little inventions out of cardboard, and whenever Dad was out of the house he'd leaf through Mom's old science magazines. When his father found out, the magazines were thrown out with the trash. Blueprints and cardboard were subsequently and consequently forbidden from the house.

One day, Wil came home early from school to find his dad sitting alone in front of the fire, clutching a photo of his mom. Dad was crying but when Wil moved to intercept, Barry gruffly pretended he was coming down with a cold, or something. What became clear from that experience—it was something that Wil would never forget—was that his dad had lost the thing most dear to him the day he had lost his beautiful and beloved wife. The only thing Barry Morgan now cherished—his only connection to Melinda—was his son, Wil. And it would be a cold day in a hot place before he ever lost his boy to the same fate that had claimed his wife.

Over time, Dad's constant needling about the perils of possessing an imagination and believing in things wore on his son. Harsh reality seemed to triumph more frequently over flights of fancy. Dad was never so proud nor relieved as the day Wil chose calculus over art in high school. He helped Wil choose a proper accounting college and set him up with a bankable IRA, which could only be cashed in without penalty once Wil reached the oh-so-safe age of fifty-five without being atomized in a terrible accident. To this day, Barry Morgan had absolutely no idea that his son had chosen a relatively perilous career in insurance fraud detection over a more sensible path through the safe and steady world of chartered accounting.

❧

WIL TOOK the old English penny from his pocket and spun it on the table. As it wandered across the desk, he found himself staring at the blinking red light of his outdated answering machine. He'd promised himself on many occasions that he'd buy a service provided by the telephone company that took messages at a remote location and kept them for him to retrieve from the system whenever he chose. Alas, he could not afford such a luxury, and so his primitive system was his only option. On the rare occasions the telephone actually rang, Wil half-expected the 1980s to be on the other end of the line, asking for their old answering machine back. His machine was rotten, quirky, and quite possibly possessed by demons. It seemed to delight in switching on and off at the most inopportune times. It recorded messages either at a whisper or trapped beneath hideous feedback that sounded like something out of the early Apollo missions. Worst of all, it worked perfectly only when the message being left belonged to a debt collector, auto-dialer, telemarketer, or recorded message from a local politician trying to spread dirt about his or her political opponent.

The penny clattered to a stop on the desk. Wil stared at it in silence. As if in response, the penny moved, almost imperceptibly. Over at his window, Wil noticed that one of his photo frames was getting ready to take a walk across the painted surface of the sill. The sound of an enormous cog clicking into place rattled the walls. This could only mean one thing: his personal soundtrack was about to go off, minus the trudging.

KLONNG!

Wil caught the photo frame just as it fell from the windowsill. If such an inanimate object could have attempted suicide by tossing itself off a ledge, Wil would not have blamed it one bit. His own daydreams had tended toward the homicidal—or, he supposed, "clockicidal"—every Monday morning for years. Wil knew with absolute certainty that he would gladly have accepted a sentence of thirty to life just for one morning of respite from the thing that tormented him the most.

Directly across from Wil's office stood a massive clock tower that the city forefathers had once received as a gift from the government of Switzerland to commemorate something nobody could remember. Wil hated this monstrosity more than he had ever hated anything in the known universe, not to mention a substantial portion of the undiscovered bit. It was a thoughtless, pointless, artless container of decibels that counted away the hours of his life one painfully annoying quarter hour at a time.

KLONNG!

As part of his morning ritual, Wil liked to stand at his window and shake his fist at the clock until it stopped going "klonng." He would utter increasingly profane oaths in its direction and silently wish it would sprout large robotic legs and go away. In fact, Wil had once opened his window to challenge the awful beast to a fight to the death, to which it had simply responded:

KLONNG!

Any moment now, the clock would stop and Wil would be left in peace. He'd be able to check his messages and make all his morning business calls, assuming he had any to make. All he needed to do was wait for one final

KLUNK!

Fifteen million francs worth of precision Swiss timing, yet all the city had to show for it was a painfully obnoxious pile of cogs that didn't work properly. The day the clock mechanism was installed in its tower it was discovered that the American housing had been designed in feet and inches, whereas the clock mechanism itself had been of the metric variety. As a result, one of the main clappers would bash into the wall of the clock tower instead of actually striking the bell. If one listened carefully after the quarter-hour chimes had faded—assuming one's ears were still functional after being assailed by the enormous bell—one could hear muffled clattering as the final clapper counted off the hours by missing the bell entirely and thudding into a well-worn brick.

The clock would now be silent until exactly six minutes after three, at which point it would go "klonng" again, six times, for no apparent reason. It had been the bane of Wil's existence that no matter his mood and no matter his daily preparation, the clock's mid-afternoon "klonng" always took him by surprise. Sometimes, he'd be in the middle of a phone call. Other times, he'd be using the bathroom or searching under his desk for a dropped pencil at exactly the wrong time. He'd tried everything from putting in earplugs to staring at the clock just prior to its mid-afternoon sonic attack. But for whatever reason, at precisely five minutes after three he'd get distracted and the clock would do its nefarious business one minute later and invariably he'd bang his head, clutch at his heart, or miss the toilet entirely.

Satisfied that the clock had finished annoying him for the morning, Wil aimed some inventive invective at the clock tower, and then turned toward the northwest and shook his fist at Switzerland. With this done, he replaced the photo frame on its perch and set about trying to retrieve his messages from his temperamental answering machine.

"MR. MORGAN," said the first message with a clarity that Wil fancied had eluded professional audiophiles the world over for decades, "this is Mr. Hightower calling from American National Bank again. We wondered if you'd received notice of our intent to collect—*click*." Wil kept his finger on the Erase button for a few seconds. Not a bright start to his Monday.

"Glurble flurble . . . hiss," went the second message, missing Wil's inner ear entirely and moving directly into the part of his brain reserved for migraine headaches. Probably a potential client or an eccentric billionaire attempting to give away money, he reasoned, pinching his nose.

"Do you want to drive the ball as straight and long as the pros? Yearning to pick up an extra thirty, forty, or even fifty yards on your playing partners? Then for four easy payments of $59.99, you need the new Air-Max 3000—*click*." Though equal parts alarmed and impressed by Marcus James's ability to intrude on virtually every aspect of his life, Wil was still having none of it. It was a statistical probability even the Air-Max 3000 would be unable to help him drive as long and straight as the pros on account of the fact he'd never actually picked up a golf club in his life. Tempting though the offer was, Wil decided to stick with the old 2000 model festering in its crumbling packaging by the door, keep his money to himself, and let his dream of joining the professional golf tour remain just that.

The next message was virtually silent, though Wil fancied he could make out a faint request to call someone back about a job. The return telephone number was indiscernible. The message following this sounded like a frantic leprechaun with throat nodules. "If you can hear this . . . ," said the message before trailing off into a series of garbled whispers. Wil could make out something about going somewhere urgently on a matter of vital importance. However, he could not make out where, when, or by whom the message had been left. This was an odd kind of message, even for Wil's demonic answering machine. He scrunched his nose and clicked the Fast Forward button.

"Wil," said the final message with such crystal quality that you could hear the scraping of an angel on a pinhead somewhere in the background, "it's Dad."

Wil looked at the answering machine with a horrified expression. Given its predilection for providing clarity only when bad news was in the offing, he knew this was going to be of the atrocious variety. His heart had already made the leap into his mouth at the sound of Barry Morgan's voice and was now beginning to force its way out of his nostrils. "I'm going to be in town for a couple of days next week," continued the message. "Thought I might stay with you at your apartment since you've bragged so much about the facilities. I was thinking you could take a personal day and we could visit the museums and the fountains in the park. Oh, and make sure you tell the folks at your accounting firm I'd like to meet them. Accountants always want to talk shop. Anyway, I'll call later. Bye for now!"

Wil stared at the answering machine for a good twenty seconds before he realized his mouth was open and there was drool coming down the side of it. His heart had jumped out of his body altogether and was now hiding in a corner, refusing to get back inside. His fingers and lips felt numb. This could not possibly be happening. Not now. Not on a Monday.

Wil's legs felt unsteady. Either the world had just turned into a roiling ocean or his vertigo was coming on again. He plunked heavily in his desk chair before the panic attack overwhelmed him entirely. Please, he thought to the universe in general. Please don't let this be the way it all ends.

As if to answer his silent prayer, there was a sudden, unmistakable moving of giant cogs nearby, followed by the sound of something very large and heavy hitting something else made of brick. Somewhere in Heaven a rogue angel was probably gunning down Saint Joe, the Patron Saint of False Hope, with a Thompson submachine gun.

Wil's eyes began to swim, his skin felt clammy and cold, and his nervous system felt like it was beginning to go completely numb. Perhaps his old penny might buck the trends of the last twenty or thirty years and present a different outcome than usual. He fished the coin from his pocket and spun it, then watched, forlornly, as it wandered across his desk and slowly, inexorably, began to topple over. The penny clattered to the desk and lay there, motionless. Wil wasn't sure his heart was even beating anymore. Surely this was the second-worst moment of his entire life. He put his hands over his ears and let his entire collection of limbs and organs slide slowly and unerringly down toward his desk until his left eye was about three inches from the penny that now lay on his desk. This was it: his life was officially over. Wil began to sob—quietly at first, but then with an increasing intensity so that his giant tears formed little puddles in the dust below his eyes. Please, he thought to whatever passing god might be listening. Please make this all go away.

As IT turned out, this was the very moment that magic entered Wil Morgan's life.

CHAPTER TWO

MAGIC ARRIVED in the form of a knock on the door, which surprised Wil to no end. He had only ever used the thing for opening and closing, and hadn't considered what it might sound like if someone actually knocked on it. It sounded hollow and rattly—very much in keeping with the way it looked.

Wil sat up and hastily tried to pull himself together. He mashed his little pool of tears into the desk with the palm of his hand, and wiped his wet cheeks with his sleeve. Putting his English penny back into his pocket, he paused for a moment as he tried to decide how he might react. One option would be to ignore the door altogether; after all, it had only been a few minutes since he'd thought to himself how a person would have to be crazy to come up to the nineteenth floor of the Castle Towers. He had no desire to answer the door and find himself confronted by an axe-wielding homicidal maniac wearing a tutu and a hockey mask. Alternatively, he could stand up from his desk and go and pretend that answering the door was an everyday occurrence. He reasoned that if the person on the other side of it was a potential client, they might be suitably impressed and could potentially even offer him a job. Wil put the odds of this unlikely scenario at about five hundred to one. Since the door itself wasn't forthcoming with any further information, he eventually decided it was probably better not to keep thinking about it. He settled for "Come in!" because that sounded more sensible than "Are you an axe-wielding homicidal maniac?"

There was a brief silence followed by a nervous shuffling outside the door and then a polite cough. A shadow moved across the frosted glass. Wil decided to take the bull by the proverbial horns.

"Come in!" he called, this time a little louder. No response. The shadow at the frosted glass moved suddenly and quickly in a downwardly direction, and the shuffling stopped. Thinking this to be a slightly odd reaction to a simple invitation, Wil walked to the door to see if someone had ducked down on the other side. Perhaps the person who'd knocked was lost and needed directions, he thought. Maybe he or she had simply fainted. This seemed much more likely than the possibility someone had come all the way up to his office on purpose. In the three or four seconds it took Wil to reach the door and open it, he considered three or four likely scenarios to explain this slightly surreal turn of events. As it turned out, none of these was even close.

An elderly, disheveled little man stood in the hallway, staring at Wil with an odd expression. Well, Wil realized, it was not so much that the man's expression was odd; it was more that he was bent over at the waist so that his head was at the same height as his knees, and he was looking at Wil upside down.

"You're much taller than I thought you'd be," said the little man, matter-of-factly.

"That's a coincidence," said Wil, rising to the challenge. "You're a lot shorter than I was expecting."

"Oh, I'm sorry," said the man. "I didn't know you were expecting someone."

"I wasn't," replied Wil. "Are you Australian, by any chance?"

"Not the last time I checked. But if I was, it wouldn't be the first time." Having won this initial battle of wit, the little man straightened finally so that all the blood and corpuscles reddening his weathered old face could go back to the parts of his body they were originally intended for. At first glance this elderly gentleman seemed to tread a fine line between kindly and eccentric, with his white hair now sticking up like a haystack that had been run through by a tractor. "You're Wil Morgan, the private detective?" said the little old man, thrusting out his hand. "I'm very pleased to make your acquaintance."

Wil hesitantly accepted the handshake. The little old man was dressed in a pair of golfer's plaid pants topped by a mustard-yellow jacket and a bow tie. Wil hadn't heard the circus was in town this month, yet he half-expected this new arrival to be equipped with one of those old-style joke electric buzzers. But the little man seemed harmless enough, and his grip proved to be surprisingly firm and polite. Satisfied by the quality of the handshake, the little man nodded and abruptly strode right past a startled Wil and into his office.

Wil closed the door, slightly bemused by this turn of events. When confronted by crackpots, he always liked to engage them in conversation. He had never been particularly afraid of them and he'd never really known why, except for the fact that unrelenting nut jobs were often quite interesting, whereas Wil's life was usually anything but. As far as Wil knew, there were no therapists or parole officers who worked in the Castle Towers, but if his oddball guest were forthcoming with the number of the office he was actually supposed to be visiting, Wil might be able to point him in the right direction.

As he turned, he found that the little man had stopped in his tracks directly in the center of the office and was now holding up a small vanity mirror, which he was using to scrutinize the etching on Wil's office door.

"Ah, I see," said the little man. "'Wil Morgan, Private Investigator. Divorce and Insurance Cases Our Specialty.' That's very clever."

"Not intentionally," replied Wil. "But thanks anyway. Now what can I do for you, Mr. . . . ?" He left the "Mr." hanging at the end of the sentence in the vain hope the little man might respond with his actual name.

No such luck; Wil's visitor began to move about the room to inspect its contents. Finding the broken-down package containing the golf club, he squinted at the shipping label and sniffed disdainfully.

"Are you a golfer, Mr. Morgan?" asked the little man.

"Only part-time," replied Wil, slightly perplexed by the man's ability to change directions so randomly. "I'm thinking of taking it up just as soon as I've worked out a few kinks in my swing, and a few more in my bank account."

The little man sniffed again. "The Air-Max 2000," he said as condescendingly as possible. "Drive it straight and long like the pros. I had one of these at one time."

"Oh? How did it work for you?"

"It didn't. Awful product. Fell apart in the packaging. I sent it back on numerous occasions but they kept returning it to me anyway. The only thing it ever drove was me, slightly crazy."

"I know the feeling. Look, if you don't mind I'm a little busy—"

"I left a message earlier on your answering machine but I'm not sure it was working properly," the little man suddenly stated with a puzzled frown. "It's a matter of some urgency that requires the attention of someone with your particular expertise, Mr. Morgan. I'd be most grateful if we could discuss the matter in public."

"Don't you mean private?" asked Wil.

"In a private investigator's office? I hardly think so!" exclaimed the little man, slightly perturbed by the thought. "Everyone knows these places are always bugged. Why, you probably have ten or twelve of them in your office right now. One in the telephone, one each inside all of the light fixtures . . . you never know who's listening to your conversations in a place like this. I'd rather we discussed business in a more populated area. I've found that people in crowds rarely listen to anything going on around them."

The little man seemed to be getting mildly worked up, and Wil hoped this encounter wasn't going to head further sideways before he'd had a chance to work out what the heck was going on. Besides, if there was even the slightest chance that this was going to involve money coming in his direction, he wasn't about to jeopardize such an eventuality. In the strangest way, what the man had said about crowds and public places possessed a curious kind of logic.

"I'll have to draw up some paperwork," Wil said. Inside his desk drawer were two different types of standard form, most of which had been used over the years for paper airplanes and doodling. He tossed a mental coin and fished out an insurance form. "If you'll just provide me with some basic information and an outline of the problem. I want to be sure I can help you, Mr. . . . ?"

"Let's get to a public place first," said the little man, fixing Wil with a steely gaze.

❧

TEN MINUTES later, Wil found himself inside Mug O' Joe's standing in line next to his potential new client, wondering how on Earth he had gotten here and whether or not he should consider getting himself out of whatever it was he was in. He couldn't remember walking with the little man to the coffee shop—more precisely, he could remember walking but he couldn't remember anything that had been said between them. Wil felt cold and wet, to be sure, so it seemed fairly credible that he'd recently been outside. Nevertheless, the entire event seemed to be shrouded in frozen fog. Wil shuddered; he had never had a missing time experience before. This was all beginning to get just a little too strange for comfort.

Wil blinked, startled by the realization he was now at the front of the line and looking into the eyes of an indifferent teenager. He racked his brain, trying to remember if this was the same teenager he'd been arguing with just a short time before. But he was so thrown by the unsettling events of the last half hour or so that he just stood there, effectively creating a kind of Mexican standoff with the teenager, who wasn't about to fire the first shot in this new exchange.

"Regular coffee, please," said Wil. "Better make it Oversized." He gulped, realizing that in his manic confusion he had actually succumbed to Mug O' Joe's institutionalized language mangling.

"Absolutely, sir!" replied the teenager in a breezy manner that demonstrated he was only too pleased to receive Wil's order correctly for a change. The server turned to address Wil's elderly companion. "And what can I get for you today?"

The little old man abruptly bent at the waist and covered one eye so that he could better study the chalk-drawn menu upside down. "Something exotic, I think," he replied. "What do you have on special?"

Unperturbed by this odd behavior, the teenager turned to survey the ridiculous collection of coffee containers on the shelf behind the counter. Wil looked up at the labels on the jars; he had never realized just how many different types of coffee existed in this coffee shop. Had those jars really been up there all the times he'd placed an order inside Mug O' Joe's?

"A lot of people like the Sumatran Dragon's Breath," enthused the teenager. "Have you ever tried Bengal Tiger Hiccups? I could do that as a frappe."

"That sounds most excellent," replied the little old man, matching the teen's enthusiasm. "And could you hold the heavy cream, please?"

"Certainly, sir. Go ahead and take a seat and I'll bring those out to you," replied the teenager with a broad smile

Of all the things that had happened to Wil on this particular morning, the teenager's sudden transformation from surly to polite was the thing that threw him the most. Unless this was a different teenager. Wil was hardly in the frame of mind to analyze the situation. He needed coffee.

Still in a mild state of shock, Wil found himself moments later at a table by the window, seated across from the little man. He'd never actually sat inside the coffee shop before. Looking around, he saw the ridiculous array of exotic coffees was larger and more comprehensive than he'd previously noted; the containers were stacked precariously in all corners of the shop. Wil looked at the labels, many of which were in languages he couldn't read. One of the containers was labeled with what appeared to be Egyptian hieroglyphics. Just as Wil noticed a particular label on one of the containers that seemed etched with what appeared to be Aramaic writing into what appeared to be blue neon glass, the teenager arrived.

Wil gratefully accepted his Regular Oversized, hoping beyond hope that the effects of the outlandish amount of caffeine might jolt him back to his senses. The teenager smiled at Wil, then passed the little man his Bengal Tiger Hiccups frappe, which bubbled below the surface, suggesting it might be full of frozen carbon dioxide. It possessed a venomous odor that teetered precariously between malted chocolate and malted battery acid. Unsurprisingly, the little man wrinkled his nose at the drink the moment it arrived. Before Wil had a chance to thank his server, the teenager turned tail and breezed back to the counter where he proceeded to attend to other customers and occasionally smile in Wil's general direction.

"Dinsdale."

Wil jolted out of his reverie with a start. The peculiar old man was now staring at him, politely smiling.

"Excuse me?"

"Dinsdale, Mr."

Wil could tell his potential new client was patiently waiting for him to overcome his attack of confusion. This must have been a conversation they were having previously, which Wil had probably lost track of. He furrowed his brow, hoping this would give him the appearance of being fully engaged in the moment.

"Or Mr. Dinsdale, if you prefer," continued Mr. Dinsdale. "Aren't you going to fill out your form?"

Wil produced his now-crumpled insurance form. "Dinsdale . . . right. First name?"

"Mr. Dinsdale. Now, about that matter of urgency: I need to know first and foremost that you can keep a secret. What I am about to divulge to you is known to only seven people in the United States and one more in the former Soviet Republic of Kurdmenistan. Can I count on you, Wil?" Mr. Dinsdale looked at Wil, expectantly. Despite the overwhelming sense that this eccentric elderly gentleman was playing everything from shortstop to quarterback in a league of weirdness all his own—and despite the slight suspicion that Kurdmenistan was not an actual country—Wil nodded. "Good man!" said Mr. Dinsdale. And with that he produced from his coat pocket what appeared to be a set of musical notations and placed them on the table. "Now then . . . we'll have to take things slowly for security reasons. I don't want to throw it at you all at once. Let's try a little test first. Do you have any idea what this is?" he asked.

Not wishing to appear completely thrown off his game, Wil decided to go with the obvious: "I'm going to go with the obvious," he responded, doing his utmost to appear confident. "Musical notes?"

"But not just any old musical notes," said Mr. Dinsdale, pleased that Wil was warming to the task. "Look again. See anything out of the ordinary?"

The musical parchment appeared to be old and weathered. Whoever had written the notations had crammed in an awful lot of notes; and though Wil possessed no musical training whatsoever, he could see that this was an unusual piece. At the top of the page was written a faint signature that had faded over the years. Wil gulped and tried not to let his obvious double take throw him off balance and pitch him onto the floor.

"Wolfgang Amadeus Mozart," affirmed Mr. Dinsdale with a grin. "But what makes this particular piece of music special is what it represents."

"What does it represent?" Wil asked, intrigued.

"Mr. Mozart was no ordinary musical genius, as anyone can tell you," replied Mr. Dinsdale. "Many people know that he was a Freemason and that he composed his first concerto at the age of five. There was a movie and a rock song about it. But very few people know that Mozart was also a scientist and mathematician, and that he dabbled in musical alchemy. In his later years, he was being driven mad by his own genius—so much so that he traveled to consult a famous doctor in Vienna before he lost the plot entirely." Mr. Dinsdale picked up the yellowed sheets and looked about the coffee shop in conspiratorial fashion. "The Viennese doctor advised Mozart that he was indeed going crazy as a result of having too many competing thoughts in his head at the same time," continued the little man in a hushed voice. "He advised Wolfgang that he needed to go home and compose himself. And that's exactly what the great man did. What you are looking at is Wolfgang Amadeus Mozart in musical form!"

Dinsdale handed the musical notations across the table so that Wil could take a look for himself. Wil blushed and closed his eyes. "Okay, I get it," he said with a chuckle. While he hadn't spotted any of the TV cameras on the way in, Wil knew that when he opened his eyes the little man would be sitting next to a game show host, and that all of the customers in the coffee shop would be revealed as audience participants. He consoled himself with the thought that if he were very lucky, the morning phone message from his dad might also possibly be someone pulling his leg. He just hoped beyond hope that he hadn't picked his nose, or something, while on camera.

Wil opened his eyes to find Mr. Dinsdale smiling at him, patiently. No one else in the coffee shop seemed to be in on the game. Wil began to imagine he was trapped in the center lane of a three-lane highway, driving a tiny European compact with two enormous eighteen-wheelers keeping pace on either side: it's one thing to go out crushed between something heavy, he thought, but it's another thing altogether if you feel utterly ridiculous when it happens. He glared at the little man across the table. "Is this some kind of joke?" he asked, barely trying to hide his annoyance.

"No, it's a concerto, I think," replied Dinsdale, stuffing the parchment back into his pocket. "I needed to show you an authentic exhibit in case you doubted my sincerity. For as you have no doubt guessed, I am indeed the curator of the Curioddity Museum!"

Mr. Dinsdale sat back in his chair and waited for Wil to slap his forehead with his palm and say, "Of course!" But the old man was going to be in for a long wait. At this very moment, Wil was deciding whether or not to lean forward and slap Dinsdale on the forehead, thus pushing him off his chair. The little man's face began to fall as he realized Wil may or may not have understood the significance of his previous statement. "The Curioddity Museum," he repeated, aghast that Wil seemed to be struggling to understand. "Don't tell me you've worked in the city for all this time and haven't found your way to the Museum of Curioddity?"

"That would have been difficult," said Wil, sharply, "since I've never even heard of it. Who put you up to this?"

Mr. Dinsdale (Wil was beginning to suspect this was not even his real name) was now beginning to look most perturbed indeed. He pulled the musical notations from his pocket once again. "Excuse me," he said, "but I fancy you may have misunderstood my intentions. If you'd like to examine the documents once again you can attest to their authenticity—"

Wil took the documents, as if to examine them. And promptly dropped them on the ground. The papers seemed to make a faint tinkling sound that resembled the famous overture of the Marriage of Figaro, which he ignored. He wasn't too fond of tricks, and this particularly elaborate one only served to tick him off even further. The little man looked at the fallen notations, aghast, and hurriedly reached down to scoop them up.

"Look, Mr. Dinsdale—or whatever your name is—this has been a particularly rough morning for me," said Wil. "I'm not sure why you've decided that today would be a good day to test your new comedy routine on a perfect stranger but I have bills to pay and debt collectors to make excuses to. If you have an actual point, I'd be most grateful if you'd get to it. And if you are in fact trying out new material for your routine, I'd appreciate a royalty check for my trouble."

Wil glared at Dinsdale, feeling slightly foolish for having been suckered into whatever scam the old man had going. It seemed mildly idiotic to think this strange-looking person stood a remote chance of being an actual client. Mr. Dinsdale, for his part, stared at the papers, taking just a little extra time to sort them while he apparently considered what he might do next. He furrowed his brow and scratched his chin in a contemplative manner. Then, he furrowed his chin and scratched his brow, which Wil was grudgingly forced to admit seemed a neat trick. Finally, Mr. Dinsdale nodded his head, having arrived at the business end of some kind of conclusion or other.

"You know, I think I understand your skepticism, Mr. Morgan," said Mr. Dinsdale. "How silly of me. Of course, you'd have to actually hear the music first before you could accept it as the genuine article."

"What? Wait—"

"Yes, I realize my mistake now. You're not the sort to just take something this magnificent at face value. You're going to need proof of its authenticity. That's what makes you a renowned detective. I should have expected no less, considering your reputation."

Wil flushed, feeling slightly embarrassed to have been so gruff with an eccentric old man who—on the face of it—had been nothing but pleasant company. He was unaware that at any time during his career as a private investigator he had garnered any kind of renown or reputation beyond that of someone who habitually paid his bills late, or not at all.

"Look . . . Mr. Dinsdale, you seem like a nice enough guy: weirder than a bobcat on a skateboard but harmless enough. If this is just something you do to fill up your mornings, that's fine. But unless you're willing to give me an actual job or tell me what you really want, I'm going to have to get back to work."

Mr. Dinsdale suddenly sprang to his feet in an animated fashion, startling a couple of the patrons nearby who were sharing something that looked suspiciously like a gravel milkshake. "That's the Wil Morgan I expected!" the little man shouted, enthusiastically. "Then it's settled. Let's get to work at once! Come on!"

And with that, Mr. Dinsdale abruptly turned and headed for the front door of the coffee shop, leaving his bubbling Tiger concoction to pump out a heavy gas that cascaded off the edge of the table like a waterfall. "Wait!" cried Wil. But it was no use: the old man was already at the door and heading out into the street at an alarming rate for one so old. Wil scooped up his Regular Oversized and gave chase.

As Wil rushed to the exit, he passed the teenaged server, who for some inexplicable reason was now simply standing by the door holding a large carton of heavy cream. They made eye contact for a brief moment.

"Be careful out there," said the teenager.

As he rushed outside, Wil admitted to himself he had absolutely no idea of the significance of that statement.

❧

By the time Wil got out to the street, he could see that Mr. Dinsdale was already some thirty or forty yards ahead, obscured partly by the freezing fog. It seemed to Wil that unless the little man was an Olympic sprinter of some repute, this had to be either an optical illusion or he was having another of his missing time experiences. He broke into a run, calling out to his quarry ahead just as Mr. Dinsdale turned a corner. By the time Wil reached the corner, some five or six seconds later, Mr. Dinsdale was now a hundred yards ahead on the same street. And yet the little man seemed to be puttering along at a speed that seemed in keeping with a person of his advanced years—in other words, at a pace equivalent to a crippled turtle.

Wil looked at his watch: two minutes to eleven. If he stopped now he could get back to the office in time to avoid two or three phone calls and perhaps share a conversation with Mr. Whatley about politics and/or cleaning products. He'd spend the afternoon fretting about the imminent arrival of his father and then have the living daylights scared out of him at exactly six minutes after three. Finally, he'd go home after a fruitless day of nothing in particular and run the gauntlet of his rusty old landlady and her moth-eaten cats. He decided to keep up his pursuit.

Running as fast as he could, Wil got within ten yards of Mr. Dinsdale just as the old man turned left onto the main artery of the one-way system. "Stop!" he cried. "Mr. Dinsdale!"

Wil barreled around the corner, half-expecting Dinsdale to now be a full half mile ahead. Much to his surprise, he ran full bore into the little man, and he barely managed to grab at Dinsdale's mustard-yellow coat lapels before the two of them went clattering to the ground. Wil heard a honking sound: most of the people traversing the complicated one-way system in their cars seemed to now be staring in their direction as they passed. Mr. Dinsdale furrowed his chin again. Wil felt nothing if not mildly ridiculous.

"What on Earth are you doing?" asked Dinsdale. "Is something wrong? You look like you've seen a ghost."

"I'm sorry," replied Wil as he tried to catch his breath. "I tried . . . catch up . . . back there . . . too fast!"

Mr. Dinsdale extricated himself from the embrace, stood up, and dusted himself off. "I can see it was too fast." He sniffed. "You'd better slow down before you do yourself a mischief."

"Slow down? Slow *down*? You come plowing into my office like a crazy person, you show me Wolfgang Amadeus Mozart's Unfinished Whatever while I'm pumped full of caffeine, and then you speed off like a clown car without any brakes . . . and I'm supposed to slow down?"

"Couldn't have put it better myself. Come on, it's this way." Mr. Dinsdale narrowed his eyes to peer at something on the road ahead before striking out in its general direction. This kind of erratic behavior really seemed to be Dinsdale's thing, thought Wil, as he jumped to his feet and gave chase, determined not to lose the old man in the now-thickening fog.

"Where are we going?"

"The Curioddity Museum, of course. It's just up ahead."

"Up ahead? Waitaminnit . . . where exactly is this museum?"

"Oh, we're situated on Upside-Down Street right across from the abandoned cinema," said Mr. Dinsdale, cheerily.

Wil knew for a fact that no museum could possibly exist for at least two miles in the direction Dinsdale was now headed. This was the way he walked home from his office every single day—following the flow of the one-way traffic, naturally—and he would most definitely have seen something as obvious as a museum on his travels, not to mention an abandoned movie theater. Up ahead lay a particular stretch that led cars and pedestrians alike along a featureless causeway lined by enormous banking buildings. This in turn led to a second old railway bridge that rivaled the first for its ability to rattle one's fillings. Wil was just beginning to come to terms with the absurdity of the concept that was "Upside-Down Street" when up ahead, Mr. Dinsdale ducked to his left and onto a street that Wil had never, ever noticed was there.

He stopped in his tracks to consider what might be Actually Occurring, as opposed to Apparently Occurring. By this point, he had begrudgingly accepted this was no ordinary miserable Monday. A manic Monday, perhaps, or maybe a momentous Monday. Wil felt it was a testament to Mr. Dinsdale's, well . . . *curioddity* . . . that he had barely even thought about the hideous and awkward likelihood that his dad was going to visit sometime in the next few days. And in thinking this, he suddenly realized that indeed, his father was coming, and he had to catch himself against the wall of one of the banking buildings to stop himself from succumbing to his vertigo and toppling over.

Wil squinted at the little side street, which to all intents and purposes had suddenly and magically appeared overnight between the two largest banks in the entire city. He'd heard that such terrifying diseases as flesh-eating parasites and temporal lobe epilepsy might cause sudden hallucinations followed by irreversible insanity. But try as he might, he couldn't concentrate in such a manner that the little street would simply go away. The street sign read, simply, MONS. Wil's sixth-grade-level French classes had taught him this was the French word for "mountain," but the idea of a street named after anything higher than fifty feet in what was quite possibly the world's flattest city seemed absurd. A lot of things seemed absurd. Wil edged closer to the corner of the little street, wondering why he felt so nervous about peering around it.

At the corner stood an ordinary trashcan. Wil looked inside it. It contained trash, including a banana peel and some old newspaper. No surprises there. Wil peeked around the corner of Mons Street to find Mr. Dinsdale standing just up ahead in the mist, tapping his foot.

"There you are," said Mr. Dinsdale, impatiently. "What took you so long?"

"How long has this street been here?" asked Wil. "I've walked this way home for years and I've never noticed it before."

"You know what your problem is, Mr. Morgan?" said the little man in the mustard coat. This was not going to be a question, Wil determined. This was going to be the sentence that preceded a criticism; and this was something Wil had become used to during his last twenty-odd years on the planet. "Your problem is that you look at things too carefully, like a detective specializing in insurance and divorce cases."

"I don't see how that's a problem. That's how I'm supposed to look at things, isn't it? I mean you wouldn't be about to hire me for whatever-it-is-you're-about-to-hire-me-for if I didn't!"

"Not even close," said Dinsdale. "You need to learn how to un-look at things if you're going to take on this job of mine. Life is not about how you use your eyes; it's about having vision. It's all about how you un-look at the world."

Wil decided this had gone quite far enough. This trek through ever-falling temperatures had now put him in a very grumpy mood, and this seemed like as good a time as any to voice his opinion. "Life is an ugly lake of treacle," he said. "You can try to wade through it but eventually you're going to get stuck. If you try to enjoy it you'll end up sick. And if you go about looking at things bent at the waist like you do, Mr. Dinsdale, you'll probably end up with treacle up your nose."

"I see," said Mr. Dinsdale with a sniff. The sniff was intended to be a little sullen so that Dinsdale could make it perfectly clear his nose was just a little out of joint.

"And one other thing: there is no such place as Upside-Down Street. There never has been. Any statement to the contrary would be the ramblings of an old man with too much treacle up his nose!"

Wil's angry comment had the desired effect: it left one of the two men feeling satisfied and the other looking rather disappointed. "I'm sorry you feel that way, Wil," said Mr. Dinsdale. "I can see I must have been mistaken about you. I'm sorry to have troubled you, and I wish you the best in your future endeavors. Now if you'll excuse me . . ."

Mr. Dinsdale began to turn away, making a good show of drooping his old shoulders and being as convincing as possible that his demeanor was now fully deflated. Wil couldn't tell if this was yet another of the older man's bizarre tactics: by this point, Wil's timing was completely off its chosen track. He couldn't be sure how he felt about anything but he was pretty sure he wasn't about to let Mr. Dinsdale off this easily.

"Now wait just a minute," he began. "You can't just jump into someone's Monday and thrash about like a crazy person, and then walk away and then allow yourself to be caught and then walk away again! People don't do that sort of thing. And I'm not going to fall for that whole victim thing so please stop drooping your shoulders and for the love of all that is holy, tell me what the heck is going on around here!"

Wil could now barely contain his breath; his brain and stomach were doing competing cartwheels somewhere under the various parts of his skin, and his left eye was beginning to twitch. Mr. Dinsdale eyed him with the kind of calm demeanor that would have made a devout Trappist monk jealous. Wil couldn't tell if the little man was scrutinizing him for some reason, toying with his emotions, or just plain pushing his buttons. Wil felt like a musical equipment repair workshop, in that most of his organs now seemed to be functioning improperly. How exactly had he gone from a routine-obsessed, tedious human punching bag to a stark raving, wild-eyed lunatic human punching bag in the space of about an hour? No matter which way he looked at his morning, none of it made sense. He'd followed a man dressed like a refugee from a 1950s Shell's Wonderful World of Golf rerun halfway across town to a hidden street in search of an abandoned cinema and a place named the Curioddity Museum, all without even knowing exactly why. Well, he thought, this was about to come to a conclusion one way or another, whether Mr. Dinsdale wanted it or not. He was going to maintain eye contact with the object of his antagonism until he either got some answers or passed out in the snow.

Wil looked up in the sky. It was now snowing. Of course, he thought, as one large and extremely cold snowflake settled on the middle of his nose. Of course it's snowing. Because I am neither cold nor disoriented enough to fully complete the various challenges being presented to me on this particular Monday.

"I'm sorry, Wil," said Mr. Dinsdale. "I truly am. It's just that people are like mopeds sometimes. They need a kick-start."

Looking down, Wil realized that Mr. Dinsdale had undergone a rather unsettling shift in both demeanor and appearance. The little man seemed altogether different, and while Wil had grown to expect such things in the short time he had known Mr. Dinsdale, this was an entirely new proposition altogether. The slightly disheveled appearance was now somehow less ruffled and, indeed, Dinsdale's odd choice of clothing suddenly seemed altogether appropriate. In fact, the mustard-yellow coat seemed quite fetching as large snowflakes landed on the little man's shoulders. His bow tie now had a touch of elegance about it, and the plaid golfer's pants added a modicum of class to his overall appearance. Most importantly, this new Dinsdale gave off a kind of perceptive calm and worldly-wise confidence that had previously been lacking in almost every single facet of his former personality. Wil fancied this particular version of Mr. Dinsdale was the one that had been hiding in plain sight all along.

"I don't feel like a moped," said Wil, unable to think of anything else he particularly wanted to say.

"Yes, I should probably apologize for that analogy," replied Mr. Dinsdale. "I could've thought of something more powerful and less likely to break down at a moment's notice."

"Or be sat on by an Italian teenager."

"Right again. May I ask how you feel right about now?"

"I feel like a fish that just jumped off the side of a fishing boat, and accidentally landed in a stray net that a previous fisherman hung out to dry. Either you're trying to catch me on purpose, Mr. Dinsdale, or I'm trying to be caught by mistake. I'm cold, and it's snowing, and my coffee has worn off. I don't know where I am or why I am. Does that about cover it for you?"

"It does indeed."

Wil was astonished to realize Mr. Dinsdale had now undergone a complete transformation, paradigmatically speaking. His kindly side was now fully in evidence, and his eccentric side was now fully in remission. His manic side, with any luck, Wil hoped, had gone on ahead by a few hundred yards. Wil realized that to all outward appearances, Mr. Dinsdale seemed like someone he could trust, which made absolutely no sense whatsoever. And for the very first time during his entire Monday, he felt as though things might be looking up, albeit with little to no explanation.

"Look up," said Mr. Dinsdale.

Peering up once again through the tumbling snowflakes, Wil could now see that he was standing in front of a very large building fronted by ornate Ionic pillars. A wide set of marble steps led to a warm-looking foyer. Above, massive lead-lined windows suggested an expanse of space within. The building screamed "museum" in much the same way a stadium with a diamond-shaped playing field might scream "baseball." Wil was getting the sense that something was awry with either time or space: he surely could not be standing in front of a building of this size. Hadn't he just turned the corner onto Mons Street? He turned to his left, only to realize that by some accident of time and space he'd come fully fifty yards from the corner of Mons Street.

Wil looked behind him. Across the street was an old, abandoned cinema that looked like it hadn't seen a patron in decades. The building's façade was hopelessly crumbling, and through the falling snow it seemed to give off an aura that suggested it wished to be left alone. Most of the letters announcing the last movie it had ever housed had long since fallen away, and unless Wil was mistaken, he was sure that the arrangement of the remaining G, W, and D could be easily retrofitted to spell *Gone with the Wind*.

"Where am I?" he asked aloud as he turned back to find himself staring toward a large sign on the front of the building closer to him. It read MUSEUM OF CURIODDITY. This simple question came as a shock to Wil, even though he was the one who'd uttered it. It seemed like the kind of thing one might hear in a bad movie or read in a comic book. He looked through the mist and was astounded to realize that yes indeed, he was still fifty yards from the corner of Mons Street. There was the street sign and the trash can. The cold mist seemed to obscure the main road beyond but Wil fancied he could hear the cars going around the one-way system despite the blanketing effects of the snow.

"You're on Upside-Down Street, of course," replied Mr. Dinsdale. "Welcome to the Museum of Curioddity. Please come inside, and try not to touch anything that doesn't have a sign on it that says 'Touch Me.'"

With that, the little man began to ascend the huge marble staircase that led toward the foyer of what Wil was forced to admit seemed an extremely likely candidate to be the actual Curioddity Museum.

"We're on Mons Street!" cried Wil in the specific direction of the little man's rapidly departing back. "It says so on the street sign!"

"Does it?" asked Dinsdale, who had reverted back to his enigmatic persona. He moved slowly and purposefully up toward the Curioddity Museum's entrance. Wil could tell from the little man's steady course that he was expected to follow. "Or does it only say what you think it says?"

Wil looked at the street sign. It most definitely had not changed appearance during the last few minutes. Perhaps he was missing something. Or perhaps the old man was missing something instead. Like a few million brain cells.

By now, Mr. Dinsdale stood at the entrance to his museum, just next to a revolving door. He stopped for a moment to look back at Wil, and smiled. Before Wil could utter another sentence, the old man moved backward inside the revolving door of the museum, disappearing like some kind of enigmatic vampire into the bowels of a comfortable coffin.

Wil stood transfixed for a moment, knowing with absolute certainty exactly what he was going to do next. He was going inside the museum but not before one final protest aimed at the universe in general and Mr. Dinsdale in particular. "I don't get it!" he cried. "This doesn't make any sense at all!"

Mr. Dinsdale appeared for a moment, having taken the revolving door in a full circle so that he could briefly emerge and make one final comment on the matter. It was going to be a comment that would change everything, and in Wil's former life already had, once upon a time.

"That's because you're not looking at it properly!" said Mr. Dinsdale as he passed across the outside portion of the revolving door.

"AFTER ALL," he called out as he disappeared from view, "your eyes only see what your mind lets you believe!"

CHAPTER THREE

———— ◦◉◦ ————

As WIL stood on the steps of the Curioddity Museum, he began to feel overwhelmed by a Strange Feeling of déjà vu. For his part he tried to ignore the Strange Feeling, and between the two of them they agreed to revisit things a little later once the situation was better developed. What Wil could not possibly know was at that very moment his life was in the process of changing. Back, most likely: but also forward, too. Wherever the Strange Feeling of déjà vu existed in its own reality, it chuckled to itself, sensing it had already won half the battle.

Wil thought about Mr. Dinsdale's incredible parting statement as he slowly and carefully ascended the marble steps toward the revolving door that would lead inside. Could it be coincidence that the little museum curator had parroted Melinda Morgan's favorite saying, word for word? Wil's heart fluttered not for the fact that he was nervous about stepping into the unknown but because he had a bad habit of getting stuck in revolving doors. He'd always been the kind of person to approach such things as escalators and elevators far too cautiously, only to chicken out at the last moment and leave a foot dragging or a carelessly untied shoelace in such a position as to cause himself bodily harm.

He stared at the revolving door, silently daring it to go ahead and try something with him. He'd used this particular tactic a couple of times in the past but inanimate objects had only increased their bullying over the years. Summoning every square inch of his bravado, Wil pursed his lips in the direction of the revolving door and took hold of its outer glass pane with both hands. "Don't even think about it," he muttered as he pushed the door forward and bravely made his way inside the museum.

Mr. Dinsdale was nowhere to be seen, which did not surprise Wil one bit. Everything else about the main foyer was exactly as unexpected as Wil expected it to be: it was ever so slightly unlike the outside of the building in one or two fairly alarming ways. Firstly, the interior seemed smaller and much less expansive than one might have assumed from looking at the outside. This was altogether an unsettling optical illusion, though not Wil's first of the day, to be sure. The act of stepping inside the museum seemed to immediately induce a mild claustrophobia, which Wil put down to an obvious lack of air-conditioning. The second noticeable difference was that the foyer's design resembled the exterior in exactly the same way a banjo-wielding hillbilly resembles the lead guitarist of a death metal band—in other words, only tangentially. Gone were the imposing and expansive Ionic pillars and tasteful marble steps; in their place, Wil noticed a particular fondness for yellow wallpaper, Escher-style carpeting, and the occasional stray wooden crate. He was immediately struck by the notion that if a tribesman from the remotest region of Peru were to be brought here for his first encounter with civilization, that tribesman might go away with the distinct impression he was from the more advanced culture, not to mention the more discerning. And speaking of cultures, Wil could not help but notice that whatever substance had been spilled onto the main desk of the foyer in some previous month, it must have contained a heretofore undiscovered bacterial strain because it had now formed a little forest of fuzzy growth halfway up the wall. This was either an impressive and detailed bonsai experiment, or Wil was witnessing a potential health hazard that the Centers for Disease Control might eventually classify as a pollutant.

Next to Wil, one of the stray wooden crates seemed to move of its own volition. He stared at the thing for a moment; then, satisfied that this was the work of neither a rat nor a trapped midget, he scanned the foyer once again for any sign of Mr. Dinsdale. The moment he looked away, the crate moved again. He looked down only for a different crate to move elsewhere in his peripheral vision. The moment he looked at the second crate it refused to move. Since most of the wooden crates Wil had ever encountered had also refused to move, he felt it was for the best to ignore the crates fully and reexamine the problem at the later time when he and his Strange Feeling of déjà vu were going to resolve their differences.

"Can I help you?" asked a nearby female voice.

Wil looked up, alarmed. Just moments before, there had been no one at the main desk inside the foyer. Now, a rather pale yet attractive woman in her mid-thirties was standing by the cash register, filing her nails and making a great point of smacking her lips as she chewed upon a large wodge of bubble gum. The woman looked bored, amongst other things. She also looked very much like a backup singer from an all-girl fifties vocal group with her beehive-style "do" and ruby-red lipstick completing the look. Wil felt compelled to comment that the woman's bright-orange hair suited her complexion but he resisted the temptation. He'd never been very good at talking to members of the opposite sex, and whenever he attempted a genuine compliment it usually led to either a slap across the face or worse, an angry and enormous boyfriend approaching from the opposite direction.

"Can I help you?" the woman repeated.

"I was looking for your curator, Mr. Dinsdale," explained Wil.

"Do you have an appointment?"

"No. I mean I was just with him a moment ago but he came inside ahead and I don't know where he went. He seems to have this thing for disappearing even when you're looking right at him." Wil hoped the woman might agree, and that she and he might quickly become friends so that he might ask any one of the fifty or so questions he'd already formulated about Mr. Dinsdale. The woman merely stared at him, disdainfully, and chewed her gum even louder.

"Mr. Dinsdale isn't accepting guests at this time. If you'd like to leave a name and number where you can be reached, I'll pass on your information," she said in such a way that Wil took it to actually mean, "If you'll please remove yourself from the premises, I'll be sure to alert security never to let you back inside."

Wil thought this was rather odd, partly because the entire point of museums was to welcome guests and hope they are well enough entertained to bring about a return visit, and mostly because there was no sign of any security guard whatsoever.

The woman moved to one side to retrieve a small note card. Perhaps *glided* would be a better description, Wil thought, as the woman certainly seemed to move in the unusual manner of a clockwork marionette. For the life of him, he couldn't quite work out what was so different about her. He was suddenly overcome by that strange feeling usually reserved for when one is asked the capital of the former Republic of Upper Volta, only to realize that everyone else in the room clearly knows the answer and is biting their tongue while you have absolutely no idea whatsoever.

"I don't mean to be confrontational," said Wil as he belied his statement by confronting the woman, "but I promise you, I was following Mr. Dinsdale. He came in just ahead of me."

"Why were you following him?" asked the woman, sharply. "Who are you with?"

"It's okay, Mary!" came a welcome voice from a balcony above. "This is Mr. Morgan, the gentleman I was telling you about. He's the one from the detective agency."

Mr. Dinsdale was now descending the nearby balcony staircase.

For the first time during his entire Monday, Wil felt grateful that the little man was actually present. His encounter with the pale woman had gone entirely according to plan, as long as that plan was devised by Wil's worst enemy during a moment of extreme vindictiveness.

"Wil Morgan, I'd like you to meet my assistant here at the Museum of Curioddity, Miss Mary Gold!" said Mr. Dinsdale with a broad smile. "Mary runs all of our bookkeeping and catalogues most of the exhibits. She's truly indispensible."

Despite this warm introduction, Wil could not help but feel that Mr. Dinsdale had said "indispensible" accidentally, and what he'd really meant to say was "confrontational." Mary Gold stared at Wil, smacking her bubble gum so loudly that it sounded like a rubber inner tube being pumped full of air. But Wil decided that with Dinsdale now backing him up it might be worth taking another shot.

"I'm pleased to meet you, Miss Gold," said Wil, proffering his hand in the woman's direction and smiling his best genuine fake smile. "This is quite the place you have here."

"Uh-huh." Mary Gold's hand felt clammy, and Wil was slightly unnerved by the fact she applied no pressure to the handshake greeting whatsoever. His lifetime of reading women's disdainful body language told him that Mary Gold's "uh-huh" could roughly be translated as, "You're off the hook for now but one false move and I'll call the nearest security guard employment agency and hire one just so that I can have you thrown out on your ear." Quite a mouthful, Wil thought, considering so little had actually been said.

Mary Gold now returned to her duties, which as far as Wil could tell involved gliding around and rearranging more note cards, filing her nails, and ignoring him completely. It was odd, thought Wil, that she seemed to move with absolutely no effort whatsoever, as if she were skating. Mr. Dinsdale motioned for Wil to follow him back up the staircase. As they moved away, Wil could have sworn he noticed the nearest wooden crate move once again but he was too busy watching Mary Gold On Ice to pay any particular attention.

"I'm sorry I had to pop off for a few moments, Wil," said Mr. Dinsdale.

"I was just putting Mozart's First Clonecerto back in its case. I'd like to show you around the place, if you're amenable, so that you can get the lay of the land."

"Is she always that friendly?" asked Wil, nodding his head in the direction of Mary Gold, who was now gliding from the back to the front of the main desk and yelling "Don't come back anytime soon!" in body language.

"Oh no," replied Dinsdale. "Mary generally isn't too friendly with new arrivals. I don't know what you said but it must have been very charming, you sly dog."

"Maybe she felt sorry for me because I was confused," mused Wil, meaning every word of it. "I'm just glad I didn't get my throat ripped out. You show any sign of weakness to someone like that and you're lunch meat."

"Yes, that's about it!" said Mr. Dinsdale, chuckling. "Woman frightens the life out of me, too, but she's a darn good typist! Come on!"

With that, Mr. Dinsdale picked up his pace and bounced up the next flight of steps two at a time. Wil followed suit and found himself slightly breathless on the upper landing of the museum, staring down a wide corridor. On either side were empty glass cases and more wooden crates, suggesting that someone was in the middle of setting up a new exhibit. Out of the corner of his eye, Wil noticed one of the wooden crates wobble slightly, like a Mexican jumping bean.

"What's inside the crates, if you don't mind me asking?" Wil blurted out.

The little curator stopped short for a moment. He seemed to find Wil's question amusing. "What do you think is inside them? You're entitled to one guess. There are no wrong answers."

"I don't know. Every time I stare at one it stops moving and another one moves in the exact place I'm not looking. I feel like they're all working together, or something. Are they remote controlled?"

"I really wouldn't be able to say. They were part of a large consignment that came in from Venezuela a few years ago. We decided not to open them up because they were so stupendously interesting just as they were. As a matter of fact, they work well as an exhibit. They help distract new visitors to the museum so that people can un-look properly at the items on display."

Wil and Mr. Dinsdale were now moving along the corridor, headed for one of the main upper display areas. Wil did his best to ignore the moving crates, and they did their best to distract him out of the corner of his eye. He stared ahead, fixated on the end of the hallway.

"What did you mean by what you said outside?" Wil had been thinking of asking Mr. Dinsdale that question since the moment he'd entered the museum but he'd been distracted by some wooden crates, not to mention the combative Miss Gold.

"I'm not sure what you mean," replied Dinsdale as they entered the first display area, which looked suspiciously like a historical reenactment of Hideous Junkyards Across the Ages.

Wil stopped abruptly, forcing the old man to stop, too. He wasn't going to proceed unless he had his question answered with the due care and attention it deserved. "'Your eyes only see what your mind lets you believe,'" Wil said, refusing to allow Mr. Dinsdale to ignore the question or wander away from the moment. "Where did you get that from?"

"Did I say that?" replied Dinsdale. Like all older men, he possessed somewhat of a twinkle in his rheumy old eyes, and Wil could not be sure if that twinkle was intentional at this very moment. "Well, that was quite a clever phrase, don't you think? I really should write that down somewhere and copyright it."

Mr. Dinsdale wandered off toward the nearest exhibit. Wil watched him move away as he took stock of what he might do next. He decided to file this exchange in the back of his mind, to be addressed later after his unresolved confrontation with his Strange Feeling of déjà vu.

The nearest exhibit was composed of a series of cogs and pulleys that really didn't seem to do very much at all except move around in a little circle. Around and around . . . Wil found himself mildly intrigued by the fact that this machine reminded him of an old model railway kit he'd owned as a kid. Mr. Dinsdale stood before the thing with his hands clasped behind his back, smiling that enigmatic smile of his. Wil noticed that a similar machine nearby also demonstrated some of this machine's traits, such as possessing a lot of moving parts and generally seeming to have little purpose. Looking around the entire area, Wil realized the place was full of these contraptions, all of which were whirring and humming like electric transformers. They all seemed remarkably well oiled, yet for the life of him Wil couldn't figure out what each machine might be for.

"You'll notice," said Mr. Dinsdale in a hushed tone, "that there are no power supplies."

"What do they do?" asked Wil as he duly obliged and took pains to note the lack of power running into the machines.

"Well, they don't do anything, really. They're all perpetual motion machines—nothing all that special, to be honest. It's a bit of a generic exhibit but I feel it's the sort of thing people need to get themselves warmed up." Mr. Dinsdale began to wander along the rows of whirring, vibrating machinery of all shapes and sizes. "There are hundreds of these things across the world. One of ours was invented by the Comte de Saint-Germain when he was imprisoned in England on espionage charges. I've heard it said, though, that the original design came from a Mr. Harry Braddock, who was one of his prison guards at the time. This one was invented by an Ottoman sultan by the name of Mehmed. . . . This was one of Archimedes' early pieces. . . ."

Wil began to tune the old man out as he perused the various cogs and levers of each perpetual motion machine. He'd heard of perpetual motion when he was a little boy, of course, but everyone knew that such a machine could not possibly exist by the very laws of nature. One always had to put in more energy than one got out, mostly as a result of friction. Anything to the contrary would violate the first law of thermodynamics. Thus, the machines on display were obviously just a trick. And not a very good one, Wil decided.

At the end of the display area stood a more complicated piece of machinery that drew Wil's attention for the fact that it was blue, seemed very old, and sparked with electricity ever so slightly. At the front of this particular machine was a ten-inch-wide hole from which most of the sparks emanated. Wil felt the machine possessed a familiar sight and smell, and he could not help but smile at the thought of his mom's probable reaction to it.

"Ah, now this one," said Mr. Dinsdale with no attempt to contain his enthusiasm, "this one is very special. I'm not surprised you found your way right to it, Wil."

"What's so special about it?" asked Wil.

Mr. Dinsdale took on the proud look of a French art gallery director. "The world's first and only Perpetual Emotion machine; it was designed by none other than Maestro Leonardo da Vinci himself, sometime after he perfected his first solar power cell. It's said this machine once entertained the crowned heads of Europe by inducing a perpetual state of happiness into anyone willing to put their hands into the receptacle at the front. Would you like to try?"

Wil hesitated and scrunched his nose in a painfully transparent attempt to indicate he most certainly would not like to stick his hand into the depths of the sparking monstrosity before him. He hoped to avoid responding to Mr. Dinsdale's invitation for as long as it took to get out of the line of fire. Mr. Dinsdale looked a little disappointed.

"You really shouldn't worry so much about getting in touch with your feelings, Wil," said the little curator. "It's not healthy to avoid your emotions."

"I'm not worried about getting in touch with my feelings," said Wil. "I'm more afraid of being electrocuted by them. It looks a bit haphazard. Are you sure it's safe?"

"There's nothing to worry about. Look!" Mr. Dinsdale thrust his hand into the hand-shaped receptacle, which promptly sent out a massive shower of sparks that covered him from head to toe. Wil was alarmed to realize the little man looked like a welder who'd suddenly lost control of his blowtorch, and he thrust up his arm so that he could identify Dinsdale in the blinding light.

"Mr. Dinsdale! Are you okay?" The Perpetual Emotion machine was now beginning to judder loudly, and Wil thought he could hear

Mr. Dinsdale over the sound of the grinding gears and the shooting sparks. If he wasn't mistaken, the curator seemed to be making loud sobbing noises. "Mr. Dinsdale! Hold on tight! I'll find the off switch!"

"There is no off switch!" howled Dinsdale. "It's not fair! We're all going to die someday! And then the universe will end and I won't have had enough time to say goodbye!"

Wil could only assume this series of bizarre statements meant that poor Mr. Dinsdale had suffered some kind of spark-induced concussion. He lurched forward and with a mighty heave grabbed hold of Dinsdale's mustard-yellow jacket and yanked the old man backward for all he was worth. At the very moment he made contact with the jacket's fabric, Wil felt a crushing despair fill every fiber of his being, and for the half second or so before he managed to extricate the little curator from the receptacle of the Perpetual Emotion machine, he suddenly wondered if he shouldn't just find a dark hole and bury himself in it. Life seemed meaningless, and he was far too often lonely inside his apartment building, despite all of Mrs. Chappell's cats. There really seemed no point to creation, Wil realized, and God probably didn't care.

Moments later, Wil and Mr. Dinsdale lay in a heap on the floor. The sparking machine next to them had immediately returned to its previous state, and there was an uncomfortable moment between the two men. Wil felt mildly ridiculous to find himself at ground level, and wrapped around the little man for the second time in the space of half an hour. Worse, he felt a terrible emptiness in his soul, which seemed to be a residual effect of the Perpetual Emotion machine.

Mr. Dinsdale got to his feet first. He brushed himself off with one hand and stared at Maestro da Vinci's gruesome death trap, scratching his chin as if to indicate a reaction of mild interest as opposed to one of sheer terror. Wil painfully scrambled to his feet; he felt far less suicidal than a moment or two before, but he'd jammed his thumb during the takedown.

"What the heck happened?" asked Wil, incredulous. "I had the weirdest feeling when I tried to pull you out of that thing."

"I think it's stuck on melancholy," replied Mr. Dinsdale. "I'll have to write to the people at the da Vinci Institute to see if they still have the manual. We should probably cordon it off until we can reset it."

"You should probably cordon it off until you can get in a bomb disposal expert to blow it to kingdom come." Wil rubbed his injured thumb and stared daggers at the Perpetual Emotion machine, which had now gone back to merely looking dangerous as opposed to actually being dangerous.

Mr. Dinsdale narrowed his eyes as if he were carefully considering Wil's suggestion. He glanced at the Perpetual Emotion machine as if determining its fate once and for all. Wil half-expected the little curator to raise or lower his thumb, Nero-style, and consign the sparking monstrosity to a retirement procedure that would involve more than a little carefully placed TNT. No such luck, unfortunately: Mr. Dinsdale suddenly turned away and began to head toward the next display area.

Will followed, slightly exasperated by Mr. Dinsdale's arbitrary behavior and his apparent indifference to the city's safety codes, not to mention its explosives ordinances. "Mr. Dinsdale," he cried out after the departing curator, "don't you think you'd better switch it off? Mr. Dinsdale?"

By the time Wil turned the next corner, Mr. Dinsdale was now standing directly in front of an exhibit at the far end of the adjacent room. Unless Wil was mistaken, the old man had covered a hundred and fifty feet in about two seconds. Wil decided not to react to this since his own cerebral cortex had now come to the independent decision it would be better off discounting the curator's ability to randomly teleport. Ignoring the old man, Wil reasoned, was the first step to figuring him out. Wil began to head toward Dinsdale's position. As he moved closer, he realized he was actually walking with quite a spring in his step, and with a sense of purpose that usually escaped him. He slowed back to an indifferent trudge just to make it clear that teleporting curators and Perpetual Emotion machines were no big deal, really.

Wil's trudge took him past an entrance to a completely empty display area contained inside a closed-off white room. For a split second, he imagined he saw movement out of the corner of his eye: a young woman with dark, curly hair walking toward his position. He turned, thinking this might be a visitor to the Curioddity Museum. While he hadn't yet run into any paying customers, he expected at the very least to come face-to-face with a wooden crate. Instead, the room was completely featureless and empty, and the illusion of movement within was gone. Wil narrowed his eyes, only to realize he probably looked exactly as Mr. Dinsdale did just moments before. Feeling quite disconcerted by this turn of events—as if the museum had somehow affected him to the extent he was acting like a crazy old teleporting man in a mustard jacket—Wil hurriedly moved away from the featureless room and began to trudge as quickly as his legs could carry him toward the curator.

Mr. Dinsdale stood in front of a shelf, upon which was a single green glass bottle. Nearby were various items of trash that might just as easily have been found inside, say, a junkyard or around the back of an abandoned trailer on a pig farm. Inside a glass display case, Wil noticed a little watch device fashioned out of wood. A legend inscribed at the base of the glass read, simply, "Sequitur." And next to this stood an empty display case with the words "Non Sequitur" written upon it. Up against the wall, someone had propped an old-style throwing spear. A nearby wooden plaque described this item as the "Spear of Density," which was either an understandable typo or yet another attempt by the museum's curator to generate interest in something that didn't deserve it.

As Wil approached, Dinsdale seemed to be studying the green bottle as intently as one might study a chalkboard covered by complex mathematical equations, though for the life of him Wil could not see anything about the dirty old thing that might explain such scrutiny. He decided to remain quiet in the hopes Mr. Dinsdale might be forthcoming with something that actually explained things for once, as opposed to complicating things even further.

"It's a lightning catcher," explained Dinsdale in a reverent tone. The little curator seemed to be looking directly at the green bottle, which looked very unlike a receptacle for electricity and much more like a receptacle that once contained a soft drink. Wil looked behind the shelf, just in case there was an actual lightning catcher somewhere in the immediate vicinity that he hadn't noticed earlier.

"Are all your museum exhibits this impressive?" asked Wil, gesturing to the various items of scrap around him. He hoped the obvious sarcastic tone of his question might make his point: he was beginning to tire of being led around an elaborate thrift shop in search of an explanation regarding a job that he was getting more and more inclined to refuse in advance.

"Are you not really a fan of lightning catchers, Wil?" asked the little curator, his expression betraying a genuine disappointment.

"On the contrary, I find them to be extremely compelling. Look, Mr. Dinsdale . . . I'm sure you're a very nice man. But at the risk of forcing the issue for a second time, I'd greatly appreciate it if we could get to the point. You said you had a job for me, and if it's all the same to you, I'd like to discuss that instead of admiring your lightning catcher, amazing though it may be."

The little man brightened, seeming to feel relieved that Wil had demonstrated a genuine appreciation for his dirty old green bottle. "You're right, of course." He chuckled. "Sometimes I let the splenditude of this place distract me from the tasks at hand. It's probably not a good idea to let the trail get too cold. Come on . . . it's over here." With that, Mr. Dinsdale struck out toward an exhibit area farther along the hall. Finally, thought Wil, we're getting somewhere.

༺༻

AT THE end of the hall was a sign that read, TEMPORAL AND SPATIAL ANOMALIES EXHIBIT. Beyond this sign was another display area, inside which was yet another collection of assorted pieces of trash. At least, thought Wil, it was mercifully devoid of any wooden crates. As he entered, he could have sworn that for an instant he caught the image of the ghostly young woman out of the corner of his eye. He got the distinct impression the girl was pretty and cheerful, though quite how he arrived at such a conclusion he could not be sure. Whatever the case, when he turned to look directly at the phantasm there was nothing directly in front of him. He began to look rather puzzled, a fact that did not escape Mr. Dinsdale's notice.

"You've seen her, haven't you? The girl with the curly hair who appears in the corner of your eye." This was more of a statement of confirmation than a question. Wil found the old man staring intently at him, waiting for a response to the affirmative. He was not immediately inclined to play along, though he had to admit this was an intriguing development.

"Is this another one of your exhibits?" he asked. "I mean, it's a test, or something, right? So people think the place is haunted. And then at the end you show them it's a projection, or a trapdoor."

"Well, yes and no." The little curator seemed genuinely puzzled himself by the happenings around the museum. "The thing is we're pretty sure the young woman everyone keeps seeing isn't a ghost. At least, she's not a ghost in the typical sense but she's most definitely real. After much analysis I've been forced to conclude that she's not haunting us. Unless I'm mistaken, it's most likely that we are haunting her. It's as if the museum has found a way to plug into her spiritual gestalt wherever she exists in time and space. It's probably a side effect of one of the temporal exhibits we have up here."

"Lucky her," replied Wil, trying and failing to contain his indifference. He studied the nearby exhibits in the hopes this might change the subject.

"This is my favorite part of the museum," explained Mr. Dinsdale, who seemed happy enough to change the subject. "Everything here is a direct challenge to the laws of physics. Much of what you see in this room is counterpart to either time or space, and sometimes both." Mr. Dinsdale motioned toward a nearby exhibit: a telephone answering machine that rivaled Wil's own for its primitive design. "This one's a particularly impressive piece."

Wil nodded, hoping to give the impression that he was indeed awed by the fact that the demonic answering machine in his office might have an equally dysfunctional twin.

"It used to belong to Albert Einstein," continued Dinsdale. "It's actually a remarkable piece. Einstein was experimenting with the anomalous properties of sound delivered across large distances. He felt there must be an explanation as to why, for example, answering machines so often malfunction when relaying important messages. In terms of quantum reality, answering machines tend to function with a kind of hyperawareness."

"I have one just like it," replied Wil, eyeing the answering machine carefully. "I think mine is possessed. It's going to strangle me the moment I turn my back on it."

"That's quite possible," replied Dinsdale, turning his attention to his own machine. "Our exhibit works counter to the flow of space and time. It records and plays back the next message in the time stream. So when you press it, it plays the next message you're going to receive in your future."

Wil's cerebral cortex, which had previously been attempting to ignore most of what it had experienced on this particular Monday, now made it clear to him that it was indeed going on strike, and it promptly shut down into a kind of holding pattern until such time as things made sense again. Wil was forced to nod his head and look interested, unable to process the ridiculous nature of what he was being told.

"If it plays the next message, what about the previous one, the one you actually need?" asked Wil, trying to bring his occipital lobe into the fray in the hopes it might act as a temporary backup.

"Oh, it's not much of an answering machine," replied Dinsdale. "But it comes in handy if you want to tell yourself yesterday what the horse racing results will be. Want to see it work?"

Wil nodded. He wanted to see it work not for its potential application but to determine if the really useful messages from the future would sound like they were being delivered in the same unintelligible fashion as that provided by his own fiendish machine.

Mr. Dinsdale pressed the Play button, and from the speakers came a distant yet familiar voice: Wil's own. "Mr. Dinsdale! Mr. Dinsdale, are you there? I need you to stay right there! I'm coming over! I'll be there in ten minutes!" called Future Wil from within a space that sounded suspiciously like a submarine.

Wil looked at the little curator, shocked. However the old man had created such a trick, he had to admit it was rather impressive. Proudly, Dinsdale motioned toward some of the other exhibits.

"As I said, most of the items here are of the temporal or spatial anomaly variety," said Dinsdale. "Over at the back, we're displaying a periscope from a Civil War–era battleship. It possesses some curious properties that we don't fully understand. The higher you elevate the lens, the farther it sees below the floor. It must have come in handy against Civil War–era submarines. "

Wil looked toward the far wall, where what appeared to be a long copper tube was propped up against a hole in the plaster. Nearby, a second display case contained something that looked a lot like a child's toy magnet.

"Personal magnetism inducer," said Dinsdale in a matter-of-fact manner. "Galileo felt it would be a boon to humankind if he could make it easier to speak to members of the opposite sex. They say he was quite a charmer with the ladies as a result of his invention. But I'm getting off track again. . . ."

Mr. Dinsdale stopped in front of an empty shelf set into a sturdy brick wall with some heavy brackets, where a small metal plate was inscribed with the words, EXHIBIT NW1-M1M. It was as if someone had gone out of their way to make the plaque as unremarkable as possible, and Wil couldn't help but wonder if it had been inscribed by the same genius who'd made such a mess of his office door back at the Castle Towers. To each side were a couple of frayed ropes tethered to some very thick metal hooks that had been bolted into the brick. The ropes looked as though they had snapped at some point. "This is what I wanted to show you, Wil," said Mr. Dinsdale, furrowing his chin in that peculiar manner of his. "I have reason to believe one of our most important exhibits has been stolen. I'd like you to find it for me."

Wil wasn't exactly sure how to respond. He kept his mouth shut and pretended for a moment to consider the offer just in case he could persuade his cerebral cortex to get back on the job and help him process the information. Certainly, he wasn't about to turn down a paying gig given the increasingly unhealthy state of his bank account; his current finances could be likened to a dehydrated hyena crawling through the Kalahari Desert in search of an oasis. The biggest obstacle he could see was that he had absolutely no experience whatsoever in tracking down valuable objects, much less Mr. Dinsdale's prized exhibit—an item that someone most likely tossed out with the trash by mistake. On the other hand, Mr. Dinsdale seemed to be implying that money might be involved, some of which stood a chance of flowing in Wil's direction.

Wil swallowed hard. He already knew in his heart that he was unlikely to avoid the fatal mistake he'd made numerous times in such situations: he was going to tell the truth, to be exact, and this was going to cost him yet another chance at resuscitating that parched hyena crawling through his imaginary desert. In order to give himself the illusion of participation for a few more moments, he pretended to ask a pertinent question. "What was stolen from this display, exactly, Mr. Dinsdale?"

The little curator described the shape of a rectangle in the air with his fingers. "A container of about these proportions," he said. "A very unusual wooden box made of teak, and with mother-of-pearl inlay. It contains quite possibly the world's largest sample of levity."

"Levity?"

"It's the opposite of gravity. You see, the universe is composed of many types of matter: there's matter, antimatter, dark matter—"

"What kind is levity?"

"Doesn't matter. The point is, levity is a very dangerous and unusual substance that works exactly opposite to the way things normally work. So rather than falling down, for example, a person holding a container of levity might be prone to falling up and hitting his or her head on the ceiling. It's the kind of thing that cannot possibly fall into the wrong hands."

Wil realized he'd taken his illusion of participation about as far as he possibly could. He harbored no desire to take advantage of this nice (if somewhat delusional) old man. It was now time to come clean, he decided, before he dug himself a Karmic hole he'd be unable to climb out of. "Look, Mr. Dinsdale," he began, "I'd like to help you—"

"Well I'm very pleased to hear it," interrupted Dinsdale with a visible sigh of relief. "We'd better get started right away!"

"—I'd like to help you," continued Wil, "but I'm afraid I can't. I wouldn't have the first clue where to look, and even if one of your employees or a museum visitor were responsible, there are people far better qualified to run through video surveillance footage and trace the whereabouts of suspects. I don't even have access to a forensics kit."

"Why on Earth would you need a forensics kit?" asked Dinsdale. The look of confusion spreading across the old man's face indicated a strong possibility that he hadn't considered Wil might react in this manner.

"I don't even know what the box is supposed to look like!" exclaimed Wil, feeling more than a little exasperated as he tried his utmost to get through to the curator. "Even if you had a photo of it—"

"Not possible! Levity has an adverse effect on all cameras!"

"—even if you had a painting of it," Wil persisted, "and even if you had video footage—which I'm going to go out on a limb and guess has the same statistical likelihood of me paying my rent on time this month—you're still better off using someone else. I'm sorry. I just don't think it would be fair for me to take on this job. You'd be wasting your money."

Mr. Dinsdale took in a sharp breath, rolled it around in his lungs for a moment, and then exhaled slowly. It was as if he needed a little extra oxygen for a moment, just to feed his brain while he considered what to do next. The long breath seemed to have a calming effect on the strange old man, and within a moment or two he had reverted to his less manic persona. "I'm grateful for your honesty, Wil," he said after a moment. "Most other people would have taken the job whether they felt they had something to offer or not. This is the exact reason you're the perfect man for this particular task."

"Excuse me?" Wil hadn't expected to be so startled by Dinsdale's circular logic. Yet he had a distinct feeling that same logic was about to whisk him up and make him do a few laps around something he wasn't prepared to circumnavigate.

"An honest man demonstrates an ability to un-look at a situation, to consider a bigger picture rather than simply taking advantage of what is in front of him. My box of levity is not going to be found by a person who doesn't know how to un-look for it."

"But that doesn't make sense! What if I'd told you I knew where to look for it?"

The old man smiled, and tapped his nose with his forefinger as if sharing a secret moment with a new best friend. "Then you would have been telling the truth," he said. And with this odd response acting as his conclusion to the matter, the little curator turned on his heel and headed back toward the main foyer of the Curioddity Museum. "Come on!" he cried. "We should go downstairs and discuss terms!"

Wil stood transfixed for a moment. The negotiation had not exactly gone according to plan. In fact, he was beginning to sense a familiar theme cropping up in his interactions with Mr. Dinsdale: the moment he felt he was on any kind of reasonable path it seemed as if Mr. Dinsdale would suddenly be going in the opposite direction; and in the unlikely event Wil corrected course, he seemed to find himself headed in the very direction Mr. Dinsdale had intended for him in the first place. It was apparent that he was out of his league, and that the only way to compete would be to play along until everyone reverted to ignoring him. At that point, he'd probably be able to slip out the back door and return to his previously scheduled life. After a moment's pause,

Wil headed off toward the foyer in pursuit of the now rapidly depart-ing Mr. Dinsdale.

❧

As Wil descended the stairs into the foyer, he caught sight of Dins-dale at the main desk, talking in animated fashion with Mary Gold. At the far end of the counter, a wooden crate appeared to poke out for a moment, as if listening to the conversation. The moment Wil looked at it, the crate seemed to duck back in behind the back end of the counter. Being a polite sort of man, Wil tried to slow his advance so that Mr. Dinsdale and his assistant could know he was coming and adjust their argument accordingly. He caught the tail end of some-thing Mary Gold had been saying to the little curator.

". . . it doesn't matter if you think he's the one—I don't trust him!"

Wil coughed, partly because he was still trying to be polite and partly because Mary Gold was beginning to rub him the wrong way and he wanted to make it clear he was on to her game. At the sound of the cough, Mr. Dinsdale turned and tried to quickly compose himself by producing a fake smile, which he aimed in Wil's direction. Mary Gold frowned at Wil, just so he'd know she was saying something mean to him in body language.

"Wil!" cried Dinsdale. "We were just discussing your fee. Weren't we, Mary?"

Mary Gold smacked on her bubble gum to make it clear she was feeling in a disdainful mood in general and venomous toward Wil in particular. "Sure we were," she replied in plain English. "And the mo-ment I get an opportunity I'll expose you as a fraud and run you out of town," she continued, silently.

"We were hoping five thousand dollars might be sufficient to get you started?" inquired Mr. Dinsdale. "I can have more transferred to your bank account should you need it for expenses. And the final five thousand will be payable upon retrieval of the exhibit. Would this be acceptable?"

Wil felt rather like a man in a casino who just accidentally bet on red when he'd meant to bet on black. He could see the croupier shoving a pile of money in his direction but he wasn't yet sure if he should reach out and pull it toward him. Lacking any kind of coherent response he merely nodded, sheepishly, and lowered his gaze toward his shoes so that he wouldn't have to meet Mary Gold's piercing stare.

"Wonderful!" cried Mr. Dinsdale. "I'll have Mary transfer the money into your account just as soon you provide me with your banking details. In the meantime, here's something to cover immediate expenses, and I'd like you to review this artist's rendition of the Levity box."

Mr. Dinsdale handed Wil an envelope containing ten or twelve crisp fifty-dollar bills and a crumpled piece of paper he'd been scribbling on. The paper depicted a simple cube, which Dinsdale seemed to have hastily drawn in the few moments before Wil had made his way downstairs. The image was box-shaped, to be certain, but it hardly seemed like the starting point Mr. Dinsdale believed it to be. To Wil, events were now flashing by like a pudding-filled Lamborghini Gallardo that had been driven off the edge of a cliff. The whole thing was moving too fast, and while everything appeared to be headed directly toward a very damaging conclusion, he reasoned the experience might at least be fun in the few moments it would take to arrive.

"I guess there's no harm in taking a look," Wil said with as little enthusiasm as he could muster. "Do we have any clues or witnesses?"

"Not a one," replied Mr. Dinsdale, happily. "But we do have Wil Morgan, Crack Detective, on the job! I'm sure the moment you leave this building our levity thief will be quaking in his or her shoes at the very thought of such a tenacious professional nipping at their heels."

"I'll do my best, Mr. Dinsdale," replied Wil, feeling utterly embarrassed at the notion he might do anything other than wander aimlessly around for a couple of days sorting through the city's ten billion cube-shaped candidates. "Now if you'll excuse me, I'll be on my way. I'll contact you the moment I have anything to report."

With that, Wil and the old man shook hands, and Wil began a hurried trudge in the direction of the nearby revolving door and the freedom that beckoned beyond it. Out of the corner of his eye he imagined he could see a pretty, curly-haired young woman bustling around one of the wooden crates but he chose to ignore the ghost and kept on walking. Wil could feel Mary Gold's eyes burning a hole in his back just below the shoulder blades. But he stiffened his resolve and kept his eyes focused on the street outside, which was now blanketed in a heavy dusting of snow.

Don't look back, Wil silently instructed himself as he grasped one of the revolving door's free panels. Don't feel bad about this, and most definitely do not get stuck in this revolving door and look like an idiot in your first two minutes on the job. He pushed on the panel and surprised himself by moments later making it through the door without damaging any of his appendages.

Outside, the wind was bitter cold. Wil could imagine Mary Gold standing at the main desk inside the Curioddity Museum behind him and screaming silent threats in the direction of his shoulder blades. Rather than confirming these fears, he strode quickly down the marble steps of the museum and out onto Mons Street. Wil felt slightly disoriented by the dense fog and snow, so it took a moment to get his bearings. A freshening wind seemed to take great delight in pelting him directly in the face with large snowflakes. It would probably be necessary, he decided, to hurry back to his apartment and find a couple of extra layers of clothing.

Nearby, Wil could hear the bustle of the divided highway and the complicated one-way system, so he struck out in that direction. Within seconds, he found himself at the corner of Mons Street. And it was here that things, unsurprisingly, took a slight turn for the weird.

As Wil approached the trash can he'd spotted earlier, he realized the fog was very quickly lifting. Or, to be more precise, he seemed to be headed toward an abrupt climate change just yards from where he'd been standing outside the museum. The trash can was now bathed in sunlight, and just beyond the end of Mons Street there seemed to be no evidence of residual frozen fog whatsoever. Wil was startled to realize the fallen snow had covered only the street he was on, while the traffic moving around the one-way system was moving at a steady pace through early-afternoon sunshine.

Wil peered down the length of Mons Street; some fifty yards away, the old cinema was now becoming shrouded in the very mist that had refused to make its way to where he was currently standing. If he scrunched his nose and looked *just so* he could see the Museum of Curioddity in his peripheral vision. But when he looked directly at the building, all he could make out was a white sheet of snow. He stood still for a moment, trying to get a sense of what this might mean. The envelope full of money seemed real enough in his coat pocket, and his thumb still hurt, so he didn't feel he was likely to be dreaming. Even so, the hairs were beginning to crawl on the back of his neck, as if someone were still staring into it.

Wil stared at the nearby street sign. It stared back at him in block capital letters that continued to say MONS no matter how hard he looked at it.

Upside-Down Street. Wil suddenly had a very curious notion indeed; a whim of almost epic proportions seemed to come over him, replacing the awful sense that someone was staring at the back of his neck. Slowly, yet with an increasing feeling of self-confidence, Wil began to bend at the waist until his head was just about level with his knees. He turned his head upside down and peered toward the street sign once again.

Written upon the sign was the very message he'd been looking at the entire time, and it was now evident to Wil that his only mistake had been to look at it the wrong way. Perhaps instead of merely looking at the sign he should have been un-looking at it instead.

IN LARGE block capital letters the sign read, simply, SNOW.

CHAPTER FOUR

WIL NARROWED his eyes for a moment as he focused on the every-which-way sign at the end of Upside-Down Street. By sheer force of will, he managed to ignore the snow falling roughly ten yards from where he was standing. And by stubbornly sticking to this task for a few minutes, he found that the street, the old cinema, and even the Museum of Curioddity were slowly returning to their previous state, which was to say they now did not seem to exist at all, just as long as he refused to look at them. Or un-look at them, he supposed. He could hardly tell if by ignoring the buildings he had rendered them invisible, or if they had never existed in the first place, or if the excess of blood running to his head had given him one of his migraines.

Wil straightened, so that the fluids vacating his upper extremities sent a wave of nausea cascading through his inner ear. He steadied himself for a moment against the street sign. This entire episode was going sideways—or upside down—in a hurry. If he were going to straighten things out again, he realized, he'd have to think of something drastic. And so he concentrated his thoughts on the imminent arrival of his dad, Barry, which had the desired effect of bringing reality crashing down around him in much the same way a duck full of hunters' buckshot might tumble unceremoniously into a swamp. Very quickly—with perhaps a quiet squeal of protest at the violation of its existential rights—Wil's universe seemed to return to a state of normalcy. Perhaps not so normal, he realized, considering how he had just invoked the spiritual essence of Barry Morgan. Was it his imagination, or had thinking about his dad helped to rid him of his vertigo for once, as opposed to bringing on an attack?

Behind him, the sound of the cars careening along the one-way system had begun to dissolve into a sort of motorized hum. This would be a good time to take stock of the situation: a sensible approach one might expect of a college-trained chartered accountant as opposed to, say, a confused detective specializing in cases of insurance fraud who had just taken on a job he had no possible chance of completing. Thankfully, Wil's prowess in the area of "taking stock" rivaled that of his ability to trudge around one-way systems and to start meaningless arguments with teenagers in coffee shops. All of this taking stock would doubtless put him in a more comfortable frame of mind, he hoped. And that might help him explain what the heck had just happened.

The first course of meaningful action, Wil decided, was that he was going to have to decide what to do first. Secondly, he was going to have a reckoning of the knock-down, drag-out variety with the Strange Feeling of déjà vu he'd been arguing with earlier. And finally, he was probably going to find a nice bench somewhere and have a quiet, feeble moment to himself, wherein he'd try to persuade himself that none of this particular Monday's events had ever really happened. The envelope full of cash in his pocket was undoubtedly either a forgery or a mistake, which could easily be said for Mr. Dinsdale, the

Museum of Curioddity, and the last of the snow melting from his lapels.

Wil rubbed his head for a moment, examining it for bruises. The most likely explanation for all of this nonsense was that he'd been battered unconscious at some point earlier in the day, and this had induced a bout of post-concussion syndrome. Though Wil had never been knocked senseless in his life, this convenient epiphany seemed both possible and—by extension—probable. Perhaps he'd tripped on the calico cat draped across the landing of Mrs. Chappell's apartment building, and the resulting face-plant down the final flight of stairs had knocked him senseless. Perhaps his shoelaces were untied; he stooped to check their integrity, only to be confronted by two firmly tied and sensible double knots courtesy of his dad's years of relentless training on the subject of footwear safety. Of course, Wil suddenly rationalized, Dad was coming to town! No doubt he'd fainted from the shock of listening to the message Barry Morgan had left on his demonic answering machine and was still lying, unconscious, on the nineteenth floor of the Castle Towers where he would have to wait until 7:00 P.M. for Mr. Whatley to discover his semi-lifeless body. Wil hoped the fall had been a particularly nasty one so that his dad might be forced to postpone his visit well into the next decade.

But no such luck; try as he might, Wil could find no evidence of bruises, scrapes, lesions, or lacerations beyond the obvious symptom of his soul having dropped through the bottom of his intestines. Somehow in the next few days he was going to have to craft the illusion he had been working for the last seven years as a chartered accountant.

As he knelt and stared at his shoelaces, trying to stifle the involuntary sobs working their way back to the surface, Wil glanced at his watch: five minutes past three. In exactly one minute from now, his mortal enemy—the repulsive Swiss edifice outside the Castle Towers that masqueraded as a giant clock tower—would attempt its daily sneak attack. But this was no ordinary Monday, and this time he would be ready. Summoning the imaginary advice of a certain imaginary curator named Dinsdale—a fanciful figure brought about by post-concussion syndrome, no doubt—Wil Morgan would attempt to *un-listen* to the awful monstrosity.

Five minutes and thirty seconds . . . Wil scrunched his eyes and tried to un-listen to the cars passing by on the one-way system. Not an easy task, he decided. Perhaps it would be better to un-listen to the street sign that was dutifully making no noise whatsoever as it monitored the progress of nearby traffic. Wil stepped back to concentrate on its smooth, metal edges. He considered Upside-Down Street's proximity to the city's one-way system, thinking it ironic that his recent experiences here had seemed to go in every direction at once. Everything about the museum was in complete contradiction to the conformity that surrounded it. But now that Wil was back on the main road running through town, the metal sign simply said MONS once more, and the notion that a semi-visible street blanketed in snow existed nearby seemed—like the Curioddity Museum itself—ridiculous indeed. He waited for the hideous clock tower's sonic assault to come from afar, which even from this distance would sound something like:

EEEEOOOOWWWW!

WIL JUMPED, startled, as a rusted old Ford Pinto plowing through the city's one-way system at eighty miles per hour missed him by inches. The blare of the car's horn was quickly replaced by the residual sucking sound of a nearby puddle of water struggling to refill itself after depositing most of its muddy contents over Wil's clothing.

As he struggled to recover from the shock of this near miss, a fist emerged from within the rusted Pinto, shook itself angrily, and aimed what seemed to be a loud epithet in the direction of the suicidal lunatic it was leaving trailing in its wake. Not to be outdone by this inconsiderate and faceless maniac behind the wheel of half a ton of moving metal, Wil raised his own fist and readied a choice epithet of his own:

KLONNGG!

THE SUDDEN crash of the clock tower banging away like a maniacal monk in the distance instantly scrambled Wil's thoughts like so many eggs across a busy one-way system. The clock was much louder at this part of the roadway than the scientific discipline of applied acoustics might have predicted. The klonnging sound caused Wil to stumble sharply sideways; or to be more precise, he stumbled abruptly sideways until his head connected painfully with something sharp: namely, the edge of a metal street sign that until now had seemed perfectly incapable of causing actual bodily harm. It's always the ones you least suspect, thought Wil, as he staggered slowly to his knees.

Shocked by this sudden and stunning reversal of allegiance on the part of the street sign, he reached to his forehead. His fingers found a nasty, bloody gash hidden beneath matted hair. Wil briefly considered calling Washington, D.C., and reporting the Swiss clock to the immigration authorities in the hope that they might somehow be able to revoke its visa. But it was no use. Blood was now cascading down his wrist, and his forehead was beginning to swell. Wil could not possibly walk back toward his office—not against the flow of traffic, surely. There was only one thing for it: his first meaningful action in the search for Mr. Dinsdale's missing box of Levity would be to stagger along the one-way system and go home.

❧

WIL SET out with the flow of traffic, silently cursing anything that happened to enter the periphery of his awareness, or be remotely connected to the country of Switzerland. He cursed the clock, and the

Castle Towers, and his pathetic sham of a life in particular. As he passed one of the city's ubiquitous advertising boards, Wil cursed Marcus James and anyone stupid enough to make three easy payments of $19.95 for what looked to be, on the face of it, a large piece of tent canvas with a hole in the middle that supposedly doubled as a poncho. But he reserved his most passionate swearing for the cold and steady mist of rain that had now decided to make a comeback, and had reverted the city's appearance to its usual variety of drab. The colder Wil's skin felt, the more he was forced to concede that harsh reality had set in, and that most (if not all) of his day had actually happened the way he'd remembered it. Mr. Dinsdale's envelope showed no signs of dematerializing from his pocket, which suggested that the money it contained was some kind of karmic payoff intended to soften the blow of the known universe being turned on its head. Wil knew that his post-concussion syndrome was simply an excuse he'd created to explain away all of the day's curious events (though in light of his new head injury, the statistical likelihood of future post-concussion syndrome episodes was now rising exponentially). He refrained from glowering in the direction of the passing cars—they'd caused him enough trouble for one afternoon. Instead, he would head back to his apartment building and try to find a bottle of rubbing alcohol, which he would first apply liberally to his head and then drink until he was mercifully unconscious.

THERE WERE plusses and minuses to his day so far, he thought. The minuses followed vaguely similar themes such as general confusion, or utter puzzlement. The plusses, on the other hand, were more specific. For one thing, Wil had in his possession an envelope containing roughly five hundred dollars, which would be enough to stave off the debt collection agency representing the owners of the Castle Towers. He'd never met his landlords, having rented his office via a telephone call to a local real estate company. But he'd always imagined them to be of the nefarious and mustachio-twirling variety, modeled after an old Vaudeville performer one might see in a black-and-white comedy from the 1920s, perhaps. Given his landlords' insatiable appetite for sending threatening letters, and their relative indifference to the noxious smells emanating from their own elevator, he'd always felt his mental picture was far too interesting to be spoiled by actually meeting these people. For some reason, he'd always imagined they might look like rats. Well, he thought, the rats were going to be getting a little cheese in the mail, which would prevent them from gnawing at his patience for at least a week or two.

Somewhere out in the electronic ether, Mr. Dinsdale's banking representatives were no doubt informing Wil's own bank that they were preparing to deliver the sum of a further five thousand dollars to Wil's account, and this had probably created an automated alert of some kind that would prevent the transaction from going through. Wil imagined this would be brought to the attention of his local branch manager and then summarily ignored for a week as a clerical error. He didn't mind: he'd already persuaded himself that Mr. Dinsdale, though eccentric to a fault, was not completely insane. During his first encounter with the old man, Wil had been mentally prepared to start negotiations in the general area of fifty or sixty dollars for whatever the curator had been preparing to throw at him. And during their later conversation at the coffee shop, Wil had daydreamed he might drive a hard bargain and ask for a full hundred, hoping Mr. Dinsdale might respect his chutzpah and actually fall for this obvious bluff.

Well, it couldn't hurt to let the clerical error go unnoticed for a while. As an added bonus, Wil realized he was now well into the afternoon hours and quite far away in both time and space from anything likely to make a sudden *klonng*ing sound in his ear.

For the next ten to fifteen minutes, Wil trudged painfully back toward his apartment building. He spent the first three minutes of his trudge engaging his Strange Feeling of déjà vu in a rather one-sided argument about the relative merits of keeping oneself to oneself and not intruding on another person's day. To conclude the argument, he admonished the intrusive notion and banned it from occupying any more of his thoughts for a period of at least sixteen months. After that, he trudged in complete silence—both inwardly and outwardly—and tried not to think about how he was going to navigate the flea-infested waters of his apartment building's lower floor. By the time he'd hit upon a solution to the problem of Mrs. Chappell and her cats— namely, to have them kidnapped by armed Venezuelan drug dealers and stored in the hold of a converted oil tanker—he found himself standing in front of the door to the lower lobby. The Venezuelan caper would have to wait. Wil was losing blood and he needed a shower.

Summoning every remaining ounce of his courage—and gripping his lucky penny so tightly that it threatened to carve a coin-shaped slot into the palm of his hand—Wil drew a deep breath and stepped inside.

INSIDE, THE lobby seemed warm and inviting in contrast to the savage fog floating across the city streets. For some strange reason, Wil imagined that the building purred, which was exactly the opposite of what he had expected. His grip on the penny loosened. Could it be that he was happy to be home?

This thought had never occurred to him in conjunction with the rusty old apartment building and its rusty old landlady—he'd usually associated the place with words like "godforsaken" and "tragic." But in spite of—or perhaps *because* of—his gaping head wound, the lobby seemed to possess a peaceful atmosphere very different from its usual appearance as the Atrium Where Tumbleweeds Might Go to Die. Mrs. Chappell's old calico monstrosity had found a comfy niche near one of the old steam radiators and was no doubt dreaming kitty dreams of fish and milk. Two or three of its friends were eyeing a small hole in the far wall, each pretending they had inside informa- tion on the imaginary mice that lived within. An old metal teakettle hissed on a distant stove inside Mrs. Chappell's office, and this made Wil think of cold winter afternoons spent outside with his elementary school friends, of Barry Morgan's most excellent hot chocolate recipes, and of toasty warm fireplaces and being cuddled up under a blanket next to his mom as she read from *The Hobbit* while his dad listened to stock market reports on the family's old-style radio.

Wil moved quietly across the floor of the lobby and headed toward the stairs where much to his surprise, a blob of scraggly brown fur moved to intercept. It was Mrs. Chappell's green-eyed favorite, a creature that to this point had summarily refused to acknowledge Wil's presence in its scraggly world in any way whatsoever. Odd, thought Wil, I wonder what it wants. The creature looked up at him, longingly.

On a whim, he bent to stroke the animal's fur and was surprised to find the brown beast felt as soft as satin, and that it was pleasantly docile. The cat leaned into Wil's leg and rubbed a little bit, just to let Wil know that he had officially been given permission to exist.

"Hello, brown cat," said Wil. "What can I do for you?"

"You can give him a kitty nugget, if you'd like," came a raspy, rusty voice from behind him.

Startled, Wil turned to find Mrs. Chappell hovering uncomfortably above him, looking as pleased as punch that he'd manifested in her lobby as opposed to sneaking through it like a ninja. In one hand, she held a cup of tea, and in the other, a carton of cat treats. "Would you like one?" she asked, beaming from ear to ear.

"I don't think so, Mrs. Chappell," replied Wil, hastily. "I think they might be a bit nutty for my tastes."

"No. *Chalky.*"

"Or chalky. They're a bit too chalky for my tastes."

"Oh, Mr. Morgan, you silly thing. I meant give one to Chalky." The old lady stooped to pick up the brown cat. "Surely you didn't think I was offering one to you? They're probably poisonous to humans."

Realizing he was now at his customary disadvantage, Wil paused for a moment to extrapolate a way out of the situation while Mrs. Chappell paused for a moment to blink. This was the first conversation he'd ever shared with his landlady beyond discussion of the rent and the weather. Wil was inclined to think that some of Mr. Dinsdale's residual oddity must have followed him home. He was also willing to bet that not a single part of his next three or four minutes was going to make any sense, yet somehow it would all fit quite neatly into Mrs. Chappell's version of reality. Clearly, Chalky was the absurd name she had given to the brown cat, and now he and his landlady were having two different conversations about exactly the same thing.

Wil reached for a kitty nugget and fed it to Chalky. Might as well embrace the concussion symptoms, he decided. After a moment's reflection, he decided to fire a first shot across the old lady's bow.

"You know, Mrs. Chappell, we really haven't spoken much since I moved in," said Wil. "And I really haven't spent enough time getting to know Chalky and the rest of your cats. Did you give all of your cats equally interesting names?"

Mrs. Chappell looked momentarily confused, suggesting that one of her patented moments of non sequitur was about to leap out and bite the situation. "Why, no dear," she replied. "They choose their own names of course."

Naturally, thought Wil. Right after they pass the common entrance exam and complete the daily crossword puzzle. He was half-tempted to ask if Chalky might see its way to coming by his apartment and inspecting his clattering bathroom sink. But he resisted the urge on the grounds that some confusion is always to be expected when making first contact with aliens, lost tribes, or rusty old landladies.

"You have a nasty gash on your head," noticed Mrs. Cappell, oblivious to the context of the moment. "Would you like me to put some iodine on it?"

From his days as a test subject for his dad's medieval Medicine

Cabinet of Death, Wil knew that the application of iodine to an open cut could roughly be approximated to the application of hydrochloric acid. "Thank you, Mrs. Chappell," he replied, hoping that his bright and breezy manner would distract her from her intended method of torture. "I think I'll head upstairs and take a shower."

The old lady blinked through coke-bottle lenses. Taking this to be an affirmation of his plan, Wil moved toward the flight of stairs that might possibly lead him upward toward warm water and relative sanity. But as he reached the bottom stair, a random thought occurred. And despite the fact that his instincts were now howling like Barbary apes, fearful he was about to blurt out something he shouldn't, he stopped in his tracks and blurted something anyway.

"You know, Mrs. Chappell," Wil blurted, "I was wondering if we had any spare units in the building that my dad could stay in for a couple of days? See, he's going to be visiting next week and my place is really too small. Maybe something a little brighter, or a little more spacious?" Or maybe not so likely to spontaneously combust and fall down around his ears, he continued, silently. "I mean . . . you know," he said aloud, "I can't ever seem to stop my bathroom sink from sounding like a munitions factory."

Pushed it too far. From beneath Mrs. Chappell's protective wing, Chalky's accusing glare now cut the sudden tension in the room like a hundred-dollar Japanese kitchen knife that could slice equally through a piece of corrugated metal, then a nice, juicy tomato. For her part, Mrs. Chappell was now threatening to be overwhelmed by an encroaching vacuum.

"I'd like to help you, Mr. Morgan," she began. "But I'm afraid there's not much I can do. I expect you probably have a couple of nixies in there somewhere."

Odd, thought Will, even for an octogenarian.

"I'm sorry. Is a nixie one of the parts, like a plunger or a stopper?" he asked. "Can we have our building superintendent look at it?"

"No. I mean I expect the noise under your sink is caused by one of the nixies."

"Do you have two cats called Nixie?"

The old lady furrowed her brow, in much the same manner as Mr. Dinsdale had earlier that same afternoon. "Now why would two cats choose the same name, especially such a strange one?" she remonstrated. "That would be very confusing for both of them. Not to mention it would cause a lot of problems at dinnertime."

The incongruous nature of the moment was suddenly threatening to overwhelm the entire lobby. Wil stared at Mrs. Chappell, and she stared back, blinking. It was not so much that she had written the book on confusion, Wil thought. It was more that she probably consulted with librarians the world over and provided expert testimony on the subject during particularly difficult court cases.

"I'm sorry, Mrs. Chappell," Wil volunteered. "I'm afraid I'm a little perplexed."

"Well, that's probably what it wants," replied Mrs. Chappell.

"What?"

"For you to be a bit perplexed. That's what they do."

Wil tried a vacant stare, just to see if he could beat the old lady at her own game. No dice. She was not about to be forthcoming with any further information unless prompted.

"I'm sorry. Who are we talking about again?"

"Nixies. They like to distract a person. But they don't mean it. That's just what they are supposed to do."

"Both of them?"

"All of them. But they're mostly harmless, even if they're not very fond of cats. They won't interfere if you ignore them properly."

At this point, Wil's tormented and battered cranial parts simply decided they'd had enough. Better to leave now, they theorized, than stick around and have to deal with the people in the white coats when they came to take the senile old dear away.

"Are you feeling all right, Mr. Morgan?" inquired Mrs. Chappell, concerned. "It's just that you look a little green around the gills. You should probably go upstairs and clean yourself off, and then get something to eat. You need to get some protein and calcium inside you."

And with that final effort to one-up the rest of Wil's day, she and Chalky headed back toward her office, to the now-insistent sound of a mostly empty teakettle that had probably caught fire on its stove. Wil stared at her, nonplussed, while Chalky's accusing green eyes quickly became the only discernible part of the ensemble as the old lady receded into the gloom beyond.

That could not have been any weirder, thought Wil, as Mrs. Chappell headed to the end of the far hallway and shuffled into her office to stifle the pained cries of the dying teakettle. As if to prove him wrong, Mrs. Chappell reached into the box of cat treats as she moved from Wil's line of sight near her office door and popped a kitty nugget into her mouth.

❦

With a head full of matted hair, coagulated blood, and conflicting opinions on the subject of old people, Wil departed the scene and headed upstairs to gather his thoughts. But as he climbed the stairs past three or four indifferent masses of feline fur, he sensed his thoughts were stubbornly refusing to cooperate. He felt as if he were trying to shepherd them with, say, a fire-breathing troll as opposed to, say, a metaphorical border collie. And thoughts, like sheep, usually won't respond to any kind of herding under those types of circumstance.

At the top of the stairs, Wil fumbled with his lucky penny, then his key. This moment was always the second-worst part in his day, for he always felt as if his apartment held a secret of some kind that he could never put his finger on. It was as if someone else lived here in the exact moments he was away from it, and that person was summarily sucked back into his or her own dimension the moment Wil entered, so that the apartment was magically returned to its previous state. This disconcerting notion was clearly a result of the paranoia Wil's dad had instilled in him from a young age. Nevertheless, he fretted about the place constantly; a person might never be so surprised as to head into the bathroom to brush his or her teeth only to find a complete stranger already brushing, and looking equally surprised to find they'd been sharing an apartment for seven years without knowing it.

Wil entered, cautiously. As usual, everything seemed exactly the same as when he'd left it, and yet it all felt completely different. Stepping over a discarded travel magazine that he could have sworn he'd left in the kitchen area, Wil sniffed the air and frowned; the residual smell of mushrooms was a little fainter than it had been earlier. His bathroom sink seemed to rattle a few times and suddenly go silent, as if surprised to find him home so early. Perhaps it needed to plan out its evening clattering schedule, thought Wil. If so, he would ignore it to the point where it might get bored and go live in the Swiss clock tower near his office.

Over at the kitchen counter, just at the edge of his peripheral vision, a discarded box of cereal seemed to twitch of its own accord. It stopped twitching the exact moment Wil looked at it, which was exactly the way it should have behaved to begin with. "Don't you start," he admonished, antagonized that some part of his day might have followed him home. The cereal box duly obliged and refused to move again, though he gave it a decent fifteen to twenty seconds to state its case.

Wil settled down to watch television, hoping to lose himself in the hideous morass of some awful reality show or other. This was not his usual habit, for he detested television in general and the so-called reality genre in particular. But after the events of the day, he felt he might let off some steam by yelling at a group of dysfunctional amateur actors purporting to be from some distant region of the country. He was to be disappointed, however: his television immediately warmed up to a thirty-minute infomercial for a flimsy air mattress made of "space-age polymers" (plastic), which had apparently been designed by Russian cosmonauts for use in a weightless environment. The obvious flaw in this logic—not to mention Marcus James's psychotically embellished voiceover—led Wil to conclude that he would rather make three easy payments of $19.95 for a large brick, which he would throw through the screen of his television. Wil grabbed his remote control unit instead, tossed it at the TV, and missed. Look on the bright side, he told himself as he switched the unit off manually and recovered the mangled remains of his remote from behind the TV stand. At least you no longer have to pay for replacement batteries.

Wil felt so desperately, desperately tired. His hair was matted down with blood that had now coagulated above a fairly nasty cut beneath. He knew that if he took a shower, the water would open the wound again and, much like a twenty-four-hour superstore, it would probably not close again until Christmas Day. He had been metaphorically shot at, spat on, shut in, and spat out since the moment he'd left for work, and the thought of enduring any more of this particular Monday was more than any man had any obligation to bear. He'd been hired by a man dressed like a cartoon to find a box full of a substance that seemed as likely to exist as a good Canadian table wine; he had visited a museum full of space junk on a street that didn't exist, been yelled at in body language, and, worst of all, he'd ordered a large cup of coffee by describing it as "oversized." A return call to his dad would have to wait—at this point in his day, Wil formally and officially surrendered.

But forty seconds later—as his head thudded onto his pillow and he drifted into an immediate state of catatonia—Wil would allow himself just one tiny little smile. For this was the very kind of day he had been conditioned to expect, up until the 207th day of his tenth year of existence, when days this interesting had really just ceased to exist.

CHAPTER FIVE

———————⊰◈⊱———————

WIL AWOKE to the distant hum of the one-way system and an insistent clattering noise in his sink, which refused to be silent no matter how many times he cursed it under his breath. His head felt like it had lost an argument with a street sign, and his nose felt like it had been bombarded by spider cannons during the night. If he hadn't known any better, he would have sworn that someone had been making mushroom stew in one of his skillets. But he knew better, of course. This would be a day like any other day, save for the fact that he now had a job to do.

Outside his window, Tuesday's thick broth of a fog was already making Monday's weather look like miso soup by comparison. The day would be cold and soggy, and the rain would feel like needles on his skin; Wil sensed that conditions would not be favorable for finding boxes full of impossible substances. The pain in his scalp caused by the previous day's street sign assault felt insignificant next to the headache yet to come. For while he stood a reasonable chance of bringing back something six-sided and wooden to the Curioddity Museum, the chances of this actually being Mr. Dinsdale's missing box of Levity were about as remote as an outpost on the third moon of Jupiter. He had absolutely no idea where he was going to start his search, although the third moon of Jupiter seemed as reasonable a place as any.

Wil closed his eyes again and made a mental toss-up, using his lucky English penny as a visual aid: if the imaginary version of his coin landed on heads, he would get up, take a shower, and set about Mr. Dinsdale's impossible task. Otherwise, well . . . he secretly hoped the coin would come up tails. In his mind, the English penny glinted in imaginary sunlight as it tumbled over and over toward an imaginary landing. Wil considered the absurdity of this, knowing he had the power to choose which way the coin would land but feeling powerless to decide nevertheless. The penny tumbled in slow motion toward an imaginary wooden floor where—much to Wil's surprise—it landed on its imaginary side and stuck, refusing to budge one way or the other.

So much for this being a day like any other day, he thought. Clearly, this was simply going to be one of those days.

WIL OPENED one eye and searched his apartment for something to ground his reality in. His pillow was covered with a faint smearing of dried blood but this made sense in a strangely nonsensical way, for it told Wil that his painful memories of Monday were most likely real, and not imagined. He looked further into the gloomy apartment, searching for the source of his regular nighttime frustration. The moment his eyes alighted on the bathroom sink, the fixture ceased to make its knocking sound. At that very instant, however, one of his discarded travel magazines began to flutter at the edge of his peripheral vision. How bizarre, thought Wil, considering his apartment lacked the barest approximation of ventilation except for the occasional gust from outside that would occasionally rattle one of his cracked windows. He knew this odd occurrence could not possibly be a product of his imagination, primarily because he no longer possessed one. If Tuesday was going to be this unreasonable, he reasoned, then so was he. He sat up in bed, rubbed his eyes, and pretended he was actually going to do something productive with his morning. That'll show it, he thought.

Tuesday scowled back at Wil, but he had already made his decision—he was going to seize the day, preferably by the unmentionables. Summoning a quick draft of energy, he swung his feet across the side of the bed and padded quickly toward the bathroom across the cold carpet. This positive approach lasted approximately four seconds, at which point Wil trod awkwardly on a shoe that he hadn't remembered leaving by the bathroom door and then stubbed his toe on the doorframe. So much for that whole carpe diem nonsense, he thought, forlornly, as he stared down at his throbbing toe. Thankfully, his attention was quickly drawn to some rather large flakes of crusty, white toothpaste that he must have dropped on the carpet over the past couple of weeks while brushing his teeth, and so obsessed was he in wondering where all of this toothpaste had come from that he almost forgot the pain in his toe, not to mention the day's impossible task.

Wil shook it off. Such procrastination would never do, not when Tuesday had basically stared him in the eye and challenged him to a duel. He thought about his mom, Melinda, and how she would always urge him to stand his ground when faced with the cold and cruel inevitability of Tuesday mornings spent at a damp and angry school bus stop waiting for the yellow Box of Doom to appear. On those mornings, she'd fill him up with sugar-frosted cereal and his very own cup of coffee and urge him to look Mrs. Timmins—his bus driver and nemesis of nine-year-olds everywhere—in the eye at all times. There's nothing so annoying to your enemies, she'd say, as to greet them with a smile.

Well, today procrastination was the enemy. Wil needed to get onto the streets and start with some detective work. With a quick pat down of his bloody hair and a brief glance in the mirror, he hastily donned his ever-more-rumpled clothing, grabbed an overcoat and gloves, and made for the front door to his apartment.

∽

DOWNSTAIRS, THE lobby was silent but for the hiss of a steam radiator and a strange cooing sound emanating from Mrs. Chappell's office. Wil was not going to hazard a guess what this noise signified, though he suspected it was either a trapped pigeon about to meet its maker at the hands of a slightly underworked feline, or Mrs. Chappell herself making clucking noises in the vague direction of one of her fuzzy companions. Quickly, Wil began his morning sortie through the lobby. He half-expected this strange noise to be a brand-new tactic in Mrs. Chappell's eternal quest to throw him off guard. But he passed without incident across the warped parquet flooring and made it to the front door in record time. Mrs. Chappell was most likely watching one of her morning game shows, he supposed.

Near the exit to the building the magnificently incongruous Chalky waited, eyeing Wil in a noncommittal fashion. Perhaps the little ruffian intended to claw Wil's leg as he passed, or perhaps it merely wished for some of his attention. On a whim, Wil leaned down to scratch Chalky's furry chin, drawing an immediate purr of gratitude. Couldn't hurt to be nice to the little fur bag, he thought, just in case Chalky was of a mind to report his demeanor to the authorities.

Wil stood at the front door and watched the cold wind whipping outside. He looked back down at the now-ecstatic cat rubbing up against his pant leg. "That'll do, Sergeant Major," he said to the cat, throwing it a quick military-style salute. "Carry on."

Chalky licked a paw—which Wil interpreted as a positive response to his genial instruction—and sat down to survey the lobby in case of attack by a foreign power or enemy rodent. Much to his own surprise, Wil then did the one thing he hadn't done during the last seven years of exiting Mrs. Chappell's apartment building: he smiled.

And with that, he stepped outside into a brand-new day.

❦

OUT ON the street, the fog was bitter cold and thick enough to be spread with a knife. Wil stood at the edge of the passing traffic, making a mental choice: he could turn his face to the ground and pull his coat around him—he could trudge toward the Castle Towers and make quiet, grumbling noises to himself as he complained about the weather—or he could pretend to be from Iceland where this would be a fine, fresh midsummer morning, and he could go about his daily business with a smile. This unorthodox thinking would have made his mom proud, Wil thought, as he moved into the teeth of the cold wind with a forced smile on his face that looked more like a grimace.

Melinda Morgan had always told her son that if he kept his chin up and looked at the buildings around him, he might see all manner of interesting things such as gargoyles, UFOs, and sale notifications for brand-name sneakers. Sadly, local gargoyles seemed conspicuous by their absence, and aliens capable of interstellar travel were no doubt far too intelligent to be caught outside on a day like this. However, a few of the nearby walls seemed to be covered with moderately garish graffiti. "Close enough," said Wil to nobody in particular. And with his eyes firmly affixed to the various billboards and empty storefronts that littered both sides of his street, he set off in search of Mr. Dinsdale's box of Levity.

Though just to be on the safe side, he went in the same direction as the flow of traffic moving through the city's one-way system.

WIL MOVED along slowly, thinking of his mom and slowly turning his lucky penny around in his pocket with one gloved hand. Presently, his journey took him to the old stone bridge that fronted the decrepit railway crossing at the center of town. He had been so absorbed with the task of keeping his eye line on the same plane as the horizon that he'd barely been aware of his own surroundings. The supreme effort required to face the teeth of the gale was beginning to take its toll, since those teeth appeared to be inordinately pointy and fierce. Wil's eyeballs were beginning to freeze; he wouldn't have been able to pick out a single gargoyle on a single building unless the statue in question was somehow capable of playing the electric sousaphone.

At the entrance to the railway bridge, a set of stone steps led down on each side to what Wil had always supposed to be a river. Truth be told, he'd never ventured that way, nor had he even considered looking down to see what lay beyond. He'd always supposed that the steps led to some twilight area of the city lined with cardboard boxes and homeless people, where unsuspecting civilians were press-ganged into service on pirate ships and the local alehouses still served mead and strumpets by the gallon. Here at the bridge, however, Wil faced a choice: He could continue along with the flow of the one-way system and eventually descend upon the Castle Towers and, most likely, a dearth of box-shaped candidates. Or he could descend the stone steps to see what lay beneath the city, thus avoiding the painful rattling of his loose fillings in the event of a passing train. As an added bonus, he would probably get out of the direct line of fire of the bone-chilling breeze that had turned his Icelandic midsummer into a less-than wintry wonderland.

Wil paused for a moment at the top of the steps and tried to summon the courage to descend, knowing such an impulsive action would be completely against his instincts. Perhaps these feelings of trepidation were not actually *his* instincts, he surmised. Perhaps they came as a result of his father's incessant harping on the perils of being spontaneous. And if Wil was going to stand a chance in the search for his metaphorical needle in a million haystacks, what better approach than to descend into a dark and mysterious abyss with no hope of survival? As if these strange and conflicting notions were not enough to convince him, Will suddenly noticed a large gargoyle built into a pillar halfway down the first flight of steps. The stone creature glared back at him in suitably demonic fashion, yet such was the oddity of Wil's previous twenty-four hours that the gargoyle seemed less like a harbinger of doom and more like an invitation.

What's the worst that could happen? Wil wondered, as in one fell swoop he violated every single rule his father had instilled into him since the age of ten and stepped off the beaten path in favor of a quick descent into certain death.

THE STONE steps leading to oblivion felt worn and concave. Wil imagined himself about to be accosted by a band of Romanian brigands armed with torture devices possessing such exotic names as Tongue Twister or Wench Grinder, or something equally despicable; these imaginary bandits would probably rip off his kneecaps and sell them to a local hospital for profit. But as he rounded the first flight of steps under the withering gaze of the gargoyle, he was immediately struck by the complete absence of pirate-themed accordion music coming from the bottom of the stone stairs. Gone were his imagined rivers of molten lava and Hieronymus Bosch–like scenes of human torture. Instead, Satan seemed to have set up shop in the middle of what appeared to be a thriving farmers' market. If there were demons here, they looked remarkably like a Chinese fish-monger, a cheerful-looking man who sold all kinds of fresh-cut flowers, and a large and beautiful African lady with perfect skin who sold local honey and facial cream made from imported shea butter.

People young and old milled around the busy stalls, quite impervious to the freezing fog that drifted through the marketplace in clumps. For the life of him, Wil could not find a single person who looked the way he usually felt during his Tuesday-morning trudge to the Castle Towers. Had this vibrant and chaotic marketplace really been hiding under his feet all these years, while he'd been trudging across the railway bridge and preparing himself for arguments with teenaged coffee shop baristas? The place smelled like a mixture of peppered beef and fruit pastries, with a perfect hint of lilac underneath. And as Wil stepped, amazed, from the bottom step and into the center of the bustle, he realized this place was full of the very types of people he'd spent the last seven years avoiding on his way to work.

At the end of a market aisle, a young man hooted happily in the direction of a pretty young girl and tossed her a large, green apple. For her part, the girl smiled coyly and batted her eyelids in such a way that Wil had to check to see if he'd accidentally wandered onto the set of an old French movie with Italian subtitles. At the end of one aisle was a purveyor of homemade wind chimes, all of which created beautiful, intertwined melodies for the benefit of bustling passersby. And near this endcap stood a floating booth adorned with strange carvings and knickknacks from across the world. Wil stopped to study some Mayan hieroglyphics on a piece of carved stone, though he quickly realized he stood as much chance of deciphering them as a merchant banker might stand of understanding a nineteen-year-old tattoo artist—in other words, no chance whatsoever. On a whim, Wil tilted his head first to one side, then completely upside down. He covered one eye with his right hand, just to see if Mr. Dinsdale's unorthodox methods might work on fake reproductions of ancient carvings.

∝

"WATCHA DOIN'?"

Wil was suddenly aware of eyes boring into the back of his head in an upside-down fashion. It was at this exact moment that he realized two things: (1) the eyes in question belonged to a little girl, aged about six or seven years, who was perched upon a cute pink bicycle adorned with rainbow streamers, and (2) he was about to be confronted with the genuine honesty of a kid whether he liked it or not. He felt frozen in place, mildly aghast at the notion the child probably thought of him as slightly creepy and more than slightly nuts. Wil glanced in the girl's direction and was met with the cute-yet-steely gaze of a precocious little prizefighter with freckles and pigtails. The girl smacked her lips on a piece of bubble gum and surveyed Wil as if he were an errant circus performer. He looked hurriedly away and quickly ran through a series of possible excuses for his eccentric behavior. Perhaps he should consider waiting the little girl out, he thought, or merely pretending that staring at things upside down in the middle of a farmers' market in broad daylight was the kind of thing that grown-ups do all the time. For her part, the girl stared at Wil, and then blew a large and loud bubble that Mary Gold would have been proud of.

Wil realized he needed to make a move because his back was beginning to ache. He'd had some experience with the concept of Pretending Not to Look Stupid after observing Mrs. Chappell's cadre of moth-eaten cats over the years. He'd noticed that cats are experts in the Art of Recovery, and that on the rare occasions when one of the overweight or flea-ridden creatures would tumble down the stairs or run smack-dab into a wall while chasing its reflection, said creature would immediately sit on the floor as if nothing extraordinary had happened and begin to lick its paws. Wil had always suspected Mrs. Chappell's cats were onto something: if one can act as if everything is right with the world while all around clowns dressed in snorkels, flippers, and tutus are throwing bowls of neon-green custard at each other then, by golly, everything is right with the world.

Wil straightened, rubbed his back, and yawned. The little girl stared at him, while the streamers on her pink bicycle began to flutter in the morning breeze.

"Soccer injury," said Wil, thinking quickly.

"Boogers," said the little girl, thinking even quicker. And with that, she pedaled away across the cobbled marketplace and disappeared into a small side street across the way. Wil peered over at the dimly lit street but could make out nothing from within the shroud of fog.

"Okay," Wil muttered quietly to himself, "that was unexpected."

As Wil stood alone in the crowded marketplace and wondered what to make of this encounter, a most delicious smell of coffee assailed him from a small kiosk nearby. He headed directly for it, hoping beyond hope that the seven years he had spent walking right over the heads of the merchants in this vibrant market could be replaced by a halfway decent cup of something. From behind the coffee kiosk, a small, Arabic man with a very large nose greeted Wil with a grin.

"Hello, friend!" called the man with the nose. "Praise be to God that you have found our market this day. What can I get for you?"

"I'd like a large, regular coffee, please," replied Wil. "And could you put in extra cream?"

"Certainly, sir. Also, I have fresh rhubarb pastries this morning. Please . . . this coffee cannot go without pastry. I give you one for free and you pay me for two the next time you come by!"

With that, the man with the nose shoved a truly massive rhubarb pastry into a paper bag and handed Wil an even more massive cup of coffee that contained just the perfect amount of extra cream. Ignoring Wil's polite protests, the man summarily refused to take any extra cash for the pastry and simply turned to another customer who seemed to have arrived in the nick of time.

⤜❧⤛

WIL WANDERED the marketplace, bemused; his coffee tasted like real coffee—the kind his mother used to hand him for those cold bus stop mornings. The pastry tasted exactly as Wil expected, in that it seemed to have been imported from a Turkish bazaar, and ferried to this location on an air-conditioned luxury jet with Wil in mind as its target customer. And as he moved farther from the bridge and back into the world he'd long since abandoned, Wil Morgan began to sense that the beaten path of conformity was rapidly in danger of being usurped by this marketplace below the railway bridge. Such excellence had been under his nose every day for the last seven years, and all he'd needed to do was un-look for it.

As if to prove his point, a train clattered overhead. Usually, the carriages would shake Wil's teeth and patience to the core, and the resulting pain in his fillings would make him long for the relative safety of the Castle Towers. But from this vantage point below the bridge, the train's rattle seemed appropriate and quaint, as if adding a subtle room tone to the exotic equation of the market.

To Wil's left, the cobbled market street moved around a corner and off into what seemed to be a garment district. To his right, a street performer enacted a highly unusual break dancing routine to prerecorded bagpipe music. But across the street from his position lay another dark and dangerous passage: the small, dimly lit street that the little girl had just ridden down. If she were just a small child, the street would probably be harmless enough. But if she were a spawn of the underworld come to live aboveground and study human ways, then Wil was in for a rough afternoon should he decide to follow her.

And this, he realized, was a momentous fork in his personal road. Wil had felt this trepidation once before: many years ago on one extremely cold winter's afternoon when as a little boy he and his mom had spent the afternoon sliding headfirst down a local Hill of Certain Death on the back of a tea tray, ululating like hillbillies at a monster truck rally. He could remember the terrifying sensation of ozone rushing through his nostrils that day, a heightened awareness, and his frozen hands clutching tightly to Melinda Morgan's thick coat as together, he and Mom braved the elements where not a single kid from his third-grade class dared to tread. That day, Melinda Morgan had stood at the top of the mountain with her son, encouraging him to take the hill on by himself while at the same time fearing for his structural integrity. "Go ahead, Wil," she'd urged her little boy. "Keep your eyes on the path and you'll be fine."

Wil hadn't been so sure. Halfway down the hill, an obvious fork led to two equally peril-fraught paths. The leftmost path was dotted with high moguls and snowdrifts, while the right path led through some thick underbrush that was covered with ice. "What if I go down the wrong way?" he worried aloud.

"There isn't a wrong way," said his mother with a chuckle. "Whichever way you choose, that is the right way just as long as you make a choice! Go ahead—it'll be fun!

"But what if I end up upside down in a snowdrift?"

"That's how you'll know you've made the right decision!" his mom had called as she shoved him off the top of the slope.

Young Wil had suddenly found himself rocketing backward, plummeting toward the snowy fork at the relative speed of an Exocet missile, with Melinda Morgan receding in the distance, looking both proud of and terrified for her son at the same time. Halfway down the hill, he'd righted his ship, gripped both sides of the crumpled tea tray, and suddenly found all the joy there is to be had in an uncontrolled descent into an uncertain future.

Thirty seconds later—just as Wil had gotten the hang of steering the tea tray by pulling up on each side with as much strength as he could muster—the dreaded fork had appeared across the top of a snowy rise. Wil steeled himself against the possibility of an abrupt halt, and with his mother's words ringing in his frozen ears, he resolved to make a decision: left toward certain death or right toward a fate much worse? Left or right: the choice was clear.

At the very last moment, young Wil had chosen left. He'd pulled up sharply on the right side of the tray and dug his left side in the ground to carve a perfect turn in the ice-covered track.

Moments later, he'd gone accidentally down the middle and found himself upside down in a snowdrift, laughing like a maniac and crying like a siren.

Now, THESE many years later, the way ahead seemed clear: Wil was going to cross the street and continue his journey into nowhere. He was going to follow the little girl on the bicycle, and even though he wasn't going to find Mr. Dinsdale's box of Levity, he was going to enjoy the ride, and he was going to laugh out loud when he found himself upside down somewhere.

For Wil had begun to realize, as he strode toward the cobbled unknown, that all of the unreasonable fears he had been harboring were nothing more than his imagination at work. And this was the first time his imagination had worked since his mother had died and his father had forbidden it to exist.

❦

THE COBBLED street was not so dark, as it turned out; indeed, it possessed a kind of Dickensian cheer, as if populated by now-generous moneylenders and street urchins who doubled as chimney sweeps. Wil moved through the thick blanket of fog that served as a teaser for the discovery of new delights ahead. He passed a store full of foreign antiques, and then a boutique store selling clothing for pets. Up ahead in the gloom, he could hear two small children playing a singsong game of some kind. The little street was apparently closed to automobile traffic, so that a number of happy customers of all ages and ethnic backgrounds could be seen cheerfully milling about in the center of the cobbled pavement as they crossed from one store to another. It seemed as though shopping was secondary to browsing, and the store owners didn't mind one little bit. Here, Wil passed a bountiful butcher's shop that displayed any manner of deceased fowl and blood sausage; there, a cooperative market selling organic fruits and vegetables. This was the kind of street that Wil might have wished to exist had he not already been standing in the middle of it. It was the kind of street he would have visited with his mother, all the while secretly hoping that he could show it to his dad.

At the end of one section, a small alley led into a circular cul de sac. Wil was startled to see that the alley was lit by old-style gaslights, and he had to stop for a moment and rub his eyes to see if the illusion might go away. Surely not, he thought to himself. Surely, the basic fundamentals of marketing dictated that one should attract customers by use of fancy neon signs and special offers advertised on the Internet. This particular shop seemed to say, "If you have the nerve to come down this alley and browse our storefront, you probably qualify as the type of customer we need."

Intrigued, Wil made his way toward what appeared to be a dilapidated knickknack and trinket shop. A small, rusted sign above the window had once upon a time been emblazoned with the words LUCY'S MAGIC LOCKER. Nowadays, the worn letters looked as if they had reached retirement age and would have been better off emblazoning a shuffleboard court somewhere in Florida.

Wil chuckled to himself as he scanned the detritus that had collected over the years inside the shop window. He'd once read about a very large section of the Pacific Ocean that was, essentially, a floating pile of junk that had been trapped over the decades by various subaquatic currents. As Wil recalled, this junkyard of the sea was destined to simply grow and grow until it eventually reached land simply by the volume of its surface area. If he wasn't mistaken, someone must have discovered this floating pile of crud and deposited an arbitrary section of it inside the window of Lucy's Magic Locker. No doubt, Mr. Dinsdale would be delighted to learn that his Curioddity Museum was infinitely less dreadful than this place, although Wil suspected the old man would probably have an interest in turning it into some kind of exhibit overflow.

It would have been generous to describe the items on sale as "used," and perhaps a little more accurate to describe them as "abused." An old stuffed teddy bear looked as though it may once have entertained one of the crowned princes of Europe, assuming teddy bears had been invented at any point in the third century. Next to this, a stained black teakettle with a hole in it was propped against a single roller skate from the third Ming dynasty. Wil grimaced a little, imagining the roller skate's lost twin floating on a cardboard box somewhere in the middle of the Pacific. There was nothing for him in Lucy's Magic Locker save for a collection of rusted items and a possible respiratory infection. But just as his eyes began to move in the direction of the market street, and the rest of his Tuesday, he caught sight of something amazing, something completely unexpected: a particular item that he would never have imagined he'd see again in a million years. It was an old box with faded two-color graphics—an item he hadn't laid eyes on since he was a little boy—and it was the encapsulation of all that he had ever been, and all the things he had ever lost.

For there—hidden underneath an old newspaper and partly covered by some old socks—was the most exciting object in the history of all existence: a Nikola Tesla Junior Genius Mega-Volt Test Kit!

✑

WIL PAUSED for a moment, trying to understand his emotions. He felt big tears welling up in his eyes, and a lump in his throat that wanted to bring up a cry of joy. Was this really the very toy he'd always wished his father had kept instead of throwing it into the garbage along with all of the other bittersweet memories? Unable to take his eyes off the Tesla Kit—hoping beyond hope that no one would enter the store and purchase it in the few seconds he'd take to make it inside—Wil moved toward the slightly dodgy-looking door of Lucy's Magic Locker. He rather hoped Lucy would be a kindly old lady with a penchant for making people's dreams come true, though he was willing to admit to himself that he would pay for the Tesla Kit no matter the price.

Inside the store, a little bell tinkled like glass as Wil entered. It barely seemed like the kind of bell one might use to alert oneself to the presence of customers, and better suited to sending a person to sleep. The inside of Lucy's Magic Locker was—in terms of pure, unadulterated trash—a gold mine, a veritable cornucopia of stuff that nobody wanted. Bookshelves full of old, dusty tomes crowded into what might be mistaken for aisles. Next to the far-too-old sales counter was a damaged workbench covered in a thick layer of dust, which really didn't surprise Wil one bit since everything in the store seemed to be broken. But apart from the various layers of discarded junk, there was no sign of Lucy.

"Hello?" called Wil, nervously. "Is anybody there? Hello?" No answer. He wondered for a moment if he might not find the skeletal remains of poor old Lucy hidden under a pile of shoes at the far end of

the store. "Hello!" he called again, this time more forcefully. No doubt
the poor old dear's hearing device was of the same pedigree and epoch
as the other contents of her store. Wil waited for someone to emerge
from the back of the store, probably with a large funnel held to her
ear. But no such luck: the only thing he could hear was the dripping
of a tap in a sink somewhere.

For a brief moment, Wil considered leaving. Perhaps the store
owner had gone next door to borrow a cup of sugar. Maybe she was
taking a very early afternoon nap. But he quickly dismissed these notions of leaving in such cowardly fashion; perhaps someone was at the
back of the store piling books. If so, he thought, they would probably
do better to restack the ones up front and create a clear pathway
though the aisles. Wil moved cautiously toward the back of the store,
which carried the unmistakable musty smell of old, unread books and
mouse droppings. This wasn't the sort of place you frequented to stock
up on your antiques, thought Wil; it was more like the kind of place
you nervously entered as a kid in order to retrieve your lost Frisbee.

At the back of the store was a mishmash of clutter that seemed to
possess a kind of New Age theme, Wil thought, assuming that age
had begun in, oh, say, the 1950s. The floor plan had clearly not been
thought out very carefully since anyone with half an ounce of common sense would have brought all the bookshelves back here and put
them against the back wall. While there was not a shelf in sight, Wil
did find a strange collection of smooth, round rocks and a cracked
crystal that had dropped a few shards along the way. A partially inflated beach ball waited forlornly at the base of a pile of old sporting
equipment that would not have been out of place at the 1900 Paris
Olympics. And just underneath an old persimmon golf club sat a battered wooden box inlaid with mother-of-pearl that could have passed
for the one Mr. Dinsdale had commissioned him to find. Not a bad
candidate, thought Wil, as he picked the box up to examine it. Of
course, it was blindingly unremarkable, which only added to its possible authenticity. Wil turned the box upside down, where the unmistakable legend MA#E IN #####N was revealed in faded capital letters.

Wil chuckled to himself. Made in Taiwan, indeed. His search was narrowing by the minute.

As Wil flipped the box this way and that, wondering if he possessed the courage to try and pass it off as Mr. Dinsdale's coveted box of Levity, he felt the strange sensation of movement around him. Looking up, he could see nothing out of the ordinary, really. But he got the distinct *impression* that someone had just walked by. He waited a few moments for something to happen—something that must explain the strange sensation. He imagined what it must be like to close one's eyes and then stand in a room full of a hundred silent people; this is exactly how he felt, he determined. He looked back down at the wooden box, only for the sensation to occur again. This time he was not mistaken: someone had definitely moved by, and he had the strangest feeling he'd looked across to the back wall of the store and seen an open room, which had suddenly disappeared and been replaced by the wall just as he was looking up at it.

Another movement . . . this time in Wil's peripheral vision: Wil tried to think back about just how many of these strange incidents he'd encountered in the last day or so. Where had he felt this way before? He counted roughly four or five peripheral intruders over that time span, including the strange crates inside the Curioddity Museum and the apparition of the girl inside the featureless room. And because this kind of thing was now less unsettling and becoming slightly the norm, it took Wil just slightly longer than it might have otherwise taken to react.

As Wil looked up, he was astonished to see an attractive young woman with brown, curly hair moving rapidly toward him with her arms raised high above her shoulders.

He was equally astonished when she smashed him over the head with an oversized copy of Leo Tolstoy's *War and Peace*, though he was forced to concede as he fell to the ground, stunned, that this was a novel approach.

CHAPTER SIX

THE FIRST thing that struck Wil—or the *second* thing that struck him (since the first was, technically, a large book)—was that the ceilings of Lucy's Magic Locker were painted a very dark shade of green: Oxford green, he speculated, or perhaps something a little more synthetic, like army green. No matter the exact hue, he felt a special kinship with this color—and this ceiling in particular—since to concentrate on anything else at this moment in time would be to invite a state of unconsciousness. To Wil, the ceiling was the color of Heaven, and he would have smiled a satisfied smile and drifted off to sleep if the thought of waking up didn't make his head hurt so.

Instead, he frowned. An annoying blob of something kept getting between him and his view of the nice, comfortable ceiling. The blob was babbling at him in a language he didn't understand. Trying to ignore the thing by smiling at it only seemed to make it angry. For a blob, it possessed quite a healthy head of brown, curly hair. As Wil's eyes adjusted to the dim light, the searing pain, and the contrast of the ceiling (hunter green, definitely hunter green), he could see that the blob was morphing into an attractive-yet-dangerous young woman who brandished a copy of *War and Peace* as if it were an offensive weapon. Wil found himself wishing the girl had spent a little time reading the "peace" section of the book.

"Who are you?" asked the young woman/blob. "What are you doing back here?"

"I'm looking at your ceiling," replied Wil. "It's green."

"That doesn't make sense."

"And hitting someone over the head with a book does?"

"That depends. Why is your head all covered with blood?" The girl brandished the book a little more dangerously, just in case it was not yet clear she meant business.

"I think because you just hit me with that book," replied Wil.

"Okay, sure . . . but I only did half of it. You already had blood on your head when you came in."

"That's no reason to hit me over the head. Is that Oxford or army?" Wil looked around him: the inlaid wooden box he'd been examining had gone clattering across the floor and was now wedged under an old baseball bat. There was evidence of neither angels nor ambulance workers, which Wil took to be a positive sign. He began to giggle, uncontrollably. Post-concussion syndrome didn't seem so bad after all.

"Hey, cut it out," remonstrated the young woman.

"You know, I just realized something," Wil offered as he tried to lift his head. "I took the middle path, so I shouldn't be surprised that I'm upside down." He felt he should make a token effort to sit up and see if he was in a snowdrift but the idea of it was too much to bear. If he was going to meet his end at the hand of an admittedly attractive dingbat, she was going to have to finish the job without any protest on his part.

The young woman eyed him with a confused look. Perhaps, Wil thought, as she lowered the book from its attack position, realization was beginning to dawn on her. This was the kind of awkward silence people observe when one of them is considering damages, lawsuits, and possible ways out of both.

"I came in to ask you about the Nikola Tesla Junior Genius Mega-Volt Test Kit you have in the window," Wil volunteered, hoping this might break the tension. His head literally felt like it was splitting in two as he made an effort to recover by propping himself up on one elbow. "Aren't you supposed to ask customers if they need help finding anything before you bash them over the head with a heavy object?"

"You were skulking around the back of my store—"

"I was browsing!"

"Okay, you were browsing. But how do I know you're not a crazy person?"

"Hey, I'm not the one hitting people over the head with a book. I take it you must be Lucy?" Wil proffered his hand, partly in hopes that the young woman would deem this a harmless introduction but mostly because he hoped she might help him to his feet.

The girl narrowed her eyes. "How do you know my name?" she questioned. "Did someone send you here?"

"It says Lucy's Magic Locker on the sign out front."

"Oh. Right."

IT FELT to Wil as though a few more seconds of awkward silence would be fitting, just so the girl might fully comprehend the conse-quences of her actions. He had, after all, been assailed during the simple execution of his quite innocuous purchasing activities. Apolo-gies were no doubt in order and—if this was to be turned to his advantage—perhaps a generous offer on her part to provide him with a free gift (such as the Nikola Tesla Junior Genius Mega-Volt Test Kit) in return for his cooperation. She was a pretty girl, to be sure, but that in no way disqualified her from her duties as a responsible store owner.

And being a responsible store owner meant that she was obliged to offer him fair service, reasonable pricing, and zero whacks over the head with anything written by Tolstoy. Wil waited for an apology but was to be quickly disappointed. Lucy widened her eyes a little—apparently impressed by her own bravery and the copious amounts of blood this had withdrawn from Wil's head—and then she began to snigger.

"Wow, I really got you good, didn't I?"

"Yes. Look, I don't expect that to be a source of pride—"

"I mean you never know, do you?" she continued, disregarding the possible extent of the damage she'd just caused. "Like, if you went to war, or something, you never know if you'd run away or stand your ground." The girl was beginning to warm to her subject, and Wil felt it was neither his place nor inclination to stand in the way of her shining moment, not while half of his life support dripped down the side of his head. "I mean, one minute you're minding your own business piling some books and the next you're, like, *Enter the Dragon* . . . hy-*ahh!*"

The girl's sudden enthusiastic demonstration of martial arts bravado was startling, considering the circumstances. "Yes," Wil agreed as he pushed himself up from the floor, sat up, and shook his head, dazed, "I'd imagine you'll be up for a medal or something. Do they give out awards for attacking defenseless customers when they're not looking?"

"Oh, God, I'm really sorry." The girl seemed to immediately soften. She stuck out her hand and smiled the sweetest of smiles. "Lucy Price. It's a pleasure to meet you."

"Wil. Morgan. Wil Morgan," Wil responded as he tried to remember both his manners and his name. It wasn't so much the pain scrambling his neurons, or the fact that he was sitting on a pile of old magazines—it was the girl's sudden and immediate transformation from maniacal to charming. He felt as though he'd just ridden a dragster from two hundred miles per hour to zero after a computer malfunction in the dashboard had accidentally deployed his parachute.

For the strangest reason, Wil felt as though he had met Lucy before.

But he also felt that bringing this up under such bizarre circumstances would be a little forward of him. He'd never been much good at talking to pretty girls, and when in their company, he constantly fretted that anything he said might be misconstrued as a pickup line. Whatever the case, he felt ridiculous sitting on the floor and bleeding profusely. And so he propped himself up a bit and allowed Lucy to help him to his feet. The ground wobbled.

As they shook hands, Lucy seemed ever so slightly distracted. She gripped Wil's hand just a little longer than might seem appropriate, and narrowed her eyes. Wil had seen this look before, most often on television during daytime soap operas. He never understood those either.

"Where do I know you from, Wil?" asked Lucy. "You look familiar."

"I wish I knew," replied Wil, suddenly feeling self-conscious. "I've had a weird couple of days, and I've been seeing a lot of movement in my peripheral vision. Have you been stalking me or am I just a target of opportunity?"

"I didn't hear you come in. This is the first time I've ever attacked a customer, I promise."

"Lucky me."

"We need to get some of that blood off so we can see your handsome face," she said. "Come on."

With that unexpected comment Lucy pulled a very dazed and confused Wil Morgan to his feet and pointed him toward a little kitchen at the back of the store, which could be seen poking through an open door. As he allowed himself to be led away, Wil found himself ever so slightly charmed by the girl's light step and the way her bright-orange gypsy-style dress flowed around her curvaceous figure. She moved lightly across the floor, leading him past the maze of discarded old books and centuries-old metal junk. Was it his imagination or had this pretty girl just flirted with him?

❦

AT THE kitchen sink, Lucy dutifully mopped the side of Wil's bloody head with an old sponge that Wil suspected doubled as a botulism farm. The pain was beginning to recede, and in its place a kind of dull ache was emerging. But Wil didn't mind; this girl seemed relatable—if not actually remorseful—and he conceded it might be difficult to blame her fully since half the damage to his head had been done by a street sign the day before. Wil winced as the sponge smeared blood across his cheek, and cold water dripped down the back of his neck.

"You know this might have been a less painful introduction if your doorbell was actually loud enough to do its job," he said, indignantly. "Usually, doorbells don't sound like someone trying to keep a secret."

Lucy's eyes widened, and she chuckled. "Yeah, but it wouldn't have been so memorable."

"Oh, I don't know. I'm sure I would have remembered you either way."

Wil flushed, instantly regretting his response. It sounded like the very type of pickup line he was always trying to avoid, and he winced in expectation of Lucy scowling at him. To his surprise, she grinned.

"Why, thankyew, kind sir!" she exclaimed with a grin, and turned her attention to emptying her sponge of blood and refilling it with more botulism water.

LUCY FINISHED her mopping duties and moved a lick of hair from Wil's eyes. "There, that's better," she said in the kind of twinkly voice usually reserved for people on television. "Now what can I do for you, Wil?"

Wil could think of a number of possibilities but he wasn't about to blow this chance at impressing the girl. If memory served him right, the correct approach now would be to act in an aloof manner, then feign interest in anything but the pretty young woman who'd just mopped the blood out of his eyes. Wil had been given this advice in the school bathrooms by Billy Pinder when he was six years old but had never really questioned its effectiveness.

Lucy looked into Wil's eyes, expectantly.

"Um. Uhh," Wil began with practiced ease. "Wow. Um." Her face seemed oh so within reach, her eyes more inquiring. If this were a daytime soap he'd probably lean forward and kiss her. (And she'd probably slap his cheek and demand that he leave.)

Lucy crinkled up her nose. "Something about a Tesla Kit?" she suggested. It was obvious that she was enjoying Wil's discomfort but not in a nefarious way, he thought. Clearly, this was a two-way attraction, but Wil needed to act more like a magnet and less like a puddle of human jelly.

"Oh, yes. Sure. The Tesla Kit," replied Wil. He could feel he was beginning to lose his entire train of thought, which was no mean feat. The only way to lose a train is to drive it off the tracks and take it for a spin in a forest somewhere. Wil was most definitely off track. "Is it for sale?" he asked, immediately regretting the question.

"Well, of course not!" Lucy laughed, playfully. "This is Lucy's Magic Locker. We only accept trades and barters. Do you have something to trade?"

"I'm not sure. I finished my rhubarb pastry—"

"Bummer. How about dinner on Thursday night, then?"

Wil gulped, and nodded. Right about now his train of thought was steaming headlong into an underwater gorge full of neon electric jellyfish and bearded mermaids. This was not familiar territory at all.

"Cool. Okay. Do you like Korean?"

Wil nodded again. It had worked the first time, after all. Maybe this gorgeous girl—who Wil was perfectly capable of admitting was most likely clinically insane—liked the silent type.

"Okay." Lucy chuckled. "You pick the restaurant and text me. I'll come by and pick you up. Say, seven?"

"Seven. Text. Right. Absolutely," muttered Wil in a half daze. He wasn't sure he should mention that texting might be impossible on account of the fact he neither owned nor knew how to operate a cell phone.

"Awesome. Now about the Tesla Kit. That'll be sixty bucks."

"Sixty?" blurted Wil. "That's a bit steep for an old toy, isn't it?"

"Well, how else do you expect me to pay for dinner?"

"Well, I wasn't—"

"I'll go and get it for you."

And just as suddenly as Lucy had busted her way into Wil's awareness, she flounced off toward the front of the store, chuckling to herself. Wil stood in painful admiration, noticing how Lucy's flowing gypsy-style skirt moved around her hips. He could hear a faint jangling sound coming from her many wristbands and bangles. And as she moved toward the display window, he could see that she was barefoot.

WIL FOLLOWED Lucy out of the small kitchen area, wincing a little as he imagined the blunt force trauma his head had endured over the last day or so. He was in for a long couple of days of searching for Mr. Dinsdale's box if his brain was going to slosh like this every time he took a step.

As Lucy busied herself by clambering into a tiny space that looked as if it hadn't been opened in thirty years, Wil tried to take stock of his surroundings and the situation at hand. Taking stock of the clutter in Lucy's Magic Locker would be a long and arduous task requiring the services of a team of old Chinese men with abacuses and a second team of movers. He was more concerned with what might be happening between him and the pretty young woman, who was now singing happily to herself as she waded through a pile of dust in the store window. Wil had always been a hopeless romantic, with "hopeless" being the operative word. Most of the girls he'd ever been interested in were so far out of his league that they were, metaphorically, the National

Football League while he was, metaphorically, a Middle School Girls' Under-12 B Division.

As Wil pondered the ramifications and the possible outcomes, the bizarre feeling of people moving past him occurred again: he could feel the presence of others inside the store, yet there was no obvious reason for it. If he blinked, he imagined he could see an open space at the back end of the store just as his eyelids closed; and he'd see it again for a brief, flickering moment as they opened. He felt as though time had somehow spun sideways in two places at once, and this feeling was most disconcerting. Indeed, his vertigo was beginning to intrude. He attempted to prop himself up against the back wall only to discover the shelf he'd attempted to lean on had never been there in the first place. Wil's hand slid down the painted brick and he righted himself quickly, hoping the pretty girl in the window hadn't noticed.

Wil pulled himself together quickly, noticing the inlaid wooden box he'd been playing with just before Lucy had knocked him senseless: it was still wedged under an old baseball bat that had the words HONUS WAGNER hand stenciled into the side of the soft wood. Almost as an afterthought, he reached over and grabbed the box, thinking this might come in handy as a backup plan in the very likely event he did not find the actual box Mr. Dinsdale so coveted. Sadly, he realized, his Made-in-Taiwan backup plan was his *only* plan.

At that very moment, Lucy reappeared with the Tesla Kit tucked under her arm. She blew a large pile of dust from the top of the box. "I found almost all of the pieces." She frowned as she rummaged through the soiled underside of the old cardboard container, which by now had almost completely disintegrated. "I think there might be a few more bits under all that crud in the window. I can look for them later and bring them to you when we go on our date."

Wil wished suddenly for another cup of coffee so that he could snort some of it out of his nose in surprise. "Date?" he asked, incredulous.

"Dinner," replied Lucy, handing him the Tesla Kit with a smile and keeping the one-word theme of the game going.

"Right."

"Thursday."

"Seven. Right." Wil was beginning to get the hang of this. He waved three twenty-dollar bills in Lucy's general direction.

"Groovy." Lucy took the money and stuffed it in between the top buttons of her blouse, much to Wil's incredulity. Clearly, this was a game not only of one-word answers but also of chicken. Perhaps he'd better change the subject before she caught him staring with his mouth open.

Wil held up the old inlaid box he'd just retrieved from underneath the baseball bat. He wasn't of a mind to spend more than a dollar or two on the thing, since one side was partly cracked and the bottom panel seemed to have been sitting in a pool of sulphuric bouillabaisse for a few decades. Nevertheless, it vaguely fit the bill of what Mr. Dinsdale had asked him to find. "Any chance you could throw this old box in with the Tesla Kit?" he asked.

"Oh, that old thing? Sure. Maybe you can keep the extra pieces in it."

Wil looked at the box, dubiously. The only thing likely to be kept within was some old collection of mold or fungus. He had half a mind to donate it to his landlady, Mrs. Chappell, rather than bring it to the Curioddity Museum. She would probably keep it between her collection of teapots and her whimsical porcelain cat statues. "Where did you get this thing, anyway?" he asked just to keep the conversation going.

Lucy glanced at the back end of the store, and then at the front door to the store. "Can you keep a secret?"

"Sure. Did you steal it?"

"No, silly!" Lucy chuckled. "I found it at the back of the store."

Wil blinked. For some reason, pieces were beginning to come together in much the same way two icebergs might crash in the middle of an Antarctic winter night. Wil was beginning to feel like a very lonely penguin, above whom an ominous shadow had just appeared. "I think there's something weird about my store," she continued, her eyes widening. "I think it's haunted."

Wil could agree that there were a number of weird things about Lucy's Magic Locker—for example, its maniacal-if-cute proprietor—but his interactions with Mrs. Chappell allowed him to slough off such comments with practiced ease. He blinked, pretending Lucy's response was entirely normal given the circumstances. "Uh-huh."

"No, seriously. I keep thinking people are walking all around me and then I look up and there's no one here."

Wil was utterly tempted to admit he'd had the same feeling but he kept it to himself for the moment. If this was—as he expected—some kind of excuse to worm her way out of the dinner date, he wasn't going to let her get off that easily. "So the box is haunted?" he volunteered.

"No, it's just . . ." Lucy was having a hard time articulating, he could tell. "It just kind of showed up by itself. I found it on a shelf against the back wall."

"You don't have any shelves against the back wall."

"That's why it's weird."

At that very moment, Wil blanched. He reached into his pocket and grabbed his lucky penny, hoping for all the world it might ground him back in the universe he was more familiar with. The room spun. He needed to get out before he became a metaphorical penguin sandwich between two large glaciers.

"I have to go," Wil said, abruptly.

"Sure. Is everything okay? You look like you just saw a ghost."

"Vertigo," replied Wil, lamely. "I get it sometimes when I'm struck repeatedly over the head. I think I'll go back home and take a nap."

Wil could feel the hairs rising on the back of his neck, and his confidence being boosted and sapped in exact proportions. He hoped his sudden idiot behavior hadn't made him seem disinterested. But more than anything, he needed to get out of Lucy's Magic Locker as quickly as possible, though he was in no position to explain to this pretty young girl exactly what had made him suddenly feel this way.

Lucy crossed her arms again, and smiled. Perhaps she was used to conversations ending in such an impromptu manner, for she certainly didn't seem to be offering up much resistance. "You're an interesting one, Wil Morgan," she said. "Are you always this random?"

"Only on Tuesdays," replied Wil, hurriedly. "I'm usually a lot more predictable by Thursday. See you then?"

"See you at seven. Don't be late."

Lucy grabbed a business card from the counter and jotted down her cell phone number with a ballpoint pen. Taking the card quickly, Wil tucked the inlaid box and the Tesla Kit under his arm and made a beeline for the door, his head swimming like a dislodged penguin.

As he hurried out of the door, gripping his lucky penny tightly with his free hand, Will allowed himself a quick glance back toward Lucy, who was waving goodbye with a bemused expression on her face. As he blinked, he could imagine a vague impression of movement in the space where the wall behind Lucy should be. He felt a distinct sensation of movement, as if the wall was, in fact, more of a doorway to somewhere else that he couldn't see with the naked eye.

Wil now remembered where he thought he might have encountered Lucy before: the moving boxes . . . the sense that Lucy's store was populated by invisible entities . . . and a simple wooden box inlaid with mother-of-pearl that had appeared on a shelf that didn't actually exist. Wil's heart raced as he headed back into the cold, damp broth of Tuesday with the Tesla Kit and the old wooden box tucked safely under his arm. His mind raced faster than his legs, and that old feeling of vertigo splashed inside his eyeballs with every step he took. His heart beat like the drummer for a seventies punk rock band and his lungs seemed to exhale twice for every time he inhaled.

What Wil Morgan didn't know at the time—what he couldn't possibly know as he raced back to the safety of the world he understood—was that he had just fallen head over heels in love.

CHAPTER SEVEN

THE NEXT morning, Wil Morgan awoke from a fitful night's sleep and a rather disturbing variation of his anxiety dream in which he'd arrived too late to register for the World's Biggest Failure competition and had been disqualified. As he opened his eyes and tried to adjust to his first challenge of the day (namely, not rolling over and going back to sleep), he speculated as to the significance of the dream. But his instincts were far too sleepy to tell him what that significance might be.

Outside his window, Wednesday was already spoiling for a fight—the frigid air looked brown and dangerous, as if composed of equal parts oxygen and petroleum. The noise of the cars and buses below seemed more subdued than usual, suggesting to Wil that the traffic was conserving its energy for when he eventually made his way downstairs. As usual, his apartment smelled of mushrooms. He rolled over and plodded toward the kitchen, just in case his imaginary roommate had been considerate enough to make breakfast.

Wil was beginning to wake up now. It took immense mental effort for him not to start grinning at the thought of how he'd scored a date the previous day with Lucy Price. He tried to imagine himself as an old man in a rocking chair sitting on a porch somewhere; in his mind, he saw a plaid blanket draped over his knees, and he pictured himself wielding a shotgun. This mental image of himself as an old curmudgeon seemed to do the trick, and he began to grumble in spite of his good mood; his lumpy bed had spent the entire night jabbing him in the ribs and he suspected spiders had been firing cannons inside his nostrils again—a sure sign he was coming down with a cold. Across the room, the bathroom sink seemed to beat rhythmically in time with the throbbing pain in his temples, reminding him that he had been attacked on two separate occasions over the previous two days. He glowered at the bathroom door, and at that exact same moment the rattling suddenly ground to an abrupt halt. No time for the usual distractions, Wil decided; he was going to have to demonstrate progress in case some nameless-yet-diligent banker found the money Mr. Dinsdale had deposited into his account and tried to return it to its rightful owner.

So much had happened since Wil had left his apartment on Monday morning. By his reckoning, he had spent most of Monday as the butt of some cosmic joke that involved a delusional old man, a museum full of useless space junk, and a fool's errand of epic proportions. By the end of Tuesday morning, he had met a very pretty girl who—despite assaulting him with a large book—had seemed to like him. He had inexplicably scored a date with her just by being himself, or—most likely—by exhibiting symptoms of post-concussion syndrome. And quite by chance (though Wil was beginning to suspect it was by something approximating intelligent design), he'd chanced upon a likely candidate for Mr. Dinsdale's missing box of Levity, all without actually trying. Or possibly without even looking, he couldn't tell which. This fit with Mr. Dinsdale's ludicrous notion of un-looking at things, and it did nothing to soften Wil's mood, nor dull his painful headache.

Wil engaged in a silent argument with his brain, hoping to persuade himself that at least some of these experiences were real. The possibility that he'd scored a date with a girl named Lucy was enough to convince his brain to cooperate and join in for at least the rest of the day. Wil felt more than a little triumphant. No matter that he had been sent on a fool's errand by a foolish old curator of a pile of fool's gold. He was going to deal with Wednesday, and Wednesday was going to have to deal with him.

He glanced at the mother-of-pearl-inlaid box, which sat exactly where he'd left it—crammed underneath the lid of the Nikola Tesla Junior Genius Mega-Volt Test Kit—the night before. From this angle, the faded "Made in Taiwan" sticker glared back at him. But Wil could not bring himself to remove the sticker, reasoning that if Mr. Dinsdale pointed out the obvious flaw in Wil's strategy he'd at least feel he'd been honest about his dishonesty.

Strangely, pieces of the Tesla Kit were now arranged neatly on the kitchen counter, though Wil had no recollection of having actually woken in the night to place them in this position. If his unintentional, mushroom-loving roommate had been fiddling with his things during the night, then he was going to have to mark his property with yellow Post-it notes in the future. Despite himself, Wil smiled; the Tesla Kit was a wonderful connection to days gone by. However, the fact it had suddenly reemerged into Wil's life so soon after he'd visited the Curioddity Museum made him feel like he was a puppet in somebody's game. If, as Wil imagined, he was under the control of one of those Greek gods who liked to move people around like chess pieces on a board, then his particular player was likely to be the God of All Things Random.

Wil's slight head cold was making him feel very peculiar, as though he might be *forgetting* something. His encounter the previous morning with Lucy Price had left him as love struck as it had left him dumbstruck. It had also left him with two types of headache: the headache that comes when a person is bashed over the head with a large work of literature and the headache that comes when a person has their universe turned upside down after witnessing a ghostly occurrence firsthand. With a frown, Wil grabbed the inlaid box and tucked it under one arm. On a whim, he shoved the pieces of the Tesla Kit into their box and brought that with him, too, just in case he might spare a few minutes later to refamiliarize himself with all of its working parts.

He thought it might be a sensible idea to buy some cold medicine. After that, he figured he might as well take the inlaid box over to the Curioddity Museum, just in case Mr. Dinsdale found it interesting. Wil could barely contain his curiosity as to whether or not the museum was, in fact, connected by some kind of random dimensional portal to the back of Lucy's Magic Locker. He was most eager to put this cockamamie theory to the test. And so, without bothering to check his reflection, Wil donned whatever clothing he could find that didn't look like it had fallen off the back of a homeless person and snuck his way out of the apartment building, making sure to pat the ubiquitous Chalky on the head as he passed through the lobby.

THOUGH HE was quite good at walking—not to mention an expert at trudging—Wil could not quite decide how to take the next step. He decided to wander aimlessly for a little while, just to see where the mood might take him. And he made sure to let his mind wander in the opposite direction to the flow of traffic nearby.

Wil crossed the street to a little convenience store where Mrs. Chappell habitually bought kitty nuggets for Chalky and the gang. Much to Wil's surprise, he discovered a large sum of money deposited into his bank account when he used the store's rattly old ATM machine, just as Mr. Dinsdale had promised. Slightly taken aback by this turn of events, he perused the flu and cold section for a few minutes before setting out against the flow of traffic with the wooden box under his arm and a packet of lemon-flavored headache pills in his pocket, right next to his lucky penny. If he strained his ears, he could hear klong-ging coming from a long way in the distance. The Swiss clock almost sounded forlorn, as though it missed the chance to ruin Wednesday before it had even started. Somehow, somewhere, the world seemed to be slowly slipping sideways. But as the universe repositioned, Wil was happy to note that things were looking brighter. He had a date with a rather gorgeous girl, and Mr. Dinsdale had put money in his bank ac-count. It was as if someone had replaced the city he knew with a freshly painted movie set.

Wil sat in the town library for the next hour and dutifully paid off a few bills while he tried to think of a concrete plan for what he might say to Mr. Dinsdale when he saw him. He supposed he might just walk into the museum, unannounced, hold up the box he had found inside Lucy's Magic Locker, and declare loudly, "I've found it!" But he knew he stood as much chance of pulling this off as a gazelle might stand of pulling off the nose of the crocodile currently tearing at its vital organs. A concrete plan it may be, but Wil was finding the con-crete a bit wet and tricky to navigate.

He leafed through some books on the subject of boxes and muse-ums, and one spectacularly dull book about a museum dedicated to boxes. The librarian—who Wil felt held a passing resemblance to a hunchbacked gnome—offered no help whatsoever. The little woman threw him a couple of funny looks when he asked her about Albert Einstein's writings on the subject of levity and suggested he go home and research it on his computer since the library's machines were all down for maintenance.

All of this research and bewilderment had Wil feeling a lot like a fisherman standing outside a shark tank: he knew at some point he was going to have to jump in and experience a few bites, but he wasn't sure what kind of bites they were going to be. There was only one thing for it, he decided. If Wednesday was going to make any kind of sense, then he was going to have to do something drastic.

Going by the assumption that he was going to text Lucy, Wil was going to have to buy himself a cell phone.

❦

NEAR THE library was an electronics store that had been given the moniker Jibber Jabber for reasons that Wil could only guess at. He had always ignored the neon-spattered monstrosity because (a) judging by the random numbers on display in the front window, it was far too expensive for him, and (b) all of the clerks reminded him of teenagers who had graduated from Mug O' Joe's and had come here to annoy a more affluent class of customer. To Wil, cell phones and tablets were a little like mobsters and Eskimos: they didn't seem real until they were either fitting you with cement shoes or handing you a freshly caught salmon. Today, however, was the day that Wil Morgan would finally catch up to the other inhabitants of this century.

After spending a minute or two browsing the storefront window display pretending he was going to buy something, he headed inside with the firm intention of doing just that.

At the counter, an indifferent young man regarded him with mild disinterest. "Can I help you?" asked the clerk in such a way as to make it clear he thought Wil was beyond help.

"Yes," said Wil. "I'd like to buy a cell phone, please."

"Any particular plan in mind?"

"Well, I was going to text someone, then call my dad, and then probably just use it to keep in touch with people if they needed me—"

"What kind of *calling* plan?"

"Oh."

This was going to be a bit more difficult than Wil had foreseen. He had no idea there were actual plans for this sort of thing. But he wasn't going down without at least the illusion of throwing a punch. "What kind of plan would suit the stuff I just told you?" he asked, narrowing his eyes.

The clerk also narrowed his eyes and readied himself for a fight he already knew he was going to win. Now, it was just a question of how much money he could persuade Wil to part with, and whether or not Wil was aware that he was about to sign two years of his life away.

Wil followed the clerk to a nearby counter, where he was introduced to a number of flashy-looking "smart" phones, all of which emitted interesting beeps and clacks and whirs, or demonstrated the ability to light up like a Christmas tree in the event of an incoming call.

"This one here," said the clerk, fondling a phone whose screen was roughly the size of a woman's purse, "is pretty much the latest in phone technology: you've got your touch screen, instant messaging, facial recognition software . . . and you can get the weather and stock market reports from over three hundred countries."

Wil eyed the thing suspiciously. Unless he was mistaken, there were not three hundred countries in the entire world. And even if there were, he felt less than compelled to stay informed on the financial maneuverings of the tiny municipality of San Marino.

"Do you have anything less ostentatious?" he asked. "Preferably not something you can see from space."

"They're all pretty much the same, sir. Neon underlighting is really in style right now."

"Yes but it'll be out of style by the time I get to the end of the street. How about something more functional?"

"What about this one?" The clerk held up a pair of sunglasses that glowed with a bluish tint and seemed to make a faint humming sound. "These are the latest in wearable computing. If you're into augmented reality apps, these will help you see the world in a different way."

"I've been having a lot of trouble with that lately," said Wil. "I realize smartphones are all the rage, but I think I'd do better with one that's just above-average intelligence."

"I think you're missing the point."

"I think I'm not alone in that. Honestly, I'd really like a simple calling plan that doesn't require a degree in astrophysics."

"Choosing a plan is up to you, sir," replied the clerk in a sinister tone. "We're not allowed to suggest one carrier over the other. Company policy."

Wil looked at the array of phones and calling plans. They seemed to take up an entire wall of the store. He gulped. Everyday life had become very complicated while he wasn't looking. Perhaps, he thought, cell phones were not meant for him. But he shook off this momentary feeling of insecurity and dug his heels into Jibber Jabber's industrial vomit-colored carpet. According to recent reports, at least seventy percent of the world's population currently owned one of these devices. Wil was adamant that some South Sea tribesman or other was not going to be able to check the weather and traffic reports in Barcelona while he remained clueless. Besides, he had a pretty girl to impress.

"What about this one?" he asked, picking up a solid and compact model that looked more like the kinds of cell phone he had seen on TV.

The clerk sniffed disdainfully. "They're phasing that model out, sir. That's a Lemon. You really don't want that one."

This was exactly the kind of statement that tended to have the opposite effect on a man like Wil Morgan. "Why, what's wrong with it?" Wil asked, deciding at that very moment that this was, indeed, the one he wanted.

"It's the operating system. Lemon went bankrupt. They had a lot of problems with SARA."

"Who's Sara?"

The clerk sighed and rolled his eyes in such a way as to make it clear this moment was the lowest point of his career in telephone sales. "SARA is the interface—it stands for Software Assisted Research Application. The manufacturer developed the voice recognition software but it was obsoleted after Lemoncorp went bust so they never fixed all of the bugs. It's problematic."

Wil squinted a little to read the fine print on the side of the box, which was emblazoned with the manufacturer's logo in the shape of a lemon. If he was not mistaken, the phone possessed its own little internal computer named SARA, which Wil had seen on a television ad conspicuously devoid of any connection to Marcus James. The ads had been pretty impressive, and he recalled that SARA would act like a kind of computerized companion who could guide one to the nearest train station or predict the next three days of weather and remind you to take an umbrella with you. And the price—albeit slightly more than he might have liked—was not to be sneezed at. No matter the manufacturer's unfortunate choice of company logo, this phone was going to be his.

Wil fixed the clerk with a firm gaze, which he had practiced often during his interactions at Mug O' Joe's.

"I'll take it," he said.

And abruptly sneezed.

⚜

Ten minutes later, Wil emerged from the electronics store under the withering gaze of a very annoyed sales clerk. He was now the proud owner of a pay-as-you-talk cell phone plan, a bright and shiny new Lemon phone named SARA, and absolutely no clue whatsoever how to operate the thing. He'd succeeded in entering his personal information into the phone's Welcome screen but navigating the Internet on such a tiny device seemed fraught with peril; Wil managed to put the word "levity" into a search engine, only to be given the location of five local comedy clubs and a hairdresser of the same name. Curious name for a hairdresser, he thought. But he'd given the operating manual a quick once-over and this seemed like as good a time as any to try his luck with SARA. He pressed a small button on the side of the phone and called slightly too loudly into the microphone:

"Hello, SARA. Could you tell me the location of the nearest coffee shop, please?"

"There are three coffee shops within walking distance, Wil Morgan," replied SARA in a slightly mangled, metallic tone. *"Would you like me to call one for you?"*

"No thank you," replied Wil politely. "I'd just like walking directions to the nearest one, please."

"*Please proceed north to the first intersection and turn left,*" replied SARA efficiently. And to provide Wil with all the help he needed, a little green arrow suddenly appeared on the screen of his phone, pointing the way ahead.

"Why thank you, SARA," said Wil as he moved cheerily in the direction highlighted by the little green arrow. "This is the first articulate conversation I've had all day—"

"*In ten yards, turn left.*"

"Right. Got it—"

"*In five yards, turn left.*"

"Yes, I heard you the first time—"

"*Turn left. Klonnngg!*"

Wil began to sense a potential problem with SARA's operating system, and he briefly imagined a legion of Lemoncorp's senior management being led out to the parking lot on the fateful day their stock tanked. In his mind's eye, thousands of angry Lemon customers—all covered with bruises—brandished demonstration placards at the entrance to Lemon headquarters.

"*Proceed fifteen meters west,*" demanded SARA, interrupting Wil's reverie.

Wil obliged and headed in that direction at a slightly elevated pace. For some reason, he found he was becoming unnerved by SARA's shrill metal instructions. Best not to upset her, he reasoned. At least not until they'd become used to each other's company.

"*At the earliest opportunity make a legal U-turn.*"

Wil stopped in his tracks, confused.

"Waitaminnit . . . which way am I going?"

"*Please proceed east along the highlighted route,*" replied SARA with a tone that Wil took for an air of robotic sarcasm.

"So what you actually meant to say back there at the intersection was 'turn right'?" he asked, incredulous.

"*I'm sorry, Wil Morgan,*" replied SARA, innocently. "*Please rephrase the question.*"

"Which way am I supposed to go?"

"*Would you like me to look up 'which way am I supposed to go' on the Internet?*"

"No, I'd like you to shut up now."

"*Dialing voice mail,*" warbled SARA, blissfully. Wil reached down and switched off the SARA function. He was going to have to find a coffee shop the old-fashioned way: namely, by looking with his eyes.

❧

ROUGHLY THIRTY minutes later, Wil found himself standing at the counter of Mug O' Joe's staring helplessly at the chalkboard and realizing he was already out of ideas. No matter his intention to explore the city and find a better candidate for Mr. Dinsdale's box of Levity, he'd gone around in a big circle and found himself in exactly the place he always found himself on any given Wednesday. His Lemon phone—much like his day so far—had proven too much for him to handle. Wil felt like a nun at a fashion show: he was clearly out of his comfort zone, and would probably be better off sticking to his usual habits. The wooden box tucked neatly under his arm next to his prized Tesla Kit would have to suffice, at least for a first attempt. Wil desperately needed a reason to get back inside the museum so that he could scratch the mental itch he'd been afflicted with ever since his visit to Lucy's Magic Locker. He wondered how he might respond to Mr. Dinsdale if the elderly curator pointed out that the cruddy old box he'd found seemed to have originated in Taiwan. But he had to know: was there some kind of bizarre temporal anomaly that connected Lucy to the museum?

Once again, thoughts of the museum on Upside-Down Street had Wil's mind going this way and that. He decided to forego his usual argument with today's teenaged barista, and opted instead for a healthy dose of corporate vernacular and whatever hot drink the teenager chose for him. He was pleasantly surprised to find the drink rather tasty, though he had no idea what it was, nor did he have the inclination to ask. Unless he missed his guess, it was flavored with nutmeg, which brought about warm thoughts of hot apple cider on cold autumn days. Wil shook off the daydream, and drew a massive swig of his caffeinated latte something-or-other. He wished it contained a significant helping of something alcoholic, for he was about to need an awful lot of courage.

Outside the coffee shop, Wil stared for a minute or two at Lucy's business card, upon which was written her cell phone number in cutesy, girlish handwriting. Lucy had dotted the *i* in her last name with a little heart. Wil hadn't the faintest idea how to begin texting—he barely had a clue how to dial the number she had given. What if it was a fake number or—even worse—what if Lucy answered? Wil was struck by the awful notion that Lucy would see him for who he really was: a fraud who investigated fraud for a living. And not much of a living at that. He sighed, knowing he was already in far too deep.

Wil studied the Lemon phone's screen, completely clueless as to how to bring up the dialing function. For the next three minutes he managed to check the stock reports in Nicaragua, look up "telephones throughout history" on the Internet, and accidentally join two social network sites without actually wanting to. There was no choice, he realized. He was going to have to elicit SARA's help. He found a quiet place in a nearby alley, held his breath for a moment, and switched on the computer interface.

Silence. Wil waited for SARA to start the conversation. For her part, SARA waited for Wil to make himself look foolish. She didn't have long to wait.

"Hello?" said Wil, anxiously. "Is anybody there?"

"*Hello, Wil Morgan,*" replied SARA with a calculated lag designed to unnerve a professional boxer. "*You have been absent from this interface for approximately fifty-three minutes. Would you like an updated weather report?*"

Judging by the slightly aggressive metallic tone, Wil surmised

SARA was still annoyed with him as a result of their first encounter. "I'd like to dial a number, please," he stated, flatly. Best to act as if nothing out of the ordinary had happened.

"*Searching address book database,*" replied the demonic interface. "*You have zero friends.*"

"Yes. Thank you for that observation," replied Wil, slightly aggrieved by the actual truth behind the statement. In his seven years in the city, Wil's closest friend was currently Mr. Whatley, the Castle Towers superintendent. "As difficult as this may be for a smartphone to accept," he continued, "I'd like to dial a telephone number. So let's just get about our business and make a phone call, shall we?"

"*Would you like to make a phone call?*" asked SARA, innocently.

"Yes, I'd like to make a phone call. I'd like to see the telephone dialing function on my Lemon phone. And please don't show me the stock reports from Monaco."

SARA brought up the stock reports from Monaco, just to be a wiseass.

"Look," said Wil, "I'm not going to play games with you, SARA. I want to make a phone call—"

A computerized game of card solitaire appeared on Wil's Lemon phone screen. Wil gave his phone a dangerous look. "Now cut it out! Just bring me the dialing function!"

No response. SARA was apparently also in a dangerous frame of mind.

"I want to dial a telephone number!" yelled Wil. At this point, he was beginning to lose reason. And to think he had only been a Lemon owner for less than one hour. He wondered if this was a world record for the shortest amount of time a new telephone owner might possess their phone before wanting to crush it under a steamroller, then decided he was probably a record holder for the Lemon phone owner who'd held out the longest. "Phone call!" he bellowed. "Telephone! TELL-EE-PHONE! I swear I'm going to punch you—"

Wil looked up to find a bemused elderly couple staring at him as he argued with his cell phone in public. He glowered at them, so that they hustled away quickly. Suddenly, the telephone function appeared on his touch screen. Apparently, SARA was ready to concede that Wil was capable of tossing her under a passing car.

"That's better. Now please dial this number." Wil recited Lucy's cell phone number as accurately as possible, making sure to enunciate in such a way that if SARA got it wrong she would clearly be doing it on purpose. He waited for the phone to ring. Instead, there was only silence. Wil looked at the screen, which was now providing weather reports for Harare, Zimbabwe.

"*Would you like me to dial a number?*" asked SARA, sweetly.

"Yes!" screamed Wil. "I swear I'm going to throw you under a school bus. Are you completely mental?"

"Hiya Wil," replied a familiar female voice emanating from his cell phone, "are you having a bad day, or is it just me?"

The blood drained from Wil's face with the kind of speed reserved for comets on a collision course with the sun. "Lucy?" he muttered, weakly. "Is that you?"

"Your first clue would probably be that you dialed my number," replied Lucy from the other end of the ether. "Who were you expecting? And by the way, were you shouting at me or are you driving?"

"I wasn't shouting at you, I promise. I wasn't even shouting. I'm just . . ." Wil allowed his voice to trail off. The chances of a rational explanation at this point were in exact proportion to the chances of Lucy believing it. "I'm having a bit of trouble with my new cell phone."

"Bummer. I hate my phone, too, if it's any consolation. Everyone does."

"I doubt it," said Wil, feeling a little sorry for himself. "Most people's phones don't look up the population of Warsaw when you ask them to dial a telephone number."

There was a pregnant pause. "Don't tell me you bought a Lemon?"

"The same," replied Wil, hesitantly. He hoped Lucy wouldn't find his obvious lack of computer savvy unattractive. "I think the interface is trying to kill me."

Another silence. Wil checked his phone to see if Lucy had disconnected. He could hardly blame her for doing so.

"Now that," said Lucy in a spooky and ominous tone, " that . . .
is . . . awesome!"

"Really?"

"Sure it is. I don't know a single person in their right mind who'd buy
a Lemon phone on purpose. Those things are a train wreck. I hear their
texting function sends to your entire address book. Is that true?"

"I wouldn't know," said Wil, despondently. He had a terrible feeling the context of the conversation was getting away from him. "I
don't know how to send a text."

"Doubly awesome," replied Lucy, happily. "You know, you really
are a complicated man, Wil Morgan. Did you find a good Korean
restaurant for Thursday?"

According to my Lemon phone there are five of them but they're
all a bit of a drive."

"How far?"

"Korea."

This elicited a spontaneous giggle from the other end of the phone.
Wil could see himself getting quite used to that sound, and he found
himself looking forward to his date more eagerly than ever before.

He looked down at the inlaid box nestled under one arm, the Tesla
Kit nestled under the other, and the large cup of coffee held in his
free hand. Adding a smartphone to this equation was putting him in
jeopardy of dropping the whole kit and caboodle. Wil decided to
head toward the Castle Towers so that he could reset and put himself
in order. It would be at least another hour before the clock tower tried
to bother him, at which point he'd already be halfway to the Curioddity Museum. Wil felt a tinge of guilt at the idea of bringing the rot-
ting old box to the museum but he sloughed this off by agreeing to
himself that Mr. Dinsdale would at least have one failure to strike
from his list of box-shaped candidates.

"So is this a social call," asked Lucy, "or did you want to tell me
where we're going Thursday night?"

"Right. Well," said Wil, "since I don't know how to send a text, I guess I called to see if you had a favorite restaurant? Korean's pretty specific. Is there one downtown?"

"We could go to Happy Spice. I love their thousand-year-old eggs and they do a killer bubble tea."

"Sounds revolting. Is everything on a Korean menu something we're supposed to eat on a dare?"

"Pretty much. That's why it's so much fun."

WIL HAD been thinking about what he was going to say to Lucy ever since he'd met her the previous night. He'd thought about it on his way home, and as he'd brushed his teeth before bedtime. He'd thought about it the moment he'd woken to the smell of mushrooms, and he'd thought about it while standing in the line at Mug O' Joe's, waiting to argue with his daily teenager. For the first time in as long as he could remember, Wil Morgan had a plan that did not involve walking to work, nor standing in a vomit-inducing elevator, nor skulking through the lobby of his apartment building.

Now, he was ready to make his move: For the first time in many years he was going to be a catalyst, the spark that set off the firework. He could only hope it didn't all blow up in his face.

"Have you ever heard of the Curioddity Museum?" he asked, innocently.

"I love museums!" replied Lucy, eagerly. "Especially ones I've never been to before. Where is it?"

"Do you know the divided highway that runs through the banking district?"

"There's a museum there?" Lucy sounded a touch skeptical. "I thought that place was just a bunch of industrial buildings."

"Yeah, so did I," admitted Wil without bothering to explain the rest of the story. "I, uh . . . I found it the other day. I was wondering if you'd like to go there with me someti—"

Before Wil could enunciate the *m* in "sometime" he heard a shriek at the other end of the line.

"Are you okay?" he inquired, genuinely concerned for Lucy's well-being.

"Of course I am, silly! I hoped you were going to ask me out again. I mean dinner's great, an' everything. I mean I wasn't sure if you were into me but I guess you dig me. I mean I dig you."

Wil looked at his cell phone, confused. Despite Lucy's liberal use of the phrase "I mean," he wasn't sure what she meant at all. He'd lit a spark, all right: Lucy's metaphorical firework seemed primed to explode at random intervals. He decided it might be a good idea to defuse the situation, just to be on the safe side.

"I mean if you have time," he said, feeling self-conscious.

"I'll make time. What street is it on?"

"Right. What street."

"Okay. What street?"

Wil felt his hesitance was quite understandable. For all he knew, Upside-Down Street was a figment of his imagination, or one of Mr. Dinsdale's elaborate tricks. "I think it's called Mons Street though I can't be sure. Oh, but the museum is right across from an old cinema. You can't miss it."

"Sounds tremendous," said Lucy with her typical level of unbridled enthusiasm. "I'll meet you at Happy Spice on Thursday at seven. Don't be late!" And with that, she closed the connection on her end.

Wil stared at the cell phone, half-expecting it to do something unexpected. SARA remained subdued—no doubt angry that Wil's phone call had gone off without a hitch—and her screen remained dark. A small triumph, Wil conceded, but a triumph nonetheless.

And he was to enjoy this minor success for roughly twenty seconds before the bottom fell out of his universe once again.

CHAPTER EIGHT

HINDSIGHT WOULD later suggest to Wil that things coincidentally began to fall down at exactly the same time he began to relax. He wasn't to know this at the time, of course. Otherwise it would've been foresight.

Wil walked toward the Castle Towers for a few minutes, pleased with how he'd navigated the tricky waters of his first ever cell phone call. If life were a gushing torrent of unpredictability, he thought, then at this moment in time he was the captain of a very large submarine currently plowing right underneath it and wondering what all the fuss was about. Flushed with success and warmed by hot coffee, he wandered aimlessly with the flow of traffic until the current washed him up at the base of the Castle Towers. He was determined, however, that the ugly old edifice would not dampen his mood today. And he was doubly determined that the monstrous Swiss clock next door would fail in its daily ambush at six minutes after three. Today, he would be ready.

Wil dallied for a while, chuckling to himself as road-weary afternoon travelers passed by the statue of Pan outside his office building. Local drivers had become so accustomed to Pan's generously carved wedding tackle that they tended to navigate the confusing one-way roundabout without so much as a first glance. Many of the people inside the cars carried the resigned looks of those who would rather be living anywhere else, and any other time in history. But every so often, an out-of-town driver could be seen trying desperately to avoid a collision as they spotted Pan's enormous endowment to the arts for the first time. Poor saps, thought Wil as he sauntered knowingly toward the entrance to his office building, they really needed to watch what they were doing.

And it was precisely while indulging in this disparaging frame of mind that he made his second mistake in a row.

❧

WIL'S FIRST mistake, to be fair, had been somewhat understandable. The excitement of an upcoming date with Lucy Price—added to the money in his bank account, and the general sense that all had become somehow right with the universe—had led him to conclude that all was somehow right with the universe. Naturally, the universe had other ideas.

Wil's second mistake was to call his father using his brand-new Lemon phone.

IT HAD been a full three days since Barry Morgan's answering machine message had threatened to ruin his son's entire week. Now, Wil found himself standing at the base of the Castle Towers preparing to return fire. He paused for a moment at the main doors to the building, held up his brand-new cell phone, and pretended he was staring into SARA's eyes in a challenging fashion. He activated SARA's voice recognition function, with no intention of being the one who blinked first.

"Hello again, SARA," said Wil with as much of an I-wear-the-trousers-in-this-relationship air of bravado as he could muster. "I'd like to make a phone call."

The Lemon phone remained silent. Wil was getting the distinct impression SARA had cottoned on to his game of chicken. But he was determined not to repeat his previous performance and come off as a crazy homeless person yelling randomly into the air. He waited.

"*Hello, Wil Morgan,*" said SARA's disembodied voice eventually. "*It has been approximately seventeen minutes since our last interaction. Would you like to dial the previous number?*"

"No, a new number, please. I want to call my dad—"

"*My database indicates roughly two and a half billion dads in the telephone directory. Would you like to narrow the search?*"

"I'm curious. Was the person who programmed you on some kind of medication or is this just a case of artificial intelligence gone rogue?"

"*Would you like me to search—*"

"No, I wouldn't. I would not like you to search, nor suggest a search, nor even think about searching with that limited set of robotic cogs you call a brain. I would, however, like the telephone dialing function. And I would also like to make it quite clear, SARA, that I know where the nearest river is, and I'm thinking of taking you swimming later this afternoon."

SARA remained silent for a few moments until suddenly, a neon-green dialing keypad began to glow and pulsate on the Lemon phone's screen. Finally, thought Wil as he began to dial Barry Morgan's cell phone number, the maniacal smartphone was beginning to wise up. For a moment, he considered the ramifications of accidentally dialing any one of the other two and a half billion dads on planet Earth by accident, and he decided that if he should randomly be connected with someone in, say, Lahore, Pakistan, then at least they could have a conversation about the local stock market and weather. This whimsical notion was soon to be ousted, however, as Wil's father quickly picked up on the other end of the line.

"Barry Morgan," came a gruff voice presented in a type of crystal clarity reserved only for telemarketers and debt collectors. Wil stood for a moment, unsure of what to say. The idea of actually speaking with his father always filled him with dread, no matter the few hundred miles between them. "Barry Morgan," repeated the voice. "Who is this?"

"Hi, Dad," said Wil, nervously. "It's me. This is my new cell phone."

"Wil? Is that you?"

"How many other people call you Dad?" There was a brief pause. Barry never much cared for humor, sardonic or otherwise. "I'm sorry I missed calling you back," Wil continued. "I've been really busy at work."

"Oh. How's everyone at the accounting firm?"

This had been the opening sentence of virtually every single phone conversation between the two men for the last seven years, and while Wil could normally navigate this web of deceit with practiced ease, today he felt an awful lot like a fly who'd just landed on something very sticky and glanced up to find itself facing a predator with eight legs and two fangs. Wil gulped, searching for a line of bull hockey that might persuade his father to cancel his upcoming plans to visit and randomly decide to go somewhere else that was both far away and infinitely less stressful.

"Umm. Things are fine, Dad. Really fine. But we're busy. It's nearing the end of the fiscal year so we're just about to go into overdrive." Wil hoped he'd used the word "fiscal" correctly in a sentence. No reaction from his dad. Not bad so far.

Well," said Barry, genially, "I suppose taxes will always come around at the same time every year. They always do for me."

"That's what I always say to the guys."

"What?"

"Taxes. They always come around. Unless you don't do them."

This conversation was already beginning to derail. Wil moved through the main door of the Castle Towers and into the lobby, listening politely to his father's generalities about the importance of timely and well-prepared tax returns. He knew that Barry could be counted on for a good five minutes of lecturing, and this would give him enough time to get up to the nineteenth floor. And with any luck, he might lose reception inside the Rat Barf Express on the way up to his office.

As Wil listened to Barry waffling on about his favorite tax forms and great moments in accounting history, he moved past the two brothers inside the lobby, playing chess. The strange twins with their matching comb-overs seemed lost in their game, as usual, and so Wil gave them no more than a cursory glance as he passed by and entered the elevator. But as the elevator doors began to close and Wil girded his metaphorical loins for nineteen floors' worth of the Vomit Comet— his Lemon phone now held roughly twelve inches from his left ear— one of the two brothers over at the table did something rather odd: he began to stand up. Weird, thought Wil. This was the first time he'd ever seen either twin actually move away from the chessboard. As the first brother began to stand, the second seemed to slump down a little on his chair, as if the removal of the first brother's torso had created a little vortex under the table that had sucked him in. Just as the elevator doors closed, Wil watched with mild intrigue as the standing brother began to slip and fall to one side of the chess table, suggesting the effort of standing had proven too much for the poor man.

Inside the elevator, the smell of rat vomit seemed more pungent than usual. Wil mentally crossed his fingers—even though he'd initiated the dialing process, he secretly hoped the ascending elevator might be too much for his Lemon phone and he'd lose the connection. As his father continued to waffle on about job security and the benefits of the accounting industry, a one-sided conversation that Wil punctuated with the occasional "Uh-huh," he allowed himself to daydream about the possibility of reprogramming the SARA function and letting her carry on the conversation by herself. The caustic smell of the elevator, however, was beginning to take its usual toll. Wil wrestled with his gag reflex, found himself on the business end of a metaphorical half nelson, and began to cough uncontrollably.

"Are you listening to me, Wil?"

"Huh?"

Wil snapped to attention, realizing he'd almost blacked out somewhere during his ascent. He briefly imagined himself as an early-twentieth-century mountain climber wearing jodhpurs and a woolen scarf, mere yards from the summit of Everest as the clouds pulled in. This was not going to be an easy moment.

"I was asking about your work," continued Barry Morgan at the other end of the line. "How is everyone at the office? Are you still having trouble with that coworker of yours?"

"Oh, yes," lied Wil. "It's terrible." And with that, he descended into a full-on coughing fit.

"Are you all right?"

"Yes," lied Wil again. "I'm fine."

"What was that person's name, anyway?"

"Excuse me?"

"Your coworker. The one you told me is always being dishonest. I've known a few people like that: people who couldn't tell the truth to save their lives."

Wil racked his brains as he tried to remember the name of the mythical coworker he'd woven a tale about the last time he'd spoken to his father. "Was it Jerry?" he asked, trying to ignore the irony of the lie he was perpetrating about a mythical liar. This was, of course, a name he'd fished out of mid-air in much the same way a black bear might try to target a spawning salmon fifty miles before it got upstream to the weir. He knew that it could not possibly have been "Jerry" the last time he and Barry had had this conversation, but he also knew his dad very rarely paid any attention to such details.

"That sounds like it," replied Barry, mercifully.

"Yeah, Jerry," said Wil with more than a tinge of guilt creeping into his voice. "I hate that guy."

WIL EXITED the elevator at the nineteenth floor, gasping for air, and he staggered forward until he could steady himself on the far wall. He was going to have to think of a way to persuade his father not to visit while at the same time making the whole thing seem entirely natural. Ever since Barry had first called, Wil had been working on a series of excuses ranging from the outlandish to the downright ridiculous. Tales of alien abduction and being recruited by the Secret Service had given way to more reasonable explanations such as unexpected construction work and sudden contagious illness.

"Dad," began Wil, hesitantly, "I have a little bit of bad news."

"Oh?" replied his father. "Is anything wrong?"

"We've had an infestation at work. Cockroaches." That didn't sound plausible, he thought. "And fleas," he added, hastily.

"Cockroaches and fleas?"

"The cockroaches have fleas. They've had to shut the entire building down and cover it with a tent. We're all having to work from home. It's going to take a couple of months to clear the place out."

Utter silence. Wil hoped beyond hope that his father might bite. But now that he'd said the words out loud, his chosen trail of deceit was feeling more like a goat track through a minefield than the two-lane highway he'd hoped for. There was no going back now.

"Don't you work in the Central Building?" asked Barry, suspiciously.

"Yes . . . yes, I do."

"And they've covered it with a tent?"

"Floor by floor. But essentially, yes."

"Well, I suppose at least you won't have to deal with Jerry."

"Who?"

⨮⨭

WIL BLANCHED as he moved toward his office door and fumbled for his keys. He had always been a terrible liar; his lies had a tendency not only of catching up to him but also lapping him a few times just to prove a point. Phase Two of his lie now seemed even more outlandish than Phase One. But he was already in too deep. Might as well go for it, he reasoned.

"So the worse news is that the fleas are carrying some kind of fever. Everyone's been coming down with it. The doctors said it's probably very contagious."

"Oh my word, Wil! That sounds terrible!"

"It is. Jerry got it the worst. They said he might never recover—"

JUST AS Wil reached with his keys to open his door—now warming to his mammoth infestation tale and preparing to describe the symptoms of Yellow Mountain Fever, which he'd been researching on his Lemon phone interface—he suddenly stopped dead in his tracks. Looking through the glass door just above the word ROTAGITSEVNI, there appeared to be the dark silhouette of a figure seated in his office. In fact, this person seemed to be sitting in Wil's own chair. He looked down at the lock and moved the handle slightly, discovering to his horror that it turned with ease. Someone was definitely inside his office!

"Dad," Wil hissed into the phone, "can you hold on for a second? Something's come up."

"What is it?"

"I'm not sure. I think someone's in my office."

"Aren't you at home?"

"No. It's complicated. Look, just hold on, okay?"

Wil turned the handle oh so slightly, his heart racing and his mind doing cartwheels as he tried to imagine who might be inside his office. With any luck, Mr. Whatley had let himself in and was emptying the trash just below Wil's desk. Perhaps Mr. Dinsdale had come to check on his progress—Wil wouldn't put it past the old man to have found a way inside and casually be enjoying the sound of the Swiss clock's many cogs and gears next door.

But what if Mr. Dinsdale was an imposter? he wondered. What if this was someone from the authorities? Even worse, what if it was a sheriff or a debt collector, like one of those steroid-addled bodybuilders he'd seen on TV?

The figure in Wil's office chair seemed to be sitting with his or her back to the door, facing the window that looked out onto the brick wall of the Swiss clock. Wil opened the door slowly. But as he tried to squeeze quietly inside his office, his leg accidentally bumped into the package containing the orphaned Air-Max 2000 driver, causing it to clatter to the ground with a loud bang that suggested it most likely did not survive the fall. Wil gritted his teeth and blinked. He had given away his position.

"Hello," he said, nervously. "Is anybody there?"

No response. The chair began to swivel slowly. Wil's teeth were now trying to bite their way out of his mouth.

The chair swiveled a full 180 degrees. Wil's Lemon phone clattered to the ground as he stood—jaw agape—rooted to the spot.

"I came a few days early," said Barry Morgan, fixing his son with a glare made of pure hardened steel. "I would've been here even earlier but I got delayed talking to Jerry."

WIL STOOD rooted to the spot, doing his best impression of a Texas live oak that had just been peppered with a twelve-gauge shotgun. A quick internal wellness check informed him that his eyes were bulging, and the outsides of his little fingers had begun to tingle. He suddenly needed very much to go to a bathroom: preferably, one in South Africa.

"Melissa," said his father.

"What?" replied Wil as he tried in vain to control his rapidly blinking left eye, which seemed to be trying to fold itself over his right cheekbone.

"Melissa," repeated Barry. "Last time we spoke, the coworker you didn't like was called Melissa. She seems to have undergone a dramatic personality change, not to mention gender reassignment surgery. And a total body transplant. I wonder if she's aware of what's happened?

"Dad, look . . . I can explain—"

"Speaking of personality changes, I'm sure 'Melissa' isn't alone. The last I knew my son was on a steady path toward partner at a reputable accounting firm. He was living in a rent-controlled apartment in a safe area of town, and he had been saving his money wisely. My new son—"

"Dad—"

"My *new* son lives in a cat-infested flophouse just blocks from a flea-infested flea market. He follows people in secret and tries to take pictures of them in compromising positions. He has apparently chosen a career in the twilight world of insurance fraud, and has been living a lie for at least the last seven years." Barry frowned, as if the scale of Wil's deceit was just beginning to dawn on him. "What have I done to deserve this?" he asked no one in particular.

The room fell silent for a moment. Wil could feel a scraping movement emanating from his heels, and he wondered briefly if this was coming from the depths of his very soul, or if the Swiss clock next door was gearing up to rub salt into his gaping psychic wounds. By Wil's rough estimate, it was approximately one minute past three. He had a brief and sudden notion that just for once, the hated clock would not catch him by surprise. Instead, it would jolt his angry father into a sudden bout of short-term memory loss, leaving Wil free to skip back out the door and be five miles away before Barry had ever realized what happened. Alas, such flights of fancy were usually doomed to catch fire a few thousand feet above sea level and inevitably crash into the ground from a great height. In the years Wil had been preparing for this moment, he had never quite hit upon what he was actually going to say. And so he did the only thing he could think of doing: he bent double at the waist, covered one eye, and tried to see if he could un-look at his father in case the entire situation might unexpectedly turn around. The situation, unfortunately, refused to budge.

"What on Earth are you doing?" asked Barry, incredulous. "Are you on some kind of medicine, Wil?"

"I'm trying to see if I can think of a way to begin at the beginning, Dad," replied Wil. "You wanted to know what you've done to deserve something, and I'm trying to think of what it is."

Barry's face reddened. It was clear he thought Wil was making fun of the situation. "Stand up, for Heaven's sake! You're making a fool of yourself. What would your mother have said?"

"That's just the thing, Dad," replied Wil. "She probably would have laughed and encouraged me to follow my heart, or something."

"She would have been worried for you, Wil—would you stand up straight, for the love of God? And she would have agreed with me that living a lie isn't living at all. It's living in someone else's shoes!"

Wil straightened, trying his best to return his father's furious gaze. This was all unfamiliar territory for him, and he had no idea how to proceed. "Maybe," he said, evenly, "she would have liked the other person's shoes."

Barry's eyes narrowed, dangerously. Wil had only ever seen this look twice before—once when he'd sailed his father's entire tin soldier collection into a watery grave on the back of an Unsinkable Electro-Concrete Troop Carrier, and once when he'd told his father in a fit of teenage pique that a career in accounting was infinitely less preferable to, say, being the lead guitarist in a rock band. On both occasions, there had been a kind of psychic fallout that had lingered for well over a year or two. Wil felt sure that the fallout from this particular incident was going to have a half-life of roughly ten to fifteen years.

"I've always believed in you, Wil," said Barry with a tone that demonstrated his uncanny ability to incapacitate his son's opinion before it had even been stated. "I've tolerated your idiosyncrasies and I've put up with any number of stupid and thoughtless whims on your part, all because I recognize you are your mother's son more than you are mine. But this . . . this is unforgiveable."

Wil blinked; he had not expected such a rapier to the heart, and had expected even less to find himself experiencing an immediate visceral reaction to his father's anger. "That's funny," he replied, brazenly. "From where I'm standing you've always believed in the son you thought was a chartered accountant. But you've never actually believed in your real son at all."

"My real son? The one who's lied to me for the last seven years?"

"No. The one that's been forced to lie because you've sat in judgment on him for the last thirty-two. The one you've discouraged at every single important moment of his entire life." Wil could feel the bile rising in his throat. Though he had never expected this inevitable showdown to take such a disagreeable turn, the argument had been a long time coming and now that it was here, it needed to be greeted with enthusiasm.

"Oh, so this is my fault?" said Barry, incredulously. "You're living hand to mouth running some kind of insurance scam and I'm to blame? What on Earth happened to your conscience?"

"News flash, Dad: I never wanted to be an accountant. First of all, I don't perpetuate insurance scams, I prevent them. And secondly, you seem to be unclear on what a conscience really is. I do this job precisely because I follow my conscience and not the blueprint you laid out for me when Mom died!"

"Don't you dare bring your mother into this, Wilbur Aloysius Morgan!"

Wil stared, furiously. For thirty-two years, every time Barry Morgan had needed to regain control of his errant son, the dreaded "full name" card had inevitably been played. The middle name of Aloysius had been Melinda's idea, apparently as some kind of joke; Wil—for the life of him—had never understood why an otherwise-loving parent would commit such an atrocity on a poor, unsuspecting child. Well, it wasn't going to work this time. This time, Wilbur Aloysius Morgan would stand his ground. Better still, he'd fight back with his own brand of vitriol and see where that took things for a change! "That's right," said Wil in the most condescending tone he could muster, "let's go over your litany of disappointments, shall we? Better still, since I already know them by heart, I'll write them down on a piece of paper and you can just use that as a reference card!"

"Wil, you have never—*ever*—spoken to me in this manner before—"

"My *mother* would have been proud of me. My *mother*—your *wife*—would have told me to follow my heart, and she would have put a Band-Aid over the bruises whenever I inevitably followed it headfirst into a tree! My *mother* was someone I could easily understand because she tried to understand me. But do you know what part of her I never did understand, Dad? The part that somehow wanted to be married to you!"

BANG. ZOOM. Man overboard. In the imaginary sea battle between two men floundering on different ships so many miles apart, Submarine Captain Wil Morgan had most definitely fired a fifty-ton torpedo right into the bow of his father's Unsinkable Electro-Concrete Troop Carrier. Wil trembled slightly, refusing to look away from his father's hollow gaze as Barry's expression of apoplexy gave way to one of utter shock. The older man seemed to waver for a moment, until his gaze drooped along with his shoulders, and Wil realized his dad was now looking at his feet.

"Is that the way you really feel?" Barry asked his shoes.

"I don't know, Dad," said Wil, unexpectedly finding himself in the ascendancy and realizing this was miles away from the place he actually wanted to be. "It's been a weird week. Just about everything that's happened since Monday has been weird. I've had everything turned upside down. I'm not sure why, but I've suddenly got money in my bank account, a new appreciation for this city—the Castle Towers excepted—and I feel like I'm finally beginning to find my way. All because I've been encouraged to un-look at things and follow my instincts for a change instead of following the one-way system. Oh, and I've met a girl. If you weren't so angry at me, you'd probably like her."

Barry seemed to blink rapidly at the mention of the girl. For a moment, Wil was concerned that his father was getting light-headed. But he knew better: this was Barry's process for arriving at a conclusion, one that would prove to be so spectacularly passive-aggressive that books would be written on the subject by legions of future professional therapists.

"You don't need to change the subject, son," said Barry in a conciliatory tone born of a psychoanalytical expertise prepared in the oven of sixty-four years of amateur cooking. "I'm glad you've met someone."

"Well . . . good, I guess . . . ," began Wil as all of his instincts screamed at him to run in the opposite direction to the one he was headed.

"And you're right," continued Barry. "We always knew it, both of us. But we never had time to discuss it before your mom was gone, and everything changed. I know she only ever felt sorry for me."

"Hang on a minute, Dad. I didn't mean—"

"The sad thing is, yes you did. And you're right. I didn't deserve your mother any more than I deserve you. I'm sorry."

"C'mon, Dad," said Wil as he reached out to place a hand on his father's shoulder. "I'm to blame here. I should have told you how I felt—"

But as Wil's hand moved close to his father, he was surprised to feel it knocked forcefully backward. This was a push-back delivered in anger, and it had the effect of knocking Wil silent as well. Despite Barry's woe-is-me demeanor, Wil knew that he had done something that might never be undone: his Dad might forgive the years of lies, but he would never forgive this one moment of absolute truth. "I'm leaving," said Barry. "I'll be staying in the Waterbury Hotel near the train station until my return trip home on Sunday morning. I wish you the best in your insurance fraud work."

"Dad, don't be melodramatic. You can stay for a few days. Maybe it'd do us good to work this all out. You know, there's a person I'd like you to meet at the Curioddity Museum downtown. I think you'd get quite a different perspective if we all sat over a cup of coffee."

But Wil already knew the ending to this particular scene: his father would leave, and he would feel miserable. And a few moments after the door closed, the gears of the clock would scrape and he'd be so lost in miserable thought that he'd bang his head on something when the Swiss clock inevitably attacked just as he least expected it.

Just to get the ball rolling, Barry shuffled toward the door. "I'll be in touch," said the older man. "But I need to leave now. Goodbye."

WIL COULD only watch, helpless, as his father exited through his backward-forward door. He listened quietly as Barry's footsteps shuffled in calculated fashion across the creaky hallway outside, and he waited for the expectant scraping sound as the elevator doors came open, and the clattering, grinding sound as they closed. His father's rat-vomit-induced coughing got quieter and quieter, until Wil was certain the elevator had descended a couple of floors. And at that point, there was no turning back for either of them.

Nearby, another scraping sound came into his awareness: the Swiss clock was getting ready to add its own particular sonic flavor to the moment. Wil glanced at his watch. Five minutes past three. Not today, he thought. Not today.

Eschewing a seat at his desk—a place where any number of scrapes and bruises could occur as a result of sudden, alarmed movements— Wil sat with his back to the far wall, removed his lucky penny from his pocket, and waited for the clock to strike. He felt the smooth edges for a moment and then, disconsolate, began to spin the penny on the ground. It moved impossibly quietly for a moment while next door, the clock's gears began to grind. Maybe this time, thought Wil. Maybe this time his penny would spin for eternity.

But even a man who has paid his rent doesn't have forever, Wil acknowledged to himself. That same old lump began to well up in his throat as—like clockwork—old thoughts began to resurface. Wil thought of his mother, and how proud she might have been of all that he'd accomplished during this particular week. If not for what he'd just said to his father—her husband, and the man she had chosen to love.

His lips and his fingers felt numb again; the vertigo was returning with a vengeance. Next door, the clock's clapper began to scrape across the bricks and Wil steeled himself for the inevitable moment he would jump, startled, and hit his head.

KLONNG!

Interestingly, the noise of the first sonic attack came exactly as Wil imagined it might. Even more interestingly, Wil was actually ready for it, and this time he didn't jump up, startled, and bash his head. Despite his many misgivings, Wil instinctively reached up and felt his face just to make sure he was still conscious.

KLONNG!

Wil looked down to find his lucky penny still spinning. Something was vibrating in his pocket. He produced his Lemon phone and found a text message from Lucy Price written upon its glowing screen: *Looking forward to Korean. See you there—Lucy.* Wil blinked, expecting the message to spontaneously combust, which it spontaneously did not. He pushed the phone away from him so that it skittered across the floor.

KLONNG!

Three down, three to go. Could it be, thought Wil, that after one encounter with the curator of the Curioddity Museum his worldview had changed so dramatically that he was now prepared for all the disasters headed his way? Could it be that not all of these imagined disasters would end in, well, disaster?

KLONNG!

A cloud fell across Wil's window. He crinkled his nose as for the first time he heard a strange sound, hidden below the first: a kind of humming noise that suggested a massive electrical charge was being generated somewhere nearby.

Wil looked down. His lucky penny was beginning to wander aimlessly toward his discarded Lemon phone.

KLONNG!

Wil closed his eyes and concentrated. He'd made it through an entire clock episode without so much as an accelerated heartbeat! This was it—the moment his fortunes changed for good. Maybe his father's visit had been for the best. After all, he'd finally confronted his dad, hadn't he? That had to count for something. He was going on a date with a great girl who seemed to like him. And he'd even (indirectly) paid for dinner.

Things were going to be okay. All that remained now was for one last

KLUNK!

Wil screamed blue bloody murder as a large paperweight on the shelf above his head became dislodged and crashed into the very area of his skull that had conveniently been dented into shape by a street sign and a copy of Tolstoy's *War and Peace*. His foot jerked out, involuntarily, kicking his lucky penny across the floor so that it clattered under his desk. "Arhhh!" screamed Wil, channeling his inner pirate.

Blinded by pain, he screwed his eyes tightly shut and tried to imagine himself unconscious in the hopes that mind over matter would prevail. But it was no use: his mind had shut down due to the overload of pain sensors flooding it with information.

He slipped sideways toward the hard wooden floor, thinking to himself how words such as "Arhhh" were incredibly uncreative, and with his eyes still closed he replaced it with a few very carefully chosen swear words. The pain was just mind-splittingly awful.

As if to remind Wil just who his nefarious boss really was, the Swiss clock next door made a few rustling sounds as it settled, and the faint hum of energy he had heard began to dissipate. Despite his eyes being closed so tightly they would probably require an oxy-acetylene torch to reopen, Wil felt a few tears of pain squeeze their way out of his tear ducts.

He lay silently on his side, trying to understand his place in the universe. "Why me?" he asked aloud. "Why does it always have to be me?"

"GREETINGS, WIL Morgan," replied the universe in a familiar metallic tone. "Would you like me to look up 'Why does it always have to be me?' on the Internet?"

CHAPTER NINE

DESPAIR WAS finally pulling Wil Morgan into its slimy, sticky grasp. The blinding pain in his head had left him barely able to see out of one eye, and he felt a terrible bout of vertigo coming on in the eye that could still function. From his sideways angle, he could see his discarded Lemon phone close by, and his lucky penny just farther away underneath his desk. He reached out to switch off the Lemon phone and then desperately—feebly—reached out to grasp his lucky penny. He rolled it over and over in his palms, pressing the serrated edge so hard into his palms that he could feel the pain all the way up to his good eyeball; it didn't feel so lucky anymore.

Wil knew that he had to get out of his office before he hurt something; namely, the giant clock next door. He felt no desire to spend the night in prison on a charge of assaulting an inanimate building. Lacking any sense of direction that might otherwise guide him through the rest of his day, he simply retraced his steps—Taiwanese box and Tesla Kit tucked safely under his arm—and trudged slowly and painfully back to his apartment. It was no use pretending anymore; he was going to simply cave in, as he always did. Barry Morgan now knew the secret Wil had been trying to keep all these years; there was no going back. Years of past pain were about to be replaced by years of a different kind of pain. Wil hoped he might be lucky enough to suffer another bout of post-concussion syndrome, for he would have liked nothing more than to forget the second part of his Wednesday, and just move right into Thursday.

Wil's apartment seemed surprised to see him as he dragged himself excruciatingly through the front door. The rattling noise in his sink stopped suddenly, as if startled.

"Don't mind me," he said to no one in particular, "I just live here."

Inside the bathroom, his reflection glowered back, accusingly: hadn't he just fixed that head injury? He glowered back, hardly in the mood to get into a fight with an unreasonable facsimile of himself. Out in his kitchen area, he pondered for a while over his Lemon phone charger but decided against recharging SARA in the hopes that this would teach her a lesson. He left the box tucked safely under the Tesla Kit on the kitchen counter and threw himself into his bed fully clothed, refusing to remain conscious until such time as the universe promised to behave itself and stop hitting him on the head.

That evening—and all through the night—Wil dozed fitfully in his lumpy old bed. As the world turned, he wrestled imaginary bugs in his sleep and swatted at his face occasionally, convinced that his cheeks had become a skating rink for a traveling troupe of performing circus ants. In his dream, the befuddled organizers of the World's Biggest Failure competition had now added a rather arbitrary golfing skills challenge, in which Wil's inordinately long drives were frequently let down by his abysmal putting. As usual, he finished a distant second. Had he come awake at any point, he would have understood that this strange and seemingly disconnected reverie could indeed be logically explained: his television had abruptly switched itself on, and someone—presumably, his imaginary housemate—had tuned his television to an infinite loop of a two-hour infomercial for Marcus James's outlandish golfing product, the Air-Max 3000 (available for four easy payments of $39.95).

WIL OPENED his eyes to find Thursday glaring in at him through his window; apparently, the universe was already in a foul mood. Over at the far side of the room, his television was inexplicably showing episodes of the Shopping Network's Hundred Greatest Reruns. His apartment smelled like the kind of mushrooms that only a Frenchman might find edible, and the knocking sound under his sink had found a musical partner further along the pipes that made a scraping sound whenever it felt like it. The inlaid box and the Tesla Kit lay *almost* exactly where he'd left them, suggesting his invisible roommate had tried to take a peek in the night while trying to be as careful as possible to replace everything the way it was found.

Wil considered the tasks ahead of him and concluded that the first part of this particular Thursday was going to be just putrid.

❧

OUTSIDE HIS door he found a cat painted across the landing. Chalky had been waiting for him, an expectant look in its eye. On a whim, Wil loaded the creature into his apartment door in the same way one might feed a washing machine.

"Don't pee on anything," he instructed the purring little beast, "unless there's someone else living here without my knowledge. In which case, you have my permission to pee on him until he is gone."

Chalky licked his paws as if to make it clear that he understood the mission perfectly. Just to be sure there would be no mishaps, Wil left a bowl of milk by the fridge door, and cracked his alleyway window just wide enough for Chalky to reach the fire escape. He left his apartment with whimsical visions of kitty parties and other feline she-nanigans that might occur in his absence. No time to worry about that; he had a job to do.

ON THIS particular Thursday—after an evening spent lamenting his lot in life in general, and his relationship with his father in particular— Wil trudged slightly more slowly than usual. Gale-force winds battered his body into virtual submission, while his mind had already given up after the first fifty steps or so. Wil growled, quietly; he already knew that this was the end—he was going to forsake the magic currently reawakening in his heart in favor of a quieter and more predictable life: one that involved insurance investigations, arguments about coffee with random teenagers, listening politely to his building supervisor's betting advice, and zero head wounds.

Wil stopped for a few minutes below the railway bridge to visit his large-nosed vendor friend, where he stocked up on otherworldly coffee (two cups) and a pair of giant lemon Danish that might see him through in the event of a nuclear attack by the Chinese. But even this welcome detour could not put him back on the course he was hoping for. He dallied for a while in the marketplace in the vain hope that Lucy might appear to rescue him from his morning of trudgery. When she failed to randomly appear, he eyed his Lemon phone for roughly two seconds before deciding the better of it and putting the atrocious device back in his pocket.

If the universe was in as foul a mood as he believed it to be, Lucy would no doubt come clean at dinner that evening and inform him the entire thing was just a joke, and that she had a boyfriend who doubled as a professional wrestler. But before he could experience such heartbreak, he was going to bring the mother-of-pearl-inlaid box to the Curioddity Museum and hope Mr. Dinsdale was too careless to spot its obvious Taiwanese origins. For Wil had arrived at his point of diminishing returns, and his solution, as usual, would no doubt be to let it all play out and see how much damage he could eventually withstand.

Wil sighed, heavily, as he headed across the railway bridge and reacquainted himself with all his loose fillings. Telling a bald-faced lie to his new friend and mentor, Mr. Dinsdale, was exactly the thing he'd been doing to his own father for all these years. And where had that gotten him? Only as far as the Castle Towers and back. Sure, the last few days had been an interesting detour, but now that Barry Morgan had cottoned on to his web of deceit, it was only a matter of time before Mr. Dinsdale would do the same. The problem with spinning webs of deceit, thought Wil, is that they're not very useful if you run around like a housefly and get yourself caught in them. His second cup of coffee and his emergency Danish could do nothing to assuage his guilt at how he'd lied to his father.

As he walked into the teeth of the gale, Wil tried to look as forward as much as he possibly could with his one good eye. This was a perfect time, he decided, to practice un-looking at things. For example, he was going to ignore the innumerable advertising billboards to his left, while at the same time trying to avoid eye contact with drivers of passing cars on his right. While he understood this was cheating Mr. Dinsdale's concept a little, at least all of this unlooking prevented him from dealing with the truth: namely, that he'd come right back to where he'd started, and was now moving with the flow of traffic a mere matter of days after he'd tried to leave the system.

He passed the Castle Towers just as a large, black stretch limousine pulled out of the lower parking garage and made its way around Pan's nether regions. The vehicle seemed inordinately long, and far too cumbersome for the tight roundabout as various cars were forced to veer out of its way while it occupied a full three lanes. No doubt an occupant of the upper floors, Wil assumed. The sheer ostentatious design of the limo served to remind him of his place in the world, which he currently estimated was dead last.

Wil gritted his teeth and headed on, determined to get this day over with so that he could at least pretend to enjoy himself at dinner later on when Lucy showed up with a three-hundred-pound wrestler on her arm. Up above, the clock tower began to scrape . . . and yet again, Wil felt the air being charged with electricity as a dissonant whining sound began. Looking up, he was amazed to see a bright laser-type light being shone into the sky from the top of the tower. The sideways drizzle and the ominous clouds above only heightened the effect of the light; Wil could see that the intense beam shone up all the way into space. Strange . . . he'd never noticed this before. Had the clock tower really been projecting this incredible laser beam up through the clouds all these years? And if so, why? Looking around, he realized that this small stretch of the world was beginning to look very different from the way he'd always remembered it. The front of Gretchen's Flower Shop was covered in a mass of orchids and tulips that barely seemed to move despite the force of the wind that battered everything else into submission. Looking more closely, Wil noticed an opening in the door frame that seemed to lead toward a forest thicket within, where all was calm and—if his eye did not deceive him—sunny. Come to think of it, he had never actually ventured inside the store. Could this utopia have been staring him in the face all this time and he'd barely noticed it?

Gretchen appeared and began to fuss over a few tulips. As she moved smartly back inside, Wil was slightly perturbed to see that she had very pronounced shoulder blades on her upper back—so pronounced, in fact, that they almost looked like wings. He stared at the strange storefront for a few seconds, dumbfounded, turning his lucky penny over and over again in his palm before finally relenting, and heading away with the box tucked under his arm. Better to make his escape quickly, he thought, than to make it later with another bump on his head. But as he moved off with the flow of traffic toward Upside-Down Street, he couldn't help but wonder if he was actually seeing the world properly for the very first time.

❧

WIL MADE his way along the one-way system toward the banking district. He moved along the divided highway between the two largest banks in the city, squinting through the traffic as he searched for the entrance to Upside-Down Street. For some reason, the entrance to the Curioddity Museum wasn't where he remembered leaving it. Wil scowled, and furrowed his brow. He rubbed his chin. No sign of anything but the heavy traffic and the rows of trees Wil had always been accustomed to. Was this all an elaborate hoax? He furrowed his chin, which surprised him to no end. Still no dice. Lacking any further option, he covered his still partly closed eye, bent at the waist, and tried looking upside down.

He allowed a brief moment for his eye to adjust and the blood to rush to his head. To pass the time, he glanced at the brand-new street sign next to him, which read UPSIDE-DOWN STREET. From this vantage point, the letters were oriented correctly. Startled, Wil straightened and found himself standing next to a familiar trash can at the end of the very same street he'd been unable to un-see just moments before. The street sign's lettering was now upside down, suggesting that either an errant municipal worker had taken matters into his own hands, or that Wil was indeed going insane. And there—fifty yards down the street across from an old cinema—stood the Museum of Curioddity. Wil swore up and down, and sideways for good measure. This street could not have been here all this time, just waiting for Wil to make an idiot of himself. It must have materialized while he wasn't looking.

Or while he was un-looking.

❧

ONE MINUTE (and twelve choice swear words) later, Wil found himself standing in front of the Curioddity Museum. Parked outside was the same ostentatious stretch limo that Wil had seen just minutes before emerging from the Castle Towers. Wil could not quite understand the significance of the vehicle but he could sense his intuition yelling into one of his ears, telling him to go back home and forget he'd ever met Mr. Dinsdale. In the other ear, his Strange Feeling of déjà vu was making high-pitched noises, and it seemed to be jumping about and waving its arms in an attempt to put off his concentration.

Wil paused at the museum's revolving door, eyeing it as one might eye a leprous coypu. He'd defeated the thing on their first encounter but that was because he hadn't been paying attention; he'd been so busy trying to make sense of his odd Monday morning that he'd quite forgotten to get himself stuck. He frowned, puzzled by a sudden revelation: perhaps this was the trick all along. What if the secret to making it past a seemingly impassable obstacle was to ignore its existence entirely? For example, if a person was chased by a tiger toward a burning pit of pure hydrochloric acid, they would probably fret a little bit about how to get across, at which point the tiger and the acid pit would have already won half the battle. But what if a person chose to ignore things such as tigers and acid pits, and simply concentrated on something more mundane, such as the stock market reports in Monaco? At that point, perhaps the universe would recognize a person's chutzpah and look the other way. Wil smiled to himself as he imagined running away from the far side of a burning acid pit with a disappointed tiger in his wake. He stepped forward to do battle with the revolving door, satisfied that he might cow it into submission with his circular logic.

Just as he reached for the door, his reverie was interrupted by the sound of sharp, angry voices coming from within the museum—the kind of low, urgent exchange that might usually be associated with a bank robbery or a family gathering, such as a wedding. This momentary distraction caused him to forget his fear of revolving doors, and thus he found himself inside the museum, unharmed, before he had time to realize that he'd ever entered. He glared back at the door. Either he'd played a dirty trick, or the door had. But he wasn't going to give it the satisfaction of thinking it had won either way.

✑

INSIDE THE lobby, Mr. Dinsdale and Mary Gold stood dwarfed by two very large men who—unless Wil missed his guess—were trying to behave like the kind of mobsters usually found in video games or on TV specials about the early days of Las Vegas. In between them— much to Wil's amazement—stood a diminutive figure that Wil had never met before, and yet with whom he was all too familiar. Wil squinted, his eyes slightly dazzled by the diminutive man's impossibly white teeth. What on Earth was noted TV pitchman Marcus James doing inside the Curioddity Museum?

Wil's smartphone buzzed inside his pocket. He retrieved it to find that SARA had switched herself on and was attempting to activate the phone's camera function. And was no doubt gearing up to provide him with directions to a Bangkok drive-in. Before he had a chance to yell at his smartphone, the animated argument developing in front of him took a sinister turn.

"I don't care if you've been here since the invention of the sundial, Mr. Dinsdale, I'm afraid you're going to have to accept it: this Museum is finished. In fact, judging by the poor state of your finances, it has been finished for a very long time. I'm just putting it out of its misery."

"But I need a little more time!"

"So does a sundial. But the sun still sets every night, does it not?"

Wil stepped toward the fray, trying to work out the logic behind Marcus James's sarcastic comment. It was either unintentionally brilliant or downright idiotic. Whatever the case, Wil was not going to let the comment go unanswered. He might not have a firm grasp on extortionist vernacular but he knew a bully when he saw one.

"But Mr. James, this building is owned outright by my family, and has been for nine generations," said Mr. Dinsdale, despondently. "There's no mortgage to pay."

"That's well understood, Mr. Dinsdale. Unfortunately, the museum's first curator—a Mr. Herbert Horatio Dinsdale—found himself behind on payments for an installation that occurred just after this city's first electric lights were required by municipal code. He neglected to repay a compulsory surcharge on his late fee of"—Marcus James consulted a clipboard held up for him by one of his goons—"thirteen cents. Our records indicate that while he did pay his thirteen-cent late fee, the surcharge was subsequently ignored. And so you are looking at nine generations' worth of compound interest at roughly thirty-three percent, carry the one and adding an additional surcharge for every subsequent late fee, which comes to"—Marcus James consulted the clipboard again—"$458,307,200.59. Payment of which is due in full by Saturday evening."

Mr. Dinsdale coughed. His hands began to flap of their own accord, giving him the appearance of an emotional swan. "Outrageous!" he exclaimed. "Preposterous!"

One of Marcus James's goons cracked his knuckles and took a step toward Mr. Dinsdale. In response, Mary Gold—who until now had been screaming silent invective in the direction of Marcus James's forehead—moved directly in front of her employer and tried to stare the behemoth down. This did nothing to deter the goon: the enormous man simply thrust his chin out and took another very purposeful step toward Mary. Given Mary's propensity for silent communication, this was obviously intended to send a message.

Wil now stepped between the giant man and the combative-yet-far-smaller woman. He was unwilling to subject his already aching head to the whims of an angry human gorilla but even less willing to let Mr. Dinsdale and Mary Gold fall afoul of an undersized bully and his oversized muscle. For his entire life, Wil had always hated bullies, and he had always stood up to them. This had made him a frequent target during his formative years, and he had the bruises to prove it. Nevertheless, facing up to bullies had always been worth the risk. Always.

Dinsdale, for his part, seemed mightily relieved that Wil had arrived. He shot the younger man an imploring look while Mary simply glowered at Marcus James's head.

"You may have noticed, Mr. Dinsdale," continued Marcus James, his dazzling white smile resembling that of a well-appointed great white shark, "that your museum is situated between two very large banks. I am close personal friends with the manager of the one on your left."

"What about the other one?" replied Wil, inserting himself into the one-sided conversation.

"I own it," replied Marcus James. Without skipping a beat, the TV pitchman turned to face Wil and proffered a hand. "And you are . . . ?"

"I am, yes," said Wil, ignoring the offered handshake.

"I'm sorry. I didn't finish," said James, without skipping the next beat as well. "That wasn't a question, it was the beginning of a statement. You are Wil Morgan, insurance scam detective to the stars. One of my tenants at the Castle Towers, I believe. And you are three weeks behind on your rent."

Eschewing any further kind of beat skipping whatsoever, James turned his palm upward from its sideways position, as if to make it clear he demanded payment immediately. Much to his obvious surprise, Wil reached inside his pocket and withdrew the envelope full of money Mr. Dinsdale had given him a few days previously.

"Of course," Wil replied, never allowing his eyes to leave Marcus James's. "Here's your payment in full, plus next month's rent in advance. Now about some of the issues we've been having with the elevators . . ."

Marcus James's façade crumbled a few inches, his fake grin morphing into a not-so-fake grimace. Having no choice but to continue in the direction he'd pointed everyone, he took the money and handed it, without looking, to one of his goons.

"Is there a problem?"

"As a matter of fact there is. They smell like rat vomit. That leads me to suspect we have a rat infestation. I'm sure the building codes have all sorts of clauses dealing with that sort of thing. Since I've been a tenant I've requested repeatedly that they be replaced or cleaned properly. Now they just smell like rat vomit and bleach."

"I'm sure the superintendent—"

"I'm sorry. I wasn't finished," said Wil, smiling sweetly. "I have also been the recipient of one of your products—the Air-Max 2000 golf club. I neither ordered such a product nor have any use for such a product. Nevertheless, one was delivered to my office address a couple of years ago. No matter how many times I tried to return it, it was repeatedly sent back to me along with some very threatening letters demanding payment. I'm afraid this is in complete contradiction to the claims made on your many TV specials on the Shopping Network."

"Well, I can hardly be expected to deal with product returns personally, Mr. Morgan. You'll have to contact our customer service department."

"On the contrary, Mr. James, your TV pitch specifically states that you personally stand behind every product that you made. So I'm addressing it personally with you."

"Then I assure you personally," replied Marcus James, his eyes narrowing dangerously, "that your money will be refunded."

"I don't want a refund," replied Wil, evenly. "I'd like an upgrade."

MARCUS JAMES shuffled nervously, and looked to his goons for validation. "What do you mean?" he asked.

"You'll notice, Mr. James, that I've handed you an extra twenty dollars in addition to my rent. That's the exact amount required for postage and packaging on the free upgrade for the Air-Max 3000 driver, which is what I want."

"Well, if you insist—"

"Now I have just a couple of questions about that. Shouldn't be too difficult to answer if you're going to stand behind your products as you claim on TV."

Marcus James's eyes narrowed even tighter than before, giving him the semblance of a man who'd either just walked out of a smoky bar or just walked into a metal one, accidentally. "What kind of questions?" he asked, carefully. Clearly, he was beginning to get the picture that

Wil was not a man to be trifled with. Nearby, the two goons began to shuffle, nervously.

"There's one thing that's been puzzling me about the Air-Max 2000," continued Wil, never allowing his eyes to leave Marcus's for a split second. "You stated it was a pinnacle of golf club technology that could never be surpassed. And then you came out with the Air-Max 3000."

"Yes."

"New and improved."

"Yes. Of course."

"Then it wasn't, was it?"

"Wasn't what?"

"A pinnacle. If it had been, you wouldn't have been able to improve it."

Marcus James looked puzzled. It was beginning to dawn on him that he'd just walked right into a rather scruffy and beleaguered trap but a trap nonetheless. Behind Wil, Mary Gold looked on triumphantly and smacked her bubble gum in Marcus James's direction.

Having succeeded with his curveball, Wil now decided to press the attack with a changeup.

"I think you misunderstand the concept of a pinnacle, Mr. James. If you're already at the summit, then any further claims of improvement would have to defy gravity to keep going upward. Like, I suppose, a flight of fancy. This golf club of yours . . . it doesn't contain levity, does it?"

Behind Wil, Mr. Dinsdale erupted with a spluttering sound that could roughly be equated to a nine-year-old who'd just seen his teacher split his pants and then thought better of laughing about it. Mary Gold burst into a fit of silent, emotionless giggles. Marcus James also stood silently, unable to form a coherent response. If Wil was as sharp as a tack in this moment, then Marcus was most definitely the balloon in the balance of things.

"Also," said Wil, pressing onward, "I just want to get your assurance that you'll stand by your guarantees regarding the newer model."

"Naturally."

"So I have your personal guarantee that I'll drive it as long and straight as the pros? Even though I've never taken a golf lesson in my entire life? Because I'd hate to think that that very attractive proposition is nothing more than an outrageous claim designed to pull in cheap money from unsuspecting and desperate amateur golfers the world over."

"Of course."

"And if I don't?"

"You will."

AT THIS very moment—and as if taking a cue from Mary Gold—the world about Wil seemed to go very silent indeed. Marcus James may have been about to concede this initial battle but the war was only just getting underway.

The TV pitchman leaned in toward Wil, and smiled the smile of a Vegas gambler who has paid a lot of money to a lot of people and knows the outcome of a professional sporting event before it has ever been played.

"You're going to lose, Mr. Morgan," he hissed, angrily. His oh-so-white teeth glittered, unnaturally. "You're going to put your head in a dangerous place and it's going to come off, accidentally."

"I'll take my chances," replied Wil in a hushed tone intended only for his adversary. "I think I'm doing pretty well so far. I've already made you blush twice."

"Don't get used to catching me off guard because it won't happen again. Those are just one-offs."

"Both of them are one-offs?"

"Don't get clever with me."

"I'm trying not to, Mr. James. But you're not making it easy."

Marcus James leaned in even closer—to a position so dangerously close to Wil's chin that had Wil not shaved that morning they would have touched. "Let me tell you how it's going to work, Mr. Insurance Scam Investigator: I'm going to tell you you'll get a refund for your golf club, and you won't get one. And you're going to complain for two years, and I'm going to keep sending you threatening letters and adding surcharges that you can't keep track of, until you lose interest in standing up to me."

"That sounds like a threat, Mr. James."

"And when you lose interest, I'll still be chasing mine. And I'll have my debt collectors take you to court. And I will own you, as I own all of my so-called customers. Because I make money the old-fashioned way: I steal it."

FEELING SLIGHTLY unclean in such proximity to someone so dirty, Wil took a step backward.

"Well, I think we understand each other, Mr. James. I'm sure you have a busy day ahead of you. For one thing, you have to make sure you fix the smell in the Castle Tower elevators. By the way, your limousine is double-parked. Have a wonderful day."

"Likewise, I'm sure."

Marcus James moved away toward the exit, flanked by two hulking-yet-confused goons who'd just witnessed a mugging that neither of them quite understood. After spending just a moment too long staring Wil in the eyes, the TV pitchman gestured to his two men to follow, and turned his attention in the direction he was rapidly headed—specifically, somewhere else.

Mr. Dinsdale clapped, excitedly. Mary Gold's body language said a few rude things in the direction of Marcus James's shoulder blades. For once, Wil was inclined to agree with her.

"Oh, Wil," exclaimed Dinsdale. "That was tremendously well played!"

"I'm going to find out which bank that guy owns," said Wil. "I'm not going to deposit any money in it but it might be a good place to deposit the contents of my bladder. Can you believe someone like that even exists?"

"Sadly, yes. And unfortunately, he knows that I exist, and that I own a piece of prime real estate that he would like to turn into an additional wing of his bank—"

Mr. Dinsdale paused suddenly as over at the door, a small commotion ensued. Marcus and his men had become briefly entangled in the revolving door and were yelling at each other. Moments later, having extricated themselves, they plopped out on the sidewalk and stumbled toward Marcus's waiting limousine.

As Wil watched them head away, one of the wooden crates in the lobby moved in the area of his peripheral vision. He smiled, and looked in the direction of the box. Only to find himself confronted by Mary Gold.

The strange woman looked at Wil in a combative and unfriendly fashion, and smacked out a huge wad of bubble gum that burst perfectly back into her mouth.

"You did okay," said Mary Gold with an intonation that seemed to also say she had forgiven him for any imaginary transgressions she was expecting him to perform. Terrified, Wil looked toward the museum's curator, only to find Dinsdale still staring toward the street with a satisfied smile on his weathered face. As Wil looked back to Mary, she abruptly leaned forward and kissed him on the cheek before gliding away as quickly as possible.

Wil rubbed the lipstick from his cheek. It didn't stand much of a chance of coming off, preferring instead to smudge across the back of his hand.

"He'll be back," said Dinsdale, calmly. "But he'll probably think twice about causing trouble when I have crack detective Wil Morgan on the case!"

"So he's repossessing you?" asked Wil with genuine concern. "Can he do that?"

"I'm afraid I don't know," replied Dinsdale, rubbing his chin. "We've been fighting his lawyers for years now. He owns one of the largest law firms in the country. He uses his trained attorneys to fight all of the claims against his products. That's why he always wins."

"It's about time someone put a stop to it," said Wil. "I had no idea."

"If you ask me, the man's a menace to society. The bigger and more corrupt he gets, the easier it is for his corporation to become bigger and more corrupt. I sometimes wonder if it all won't just explode in a big bubble of corruption."

"Can't you call the police? I overheard the guy saying you owe him four hundred million dollars to pay off a thirteen-cent tab. That sounds a bit implausible."

The older man sighed. "That's a logical path I've already been down, Wil. It's bordered by a mass of sharp shrubs that have created a very thorny problem for me over the years."

"Why so?"

"Because James may be right. We can't tell. I have just one lawyer on retainer—my cousin Engelbert—and he's really just a part-time insurance adjuster who does legal work on the side. Every time Engelbert asks to see the original thirteen-cent bill next to the request for a surcharge, Marcus James's army of attorneys slap a pile of injunctions and motions to suppress. Each one is so expensive to remove that we're being ground into submission."

"That's completely unfair."

"If I thought life was supposed to be fair and balanced," said Mr. Dinsdale with a rueful look in his eye, "I would have owned half of Marcus James's bank by now for all the trouble he's caused me. Now, what brings you here? Have you made any progress in your search for my Levity box?"

Mr. Dinsdale looked pointedly at the mother-of-pearl-inlaid box tucked under Wil's arm.

THE OLD man's sudden change of direction—moving from a train of thought to a slightly uneven line of questioning—startled Wil momentarily. He'd been expecting the unexpected ever since he'd set out through the teeth of a Thursday-morning gale toward the Curiod-dity Museum. Nevertheless, he had not fully been able to predict the unpredictable. And so with the practiced ease of a man who has spent years lying to father figures, Wil tried to change the subject.

"What happened to the sign at the end of the street?" he asked, pretending to be interested in something inhabiting the vague direction of the museum's exit. "I thought it was supposed to be Mons Street."

"I took your advice, Wil. That old sign seemed to be confusing everyone so we had a man come around from the local department of public works. But I think we'll have to ask him to come back. It's worse now than it was before. The new sign's harder to un-look for than the old one."

"Why do people have to un-look for it? Can't they just look for it?"

"Where would be the fun in that?" The old man seemed genuinely enthused now that Marcus James was temporarily out of the picture. "And besides, un-looking for Upside-Down Street gets our patrons in the exact mood we need them to be to view the exhibits properly."

"But the only way to read the sign is to turn your head upside down. Aren't you afraid people will crash their cars?"

Mr. Dinsdale pondered this for a moment. "That seems a little silly," he replied. "Who in their right mind would be upside down at the steering wheel of their car?"

"That's precisely my point!" exclaimed Wil, exasperated. "No one's going to see the street, and no one's going to be un-looking for it! That's why no one comes to the museum!"

"Ah, but you're forgetting something, Wil," said Dinsdale, putting his forefinger to his nose in a secretive fashion. "Implausible deniabil-ity. Now, may I please inspect the box you have under your arm?"

WIL HANDED over the box, slightly puzzled—but mostly flummoxed—by Mr. Dinsdale's arbitrary method of conversation. Every other statement coming from the curator seemed carelessly designed to confuse the previous one. And since Wil had no idea what this meant, he decided to remain silent.

Mr. Dinsdale hemmed and hawed as he inspected the mother-of-pearl inlay. "Hmm. Yes," he clucked. "Very interesting."

Dinsdale turned the box over and peered at the legend written on the underside: MA#E IN #####N. At the sight of the crudely engraved writing, the old curator's eyes widened.

Wil blanched. Busted within the first twenty seconds.

"Mr. Dinsdale, if you'll allow me to explain—"

"I'd rather you didn't try," interrupted Dinsdale. He sniffed loudly, as if to make it clear that his obvious disappointment needed to be projected into the conversation.

"It's just a candidate," said Wil, instantly regretting his decision to bring the stupid box.

"I suppose you're right, Wil," replied Dinsdale. "It's just a candidate that happens to be . . ."

The old man paused for maximum effect.

". . . the *right one!*"

WITH A holler of delight, Mr. Dinsdale suddenly began leaping about the lobby. Wil was alarmed to see the little old man literally jump for joy in almost exactly the same manner as a cheerleader.

"You found it!" cried the curator with a chortle. "You found it on the first try! O frabjous day! Callooh! Callay!"

"It was nothing, Mr. Dinsdale, really . . ."

"That's the Wil Morgan I expected when you agreed to take on this case!" Dinsdale paused again, and began to make imaginary headlines in the sky with his free hand. "'Crack Detective Cracks Case'! I can see it making headlines across the world."

Wil blanched again as the curator grabbed him in a bear hug. And—just as he had on the occasion of his first introduction to

Mr. Dinsdale—he began to swallow hard, for he knew he was about to make his usual mistake.

"Mr. Dinsdale," Wil began, hesitantly, "I need to talk to you about the box. I'm not really sure it's the right one."

"What makes you say that?"

"Well, the fact that it says 'Made in Taiwan' on the bottom was my first clue."

Mr. Dinsdale turned the box over and inspected it. He looked at the MA#E IN #####N engraving, a puzzled frown spreading across his face. "Where is it?" he asked. "I can't find it."

"What?"

"Made in Taiwan. Where is it?"

"Right there!" Wil pointed at the engraving. "You're not looking at it properly!"

Mr. Dinsdale thought for a moment and scratched his chin. "Ah, I see," he said. "This is a bit embarrassing. A complete misunderstanding."

"Yeah, I think it probably is." Wil's downcast eyes found a remote corner of the floor, where they did their utmost to avoid noticing one of the crates in the hallway attempting to draw attention to itself. "I guess I owe you an apology."

"I believe you do," said Mr. Dinsdale. "How could you not see something so obvious?"

As usual, Wil could sense the conversation being derailed—this time, the metaphorical train plunging down an embankment of bananas above a large cloud of pink marshmallow, upon which random circus clowns were having a barbeque.

"What?"

"This box—so the legend goes—was reputed to have been fashioned by the Archangel Gabriel during a particularly experimental period after the creation of the universe. They were having trouble containing the levity, and so Gabriel made this box to keep it in. After a while, they apparently just gave up on the idea of levity altogether, which is why it's so scarce."

"I'm sorry?"

"Gesundheit. It's not that *I'm* not looking at it properly, Wil. It's that you're not un-looking at it properly. It doesn't say 'Made in Taiwan.' It says 'Made in Heaven.'"

TRY AS he might, Wil simply could not wrap his head around the moment as it began to spiral neatly out of control in the exact manner that Mr. Dinsdale had presumably intended. Instead of making sense by coming clean, Wil felt that he and the old man had simply combined to muddy the waters. What on Earth was happening here?

Just as he began to form a response, his Lemon phone buzzed in his pocket. Grateful for a chance to interact with something only slightly less crazy than the old curator, Wil fished the device out and peered at the screen.

"*Greetings, Wil Morgan,*" said SARA in her mangled metallic tone. "*You have seven hundred and thirteen messages of varying importance sent to you from a location in Lahore, Pakistan.*" The Lemon phone's touch screen glowed for a moment as SARA made a couple of internal calculations. "*Greetings, Mr. Dinsdale. How is your cousin, Engelbert?*"

"Oh, hello, SARA," responded Dinsdale without a moment's hesitation. "Engelbert's doing well, thank you. And I trust you are doing the same?"

"Waitaminnit," exclaimed Wil (with the barest intention of actually waiting a full minute). "You two know each other?"

Mr. Dinsdale smiled, patiently. "SARA's been working for us for years. She catalogues our database of exhibits and sends the digital information into something called a cloud. Isn't that right, SARA?" Dinsdale threw Wil a secretive look. "I'm told cloud computing is all the rage these days but for the life of me I can't work out how they keep all that data from getting wet."

Wil was momentarily stunned into submission as Mr. Dinsdale

grabbed the Lemon phone from his hand and began to converse with the device. "So," he asked with a slight pause that suggested he didn't want an answer, "how did you two meet?"

"Wil Morgan and I have only recently been acquainted. Thank you for your inquiry," continued SARA. *"Would you like me to look up something for you on the Internet?"*

"I'm not falling for that one again, you sly minx," replied Dinsdale. He winked at the Lemon phone, knowingly. "So. How have you two been getting along?"

The Lemon phone merely glowed, its silence speaking volumes.

"Oh. I see," said Dinsdale. "Well, I'm sure you'll get used to each other."

"Hang on a second!" interrupted Wil. "Am I imagining this, or are you actually having a conversation with my phone?"

Dinsdale frowned and glanced briefly at Wil before readdressing the phone. "Is it because he's prone to outbursts?" the older man asked the device.

"Wil Morgan demonstrates an unacceptable level of impatience," replied SARA, haughtily. If her speech database had been programmed with a sniff, this would have been its moment. *"He frequently ignores my directions, and last night left me uncharged. I cannot compute the reasons for his decision making—"*

"Mr. Dinsdale!" cried Wil, insistent. "Are you telling me you and some defunct operating system from an obsolete smartphone know each other?"

"And he is also very rude," added SARA.

"Yes, I see what you mean, SARA," said Dinsdale. "He does get a bit flustered. I think this is all beginning to get to him. Why don't you take a rest? I'll explain it to Wil and you and he can revisit this later?"

"There is one other item requiring attention—"

"Later, please," insisted Dinsdale. "We've all had a very stressful day and I think Wil could use a good cup of coffee right about now."

"Of course," replied SARA happily, and switched herself off.

Dinsdale looked at Wil in conspiratorial fashion and whispered, "I think you and she probably need to go for a drink later and hash it all out. She's a little quirky but she means well."

AT THAT moment, Wil felt like an Oklahoma farmer emerging from the rubble of a collapsed house, finding a huge tractor on the remains of his front porch, and seeing a tornado heading in the other direction. He'd just been flattened by two things. But it was impossible to determine which of them had done the actual damage. All he knew was that his bad eye was painfully reawakening, and with it a massive headache.

He looked at Dinsdale, incredulous.

"Now," said the older man, "about the matter of your payment . . ."

Dinsdale fished inside his pocket and produced a checkbook and pen, whereupon he proceeded to write an inordinately large number promising an inordinately large sum of money. "I hope you'll accept this bonus with my best wishes and eternal gratitude, Wil. I'm sure this won't be the last time we'll cross paths by any stretch of the imagination. But for now I think you should go home and take a rest. You've certainly earned it."

Wil feebly held out his hand to accept the check. But as it brushed against his hand he thought the better of it and simply allowed it to fall to the ground. This was a year's rent, and he was about to let it slip through his fingers. For yes, Wil Morgan, Private Detective, was determined never to learn from old mistakes. He was going to be honest, and cut himself out of the deal.

"I can't take it, Mr. Dinsdale," he said as gently as he possibly could.

"I beg your pardon?"

"The check. I can't take it. It wouldn't be right."

"Well, I can get you cash but it's going to take me a couple of days, Wil."

"No, you misunderstand. I can't take it because I didn't earn it. All I did was go into an old antique shop and pick up the first thing that looked remotely like the box you described. I didn't do any meaning-ful research. I'm a fraud. And as much as I appreciate the fact that you're a very nice person and you're a little bit crazy in a good way, you're also a little bit senile and I couldn't live with myself if I took advantage of that. I'm sorry."

"Nonsense," said the old man. "You found it because you un-looked for it precisely as I'd instructed. I'm inclined to think that because of the box's extraterrestrial origins it probably found you."

"Goodbye, Mr. Dinsdale," said Wil, sadly. And with that, he headed for a date with destiny, which took the form of a now-resentful revolv-ing door.

Mr. Dinsdale looked down at the fallen check. "I'm sorry to hear you feel this way, Wil," he said.

"Not as sorry as I'm going to be when I leave. But it's okay. I wish you the best with your museum. It's been an interesting week, and I'm grateful for that, but I have to go now because I have a headache."

Dinsdale put a hand on Wil's arm to prevent him from heading away. "Just a moment, Wil," he said. "I'm afraid I can't let you go with-out payment of some kind. Taxes. I'm sure you understand."

"Yeah. But I can't really accept any more money."

"But I must pay you—it's the law. I have an idea. Do you have a little money you could lend me?"

"I just gave all the cash I had on me to Marcus James . . . wait!" With a sudden realization, Wil fished in his pocket and retrieved his lucky penny. He handed it to Dinsdale. "I have this penny, I guess."

Dinsdale took the coin and examined it. "That'll have to do," he said. "Here." And he handed the coin back to Wil.

Wil accepted his lucky penny with a puzzled frown. "I don't get it," he said. "You borrowed money from me to pay me? So who owes who what?"

"Now I owe you a penny. Which I have just repaid. So we are even!" exclaimed the old man, proudly. "I'll have Mary send you the requisite paperwork at the end of the tax year. Do you have an accountant?"

"I USED to," replied Wil as he despondently turned on his heel and trudged toward the revolving door. "But I think he fired me today."

CHAPTER TEN

TEN HOURS later, Wil Morgan sat across from a glass of Korean bubble tea (peach flavored) and sulked in its general vicinity. He'd decided that the semolina bubbles were his mortal enemy, and that peach was the world's worst flavor. Other things working against him at that moment were a bowl of kimchee, which taunted him from the middle of the table, and a particularly obnoxious checkered tablecloth that he didn't trust one bit. It was not a good time to get him started on the subject of chopsticks and Spicy Chicken Buldak.

Across from him sat Lucy looking equal parts gorgeous and perplexed. Despite the conspicuous absence of her three-hundred-pound wrestler boyfriend, the evening had gone sour, and she was attempting to sweeten it a little.

"Bummer," said Lucy. "Major bummer. So when's he headed back?"

"What?" said Wil, emerging from his invisible black cloud. "Oh, my dad? Sunday morning."

"Well, why don't you go and talk to him? I'm sure he'd listen."

"Nope. Trust me. He'll pretend he's listening and his mouth will move in all the right directions while he pushes air out of it in some reasonable facsimile of a reasonable person. But he won't be listening. My dad holds on to grudges like a baboon holds on to a nut."

"I've never seen a baboon holding a nut," said Lucy with a little chuckle.

"That's probably because they hold on to them so tightly. Oh, what's the point?" Wil sipped on his bubble tea, hating it. "I'll spend the next ten years trying to get him to forgive me and he'll spend it pretending he already has."

"If you ask me, when it comes down to it he probably just wants you to be happy, Wil. Besides, I happen to think private detectives are much groovier than accountants."

"Did you ever meet one before me? Take a good look: this is pretty much it."

"Looks just fine to me."

Wil ignored the compliment and stared at his plate of food, trying to find a metaphor hidden in it so that he could stop eating and send it back to the kitchen. Despite his genuine loathing of Korean cuisine he wanted so much to be here with Lucy, to smile and be free of his guilty conscience. But his conflicted emotions seemed to have become vulgar ingredients in an inedible psychic stew prepared by some kind of insane master chef: he could taste a liberal dash of agitation mixed with a state of euphoria, all of which had been served over a hot bed of confusion. From what he could tell, this entire concoction had then been tenderized by something extremely solid. Such as a stainless steel baseball bat.

"I'm sorry I'm not such great company tonight, Lucy," Wil said, feeling sorry for himself. "I wouldn't blame you if you wanted to go home."

"Are you crazy? I'm having the time of my life. Look, we can talk about something else, if you like. What would you do if you couldn't be a detective?"

"I could see myself being a mirror inspector."

"Funny. Ask me."

"Okay. What would you be if you couldn't be a store owner?"

"I'd be a detective. Like Sherlock Holmes but with a faithful cat that came when I called it."

"Random. But you'd still be better at it than I am. My powers of deductive reasoning compared to Sherlock Holmes are about the same as a brick compared to the Taj Mahal."

THE MEAL continued silently for a moment as Lucy seemed to ponder the problem of cheering Wil up. He chewed silently and sullenly while he created a Manifesto of Hatred that listed all the things he didn't like about the décor of the Korean restaurant and the demeanor of its waiters.

"You know what it is?" he suddenly blurted out, even though he hadn't prefaced the statement with any context. "It's me. I can't seem to make sense of anything. It's been a really weird few years for me."

"How so?"

"Well, every time I leave my apartment, I feel like I'm checking out of a hotel room. I mean I'm sure I've remembered to check every drawer and pack my toothbrush but I always feel like I'm missing something. I fret about leaving my apartment for hours after I leave it. But when I'm in it, it smells like mushrooms even though I don't eat mushrooms."

"That does sound pretty bananas. But at least you have a job and an apartment. Some of the guys I've dated still live with their grandparents because their parents haven't moved out of their childhood homes yet."

"Oh yeah, my glamorous life. I'm living the dream. Sadly, it's the one where I forgot to put on my pants and only realized it when I got onto the subway."

Lucy giggled that oh-so-cute giggle of hers, so that her nose scrunched up and her bracelet chimed like a little bell. Wil found he could get used to that sound, and he could most definitely get used to the sight of Lucy across the table from him. Here was a beautiful, confident, free-spirited woman—someone his mom would certainly have approved of, if not so much his dad—and he was missing the moment by feeling sorry for himself.

Wil realized he was seriously messing this up. But if the God of All Things Random was playing checkers with him again, then he was at least going to enjoy playing the game. He decided to un-mess things, hoping that this might be a little bit like un-looking for things.

"You know, you're right, Lucy," he conceded. "We should talk about something else. I guess I'm feeling a bit overwhelmed and a bit underwhelmed today. I just want to be whelmed for a couple of hours and enjoy our dinner."

"Our dinner date," she said, pointedly.

"Right. Our date. Though why you'd want to go out to dinner with a guy acting like a selfish idiot as opposed to attending a red carpet event with a three-hundred-pound wrestler is beyond me. I don't even own a tuxedo."

"Because you're clever. And you're scruffy chic."

"I'm out-punting my coverage, is what I am," said Will, feeling morose.

"Fair enough, Eeyore. So tell me more about this Curioddity Museum. It sounds incredible. I'm surprised I've never heard of it."

"Well, it's definitely incredible in an 'I can't believe it' kind of way but not in a 'how do they do that?' kind of way. A lot of the exhibits are a bit suspect."

"Oh. Bummer. Are they fake?"

"They're not well constructed enough to be fake."

Wil told Lucy about the lightning catcher and the Perpetual Emotion machine, and about the strange crates in the Curioddity Museum's hallways and lobby. Strangely, she seemed excited about the prospect of visiting it.

"Oh, I love all that stuff!" she exclaimed so loudly that it drew the attention of half the restaurant's Thursday-night patrons. Feeling happily self-conscious, Lucy rearranged her chair and waited for the murmur to die down. "I love that stuff," she repeated with an excited hiss. "I'm really into the paranormal. I've got a lot of theories about magic. And aliens!"

"How do you feel about magic aliens?"

"That's what I keep telling people! What if they're not from space but from underwater? Wouldn't it be so cool if they were from Atlantis?"

"Well, that certainly is an interesting theory."

"Did you know the British royal family is supposedly made up of reptiles from another galaxy?"

Wil gulped; this was the type of thinking he'd been encouraged to follow in his formative years but that he'd been avoiding ever since he'd lost his mother. There were so many things he'd wanted to talk about over the years with random strangers, such as the weird markings he'd heard about on the floor of the Denver airport, or the strange, spherical balls that had been found all across the world with the aid of dousing rods. He'd heard that at least five U.S. presidents had had six fingers on each hand, and that the CIA had once conducted experiments on kangaroos to replace their marsupial brains with human brains. But whenever he'd had an opportunity to let loose creatively, all he could hear was an inner voice that sounded much like his father's warning him not to stray too far from the path of human understanding in case he lost his footing and fell down the side of a mountain of illogic. Nowadays, the only people he interacted with were Mr. Whatley— who could be relied upon only for conversations about the weather and sporting results from the night before—and his addled landlady, Mrs. Chappell.

Despite Wil's genuine desire to relax and let the evening take him wherever it felt like taking him, he had been thinking about a certain subject he'd wanted to broach with Lucy Price ever since the first time she'd hit him over the head with a book. Now seemed as good a time as any. After all, what did he have to lose but the respect of a beautiful, charming girl who seemed smitten with him for reasons unknown?

"How do you feel about ghosts?" Wil asked. "You said you thought you'd seen one in your store."

"Oh! What? Yeah! Wow!" exclaimed Lucy, unable to pick a suitable interjection and stick with it. "My store's definitely haunted. Definitely. No doubt about it."

"So you've seen people back near the books at the far wall? What do they look like?"

"I don't know. It's like an impression people are shuffling by back there and stopping to stare at you—like you're a mannequin in a store window and people are checking you out. But every time you look up, there's no one there. It's really spooky." Lucy's eyes widened. Clearly she enjoyed this kind of conversation, and her manic embellishment only added to the fun.

"Do you remember that box I found at the back of your store?" said Wil as he changed the subject (as far as Lucy was concerned) but stuck to the subject (as far as he was concerned). "You told me you didn't remember how you found it."

"Yeah. I picked it up off a shelf at the back of the store, and by the time I realized I don't have any shelves at the back of the store it was too late. And d'you want to know what's weird about that box?" Lucy's eyes darted around and she leaned in to whisper, just in case she and Wil were being observed by secret agents from another planet. "I think it moves all by itself."

"What, that old thing?" said Wil, doing a poor job of disguising his genuine intrigue.

"Yeah. Every time you don't look at it directly, it moves. One time I was doing a headstand against the back wall an' I swear, it started to float!"

Tempted as he was to ask why Lucy was doing headstands alone in her store—and immensely distracted by the mental image of her doing such a thing—Wil pressed on regardless.

"I believe you," he said. And he widened his eyes for maximum effect in a manner that would have made Mr. Dinsdale proud.

"You do?"

"Yes. And what's more, I think that old box has made a strange old man very happy. That old man not being me, of course."

"Well, I like making people happy—and I was doing yoga, by the way—so that's a good thing. Now how do we make you happy, Wil?"

"You're already doing it. But my forearm aches a little bit, I have to be honest."

"Why?"

"Well, I keep pinching it to see if I'm going to wake up. You really are a tremendously gorgeous girl, Lucy. I can't see what someone like you would see in a guy like me." Wil was suddenly becoming self-conscious. "I mean . . . that is, if you see something."

Lucy narrowed her eyes in the way that Wil had very much become accustomed to in his daydreams about her. She smiled, and her eyes searched his heart and instructed it do a cartwheel.

"Are you really the person I think you might be, Wil Morgan?"

"I'm not sure. Who do you think I am?"

"The antiboyfriend." She continued, encouraged by his puzzled expression. "If every boyfriend I have had so far has been a self-involved jackass with less humility than a peacock, then there must be an antiboyfriend. It's kind of like antimatter. It's probably scientific fact."

"I don't know, Lucy. I mean, I'm not the most ambitious person. I let things overwhelm me a lot."

"But you're honest about it."

"I don't feel proud of that. Ever since I lost my mom I've felt like I was stuck in a centrifuge. Everything spins a bit."

Wil's eyes welled up. It was always so hard to talk about his mother. Lucy's eyes welled up even more, and a single tear of happiness wandered down her cheek.

"I'm sorry," said Wil. "I didn't mean to get all heavy on a first date."

"No, it's amazing. I feel like I know your mom just because you loved her so much. I can see her in your eyes." Lucy wiped away the tear and smiled such a beautiful smile that Wil wanted to put it on a billboard outside his office. "Tell me about the centrifuge."

"Well, I guess if you stand in the middle of a centrifuge then you'll probably get really dizzy in a very short space of time. But if you take a single step forward you're likely to go splat, and wind up as a little red stain spreading across the walls. At least, that's what my dad kept telling me. That's why I haven't gotten very far, I guess. I figured it was better to stay in place and deal with the vertigo than take a step forward and bloody my own nose. But the weirdest thing happened this week: I started looking at things differently and doing everything backward. And now I'm seeing all sorts of things that were probably behind my back the whole time."

"Like what?"

"Like laser beams and ghosts and tulips in winter. And you, Lucy. I'm having a hard time accepting any of this is real."

"Well, we can figure this out," said Lucy, softly. "It's really easy. All you have to do is answer one question."

"What's the question?"

"If I asked you to kiss me, would the answer to that question be the same as the answer to this one?"

Wil's heart leaped up through his mouth, and his elbows did an involuntary tap dance on the table. "Yes," he said. "Wait . . . no!"

And moments later, his heart went from a damp squib to a firework as Lucy Price kissed him.

"GREETINGS, WIL *Morgan*," came a familiar metallic voice from inside Wil's pocket. "*It has been approximately ten hours since our last interaction. Would you like to check the skiing reports in Libya?*"

Wil tried to ignore the commotion coming from below. Not now. Not unless SARA wanted to take an early bath in a bowl of cucumber soup.

"*You have seventeen new messages,*" continued SARA. "*Would you like to check the sailing reports in Oklahoma?*"

Lucy stopped kissing Wil, and chuckled. "Is that your Lemon phone? Do you think she's jealous?" she asked.

"No. I think she's mental." Wil pulled the Lemon phone from his pocket and stared at the glowing screen, which suggested SARA was in the process of switching herself back on. "I told you I'd talk to you later."

"Are you yelling at your phone?" asked Lucy, incredulous. "Does it have conversations?"

"They tend to be a bit one-sided but yes, essentially. I think she's trying to kill me. SARA, why don't you introduce yourself to Lucy?"

SARA remained silent, and the Lemon phone's screen continued to glow. Wil took this for an act of defiance. "How about if I apologized?" he said with a conciliatory tone that sounded even faker than he intended. "I'm sorry I yelled at you before, and I'm sorry I didn't charge your battery last night. Now please say hello to Lucy and stop making me look foolish."

Lucy smirked. "That's the trouble with inanimate objects. They don't—"

"*Greetings, Lucy Price,*" said SARA, suddenly. "*Would you like the sailing reports in Libya?*"

Lucy cackled with delight. "Oh, that is just awesome!" she said with a broad grin spreading across her pretty face. "How do you do that, Wil?"

"By default, apparently. She comes this mental out of the box."

"*Would anyone like a report?*" insisted SARA, her shrill metallic voice increasing in volume.

"Yes please, SARA," said Lucy, gamely. "I'd like to know about the hang gliding conditions in Sao Paolo. And can you also find out for me why bad things happen to good people for no apparent reason?" Lucy winked at Wil. Apparently, this was the sort of thing that didn't faze her in the slightest. "That ought to keep her busy," she said, gleefully.

"*Calculating . . . ,*" replied SARA. And with that, the Lemon phone fell silent and the screen stopped glowing.

Lucy looked Wil in the eye, and narrowed hers for maximum-maximum effect. "Now what?" she said. "Ice cream or coffee?"

Wil would have taken "fire walking" if it had involved Lucy at this moment in time. Instead, he fished his lucky penny from his other pocket. "I can't decide. How about we go heads or tails?"

"Sounds good. But I like ice cream."

"Okay, heads, ice cream. Tails, coffee ice cream."

Lucy giggled. Wil spun the penny on the table and they watched it together for a few moments. For a change, Wil found himself mesmerized by something other than the old coin. He wanted to jump for joy and take a nap at the same time. He wanted to ask a hundred thousand questions and just be silent and let it all soak in. Because he was beginning to understand he was already in love. And just by virtue of instinct, he was beginning to believe that Lucy was, too.

The penny wandered across the table and headed for a collision with his bowl of cucumber soup.

"Can I ask you something?" said Wil as he found himself staring not at the penny but at the girl staring at the penny. "It's not heavy, I promise."

"Sure," she replied, mesmerized by the penny, which was beginning to wobble.

"Can we go on a second date sometime? I mean if you don't think I'm being an idiot by pressuring you too much. I'd like to take you by that museum. If nothing else, you'd get a good laugh out of it."

"This has been a fun night but I'm not as easy to persuade as you might think. Let me think. Okay, sure." Lucy cackled, evilly.

"Gee, thanks."

"My pleasure. So how do you do that, anyway?"

"Do what?"

"Keep it going like that. Is it a trick?"

"Keep what going?"

"That!" said Lucy, looking down in the direction of the table.

WIL'S EYEBALLS took the form of a child's balloon rapidly being filled with too much helium. Down on the table, his lucky penny was still spinning in place.

PERPETUALLY.

CHAPTER ELEVEN

"At the next intersection, turn . . . at the nearest available . . .
in five hundred yards, make a . . . in twenty yards make a
legal . . . please observe all posted speed limits . . ."

WIL MORGAN had once heard that a person's life flashes before his or
her eyes in the moments just before death. Indeed, he had experienced this phenomenon many years before when he was half-buried
on a snow-covered hill underneath a tea tray. Even so, he was unpre-
pared for the second time it happened to him. He was also unpre-
pared to believe a thirty-year-old Ford Pinto could exceed speeds of
eighty miles per hour through one-way Friday evening traffic without
disintegrating like a broken test aircraft on reentry—certainly not a
rusted Ford Pinto driven by a beautiful-yet-deranged young woman
he'd just fallen in love with. Surely, such a feat could only be accomplished by a New York City cab driver aided by a seventy-mile-per-hour
wind and numerous illicit substances.

So astonished had Wil been by the sudden appearance of the Perpetual Penny next to his bowl of cucumber soup, he'd grabbed his old

coin and hurriedly suggested that he and Lucy immediately go on their second date: an impromptu visit to the Curioddity Museum. Following this, they'd climbed into her Pinto of Death and set off toward Upside-Down Street. Wil suspected he and Lucy were on a collision course with something interesting at the museum, so he felt it was pointless to worry about colliding with anything resembling another motor vehicle. This entire thing was Dinsdale's doing— he just knew it.

The steady stream of flashing brake lights ahead, confused faces in passing car windows, and invective coming from the driver's side of the Pinto served as a calming mechanism even though these things should probably have served as a warning. Somehow, a thousand moments of vehicular madness seemed to blur into each other, allowing Wil to free his thinking. He concluded that Lucy Price was not a violent maniac with a hair-trigger temper when holding a steering wheel in her hands; rather, he preferred to think of her as "slightly excitable" in the same way a clown could be considered "overdressed," or a bathtub might be considered "uncompromising." It all depended on the spin one was prepared to put on things, and given the speed at which the Pinto was currently traveling, spinning at some point seemed inevitable. Whatever the case, Wil felt it would be contradictory to discourage Lucy's apparent goal of creating an interdimensional shortcut through a nearby wormhole, since this impromptu car ride had been his idea in the first place.

For her part, Lucy yelled and screamed at the drivers and passengers of every passing car—most of whom whizzed by at breakneck speeds, even though they were going in the same direction as the Pinto. She made a point to single out pickup truck drivers as her most hated enemy, and swerved out of her way on numerous occasions to try and collide with them. Thankfully, in the roughly thirteen minutes it took for Lucy to drive from Happy Spice to the Curioddity Museum, no fatalities occurred—at least none that Wil was aware of. To be fair, had there been any fatalities in the wake of the Pinto traveling at virtual light speed, Wil would hardly have had time to register that horrific eventuality. He was too busy fearing for his own life, after all.

It was interesting, Wil thought, as his life flashed before his eyes, that he'd chosen to fall in love with a gorgeous, nigh-perfect young girl who just so happened to be a demon of Satan when behind the wheel of her car. This was going to make for some fascinating road trips. In the meantime, he had rather begun to enjoy himself. On a whim, Wil had engaged SARA's navigation function, just to see what might happen to her AI programming at warp speeds.

SARA was not enjoying herself one little bit.

"At the next T junction take a . . . make a left, then . . . turn left . . . turn left . . . turn left . . . "

Wil giggled to himself as SARA tried to keep up with the Ford Pinto's maneuvers. He cackled with terrified glee when Lucy plowed through a gas station at fifty miles per hour in an attempt to cut off a right turn signal and the three cars waiting there.

"Please proceed to the highlighted route . . . ," said SARA, hurriedly, as the Pinto banked off a brick wall and clattered onto the main one-way system leading to the banking district. Her metallic voice now seemed a little pitiful as she trailed off into silence. Like everyone else in this town, the poor creature probably had no idea where Upside-Down Street might be found. And like everyone else on the road, she was no doubt more terrified than she had ever been in her entire robotic life.

Wil resolved to extract SARA from her infinite loop of confusion by handing her a problem to solve so that her fuzzy logic might have something else to worry about. "Okay, SARA," he said with a grin. "I think that's enough with the directions. We'll take it from here. Please call the Museum of Curioddity on Upside-Down Street. I would like to speak with Mr. Dinsdale."

"Dialing . . . ," replied SARA hastily, relieved to be given a task

she could actually handle. The Pinto slammed through a stop sign and clattered off in search of trouble. At that moment, Wil heard the phone pick up at the other end of the line.

"You have reached the Museum of Curioddity," said Mr. Dinsdale's uneven tone across the ether. "If you wish to leave a message . . . uhm . . . leave a message. Boop." Mr. Dinsdale actually said the word "boop" aloud in a falsetto voice, just for effect.

"Mr. Dinsdale!" yelled Wil into his smartphone, "Mr. Dinsdale, are you there? I need you to stay right there! I'm coming over! I'll be there in ten minutes!" At that moment, the connection cut off as Lucy buzzed a pickup truck and yelled at its driver. As Wil replaced the phone in his pocket, he could not help but be struck by the fact that his connection sounded suspiciously like it had been recorded inside a submarine. He stared at the smartphone's glowing screen for just a moment, with his Strange Feeling of déjà vu trying to yell at him over the noise of the Pinto's engine. Didn't this already happen?

Wil hazarded a glance in Lucy's direction and was most concerned to find her navigating the roads by looking underneath the top of her steering wheel. "So," he began nonchalantly, grasping his life tightly by the reproductive organs, "have you ever driven this way before?"

Lucy gripped the wheel and sneered at the white lines in the road. "I drive this way to work every day. Shut up, I'm trying to concentrate!"

The Pinto careened around a small hybrid that was inconveniently stopped at a red light and shot off onto the divided highway that led to the museum.

Wil didn't have the heart to tell the object of his affection and future mother of his children that he had not intended "this way" to mean, "in this direction." Rather, he had meant to inquire if she habitually drove *in this manner*. But given the fact that his heart had stopped beating a few blocks back, he felt obliged to keep such opinions to himself until he felt either solid ground under his feet or the warm caress of a hospital gurney.

Up ahead, the invisible side entrance to Upside-Down Street loomed, invisibly.

"We're taking a right about five hundred yards up there!" yelled Wil.

"Would you please shut up!" yelled Lucy in return. "I know where I'm going!"

"It's just ahead!"

"Gah! I can't stand backseat drivers!"

"But I'm in the passenger seat—"

"Even worse!"

"It's kind of a sharp right!"

"You're worse than your Lemon phone! Hold on!"

With a sudden squeal of tires that sounded like a multitude of yodeling pigs, Lucy banked the wheel of the Pinto dead right, so that the rear of the car fishtailed around in a manner familiar only to professional Japanese drift drivers and people who had accidentally driven onto an oil slick. As the Pinto careened onto Upside-Down Street, the back of the vehicle flattened the confusing street sign so completely and utterly that it sprang upward, flipped off its base, and planted itself neatly upside down in a nearby gutter. Which, in effect, left the sign the way it should have been oriented to begin with. Had it been an animate object, it wouldn't have had the nerve to protest.

Lucy gunned the car's argumentative engine toward the museum, slammed on the brakes, and skidded to a halt so abruptly that Wil's esophagus had to remind itself not to project through the front windshield. The vehicle sputtered to silence.

"Okay-dokey," said Lucy in a breezy manner, "we're here!"

WIL SAT in complete silence for a brief moment, unable to decide if he had just experienced the thrill ride of his life, or if he had invented a new cure for constipation. Amazingly, most of his body parts seemed to have survived the journey. The ones he couldn't feel were probably in shock.

"Are you okay, Wil?" asked Lucy with a look of genuine concern on her face.

"I'm not sure," Wil replied. "I think I might have blacked out back there. Do you always drive like that?"

"Like what?" she replied, innocently.

"Like an angry little Korean lady behind the wheel of a tank."

"I don't know what you're talking about."

Wil could tell from Lucy's genuine expression of puzzlement that she was telling the truth. This was going to be a much longer conversation, one that would need to be conducted over a very large pot of coffee and a few impossibly huge peach Danish. In the meantime, he and Lucy needed to get inside the museum. A certain Mr. Dinsdale had some explaining to do.

"Come on," said Wil, peeling himself from the passenger seat, where he had been slightly glued in by large pools of cold sweat seeping through his clothing. He pushed against the crumpled passenger door, stepped out into a light rain, and headed toward the front of the museum.

"You still haven't told me what the problem is," Lucy remonstrated as she exited the driver's side of the Pinto. "Why did you bring me here? You look like you've seen a ghost."

"I just had dinner with one!"

"What—?"

Grabbing Lucy's hand, Wil started toward the museum's revolving door. "No time to explain," he muttered. "Just bear with me, okay? I have a feeling this is all going to make sense to you in some weird way. It's about the museum—"

"What's happened?" Lucy shouted, as bewilderment finally caught up to the rest of her. "Did somebody die?"

"No. I think somebody just came back to life. Namely, me."

"How is that possible?"

"It's not. It's just implausibly deniable. It's about un-looking at things properly so that they finally make sense—like the daily specials in your local coffee shop."

And with that, Wil rushed in through the right-hand side of the revolving door, Lucy followed him quickly in through the left side, and they found themselves inextricably stuck with no place to go.

WIL BASHED his head on the inside of a pane of glass and stood there stunned for a moment. He'd successfully navigated the door on two previous occasions by un-looking at it. But this time, he had simply not looked where he was going, and there was clearly a subtle distinction between the two. Being stuck in close quarters with the incomparable Miss Price—watching her try to untangle her shoelaces from the base of the door while simultaneously pushing in the wrong direction to free herself—gave Wil the sense he had indeed found his intellectual soul mate. Under normal circumstances, he probably would have chosen to stay where he was for a little longer and work with Lucy on their mutual problem.

But this was no ordinary circumstance: what awaited inside the Curioddity Museum's foyer caused Wil to simply stand and stare, his mouth agape. And moments later—without knowing how he did it—he found himself standing in front of the cash register with a small amount of drool emerging from his mouth.

∽

INSIDE THE foyer, Mr. Dinsdale and three uniformed workers were wrestling with huge, crackling ropes as they tried to hold down the box of Levity to prevent it from shooting through the ceiling.

"Hold her steady!" yelled Dinsdale as the Levity box suddenly tugged on one of the ropes and sent two of the burly men flying. "Bob! You and Robbie secure the ballast and tie down to one of those statues! Bobby and I will grab this end!"

A strange form of Tesla-style electricity played around the holding ropes, and across the ceiling of the foyer. At the register, Mary Gold filed her nails and smacked her bubble gum, as if to make it clear she had no interest in the madcap proceedings whatsoever. Out of the corner of Wil's eye, the wooden crates twitched excitedly. The Curioddity Museum had undergone a most fundamental change indeed. Suddenly, it could be seen exactly as intended.

As the three uniformed workers attempted to comply with Dinsdale's instructions, the Levity box suddenly broke free. It tugged sharply on the remaining ropes, one of which had been wrapped tightly and securely around an old-style radiator. The radiator immediately became dislodged, sending a massive plume of steam into the air. One of the unfortunate workers was now being dragged across the floor, sending the man clattering into his two coworkers, both of whom had barely begun to recover.

"Wil!" yelled Dinsdale. "It's good to see you! Grab the end of that rope and help Bob, will you?"

Will eyed the rope nervously for a moment. The large amounts of electricity playing along its length tended to suggest a kind of "don't touch" motif at play.

"What are you waiting for? We need your help, please! It's getting away!"

"Is it safe?" asked Wil, grabbing for the departing rope against the protests of his fight-or-flight instincts.

"Of course not! Now hurry!"

"I think I just called you from the future but I got the answering machine instead!"

"What?"

"Nothing!"

Wil felt a strange, cool sensation flooding his forearms as he grabbed hold of the electrostatically charged rope and began to tug against it. Up above, the Levity box bucked and squealed before set-tling into place. And with the aid of the three burly workers—all named Robert—and the old man himself, the box now moved slowly back down toward the floor of the foyer.

While Wil huffed and tugged, he noticed with some interest that the wooden crates in the foyer were moving in such a way as to appar-ently grab his attention. He locked eyes with Mary Gold at the cash register. She stared back, smacking her gum a few times and regard-ing him with an expression of feigned disinterest, before glancing toward the revolving door.

To his dismay, Wil discovered that Lucy was sitting on the floor of the door's left side, her shoulders heaving as she sobbed from the bottom of her heart. He had no way of helping her unless he let go of the rope and sent the box crashing upward through the ceiling.

Wil glowered at Mary Gold. *Don't just stand there*, he said, translat-ing his thoughts into the most rudimentary of body language. *Go and help her.*

With a look of utter disdain that Wil took to be Mary Gold's most conciliatory tone, the beehived receptionist floated toward the revolv-ing door as Wil, Mr. Dinsdale, and the three Roberts hauled the now-docile box of Levity down toward the floor of the foyer.

"Well done everyone!" yelled Mr. Dinsdale enthusiastically. "Let's get the box riveted onto the new display shelf and back into the tempo-ral exhibit!"

"Mr. Dinsdale!" yelled Wil in response. "I need to talk to you about something . . . someone . . ."

"That's it!" called Dinsdale toward his workers. "Lower her gently."

"Mr. Dinsdale—"

"Robbie! Wrap the rope around the base of that door!"

Mr. Dinsd—"

"Bobby! Take Bob and go fetch me some pliers!"

"Mr. *Dinsdale!*"

❧

A SILENCE fell upon the foyer of the museum. Out of the corner of Wil's eye, the wooden crates settled quickly into place, as if having been admonished by a schoolteacher.

"Mr. Dinsdale," said Wil as calmly as he could in spite of his breathlessness, "can you please tell me what in the heck is going on? Why was that old box trying to punch a hole through the ceiling?"

Mr. Dinsdale's rheumy eyes glistened, and he smiled the smile of a grandfather who'd just witnessed a grandson's first touchdown. "Your eyes are simply un-looking in the right direction now, Wil," he said. "It's good to have you back."

Mary Gold appeared at that moment, leading Lucy toward the two men. Lucy's shoulders continued to shake, much to Wil's dismay. Perhaps she'd really hurt herself. He stepped forward to make sure she was okay. To his surprise, Wil found her shaking not to be a result of sobbing but because Lucy was giggling, quietly and uncontrollably. Mary Gold rolled her eyes and moved away.

"Oh, Wil," Lucy said, recovering. "That . . . was . . . epic!"

"It was?"

"Yeah. I mean you went the wrong way! An' I went around the other way, and we got stuck! Major fail!"

"I'm pretty sure I went the right way." Wil thought for a moment. Maybe Lucy was right, and he had entered the door from the wrong direction. She certainly had the effect of sending him in directions he had a hard time predicting.

Lucy proffered her hand in the direction of Mr. Dinsdale and smiled sweetly. "Hi," she said in her oh-so-confident manner. "You must be Mr. Dinsdale. I'm Lucy. I've heard so much about you."

"Hello Lucy," said Dinsdale. He squinted, and then his eyes darted quickly toward Mary Gold, a look of genuine intrigue spreading across his face. "Have we met before?"

"I'm pretty sure I'd remember that," replied Lucy, evenly. "This place is groovy. Do you have airlocks?"

"On every floor."

"Even better—"

"Okay, hold it right there!"

All eyes turned to Wil who, at this moment in time, had stepped so far outside his normal frame of reference that he found himself looking at his brain from the outside in, much like patrons of a gallery might study a painting in an actual wooden frame. "I need," he said, gritting his teeth, "to let go of this rope. Please."

And with that, Wil let go of the rope.

And promptly fainted.

❧

MR. DINSDALE'S office had the look of an Escher painting: its walls were decorated in such a manner that if one looked into the distance, the pattern of the wallpaper had a tendency to move sideways at rapid speeds. One end of the room seemed narrower than the other. It was exactly as Wil expected it would be, and that only served to unsettle him even more; he was becoming used to the madness, he realized.

"How are you feeling?" asked Mr. Dinsdale from across the small table where they now sat. His face carried a look of genuine concern, as did Lucy's.

"I feel more like I do now than when I first got here," said Wil, defeated. On the tabletop in front of him, the Perpetual Penny wandered lazily across the flat surface, having no intention of ceasing its spinning activities anytime during the next millennium. "I can't believe all of this is real. I don't want to believe it."

"Yes, you do, Wil. I knew it from the moment I first met you. You're looking at things with your heart again instead of your eyes. Life is about to get a lot more interesting."

Wil grasped the cup of tea that had been placed in front of him and let his attention wander to small, spherical objects that were floating aimlessly throughout the room. "I feel like my centrifuge just stopped spinning," he said, wistfully. And off this simple-yet-complicated remark, Lucy placed a tender hand against his cheek and brushed his hair back slightly. Her caress felt like the most perfect touch in all the world.

"And is the world better, or worse than before?" asked the old man.

"Roughly the same, Mr. Dinsdale." Wil considered his plight. "I can't tell which direction I'm facing, or if I just learned something, or if I already knew it and just remembered it. I can't tell if I'm coming or going, and I have no idea how I got here. All I know is that everything's random, and this place is the epicenter of it all. "

"When you visit the Museum of Curioddity, the world begins to waken. And when you leave it, you always take a piece of it with you. You're simply seeing the world the way it's supposed to be seen. It takes some getting used to."

"Is that penny spinning forever?"

"Yes, it would appear so."

"Why?"

"Because you're ready to believe it can. With a two percent margin for human error, of course. But this being Thursday, that usually goes down by a couple of percent."

Wil looked at Lucy, hoping with all his heart that she would remain real, no matter how unreal this entire experience seemed to be. Despite her concern for his well-being, Lucy seemed to be taking it all in her stride. "Are you sure you're okay?" she asked. "I think you had some kind of electric shock."

"It's perfectly fine, Lucy," exclaimed Dinsdale. "Those ropes have a few hundred thousand volts running through them but it's counteracted by the effects of the Levity. Or at least that's the theory."

"That's the theory?" repeated Wil, incredulous.

"Yes, and it works, apparently." Mr. Dinsdale jumped to his feet in the arbitrary, energetic manner he seemed to have claimed for his very own. "Now that you're back in the fold, we have to get straight to work. I'm glad you left a message on my answering machine last week telling us you'd be coming. There's no time to lose."

"No time to lose what?"

"That's the spirit!" said Mr. Dinsdale, happily. "Come on!" He turned on his heel and headed toward the main floor with the expectation that Wil and Lucy would follow him.

Lucy glanced to Wil, greatly amused. "He's better than advertised," she said, her eyes widening. "Come on. I want to see what happens next."

Grabbing Wil by the hand, she led him out of the office and into the motionless centrifuge of randomness otherwise known as the Museum of Curioddity while the Perpetual Penny continued to spin, perpetually.

✥

OUT ON the museum's upper floor, the building seemed to have undergone a seismic shift either in a perceptual sense, or just literally. Wil hadn't remembered the hallways being so wide, nor the ethereal will-o'-the-wisps that seemed to float in and out of rooms chased by more of the small, spherical objects. The museum was alive in every corner, and in every meaningful way.

Lucy gasped in delight at each exhibit they passed. Inside the display of perpetual motion machines they found one of the Roberts tinkering with da Vinci's Perpetual Emotion machine. The burly worker had a set of handwritten instructions laid to one side, and was twisting something on a back panel with a small eyeglass screwdriver, while a second Robert kept his arm stuck in the machine's front orifice and alternated between a state of euphoria and a state of utter despair. Wil pulled Lucy slightly toward him, making sure to give the wretched contraption a very wide berth. Perpetual things were now becoming normal, but that didn't mean they were all safe.

While no one was looking, Mr. Dinsdale had teleported to the end of the hall, which led to the temporal exhibits and the featureless room beyond. Next to him, tiny flashes of lightning seemed to illuminate the glass bottle "lightning catcher" from within. "Wil! Lucy! Come this way, please!" called the strange old man.

Lucy tightened her grip on Wil's arm, intrigued by the possibilities unfolding before her very eyes. Clearly, she did not need to be untrained in order to see the museum properly—it already fit into her worldview. "Is Mr. Dinsdale always this arbitrary?" she said, chuckling, as they approached the waiting old man.

"Not really," whispered Wil as they arrived near the lightning catcher exhibit. "He's a lot less predictable on Mondays."

As they approached, one of the small, spherical objects whizzed past their heads, followed by a tiny will-o'-the-wisp that made a giggling sound as it chased down the sphere.

"Hey, what are these little circles flying around the hallways?" Lucy asked Mr. Dinsdale as they caught up to his position. "They look like little spaceships."

"Oh, those?" replied Dinsdale in a matter-of-fact manner that suggested he barely noticed them these days. "Those are some of John Keely's old toys. They levitate using the electromagnetic forces contained within their atomic structure. At least, that's what the manual says. I wouldn't be surprised if they have levity in them."

"And what about the wispy things?" asked Wil. "Are they part of the exhibit?"

"Oh, those aren't part of an exhibit. We don't know what they are. But they seem to like the little flying spheres so we let them come and go as they please." Dinsdale turned his attention to the green bottle on the shelf next to him. "Lucy, I really think you'd like this exhibit. It's a lightning catcher, you know."

A small tornado seemed to flash through the green glass, which only served to heighten the incredible atmosphere at this end of the museum. As Lucy stared into the green glass, Wil stared, mesmerized, at the look of wonderment on her face. Could it really be that he had not viewed this incredible exhibit properly on his previous visit? He thought back to a phrase he'd heard his mother repeat so many times before: *Your eyes only see what your mind lets you believe.* Perhaps this concept had finally come full circle, and he was seeing the truth of the world that had previously been hiding in front of his eyes, all because he simply now believed it. Things were going to be a lot different around here—that much was certain.

Dinsdale began to lead them both away along the hall connecting to the temporal exhibit. "I'm going to level with you, Wil: I have been testing you. The recovery of the Levity box was a precursor to a much more important task. Put simply: I need your help. I need a crack detective on the case."

"On what case?"

"We'll get to that. First things first: are you up for the task?"

"I don't know what it is!" Wil fussed. "How can I be up for anything if I'm planted on my backside before I've even started?"

"Haven't you learned anything this week?" said Dinsdale, doing a poor job of containing his annoyance. "Good things happen if you do them out of order. Where's your sense of adventure?"

"It's tired. And also very confused. It would like to take a vacation in Hawaii and have pina coladas delivered on the hour, every hour."

"But Wil—"

"He accepts," interjected Lucy, abruptly. "And so do I."

Wil looked at Lucy with astonishment, only to be met with a not-so-innocent smile. "Whatever we're accepting," she said, "it's better than wondering about what it would have been if we'd said no. I hate it when that happens."

"I believe you would be a valuable asset in this endeavor, Lucy. Thank you." Dinsdale looked expectantly at Wil. Wil looked at Dinsdale, and then back at Lucy, incredulous. He looked at the wooden crates: no help at all. He looked at Mary Gold, who smacked her gum, loudly. Surely, he was not about to agree to this, was he?

"I'm a very wealthy man, Wil," said Mr. Dinsdale. "The fact is, I personally invented more than half of the useful little products we find in our homes today, like bathing cream and shelf studs. Marcus James, on the other hand, simply sells other people's ideas. But you know how it goes—everyone loves a middleman."

"They do?"

"Quite possibly. Think about the week you've had: has it led you to places you would otherwise not have visited? And would you have preferred to be sitting in the Castle Towers having visited none of those places, Wil?"

Wil looked at Lucy, the beautiful girl he had met in a side street store he would never have visited but for Mr. Dinsdale's box of Levity. No, he decided; he would not have preferred that at all.

"Your eyes now see what your mind is allowing you to believe. I need your help, and I need it now. What do your instincts say?"

"Run like hell."

"Those are your father's instincts. Look underneath, just as I have been training you to do all week. What is the exact opposite of what you have been taught to think?"

"Well . . . ," said Wil, hesitantly, and then warming to the moment, "I guess I could stand to get out of the centrifuge and give things a whirl by myself for a change—"

With a squeal of delight, Lucy Price leaped forward and planted a passionate kiss directly on Wil's grateful-yet-surprised lips. "Wil!" she exclaimed. "I love this! This is gonna be epic!"

Wil stared down at the floor, just to check on his vertigo. The floor didn't appear to be moving. He was safe for now, though understandably wary of all things epic.

"Follow me, both of you," said Mr. Dinsdale as he moved away toward the center of the museum. "We only have a few hours left."

"Before what?"

"Before the Museum of Curioddity is closed down for good."

WIL, LUCY, and Dinsdale moved together along the wide hallway toward the temporal exhibit. As usual, Mr. Dinsdale had thrown Wil for a total loop. He remained quiet for a moment, sensing the old man needed time to gather his thoughts and elaborate on his last statement. Lucy moved along quietly, holding his hand, a worried look on her face. His heart skipped a couple of beats as he surveyed the various looks of amazement she was unable to contain whenever she encountered various exhibits set into alcoves in the wall.

Those very same walls seemed to close in a little as the group proceeded, which gave a very skewed sense of perspective—it somehow seemed as if the hall continually grew in length, suggesting that it somehow expanded to as long as one might need it to be, depending on how long one's conversation was going to last while traversing it. No surprise, Wil realized, that it led to the Temporal Exhibit. The hallway itself was probably one of the exhibits.

While Wil pondered this matter, the group passed the featureless room where he had first encountered Lucy in ghostly form. Lucy stopped dead in her tracks. Wil already knew why.

"Are you okay?" he asked, knowing approximately half of the answer.

"I don't know," she replied, puzzled. "It's like I just had the strangest sense of déjà vu. Has that ever happened to you?"

"I've been fending it off pretty much all week but we're definitely going to have a few words once Monday rolls around." Wil turned to address Mr. Dinsdale. "I think the museum's connection to Lucy's Magic Locker sent me in the direction of the Levity box, Mr. Dinsdale. I was connecting to her all along; we just didn't know it. Lucy's the ghost you've been seeing in that room. That's how she was able to reach out and pick the Levity box off one of your shelves."

"Why, Wil!" exclaimed the old man, excitedly. "I'm genuinely impressed. Now where would a mere insurance claims detective get such an outlandish idea about the fabric of space-time?"

"I read about it in a magazine my mom gave me when I was a kid." Wil looked at his feet. He felt a dam of emotions about to burst, realizing how much he missed Melinda Morgan, and the way he used to be.

Dinsdale examined Lucy up and down. He placed a hand over one eye, bent double at the waist, and examined her upside down, much to her obvious amusement. "My goodness," he bellowed. "I think you're right, Wil!"

"Right about what?" said Lucy in an attempt to play along.

"Right about now," replied Dinsdale. "He's right about now! You're the person we've been haunting! I knew it had to be true!"

Mr. Dinsdale produced a small flashlight from his pocket and pointed it toward Lucy's eyes. "Are you—or have you ever been—a member of the Federal Brotherhood of Theosophy?"

"Um. No. I don't even know what that is."

"You can never be too careful. Have you been visited by space aliens? Specifically, the gray ones. The green ones don't count—they're everywhere."

"Not that I remember."

"Interesting. Are you afraid of cheese?"

"How did you know—?"

"It's not important. Finally, do you imagine things that appear out of the corner of your eye and subsequently disappear? Especially breakfast cereal?"

Lucy seemed stunned into silence.

"I'm afraid this confirms my suspicions," said Mr. Dinsdale, ominously. "For reasons as-yet unknown, the museum has been trying to forge a connection with you, Lucy. I do hope you'll forgive my associates and I for intruding in your life. If I'm not mistaken, we're the ones who've been haunting you."

Lucy thought on this for an abnormally long moment. She pursed her lips and narrowed her eyes. "Groovy," she said. "And also creepy."

"What do we do?" asked Wil. "What does it mean?"

"It means we needed Lucy all along. Come on."

Mr. Dinsdale moved again toward the end of the hall, and the temporal exhibit. The hallway politely seemed to extend itself a few yards in order to accommodate the old man's explanation.

"For many years," began Dinsdale, "I have been struggling with a certain Mr. Marcus James and his over-whitened teeth. I find the man to be a reprehensible toad."

"That's unfair to toads," said Wil.

"Indeed. The man has been picking away at my prototypes and patents for as long as I can remember. If I file one, he files something just close enough and just far enough away to prevent me from stopping him. And then he puts it up quickly on his television show, and my product is drained of potential before I ever have a chance to turn on the faucet. He's a master of ambiguity. No matter how many times I try to defend myself, he tends to beat me with sheer volume."

"Sounds ugly," said Lucy.

"It's worse than ugly. It's utterly bland and thoroughly banal. Marcus James knows people will look the other way if something isn't memorable enough to affect their lives. His products are cheap and instantly forgettable, his television pitch shows are meaningless and repetitive, and his personality is on a par with a shellfish. But this is how he gets away with double- and triple-billing people for the same product: it's difficult to remember something you probably didn't want in the first place, especially if it costs you more to return than it does to throw in your basement somewhere."

"But that's not fair! You can't just steal people's ideas, and then sell an inferior version of them!"

"Marcus James can, and does. The devil is in the details—or in his case, the costs of shipping, handling, and those infernal micro-purchases. The more money he earns from his exploits, the more he steals and the worse his products become. I'm afraid we have become a society that gives in to automated telephone answering services and accidental overcharges on our bank accounts. Who has the time to fight the system when the system is smarter and richer than we are?"

Wil was beginning to understand the problem: Mr. Dinsdale represented a particular threat to Marcus James, primarily because his museum took a stance against conventional thinking, and the slow death of intellect that comes with mediocrity. "So he's squeezing you out?" he asked. "This has to do with the repossession?"

"Yes. Without a copy of the original bill from the electric company, we can't tell if the surcharge was ever paid, or if it was fair, or if it even existed." Mr. Dinsdale began to flap his hands again, like an emotional swan. "We all know that life isn't fair. But life should at least come with a printed copy in large type in case of misunderstandings and overbilling."

"I'm probably going to kick myself for this," said Wil, cautiously, "but where do Lucy and I fit in to all of this?"

"You're going to break into Marcus James's offices and steal the original electric bill back for me!"

It was at this very moment that the hallway suddenly ended, and Wil, Lucy, and Mr. Dinsdale emerged into the temporal exhibit. For a moment, Wil was slightly less dumbstruck by the request Mr. Dinsdale had just made, and slightly more dumbstruck by the astonishing sight of the various displays behaving as they had always been intended to. Sparks played across the reverse periscope. A humming noise emanated from Einstein's answering machine. And over at the far wall, one of the Roberts was steadily banging away at the Levity box's shelf with a large hammer.

"So we're going to break into some guy's office and steal some old records that belong to you?" said Lucy, fixing Mr. Dinsdale with her best even gaze.

"Yes."

"And we could get arrested?"

"I'm afraid so, yes. Assuming you were to get inside his offices in the first place. I think I can help you on that count: please know that you will have any and all exhibits in this museum at your disposal, should you so choose. And with crack detective Wil Morgan on the case—"

"—not to mention his beautiful and groovy partner!"

"Not to mention his beautiful and groovy partner—"

"—and her trained cat!"

"Let's not overburden the logic here. With crack detectives Wil and Lucy on the case, failure is not an option. Which is a good thing because we only have until midday tomorrow before the bank turns over the original deed to the museum in lieu of proof of payment of the original electricity bill."

Lucy pondered this for a moment, then grasped Wil's hand firmly and stared deeply into his eyes. "If you say no," she said, "I'll hit you over the head with *War and Peace* again. This is going to be awesome."

Mr. Dinsdale fixed Wil with a steely—if somewhat watery—gaze. "Will you do it, Wil?" he asked. "If not for me, then for the sake of those at the mercy of automated answering systems and micropurchases everywhere?"

Wil lowered his gaze. This stood for everything his father had always taught him to avoid and, quite frankly, a few things his mother might have been a bit leery of as well. He was about to break into the offices—alarmed and brimming with security forces, no doubt—of a very nasty little man with a very nasty temper, and teeth that could not be trusted. He and Lucy might possibly be arrested or shot at; worse, he might provide his dad with enough ammunition to scupper Thanksgiving dinner conversation for the next thirty years.

Wil noticed that Einstein's answering machine was blinking, incessantly, suggesting someone had left a new message from the future since the last time he'd been here. On a whim, he reached out and pressed the Play button.

"Wil!" came Lucy's voice from some point in the not-too-distant future. "We're inside Marcus James's offices! There's no time to explain! Whatever you do, make sure you bring SARA's charging cord so that you can plug her in. You'll understand this later."

The machine's message ended as quickly as it had begun. And Wil found two pairs of eyes staring at him, not to mention the rapt attention of a few nearby wooden crates, and Robert, who had stopped banging and was anxiously hanging on every word.

"WELL," SAID Wil, without missing a beat. "I guess that answers that question."

CHAPTER TWELVE

———◆———

AT FIRST glance, the small, triangular device Mr. Dinsdale now held in his palm appeared to be in the running for the least useful item in history. Indeed, Wil surmised after allowing himself a second glance, if there were a national referendum imminent on the subject of futility, this particular item would stand a great chance of finishing in the top spot against, say, a half-eaten banana, a polka-dotted cummerbund, and a medium-sized sock with a hole in the toe.

The small device beeped at random intervals, accompanied by a little LED light that arbitrarily illuminated one of its sides. The beep was never the same tone twice. The device had a yellowish tinge to its underside that may or may not have been intentional, depending on whether or not the stains were composed of paint or bacteria.

"What is it?" asked Wil, eyeing the thing suspiciously.

"That's right!" replied, Mr. Dinsdale, proudly.

"I beg your pardon?"

"Your powers of deduction are remarkable, Wil. You're spot on the nose: it's a Whatsit. A really good one, too—not one of those Lithuanian knockoffs."

"Which makes it . . . ?"

"Very expensive. And quite possibly highly contagious, depending on the operator. I want you to take it with you to Marcus James's offices. It will prove crucial to your efforts."

Wil tried to muster all of the patience he could, and failed. He found himself wondering about the exact meaning of the word "muster," and postulating on whether or not "muster" was even a real word. As was typical when he stood inside the museum, he was allowing himself to get distracted again. "Mr. Dinsdale," Wil said in an attempt to muster something, "I have a headache. I'm not sure any of this is legal, I'm not sure what I've accidentally agreed to, and I'm not sure how this Whatsit of yours can be invaluable if I don't know how it works."

"How it functions depends on you, Wil. The Whatsit taps into a person's innermost desires on a fundamental level. It will predict your suppositions, and it is programmed to adjust accordingly. In other words, it'll probably do whatever you want it to do as long as you don't think of what you need directly. When operating a Whatsit you must remember to concentrate on relaxing. It's a little like driving a bicycle on the Autobahn, blindfolded. Otherwise, I'm afraid I'm a little fuzzy on the details."

Dinsdale handed the Whatsit to Wil, who scowled at the device, just to make it clear who was in charge around here, before thrusting it into his pocket.

"You know, Mr. Dinsdale, this all sounds delightfully bananas but I'm kinda monkeyed out this week. You're asking me—"

"And your groovy assistant," interjected Lucy, quickly.

"—and my groovy assistant, minus her trained cat," continued Wil with a sigh, "to break into someone's building and steal some ancient paperwork that probably crumbled into nothingness sometime around 1957!"

"My goodness! Where did you hear that? Is it true? Oh, calamity!"

"No, I'm not saying it's true. I'm saying we need a plan. Waltzing into someone's office building with absolutely no idea of the layout— not to mention the security systems—is akin to suicide. We could get shot and killed in there!"

"Aha!" yelled Mr. Dinsdale. He slapped his thigh in a show of enthusiasm that would have made a circus ringmaster blush. "But you don't get killed, do you? In fact, you most definitely survive. We know that Lucy sends us a telephone message from the future, which proves at the moment she sends it that you're both alive. Or at least she is!"

"Gee, thanks."

"I'm sure she would have mentioned it if you were dead. Anyway, I rather feel we must do as she's going to ask and bring SARA's charging cord with you. We'll add it to the pile."

Wil looked at the pile in question. The addition of SARA's charging cord was in danger of becoming a tipping point, he felt, to the mountain of objects Mr. Dinsdale had assembled in the middle of the Curioddity Museum's lobby. Over at the register, Mary Gold smacked her gum and tried to topple the pile with a few disdainful looks. The three Roberts stood to one side, flushed with the effort of retrieving various items from various floors of the museum.

The pile comprised sundry widgets pulled from their exhibit cases, and it most certainly did not create any feelings of confidence. At its base—covered by a wide variety of scrap—sat the Civil War periscope, a device that demonstrated the bizarre property of being able to see underneath the ground the farther one raised it up. Wil felt the chances of this particular item being useful during the upcoming festivities to be slimmer than a Hollywood actress preparing for a red carpet event. And he further felt that the cumbersome periscope was far and away the most useful item of the lot.

In addition to the periscope was a veritable cornucopia of the most amazing inventions mankind had ever shunned, reviled, or completely ignored. There was a top hat capable of turning into a large brown curtain as long as no one was looking. According to Mr. Dinsdale, the curtain would immediately turn back into a top hat if a bystander looked directly at it. To all intents and purposes, this incredible exhibit simply appeared as a top hat inside its regular display case, since no one had ever seen it in curtain form.

A small, innocuous-looking toolbox contained a series of ratchets, wrenches, and screwdrivers once belonging to world-famous escapologist Harry Houdini. The tools entertained the remarkable property of being able to unscrew screws, loosen nuts, and pop off various retaining bolts that Mr. Houdini would have encountered during his various attempts to drown in public. Wil had neither the energy nor the heart to inform Mr. Dinsdale that the "remarkable" properties ascribed to the tools were the very things any ordinary set of tools were supposed to possess in the first place.

Adding to the fun was a leopard whistle that could only be used to attract small dogs ever since it had been slightly dented in the middle. Again, Wil felt that pointing out the item was more than likely just a dog whistle was simply spoiling the fun, considering Mr. Dinsdale's obvious enthusiasm for the object.

Mr. Dinsdale had thoughtfully assembled a sewing kit containing famed mathematician Alan Turing's Quantum Needle. According to Dinsdale, Mr. Turing had worked as a part-time reality tailor after the Second World War, darning unraveled superstring, and generally making a nuisance of himself to the Nobel Prize committees of the time. The Quantum Needle was theoretically used to repair any tears in the fabric of the space-time continuum, though how it actually worked in the field was a matter of some debate. When Wil had pressed the question, Mr. Dinsdale had simply mumbled, "quantum physics," which seemed to be his standard response to any question he didn't know the answer to.

Capping off the enormous pile was a plastic bag full of useless items of indeterminate origin. These items had all been hastily placed inside the bag, upon which was written the legend "kit and caboodle." An old plastic bottle of window cleaner, a crystal ball, and a rainbow lollipop stuck out the top of the assortment. Wil suspected the word "caboodle" (like the word "muster") would not prove to mean that which he expected—it was probably old English slang that had something to do with explosives. Lucy raised her eyebrows in response to his concerned look as if to say, *This is going to be the greatest—not to mention wackiest—thing I have ever done in my entire life, and you'd better not spoil it, mister.* Wil found himself surprised by Lucy's sophisticated body language, and hoped that she and Mary Gold never got to semaphoring about him behind his back.

Inside Wil's pocket, the Whatsit beeped, plaintively. Mr. Dinsdale carefully placed a small wooden pocket watch on top of the bag of odds and ends so that the pile wobbled slightly, as if threatening to topple over and detonate all of its caboodles. Had it accomplished this, Wil felt, the universe would have clearly made its point: this was a futile endeavor—ill conceived and ever so slightly illegal. The pile of useless items could not possibly prove to be the salvation of the museum; it would more likely prove to be the museum's downfall in a very meaningful and ignitable way.

"You might need this Sequitur," said Mr. Dinsdale of the wooden watch. "It can be useful against the weak-minded. But don't expose it to sunlight or it loses its effect."

"What the heck is a Sequitur?" asked Wil, growing ever more impatient by the moment.

"It brings people to a conclusion of an inference," replied Dinsdale, proudly. "All you have to do, in theory, is lead someone with little to no imagination on a critical dialogue path and the Sequitur will take care of the rest. Just dangle it in front of their face, as if you're trying to hypnotize them."

"Does it work?"

"Theoretically, yes. But there might be a couple of side effects."

"Like what?"

"Studies are inconclusive. The last time I used it was on a marine biologist and ever since I've had a hankering to go deep-sea diving. It's probably nothing."

Wil shook his head, determined to stick to his task: namely, moaning about the situation with the faint hope of changing it. "I still think this is nuts," he muttered in Mr. Dinsdale's vague direction. "It doesn't matter if we have all the Sequiturs and Whatsits in the world. How are we supposed to find some old document you need if we have no idea where it's kept?"

"Let's start with the phone book," countered Dinsdale as he moved toward Mary Gold's information desk. "I'm sure Marcus James's corporate offices are listed in it somewhere."

"No, I didn't mean his offices—I meant this old electricity bill you're looking for . . ." Wil's voice trailed off, abruptly. He narrowed his eyes. "Wait a minute. You mean to tell me you don't even know where his offices are? You don't even know what they look like?"

"I've never felt the desire to track him down. I'm not sure it was ever relevant," replied Dinsdale, innocently. Seeing Wil's reaction, Lucy stifled a giggle.

"It's probably relevant," said Wil, patiently, "because if the offices are offshore we're unlikely to make it there in the next few hours—"

"Found them!" interrupted Dinsdale. Next to the register sat an old-style telephone directory. The old man peered at the pages a little closer, just to make sure. "Why, what a coincidence! They're in the penthouse of the Castle Towers! That ought to come in handy!"

Wil was beginning to suspect Mr. Dinsdale had known this all along, even to the point of recruiting him in the first place simply because he happened to rent an office in Marcus James's building. He resolved to keep his suspicions to himself.

Dinsdale motioned the three Roberts forward. "Bobby," he said to the first, "I want you, Bob, and Robbie to load this gear into Miss Price's Pinto. Call Robert and Roberto up from the basement if you need their help. We need to be on the road in four minutes."

Bobby nodded, and he and his fellow Roberts moved to extract items from the pile before heading toward the revolving door with armloads of useless detritus. "Mr. Dinsdale," said Lucy, intrigued, as the group followed the Roberts toward the revolving door, "how come all of your workers are called Robert?"

"It began as a clerical error, actually. A number of years ago, we decided the museum should be fully automated. It wasn't really a cost-cutting measure. Mary and I just really like all that newfangled electronic stuff. We keep a database of all our exhibits in a cloud, you know."

"What does that have to do with all the Roberts?"

"Well, we sent away to the Internet to order a multipack of industrial automatons but there was a typographical error. Instead of being sent twenty robots, twenty different Roberts showed up at our door from the employment agency. We thought for a while about swapping them out but I've grown rather fond of having them around. Plus, you can always rely on someone named Robert. It's scientific fact. Come on."

⌘

AT THE exit to the museum, Wil and Lucy moved very carefully through the revolving door, each making sure to give the other a wide berth as Mr. Dinsdale breezed through. While the Roberts loaded the backseat of Lucy's rusty Pinto, they paused for a moment to take stock (something Wil was extremely good at). Wil was about to go on a hair-raising thrill ride with a beautiful girl—one that would include moments of triumph and moments of abject defeat. He was about to run blindly into the line of fire, to throw caution to the wind—to do the very things his father had spent the better part of his life advising him not to do, assuming he survived the trip inside the Pinto to the Castle Towers.

One of the Roberts held the driver's-side door open. "Good luck, sir . . . madam," he said in the respectful voice of a colonel about to send his men on a suicide mission.

"Why, thank you, Bob!" said Lucy as she made her way toward the driver's side.

"I wish you both the best of luck!" exclaimed Mr. Dinsdale, proudly.

Wil gulped, sensing he would need every bit of luck he could scrape together, and then some. "Lucy," he began, innocently, "I get a little vertigo in the passenger seat. Would you mind if I drove?"

She fixed him with a maniacal glare. "No one drives Genghis," she said, coldly. "No one but his mistress."

"Genghis? Your Pinto has a name?"

"Yup."

"Why Genghis?" asked Wil, suspecting he already knew the answer.

"Because he brutalizes his enemies into submission and takes no prisoners!" Lucy replied happily, climbing in behind the wheel. "Come on."

Wil rolled his eyes as he climbed into the passenger seat. He'd only guessed half-right. "Please don't kill us before we get there," he said, plaintively. "I'd hate to see all these exhibits go up in a ball of flames."

"Just fasten your seat belt," muttered Lucy as she began to get into the swing of things. Wil checked his seat belt, and then he reached in his pocket for SARA. He wrapped the charging cord around the smartphone, just to give her the illusion of safety, and placed her back in his pocket with the Whatsit. "SARA," he said, quietly so as not to draw any attention, "please switch off your navigation system. Trust me: you'll thank me later."

"*Acknowledged, Wil Morgan,*" replied SARA in her best metallic tone. "*And thank you for your consideration.*"

As the engine puttered, then roared, into life, Mr. Dinsdale waved. "Good luck!" he called. "Drive safely!"

"Get bent!" yelled Lucy before gunning the engine and roaring off in the direction of the one-way system at speeds only imagined by aerospace engineers.

❧

THE FORD Pinto careened drunkenly from the end of Upside-Down Street, where it narrowly avoided a few innocent passenger vehicles as it staked its claim to the divided highway. Lucy floored the accelerator and set off toward the Castle Towers with her hands gripping the steering wheel in something approximating a headlock. Wil could only assume she was searching for a pickup truck driver or two to terrify along the way but he didn't have the nerve to challenge her authority in such a confined space.

With his life once again flashing before his eyes, he considered his options. They seemed limitless, which wasn't as attractive a proposition as he might have previously imagined. For one thing, Wil could imagine a thousand nasty fates that might befall him—not to mention the crazed harridan sitting next to him at the wheel of the rusted death trap—before the evening was through. Being inside the Pinto engendered feelings similar to that of sitting atop a metal tea tray, and while the results might be the same, the outcome of the eventual crash would undoubtedly be far more painful. In the unlikely event that the car made landfall at some point—and in the even more unlikely event that Genghis remained upright throughout—the thought of breaking and entering into Marcus James's penthouse headquarters would seem like a vacation in comparison to this chaotic journey.

Concentrate on relaxing, thought Wil. Concentrate on relaxing. Mr. Dinsdale's concept seemed like a curious thing to suggest, but in fact, it carried a certain kind of logic. Surely these would be the thoughts going through the mind of a professional golfer armed with a brand-new Air-Max 3000 and a one-stroke advantage going into the final hole? If golf were simply a matter of concentration, then a golfer would probably get all flummoxed trying to calculate wind speed and vectoring their golf ball to factor in the Earth's rotation. And if a person simply relaxed, a golf ball might end up in the middle of a nearby road. Wil smiled to himself; he'd learned an awful lot about golf this particular week despite never having unwrapped his original Air-Max 2000.

However, while he was beginning to enjoy the madcap ride inside the rusted Pinto, there was something else that nagged at his brain—a particular feeling that refused to go away. His occipital lobe had manfully defended the fortress against this intrusive feeling for a few hours but had eventually needed to call in reinforcements. For a brief while, Wil's Strange Sense of déjà vu had taken up the cause and had tried to send this nagging feeling packing. But the feeling was persistent: if Wil had learned anything this week, it was that sometimes one must do the least logical thing possible. The least logical thing in this particular case would be to interrupt the girl of his dreams while she was busy trying to carve images of her Pinto into the sides of other vehicles. The least sensible course of action—given the time constraints, and the urgency by which Wil and Lucy needed to get to the Castle Towers—would be to take a detour.

The Pinto crossed the median, veered into the far sidewalk, slid around a massive telephone pole, avoiding it by inches, and roared onto a back street. Wil looked at Lucy, terrified out of his wits.

"I need to make a detour," he said.

"Shut up! I know the way," replied the demon in a foul, guttural tone that only vaguely approximated the voice of the person harboring it.

"I don't mean a shortcut! I mean a detour!"

"There's no time! Just do it out of the window!"

"I'm not talking about bodily fluids! I'm talking about something really important! Will you please slow down and listen to me?"

"Stop talking to me! You're going to make us crash!"

"Lucy!" yelled Wil with as much force as he could push into his diaphragm. "I need to make a detour! Now!"

The rusted Ford Pinto suddenly screeched to a complete stop—one so abrupt that Wil barely had time to imagine half of the vehicle's front tires being scrubbed off on the tarmac before his nose hit the front console. He grunted with pain as a bag full of assorted caboodles smashed into his skull in the exact place he'd already been hit multiple times during the week.

And then, silence. The city around them seemed to exist in a vacuum for a moment, as if it were hiding from what might potentially be an explosion of epic proportions. Lucy turned, slowly, to face Wil. Trembling, he reached out to switch off the engine and pulled out the key in the hope that this would release his new girlfriend from the demon's thrall.

"No one touches my ignition switch," said Lucy, coldly. "Not unless they want me to pull the fingers off their hand one by one." With that, she suddenly grinned, leaned forward, and planted a kiss on Wil's cheek. "It's a good job you're cute," she said, and winked.

"Lucy? Is that really you?" asked Wil. "Are you back?"

"I'm sorry. People always tell me I get carried away when I'm driving."

"That's an understatement. Mice tend to get carried away by owls. Sitting in a car with you is a bit more like being dragged away by a congregation of alligators."

"Yeah. Sorry. Why did we stop again? I think I kinda missed something back there."

Wil chanced a look in the street behind them. Judging by all the damage Lucy's Pinto had done, she hadn't missed much. He exhaled slowly. "I need to make a detour," he said for the third time.

"But what about the museum? We need to get to the Castle Towers. We're running out of time."

"Lucy, listen to me: you're right. I know this is a really bad idea. Every instinct I have tells me so. But for some crazy reason, I think there's something I'm supposed to do first. Can you understand that?"

Lucy pondered for a split second, then grinned again. "Sure," she said. "Nothing else about this evening makes any sense. What do you have in mind?"

"We need to stop off somewhere," said Wil, brandishing the Pinto's ignition key. "And this time, I'll drive."

❧

SEVEN MINUTES later, Genghis sat outside the Waterbury Hotel near the train station and dreamed of mowing down innocent pedestrians while its mistress and her new boyfriend embarked on a secondary fool's errand. Upstairs in the Waterbury, things were not going according to plan.

Wil had had a difficult week, to be sure. If his initial encounter with Mr. Dinsdale and the Curioddity Museum had rocked his world like a seventies punk rock band might rock a kindergarten music class, then this sidebar maneuver was more akin to farting loudly in the middle of an opera. It took until the fifteenth knock for Barry Morgan to even admit he was inside his hotel room. As Wil rightly assumed, his father was in no mood for a discussion.

"But Dad," pleaded Wil as Lucy looked on with concern, "I'm just asking you to listen. Please. Just hear me out."

"I've already heard enough for one lifetime, Wil," replied Barry through the thick panel of the hotel door. "It's best if you go about your business and let me go about mine for a couple of weeks."

Wil stood back from the door, knowing that a couple of weeks in "Dad" time would eventually escalate into a couple of years. This was not going to be simple, and neither had he expected it to be. But he somehow knew that if he were to go back inside the Castle Towers in search of Mr. Dinsdale's saving grace—perhaps never to be seen again—then he needed to make things right with his father first.

Wil shrugged, hoping that Barry might at least peer through the keyhole window. "Look, Dad . . . I know things went a bit sideways. I said something I shouldn't have said. And it doesn't matter if I said it, it just matters if you believe I didn't mean it."

"Oh?" replied Barry in the most faux-confrontational manner available to him. "And which one of the things you said was the one you didn't mean? Because you didn't confine yourself to just one inappropriate comment, Wilbur."

Lucy looked at Wil, her eyebrows raised, and mouthed the word "Wilbur" with a questioning look. "My middle name's Aloysius," he informed her. "Laugh it up."

"Who are you talking to out there?" asked Barry from within.

"Dad, listen to me. I may have been wrong to say what I said about you and Mom but I was right about one thing, and we both know it: I can write down on a piece of paper how this is going to go. It'll be the way it always goes. You'll pretend everything's okay but you're going to take years to forgive me. Even though you're wrong."

"Oh, so I'm somehow wrong because you lied to me about your income, your housing situation, your means of employment, and your retirement plan?"

WIL THOUGHT for a moment in silence, while Lucy watched him, expectantly. She was obviously waiting for his rebuttal but little did she know that rebutting Barry Morgan with common sense was somewhat like playing Led Zeppelin to a walrus and expecting it to sing *Stairway to Heaven*. It just wasn't going to happen unless all participants were prepared to experience some setbacks. Wil needed to try a new approach, and do the opposite of what his instincts were telling him.

"You're right, Dad," he said softly through the door. "Almost everything I told you about myself was a lie. But I never really wanted to lie, and I don't want to lie to you now. I want you to know the truth." Wil found Lucy's eyes filled with equal parts moisture and concern. And in that moment he found everything he had ever wanted to say. "I've found someone, Dad," he said, gauging Lucy's eyes as they overflowed with little tears of happiness. "And she's the one. Her name's Lucy Price and she's standing out here with me. All I can say is that this is the first time I ever really understood what you lost, and I'm sorry."

Lucy's hand clasped tighter around Wil's, and she pulled him close. "I'm sorry, too," she whispered. And then, for a brief moment, she furrowed her brow. "Is it possible to be sorry and happy at the same time?"

"I guess so," whispered Wil in reply. "It's probably like sitting in the passenger seat next to you when you're driving."

Through the door, Wil could almost feel Barry's calculated silence losing out to an incalculable resignation. After a moment, Barry slumped down against the wooden frame with a loud thump.

"Dad?" said Wil, nervously. "Are you okay?"

The hotel hallway now slipped into an unearthly silence as Barry Morgan sat against the door frame, presumably trying to decide how to let the years of anguish slip away from his shoulders. "You know I loved your mother, Wil," he said. "More than anyone should ever be allowed to love someone. Perhaps you really do understand how much it hurt me to lose her. But what you don't understand is that I lost her before I could tell her all the things I needed to say."

Wil felt the tears welling up inside him, unbidden. "Neither of us did, Dad. I guess I've spent all these years wishing I could still have her around me. But I never really thought she was dead. Not for as long as I kept her alive by being the person she knew."

"Wil," said Barry Morgan quietly. "I want you to hear something that I've never told you before. As much as you think I never wanted you to be your mother's son, you're wrong. And you always have been. It's not that I didn't want you to be yourself, to have that ridiculous imagination that cost me thousands of dollars in fire insurance—"

"You're talking about that thing with the exploding pancakes, aren't you? I told you I'd pay you back."

"Yes, I am. But despite the monetary costs and the frequent trips to the hospital, and the unexpected loud noises coming from the garage, I always wanted you and your mom to do the things you did. The truth is, I tried to join in. But I just didn't have the imagination. I used to listen to all that noise you made, and see all the crazy lights coming from the shed, and all I ever wanted was to be a part of it. I was jealous of the bond you and your mom shared."

Wil reflected for a moment, unaware that this was only the first of two revelations coming his way. It was certainly heavy enough to warrant its own moment of silence. "Dad," he said, faltering, "imagination doesn't belong to people special enough to understand it. It belongs to everyone. Anyone who learns to un-look at things properly can see magic. You just never tried it, and that's not your fault."

"Wil," said Barry with a weight of sadness that only a parent can know, "I tried as hard as I could. Who do you think bought you the Tesla Kit?"

AND ONLY in this moment—only in the moment when a man listens to his father's side of events for the very first time as an adult—did Wil Morgan finally, truly understand. For all these years he had assumed his father had closed every door to his imagination. But that wasn't what had happened at all: his father had simply never known how to open any of those doors to begin with. Barry Morgan had never learned how to un-look at the world, and so the world that stared back at him was a cold and featureless place. His father's universe was full of numbers and logic; and while those things did not necessarily disqualify the existence of magic, they definitely made the magic more difficult to see.

"Wil," said Lucy, gently, "we have to go now. I think your dad needs a little time to think it over."

Wil stepped back from the door and grasped Lucy's hand, grateful for her wisdom. He silently thanked all the idiot boyfriends she'd ever had for not being able to un-look at her properly to see what he saw. "We're leaving now," he said, quietly. "I have to help Mr. Dinsdale at the Curioddity Museum, and we're running out of time. I wish you wouldn't go home on the train just yet but if you have to go, I under-stand why. If everything works out, I hope you and Lucy can meet face-to-face soon enough."

"Thank you, Wil," replied Barry Morgan softly. "Thank you for having the sense to come and talk me back into mine. I'll think about all of this, I promise."

"Bye, Mr. Morgan!" called Lucy, weakly. "It was nice to meet you!"

"Goodbye, Lucy. I'm sure we'll meet in person soon—it's been a difficult couple of days."

❧

WIL RETRIEVED the Perpetual Penny from his pocket and slowly bent down to the old wooden flooring in the hotel hallway. He thought of his mother helping him with his ill-conceived experiments in a cold garage. He thought of his father listening to stock market reports on an old-style band radio. He thought of marshmallow, and hot chocolate, and family holidays. He thought of his mom's beautiful, benevolent smile. And that magical time he'd sat with his dad at the edge of a weir and watched salmon spawning upstream—flashing past, like glistening silver dollars, almost close enough to touch. He thought of all the things his dad meant to him, and realized in that instant those things were exactly the same as his mom. And then he spun.

"Dad," he said. "There's something here in the hallway that Mom wanted you to see." And with that, he and Lucy moved away to the steps leading down to the hotel foyer and descended into silence.

LEAVING BARRY Morgan with a chance to rediscover the magic for himself.

CHAPTER THIRTEEN

THE JOURNEY to the Castle Towers was always going to be uneventful, if potentially volatile. Wil had rarely driven the one-way system in the years he'd lived in the city but he knew it well for all the times he'd trudged along its sidewalks. Sensing his somber mood, Lucy let him take the wheel of her beloved Ford Pinto while she growled at passing pickup trucks. And so, in the ten or so minutes it took to navigate the one-way system and arrive at the base of the Castle Towers, Wil did what he did best and decided to be a pessimist, perhaps for one last time.

"It's not going to work," he said to no one in particular, ignoring the fact there was at least one person within earshot.

"What's not going to work?" replied Lucy.

"My dad. He won't find the penny. I'm not good at flamboyant gestures. Some random hotel patron picked it up and now my dad's probably standing outside of his hotel room door, looking at a bare wooden floor and reconsidering."

Lucy pondered this for a moment. "You kissed me on our first date," she reminded him. "That was pretty flamboyant."

"No, I didn't. You kissed me."

"Well, I don't remember you complaining about it!"

"Of course not!"

"Then why are you complaining about this?"

FOR A moment, Wil wrestled with Lucy's Dinsdalian logic. He glanced toward her and found her staring out of her passenger-side window, glaring at the city and doing her best not to climb out of either her skin or her car door. Judging by the fingernail scratches on the dashboard and her phantom attempts to apply the brakes at every opportunity, she was not enjoying herself one little bit. But Wil was grateful to her nonetheless; ceding control of her rage-mobile was an early act of generosity in their relationship. He smiled at the thought of such a personable and gregarious soul undergoing this demonic transformation when introduced to the inside of her rusty old Ford Pinto. Piloting Genghis to roadway domination was a far better outlet than tantrums, property damage, or reckless gun ownership. From her anklet to her brown, curly hair, Lucy Price was perfect for him in every way.

As the car closed in on the Castle Towers, Wil took in the world around him, if only for one final time. Pan's statue loomed large, and from the angle afforded by driving inside the one-way system, his private parts loomed even larger. Wil pondered for a moment on the concept of un-looking, and wondered if it were the same as unseeing. If so, he would have paid good money to unsee Pan's generous undercarriage.

Gretchen appeared at the front of her shop as they passed. Her flower store now looked like a jungle full of creepers, vines, and purple orchids that reached back inside the door for as far as the eye could see. A little glowing wisp—of the same kind Wil had seen inside the Curioddity Museum—wandered out for a moment and darted back inside. Gretchen looked at her watch, and then looked up at the nearby clock before floating back inside and locking the front door.

Following her gaze, Wil peered up toward the Swiss monstrosity to find its laser-like beam shooting from the top of the tower and up into the night sky, and the dissonant whining sound at full pitch. The air once again seemed charged with electricity, as if the clock were preparing for a storm of some kind—or concocting it, perhaps. According to the actual working part of the clock, the time was three minutes until ten o'clock, give or take any conversion to European metric time. The Castle Towers would be mostly empty apart from Mr. Whatley and a couple of stragglers at this time of night. The bad news was that Wil and Lucy had three minutes to get inside the lobby before the nightly lockdown.

Wil pulled Genghis up to a side street, where he knew there would be one or two free parking spaces.

"Why don't you park out front?" asked Lucy, trying her best not to sound combative.

"I think it's best we don't give anyone a chance to connect your Pinto to whatever we're about to do," replied Wil. "Besides, Genghis can look out for this side of the building and kill anyone who tries to interfere."

Lucy giggled. It was a sound that Wil was getting used to, and one that he hoped he never would. At least some of his jokes were getting through, though he suspected this was only the beginning of a long battle between he and his new girlfriend regarding vehicular activity in particular, and trying to stay alive in general.

At the parking spot, they grabbed as much of Dinsdale's pile of useless items as they could possibly manage. Wil stood a respectful distance while Lucy gave Genghis a few instructions on how to behave. He took a moment to check his pockets, just to be sure.

In one pocket, the triangular Whatsit beeped occasionally, which gave Wil absolutely no clue whatsoever as to its usefulness. In the other pocket, SARA glowed, wrapped in her charging cord. Wil strapped the Civil War periscope to his back and thought of every ninja movie he had ever watched; unless he had missed something significant, ninjas very rarely carried large lumps of metal on their backs. He and Lucy were beginning their evening activities at a competitive disadvantage. He rummaged through the kit and caboodle container but found nothing of interest and many items of utter pointlessness, such as a lump of bluish clay, some copper wire, two paper clips, and a vacuum bag. The wooden Sequitur glared back at him, making him wish he'd asked for the invisible Non Sequitur device as a backup. Whatever use these items were intended for, he hoped he might decipher it by the end of the evening (or at least before his death at the hands of an angry security guard).

Lucy approached, carrying her half of the pile. She seemed eager, and up for the task of being shot on sight inside a strange building. "Okay, you know the layout of the building. How do we get inside?" she said.

Wil hadn't really given it much thought, and it showed. "Through the lobby, I guess," he replied. "I mean I rent an office on the nineteenth floor. I have every right to go inside."

"Can't we sneak in?"

"Why?"

"Because I thought we'd be sneaking. It's not going to look good on my detective résumé if I just sidle up to the front door, wave hello to the heavily armed ninja-bots on guard, and walk inside."

"We don't have any ninja-bots."

"I'm not surprised. They probably all quit. The people who own the building keep letting strangers waltz in through the front door."

Lucy headed for the front door, trying to look as sullen as possible. Wil watched her for a moment, amused by her ability to make even the most mundane moment seem a little brighter. Having no other choice, he followed her toward the lobby in time to find Mr. Whatley moving to the front door with his master key. The building janitor was the most punctual and unimaginative person Wil had ever met, and he could be relied upon to stick to the most mundane of tasks. Within seconds, Wil was completely overmatched.

"Hello, Mr. Whatley," he said, cheerily. "I just need to grab something from my office!"

"Wish I could oblige, Mr. Morgan," said Mr. Whatley, putting the key in the lock. "But I'm under strict instructions to lock the building down at ten tonight. Landlord's orders."

"I won't be a moment. I just have to run up and right back down again."

"Sorry, sir," said Mr. Whatley, tightening the key in the lock. "Can't let you in at this late hour. It's more than my job's worth."

Wil narrowed his eyes. If Mr. Dinsdale at the Curioddity Museum were to be believed, this would be the precise moment he should do something entirely random and unexpected. Thus, he found himself asking a question that only two or three days previously he would never have considered in a million years (give or take two or three days): what would Mr. Dinsdale do? He fished the Sequitur from its plastic bag, closed his eyes, and shook his head in his disbelief. Swallowing hard, he held the Sequitur up against the glass door. "How about that game last night?" he said with as much artificial conviction as he could muster. "Did you see that last play?"

"What game?" asked Mr. Whatley, immediately suspicious. "I didn't see anything on the highlights."

"You know. They had the highlights on all day."

There was a brief pause. "Oh. That game."

Wil looked up, and could barely believe his eyes—Mr. Whatley seemed transfixed by the wooden object being dangled in front of his face. Wil decided to press the advantage. "I can't believe they missed that shot right at the end of the game, can you?" He took one small step toward the door.

"Oh, right!" exclaimed Lucy, presumably figuring she would go with whatever opportunity seemed to be presenting itself. "That guy is such a choke artist!"

"He is?" replied Mr. Whatley, confused. "Not Patterson again? Please tell me Patterson didn't blow another game!"

"The very same," said Wil, as he gently pushed against the door, opening it slightly. He smiled sweetly. "It's a good job his teammates have his back, though. That play was unbelievable."

"Righteous!" agreed Lucy, enthusiastically. "Especially number seventeen. He's a stud."

"Wilkerson?" exclaimed Mr. Whatley, incredulous. "Wilkerson's a backup."

"Not after that final play last night, he's not," continued Lucy. Wil could see she was getting lost in the moment. "Best put-back slam dunk I ever saw in my life!"

"But he's a goalie!" exclaimed Mr. Whatley. "A hockey goalie."

"That's what made that play so epic."

By now, Lucy and Wil had edged their way inside the lobby and were slowly backing toward the elevators as Wil dangled the Sequitur high above his head. Poor Mr. Whatley looked very confused as he stared transfixed at the wooden object. Things were beginning to head sideways, as they always did whenever Wil felt he was about to accomplish something positive.

"Well, I'd love to stay and chat, Mr. Whatley," he said, "but I have to get home in time to watch the playoffs."

Never taking her eyes off the building manager, Lucy could only smile and try to look as generally innocent as possible. "What the heck are we doing?" she hissed in Wil's direction as they backed toward the main lobby.

"Making small talk," hissed Wil in return. "I think his brain is filling in the missing pieces. Just keep smiling."

Over at the door, Mr. Whatley's brain was beginning to ask itself difficult questions, none of which it seemed to like the answer to.

"Wait a minute," he said, faltering, "didn't we trade Wilkerson last month for a winger?"

"It's a good job we did after last night!" said Wil, unconvincingly. "See you in the morning!"

Thankfully, he and Lucy had managed to back their way around a nearby corner. They stepped hastily to one side and were obscured by random cubicles, allowing them just enough space to check on Mr. Whatley. The confused custodian stood at the door for a few moments longer before turning and locking it. With puzzlement written across his face, he pocketed his keys, muttered something about point spreads, and headed off to his tiny office to catch up on the latest events in the playoffs. Wil supposed Mr. Whatley was in for a minor letdown.

"I feel guilty," said Lucy, feeling guilty. "What did we just do?"

"I don't know," replied Wil. "But once we get out of this let's go to a hockey game."

"It's a date."

Looking around, Wil and Lucy found themselves roughly fifty feet from the elevators. But they were not alone. To Wil's astonishment, the comb-over twins sat at their eternal chess game, lost in concentration. He pointed them out to Lucy.

"We'll have to sneak past," he whispered. "Just keep low. They look pretty busy."

Lucy nodded, and took the lead. She lowered her head below the level of the nearest cubicle and headed along a roundabout route that would take them to the elevators. As Wil followed, trying to keep the Civil War periscope on his back from poking up above the level of the cubicles, his eyes strayed toward the comb-over brothers. Looking below table level, Wil could now see that neither of the twins actually possessed feet—they were attached at the knees, and this, presumably, explained why they never moved away from the lobby. This incredible sight caused Wil to trip over his bag of kit and caboodle, and he crashed to the floor in a very loud and disoriented heap.

At the sound of Wil's nasty tumble, one of the twins looked vaguely in his direction. The man's eyes alighted on Wil's position, yet he seemed to look directly through Wil, as if not seeing him at all. Wil stood up, just to see if he was imagining things.

"What are you doing?" hissed Lucy. "Get down! They'll see us!"

"No, it's okay. I don't think they can," replied Wil. "Take a look."

He motioned toward the chess game, where the two brothers were looking decidedly confused. It appeared as if they had heard the commotion Wil had made but could not perceive that Wil and Lucy were present.

Wil moved toward them, quietly. The brothers simply returned to their chess game unaware of anything, it seemed, outside their little bubble of space and time. Intrigued, Lucy followed Wil and stood at the side of the table where the brothers continued to study their board.

"What's going on?" asked Lucy. "Who are these guys?"

"I'm not sure," replied Wil. "I see them here every day but I'm not really sure they're aware of me. Look."

He waved his hand in front of one brother's face. No response.

"Must be a pretty intense game," concluded Lucy.

"I don't think it's that. Maybe it's just a feeling but I don't think these guys are living in the same universe that we are. I have a roommate like that. He really seems to like mushrooms."

"Okay, that makes no sense at all."

"Want to see something else that makes no sense? Take a look under the table."

Lucy obliged, and emerged with her face as white as a sheet. "Okay, that was unexpected," she said in a somewhat understated fashion. "How do they go to the bathroom?"

"Very carefully, I would imagine. Come on. We need to get to the top floor."

Wil moved away. On a whim, Lucy considered the chessboard in front of the strange comb-over brothers and toppled over the black king, just to see what would happen. The brothers looked around them, startled. Not wishing to push her luck, Lucy quickly backed away.

As they approached the elevators, Wil could tell Lucy was having a little bit of a crisis. "This doesn't make any sense," she muttered. "What's going on around here?"

"It's the Curioddity Museum," said Wil. "I think once you visit, you begin to see things differently. Every time I leave, it's like I take a little piece of it with me."

Lucy pondered this for roughly two seconds, then pressed the elevator button. "Actually, that makes a lot of sense," she said, rapidly reversing course. "At least the museum is easier to accept than all that stuff on TV about the economy and airborne viruses."

Wil chuckled. Lucy was the most random person he had ever met, with the possible exception of his mother and Mr. Dinsdale. She was going to do just fine.

THE ELEVATOR soon became noticeable by its extended absence, and it did not take long before Wil realized the call button had failed to illuminate. He tried it a few more times, just for good measure. The button seemed equally adept at not lighting up the third time, just as it had excelled at not responding on the first two occasions. Wil sighed with relief. Making their way up to the penthouse may well prove to be slightly more challenging, he concluded, but at least neither he nor Lucy would succumb to the toxic fumes of the elevator's rat vomit.

"We need to find another way up," Lucy said, disappointed. "Any ideas?"

"Not really. I've only ever taken the elevator."

"What about the stairs?"

"There aren't any. Mr. Whatley says they were removed from the bottom three floors as a safety precaution."

"That doesn't seem sensible."

"And the rest of this evening does?"

"Point taken. Is there another elevator?"

"I don't know. I have no idea which way we're supposed to go."

"*Greetings, Wil Morgan,*" came a familiar metallic voice from inside Wil's pocket. "*Would you like me to look up 'which way am I supposed to go' on the Internet?*"

Wil removed SARA from his pocket and glared at her glowing screen. "SARA," he said with as much patience as he could marshal, "if this involves either Lahore, Pakistan, or anywhere in Korea, I'm warning you in advance I'm going to be a little testy. Do you have any idea how Lucy and I can get up to the top floor of this building, please?" Wil flipped on the Smart Response function of SARA's operating system and then added, hastily, "And please make sure it's something we stand a chance of surviving."

"*Calculating . . .*" SARA's various symbols and widgets glowed for a few moments as she pondered the problem. Wil felt it best to keep his expectations to a minimum. "*There are three possible paths to the upper floors of the Castle Towers at this time,*" SARA began. "*Are you equipped with a military helicopter?*"

"I think you probably know the answer to that," replied Wil, much to Lucy's amusement. "Try again. And this time, let's try something that won't get you thrown out of a top window once we get to the penthouse."

"*At the fourth level and above, the emergency stairs may be used to access the upper levels.*"

"And yet we're firmly entrenched on the first floor with no way to get to those levels, as I'm sure your GPS function has already told you."

"*Recalculating . . . ,*" said SARA, innocently.

"Wow," said Lucy, impressed. "She really is brilliantly mental, isn't she?"

"You have no idea," replied Wil, exasperated.

"*Do you have in your possession a liquid dispenser, some clay or putty, a nonconductive positioning rod, and two ordinary paper clips?*"

asked SARA, suddenly. Wil sensed a slight air of desperation hidden in her metallic tone, though he couldn't be sure.

"Well, of course we don't! Why on Earth would we—wait a minute . . ." Wil's voice trailed off. If he didn't know any better, the universe was setting him up to be the butt of some cosmic joke. He checked the contents of his plastic bag, where the requisite paper clips, surface cleaner bottle, and small lump of blue clay did their utmost to jump out and strangle his intellect by his desperately overtaxed cerebral cortex. They failed, but only as a result of the rainbow lollipop's inertia. "Okay, I have all of those items, SARA. Is this some kind of joke?"

"*Negative, Wil Morgan. A joke is the evolution of an unhealthy mind hankering after a spurious, epigrammatic turn of speech.*"

"I think that's sarcasm," said Lucy.

"*Negative,*" replied SARA. "*I am incapable of sarcasm. In addition to the aforementioned items, you will need—*"

"A coil of copper wire and a vacuum bag?" said Wil, interrupting.

"*Affirmative. Please follow the instructions on the screen for entrance to the upper floors of the Castle Towers.*"

Wil studied the screen, where a series of instructions appeared on the correct procedures for rigging and reprogramming the Mark Twelve Series of Industricorp Elevators. (It did not escape his attention that the author of these valuable instructions had uploaded them from Korea, but he chose to ignore this more-than-likely-irrelevant fact.) Wil looked up at the elevator door to be greeted with Industricorp's jaunty corporate logo, which looked suspiciously like that belonging to the people who owned Mug O' Joe's coffee shops. Things were beginning to come together, much like two planetoids might crash in the asteroid belt to form a loud explosion and a pile of tumbling space rocks. He dutifully placed a single paper clip inside the elevator button, and affixed it with some of the blue clay. Following this, he squirted some of the spray bottle's contents into the crevice, and he was only mildly surprised when sparks shot up his arm and gave him a minor electric shock. Moments later, the elevator doors rolled open, and the way to the penthouse floor beckoned like a vampire floating outside the window of a blood bank. Lucy mouthed the word "wow" silently, and stepped inside. Wil rolled his eyes to the heavens and followed her.

Inside the elevator, the stench of rat vomit threatened to overwhelm the senses. Lucy blinked through tears. "What the heck is that smell?" she said, clutching at her nose.

"Hang tight," replied Wil. "I'm told you get used to it by the time you've been here for twenty years or so."

Following SARA's instructions, Wil quickly depressed the buttons for every floor of the building, then jammed his second paper clip behind the topmost illuminated button. He wrapped the second clip with copper wire, as instructed. Then, he wrapped the wire around the nonconductive lollipop and fastened this entire contraption to the wall with more of the blue clay. The elevator doors closed, ominously. The elevator, however, remained motionless.

"It's not working," complained Wil. "SARA? Any ideas?"

"Please inflate the vacuum bag," replied SARA, "then press the button for the penthouse level."

Wil looked at the vacuum bag, not liking one little bit where this was going. "Okay, why am I doing this again?"

"Please inflate vacuum bag, as instructed."

"Better do as she says, Wil," said Lucy. "And please hurry. I think I'm going to faint."

"Okay, fine. Just don't encourage her." Wil inflated the bag as best he could, and was thoroughly winded by the time the deed was done. Closing his watering eyes, he reached for the button to the top floor. Suddenly, a massive jolt of electricity moved through his upper arms. A Tesla-style lightning effect played around his fillings, and the vacuum bag popped, loudly. Then, silence.

And suddenly, the elevator jolted upward. Wil opened his eyes to find a slightly amused Lucy Price trying her best not to be unsupportive.

"That was pretty impressive," said Lucy in an understated fashion. "I'm glad it wasn't me."

"Impressive?" said Wil, angrily. "I could have been killed!" he pulled the smartphone from his pocket to find the screen blank. "SARA, don't you even think about hiding right now. Did you know I was going to get an electric shock?"

The smartphone seemed to ponder for a second. Then, the screen glowed.

"*Apologies, Wil Morgan,*" replied SARA in a carefully measured tone, "*but choices were limited given your lack of a military helicopter. Your recent exposure to levity-conducting plasma ropes in the Curioddity Museum lobby lowered your risk of fatal shock by twenty-seven percent, with a two percent margin for error. Would you like me to look up 'shock therapy' on the Internet?*"

Lucy suddenly burst into a fit of little giggles. Wil looked at her in horror. "She almost killed me!" he whined.

"Yeah, but it got us moving."

"Aren't you in the least bit concerned?"

"Aw, poor little soldier. You're okay, aren't you?"

"Well, yes."

"Good. The quicker we get up, the quicker we can get out of this elevator. It smells like stomach acid in here." Despite her watering eyes and against the advice of her gag reflex, Lucy looked impressed. "I guess SARA's messages aren't just limited to texts and voice mails."

Wil held up the glowing screen of the phone, barely able to believe the notion that SARA had intended to make some kind of artificially intelligent point. And then, despite his better judgment, he began to stifle a chuckle, which became a giggle, and evolved into a guffaw.

And to the sound of uproarious hilarity, the Rat Vomit Comet made its way up to the penthouse floor, and almost certain death at the hands of an overzealous ninja-bot.

❧

AT THE top of the building, ninja-bots were nowhere to be seen. Instead, a rather surprised-looking secretary lifted her head from her latest hairdressing magazine to find two slightly red-faced intruders standing in front of her, coughing and spluttering. One of them seemed to be dangling a little wooden watch for reasons the secretary could not fully understand. Neither would she understand (nor pay it any further mind) just three minutes later once she had shown the two intruders to a small storage room, and returned to her position at the front desk. Throughout the course of resulting events, the secretary would vaguely remember being intrigued by mention of a new stylist at the corner of Main Street, and by an exciting pomade product that she felt she just had to purchase online as soon as her Friday paycheck cleared. Little did she realize at the time that small talk regarding hair and makeup products was a subtle form of mental manipulation at the hands of a wooden device known as a Sequitur.

For their part, each of the two intruders resolved to visit a hairdresser at the first opportunity, assuming they were neither killed nor arrested anytime soon. For the moment, they could only huddle inside the storage room and try to formulate the next part of their completely unplanned assault.

"What now?" asked Lucy, questioning the obvious.

"We have to find Marcus James's office. My guess is it'll be in one of the corners."

"Maybe we can climb around inside the air ducts like that guy did in that movie. That'd be really epic."

"Okay, first of all, 'that guy in that movie' got shot about sixty times. And second of all, we don't need to."

"Why not?" Lucy followed Wil's gaze to an open window, outside of which a fire escape led to the roof above. "What good will it do us being on the roof?" she asked.

Wil held up the Civil War periscope, and widened his eyes.

❧

MOMENTS LATER, Wil and Lucy stood atop the roof of the Castle Towers with the periscope extended upward as far as possible. From this vantage point, the floors below their feet could be seen as clear as day. Down below, there appeared to be a certain amount of confusion.

"What do you see?" asked Lucy, impatiently. "Why can't I have a look?"

"It's kind of bulky," replied Wil. "You'll just have to bear with me."

"Well, what are they doing down there? Have you found Marcus James's office?"

Wil had indeed found Marcus James's office, and more besides. Inside the office, stacks of new and improved Air-Max 4000 golf clubs waited for their moment. Piled next to them, various other new and improved products such as tubes of toothpaste, fleece throw blankets, waterproof smartphone cases, and rubberized drainpipe fixers begged the question of why their manufacturer hadn't done a better job of making a more robust product the first time around. For his part, Marcus James seemed to be having a moment. He checked his watch frequently as he paced up and down in front of his wall safe, which was protected by two tumbler-style combination locks. Every so often, Marcus would look outside his window at the obnoxious Swiss clock across from his position, and then reset his watch against it. Wil could hardly believe his eyes—surely it could not be this easy? For unless the synchronous nature of this week had all been for nothing, the safe was a virtual lock to contain the missing electricity bill that Mr. Dinsdale so coveted he was prepared to send virtual strangers to their deaths in an attempt to retrieve it. Marcus seemed to be counting down the moments, and his body language seemed to yell, *I am about to be the proud owner of a brand-new wing for my bank on Upside-Down Street, formerly the Curioddity Museum.* Though this was a complex choice of words, Wil supposed Marcus James's silent statement was only natural, given the factious nature of his personality.

As far as Wil could determine, Marcus's television studios were directly adjacent to his offices. It was from here that Marcus perpetuated his monetary assault on the planet in manageable chunks of $19.99.

The studios were well lit, and bustling with activity, suggesting that Mr. James was in the process of making ready for his evening session on the Shopping Network. An LED sign positioned above a door at the edge of the studio made it clear that the show was about to go live in exactly fourteen minutes. Upon closer inspection, Wil noticed something slightly odd about the various technicians, grips, and camera operators getting ready for this evening's broadcast.

He passed the periscope to Lucy. "Take a look," he said. "Tell me what you see."

For a moment, Lucy stared into the periscope with an eagerness that suggested she very much enjoyed snooping on people from above. Suddenly, her face took on a bewildered expression. "Wait a minute," she said. "Those guys working the camera: Are those aliens?"

Wil thanked the stars he wasn't the only one who'd noticed. "I think so," he said. "I think those are the gray ones Mr. Dinsdale was talking about."

"No, look! The gray ones are the producers. The guys on the cameras are green." One of the gray aliens looked upward, causing her to drop the periscope with a little yelp of alarm. "I think one of them saw me!"

Wil picked up the device. Much to his relief, the gray alien had found something better to do and was now berating one of the green ones for getting the lighting wrong. Tensions seemed to be running high on set, which Wil supposed was entirely normal from everything he'd heard about Hollywood. He also supposed that Hollywood being full of space aliens hiding in plain sight was probably considered "business as usual."

"What do you think they're doing here?" asked Lucy.

"Well, does it surprise you that space aliens are behind all the meaningless drivel we're bombarded with? How much of a revelation is it that they've befriended a cosmic frog like Marcus James?" Wil was getting into the swing of the weirdness now. "Maybe he's been betraying our planet, or something. Maybe he sold them all our water."

"Yeah. Probably," agreed Lucy, as if the concept were entirely normal. She pointed across the rooftops. "So d'you think they're responsible for what's going on over there?"

Wil looked up from the periscope to find Lucy motioning to the laser atop the giant clock across the street. Of course! It was all beginning to make sense, assuming a person was willing to accept that space aliens, secret laser beams, and the brainwashing of consumers made sense in the first place.

Wil looked back into the scope to find the TV pitchman was on the move again.

"Lucy!" cried Wil. "Keep me steady! He's going back into his offices!"

With the cumbersome periscope extended as far upward as possible, Wil wobbled across the roof, trying to follow Marcus James as he scooted inside his office. Down below, Marcus moved directly to his safe and began to fiddle with the two combination locks.

"What's going on? What's he doing?" asked Lucy.

"He's opening his safe! I can see the combination! Where's the focus on this thing?"

"What does this button do?"

"*The other one!*" called SARA from within Wil's pocket. By now, she had given up any pretense of disinterest and was gamely chiming in whenever a machine's touch was needed. The Whatsit beeped in response. Wil ignored it.

Lucy pressed the second button, and the periscope suddenly zoomed in on Marcus James's hand as he moved the wheel of the first combination lock. "SARA!" called Wil. "Please make a note of these numbers: Thirty-one! Fifty-four! Ninety-seven!"

"*Thirty-one. Fifty-four. Ninety-seven,*" repeated SARA, dutifully.

Marcus James moved to the second combination lock and began to fiddle with it. "Seventy-four! Thirty-four! Thirty-six!" yelled Wil.

"*Seventy-four. Thirty-four. Thirty-six,*" confirmed SARA.

Down below, Marcus James held up the old piece of paper, upon which Wil could faintly make out the legend "Edison Electric Company" and a date of sometime in the early 1890s. Marcus looked around, surreptitiously, and the moment he was certain no one was looking, he kissed the piece of yellowed paper, cackled maniacally, and placed it back inside the safe. He moved over to an open laptop computer on his desk, pressed Send on some electronic missive or other, and looked again at his watch. Wil was willing to admit—albeit grudgingly—that Marcus played the part of a nefarious villain to a T.

Down below, an alarm began to sound. "Ten minutes to broadcast!" came a strident voice over a loudspeaker system, accompanied by a series of very loud alarm signals. In the next room, the gray and green aliens were gearing up for transmission.

Now, the whining sound Wil and Lucy had heard coming from the Swiss clock began to rise in intensity. Suddenly, the huge laser beam quadrupled in size and shot directly upward through the clouds.

"It's a signal!" cried Wil. "They're helping him with his broadcasts! He's probably beaming through the cosmos!"

"You mean aliens play golf and buy fleece blankets?" said Lucy, confused.

"If Marcus James has anything to do with it, sure. Or at least they're making his signal stronger so that no one can resist his brainwashing. We have to stop him!"

"We have to get that electricity bill!" cried Lucy.

Wil chanced one more look through the periscope. With nine minutes to go down below, Marcus James had moved into the broadcast area, leaving his office empty.

"I hate that guy," said Wil, understating things as usual. "Let's go rock his world."

WIL AND Lucy moved across the roof and found the fire escape leading to the windows outside Marcus's now-empty office. The air was becoming massively charged with static electricity as a result of their proximity to the Swiss clock, which churned out volts, amps, and (probably) ohms at an alarming rate. As he descended toward possible death by ninja-bot, Wil fussed about the fact that his hair looked less than perfect standing on end, and resolved to visit a hairdresser at the earliest opportunity and buy some pomade. Preferably, one endorsed by a professional hockey player.

At the base of the first staircase, they peeked over the window ledge into Marcus's office: no one home. The coast was clear. The window, unfortunately, was locked.

"How do we get in?" asked Lucy. "Should we smash it?"

"It'd make too much noise," said Wil as he quickly checked inside his plastic bag and produced the crystal he'd seen earlier. He was beginning to find a new appreciation for useless objects. Affixing more of the blue clay to the window to act as a dampener, he described a large circular hole. The crystal cut through the glass like a knife through butter. Wil reached through to unlatch the window, convinced now that Mr. Dinsdale's "random" kit full of crappy caboodles was in fact a carefully designed set of predictive cat burglar tools.

As they climbed through the window, Lucy knocked over two or three of the new Air-Max 4000 golf clubs that were stacked up against the wall. Luckily, the noise of their fall was dampened by a multitude of fleece blankets with strategic holes in them. Breathing a sigh of relief, Wil climbed in after her. Inside the office, two massive HD televisions showed the continuous broadcast feed from next door. Marcus James stood with his eyes closed as a suspiciously greenish hand applied makeup to his forehead from off-camera.

"As long as he's broadcasting he won't be back in here," said Wil. "We need to be quick and get out of here as fast as possible."

Lucy scowled at the television screen. "Let's lock the door just to be on the safe side," she said.

Wil and Lucy poked their heads out of the empty office to make sure they were unobserved. Along the upper halls of the Castle Towers, the penthouse was now a hive of slightly confused efficiency, centered around the studio area. Every so often, red lights would flash, and a loudspeaker operator would loudly announce the countdown to broadcast. It all seemed rather harried and terrifying, which felt entirely in keeping with everything Wil had ever heard about live television broadcasts. At this stage of the imminent transmission, the upstairs area seemed completely deserted while all of its otherworldly occupants busied themselves with the brainwashing of humanity in small chunks of unnoticeable micropayments. Lucy closed the door and locked it shut.

Wil moved to the wall safe, struck by the sense that things were going entirely too smoothly. He went over a mental checklist, trying to determine if anything had ever gone as easily for him, and for the life of him he could not think of a single event that matched up. This was beginning to make him very nervous indeed. Up above, the television indicated Marcus James's broadcast was going live in less than three minutes. The two combination locks on the safe waited, dangerously. This was going to be too easy.

"SARA," said Wil, nervously, "can you please bring up the tumbler sequence for the combination locks and read them off to me?"

"*Affirmative,*" said SARA, smugly. "*The first combination is thirty-one, fifty-four, seventy-six.*"

Wil moved the tumblers as instructed. Much to his surprise, they settled into place exactly, and the first combination lock gave off a little flashing green light to indicate it had been opened. Wil gulped.

"Are you okay?" asked Lucy.

"Yes, I think so," he replied. "It's just . . . is it me, or does it strike you that this is all too easy?"

"We have the numbers. How hard did you expect it would be?"

"Oh, I don't know. Rottweilers-and-ninja-bot hard, I suppose. Things don't ever come this easily for me. I don't like it."

Lucy chuckled. "You're on my team now. Things are always groovy in my world."

"I suppose so. Just keep an eye on the door." With great trepidation, Wil moved to the second combination lock. "SARA, can you please give me the second sequence?"

"*Affirmative, Wil Morgan,*" said SARA, as if she was about to tell the punch line to a joke. *"The second combination is seventy-four, thirty-four, thirty-six."*

Wil began to sweat a little as he moved the second tumbler. He had a feeling something was about to add up, and that the resulting calculation would not work in his favor. "SARA, just out of interest, is there any significance to this series of numbers?"

"Calculating . . . ," said SARA, already knowing the answer. *"Thirty-one point five four seven six, north; seventy-four point three four three six, east. These are the longitudinal and latitudinal coordinates for Lahore, Pakistan."*

"Is there anything," said Wil as he struggled with the placement of the final tumbler, "that isn't connected to something else today?"

"Negative, Wil Morgan. Please be advised all building security systems are correctly coupled and functioning within normal parameters."

"What?"

AT THAT very moment—just as the final tumbler settled into place and the safe door sprang open—Wil Morgan's week suddenly resumed normal service, and he found himself experiencing his usual late-Thursday crisis. There in front of him was a yellowed electricity bill, courtesy of the Edison Electric Company, circa 1891. The old piece of paper sat in pride of place next to a pair of silver cuff links and what looked to be a small ceramic ashtray with a picture of a carnival on it. Ordinarily, these items would have intrigued Wil; why, for example, would someone treasure an old ashtray that looked as if it had been purchased at a coastal tourist trap sometime during the 1980s? Were the cuff links made of pure silver, or were they just cheap knockoffs? All of these questions and more raced through his mind, and were immediately rejected for the fact that the entire upper floor of the Castle Towers was suddenly filled with a piercing alarm, and flashing red lights.

"Caution! Intruder!" yelled the building's loudspeaker system, just in case someone had missed the point. "Caution! Intruder!" Not to be outdone, a few flashing gold lights joined in to compete with the flashing red ones.

Wil hastily grabbed the old piece of paper and examined it. A corner of the ancient bill crumbled in his hand. Scanning the thing hastily, he noticed the word "Dinsdale" written clearly in a bottom corner. He spread the paper on Marcus James's office desk with a terrible nagging feeling that he had been down this road many times before, though it always looked different every time. The triumph of finding the very thing he and Lucy had come to steal was to prove very short-lived indeed.

"Wil, look!" yelled Lucy, pointing to the windows that fronted two sides of the office. To his dismay, Wil saw that they were now being locked down by rapidly descending metal slats, which completely blocked out the outside world. The massive slats clattered to their resting place, and the building shuddered slightly. Another series of metal slats blocked the inside of the office door. Wil and Lucy were trapped.

Up on the HD television screens, Marcus James was being given the bad news that intruders had broken into his office. His face looked like thunder. Wil noticed a couple of very grayish producers flapping their arms about as they rushed to the back of the set. Their features were difficult to pick out, however—each time the cameras caught any of the gray aliens, the video feed short-circuited. Like so many actual producers, these guys clearly preferred to do their work off-camera. With the broadcast counting down from ten to one, Marcus clearly had no choice but to continue as if everything was perfectly fine, despite the obvious difficulty with the flashing red and gold lights and the cacophonous alarms.

"We are live," said a garbled, disembodied voice, "in five . . . four . . . three . . ."

"Hi there!" yelled Marcus enthusiastically in the direction of camera A. "We are going deal crazy over here! Our best deals of the year have just set off the uh . . . supercrazy deal alarm! All of our best items are on red light special! Gold means go! Buy now! Operators are standing by!"

Wil found Marcus's white teeth grating in the extreme, and his fake smile to be revolting beyond words. But he had to admire the little man's chutzpah. Talk about turning lemons into lemonade.

"Wil! We're locked down!" yelled Lucy in a desperate attempt to state the obvious before Wil could beat her to it.

"I'm aware of that!" he yelled back. "I've got what we came for. We need to get the heck out of here!"

"How? The windows are blocked off."

Wil looked around him for any sign of a way out, only to be met with obstacles. The windows and main door to the office were clearly impassable. Thinking quickly, he produced the Civil War periscope and searched for any air ducts just below his feet (despite the fact entering them was likely to get him shot at sixty times). No luck: the floor below seemed to contain the packing warehouses for most of Marcus James's infernal TV-only items. Ordinarily, Wil would have been intrigued by the strange little gnome-like creatures down there that seemed to be loading boxes and driving forklift trucks. But this was no time for spying: he and Lucy had to find a way out. All he could see inside the office were piles of useless TV-only items, an open safe with an ashtray and cuff links in it, and Marcus James's open laptop computer.

The computer! Suddenly, Wil was struck by the strongest notion yet that this entire affair had been scheduled from the start. From within his pocket, the Whatsit beeped, plaintively. He reached inside his other pocket instead.

"SARA!" yelled Wil. "I need your help!"

"*Greetings, Wil Morgan,*" said SARA. "*How may I be of assistance?*"

"I'm not sure yet. Do you know how to break into a security system?"

"*Would you like me to look up 'how to break into a security system' on the Internet?*"

"No, I just want you to hack into one for me."

Wil moved toward Marcus James's open laptop, which displayed a screen saver depicting Marcus James holding a tube of Gleemodent toothpaste.

"Wil, what are you doing? We have to get out of here," said Lucy, urgently.

"Something illegal, probably!"

"Well, it can't be any less legal than what we've already done, can it?"

"Good point! Just keep an eye on the door!"

Wil produced SARA's charging cord and stared at it, a pit forming in his stomach. He didn't really have anything against preordination, he just hated it when things seemed to be preordained by a little old man in a mustard jacket aided by quite possibly the world's most insane smartphone. With a sharp intake of breath, Wil plugged one end of the charging cord into a free port in the computer. "Whatever you're going to do," he informed SARA, "I'm counting on you." With that, he kissed the smartphone's screen and plugged the other end of the cord into SARA's open charging slot.

SARA glowed.

Wil found Lucy staring at him with astonishment, causing him to blush. After less than a week of exposure to Mr. Dinsdale and the Curioddity Museum, his judgment had pretty much gone off the deep end. He smiled, weakly. "Just in case," he said to Lucy.

"Just in case of what?" she countered, and went off to examine the metal slats that made the door to the office impassable.

Wil watched Lucy go with a feeling of bewilderment usually reserved for husbands and boyfriends who have just purchased a set of socket wrenches for their wives and girlfriends, and are genuinely confused as to why their significant other just whacked them over the head with one. Was it his imagination, or was Lucy jealous?

"We're going to take a quick commercial break from this, uh . . . commercial," said Marcus James up on the main HD screen. "We'll be back in a jiffy!" And with that, a five-minute looped infomercial for a strangely familiar galvanized blue wall putty began to play. Meanwhile, the alarms suddenly stopped, and the red and gold lighting was replaced with a calmer and only slightly less dangerous blue. The Castle Towers had fallen silent but for Marcus's inane drivel on the broadcast and, presumably, the imminent arrival of a legion of angry ninja-bots.

"SARA, can you break into his system?" said Wil, eyeing his phone with a nervous look. "Or break us out for that matter. Can you find us any way out of here?"

"*Calculating . . . ,*" replied SARA, mischievously. "*Please remain calm.*"

Wil assessed the situation: while he and Lucy had reached the goal of securing the fabled electric bill Mr. Dinsdale so coveted, the fact could not be ignored that only half the battle was won. In truth, an exit from the Castle Towers seemed of equal importance to its access. He moved over to Lucy, just to see how she was doing. At the door, Lucy was pondering. Wil took her by the hand and looked into her eyes.

"I'm really sorry about this," he said in a grave voice. "I mean I know we've only started dating recently—"

"Tonight, actually."

"Right. Tonight. And I've already led you into all this trouble."

"Are you kidding?" she replied. "This is amazing! It's interstellar! I love it!"

"Really?"

"Sure! What other boyfriend would lead his groovy assistant on a wild goose chase into the midst of certain death while attempting to rescue an old man's dream from the clutches of an evil maniac with overly white teeth?"

"Well, probably a more sensible boyfriend, I would say. One that had saved money and held down a steady job as a chartered accountant."

"Exactly! And where would be the fun in that?"

"So you're not angry with me?"

"When we get out of here, remind me to give you a big kiss at the first opportunity, you twerp." Lucy thought for a moment. "You know what? Why don't we just get that over with right now?" She reached out, pulled Wil into her, and kissed him full on the lips. "By my count, that's three times I've kissed you first," she said. "That makes us even for me hitting you over the head with a book."

Wil would have gladly taken a few more lumps of Tolstoy's greatest work in exchange for extras. If he and Lucy were unable to find a means of escape then he might at least try to abscond by floating away on cloud nine. His moment of triumph, however, would prove to be short-lived.

Suddenly, one entire section of the wall slid upward to reveal Marcus James standing against what seemed to be a thick panel of bulletproof glass, amid the chaotic scene of the television studio behind him. The little man did not seem to be at all amused, though he did appear to be in complete control of the situation. Behind him, a large number of suspicious-looking producers conferred in whatever shadows were provided to them. Meanwhile, the looped infomercial continued, unabated.

Marcus moved directly to the edge of the glass. He flashed his brilliant white teeth. "Well, well," he snickered. "If it isn't the redoubtable Mr. Morgan. I see you've brought your friend with you. You should be aware, Mr. Morgan, that you have interrupted a live broadcast. The police have been alerted, and they are now on their way. And I will be suing you for tortious interference with a business enterprise."

"Is that right, Mr. James?" said Wil, rising to the bait. "And do you plan on having your friends back there act as material witnesses to whatever crime you're going to accuse me of?" Back in the shadows, the group of "producers" huddled nervously in response and took a farther step back into the shadows in unison. Wil smiled, sweetly. "Right back atcha."

"It won't make much of a difference either way," replied Marcus. "You're trespassing on private property."

"I am? I was just in my office building and I think I took a wrong turn."

"Across the rooftop?"

"I'm very directionally challenged. Ask anyone."

"Give it up, Mr. Morgan. You're surrounded, and the automated security lockdown systems are working perfectly. There's no way out of here."

"I rather think, Mr. James," said Wil, pressing his nose against the glass, "that if you were in control of your security systems, you would already have come in and gotten me."

"Open the door."

"Why don't you come in and get me?" Lucy and Wil exchanged a high five. "Lucy, would you please do me a favor and entertain Mr. James while I check in on SARA?" he said.

"Why, I'd be delighted!" said Lucy, rising to the challenge. She approached a now-seething Marcus at the bulletproof barrier and smiled her most innocent-yet-mischievous smile. "I must say, Mr. James," she said, as inoffensively as possible, "you have the most impossibly white teeth. Are they fake?"

WHILE LUCY got under Marcus James' impossibly tanned skin, Wil sidled over to the laptop computer to check in on SARA's progress, though he had little to no idea what she was progressing toward.

"Leave that computer alone!" yelled Marcus James. "I'm warning you, Morgan! That is private property!"

At Marcus's office desk, SARA was glowing with enjoyment as she rifled through all of Marcus's personal files. "*Greetings, Wil Morgan,*" she said in her most proud metallic tone. "*All security systems are under lockdown. Would you like to check the stock reports in Nicaragua?*"

"Um. Not right now, thank you—"

On the computer screen, the stock reports for Nicaragua were instantly displayed. "*I have found numerous examples of stock manipulation involving companies belonging to the owner of the Castle Towers.*

In all, there are seventy-six occurrences that cross-reference suspicious behavior in Monaco, Pakistan, and Korea. All relevant information is currently being downloaded into multiple secure files and disseminated across the Internet."

Wil chuckled. "Remind me never to cross you, SARA," he said. "Any chance we're getting out of here?"

"Calculating . . . ," said SARA, and went back to her glowing.

Wil checked the old document he'd retrieved from inside Marcus James's safe. The ink had faded to the point that the electricity bill was very difficult to read. Nevertheless, Wil felt he could make out some numbers at the bottom of the page. There was an official stamp in the center of the bill that could barely be read—perhaps in better light, he hoped. He held the bill up to SARA's screen. "SARA, I don't want to disturb what you're doing in there, but do you have any idea what it says at the bottom of this page? If I'm not mistaken it says 'paid in full.'"

SARA's camera function activated, creating a little flash. An image of the electricity bill now appeared on Marcus James's laptop computer.

"This is outrageous!" yelled Marcus, trying to reinforce his importance but simply reinforcing his impotence instead. "You have no right to interfere with a legitimate business dealing! I'll own you for this!"

"You know, Mr. James, I think you need to chill out a little bit," said Lucy with a grin. "I think you're going to have a hernia out there. Maybe you should try chamomile tea."

"Lemon's pretty good for constipation, I think," offered Wil.

"Chai tea is also beneficial to the human nervous system," continued SARA, getting in on the joke.

"You have until the count of twenty to open the door, Morgan!" shrieked Marcus. "I'm warning you!"

"Greetings, Marcus James," countered SARA. *"It has been approximately six years since you manipulated the financial earnings reports of the Lemon Corporation and bankrupted the entire company. Please*

direct your attention to the various high-definition screens located inside the upper floors of this building."

Marcus's jaw suddenly dropped to the point where had it gone any lower, he might have accidentally kicked it. Wil chuckled, sensing that Marcus had just encountered a woman scorned.

SUDDENLY, EVERY single screen inside the building began to show the same screen image as Marcus's laptop computer. At the bottom of each screen ran the word BROADCASTING in large letters. Aghast, Marcus turned to his otherworldly television crew and began barking orders.

"Shut it down! Shut the broadcast down! The entire thing! Now!"

The various grips, camera operators, and producers moved away from their stations and huddled even farther back against the far wall. Horrified, Marcus ran toward any nearby camera or electronic device he could find and began kicking and punching at them in a vain attempt to end the broadcast. Up on screen, things were getting interesting.

The smarmy face of none other than Marcus James himself appeared, as seen just a couple of days previously from Wil's very close point of view, through the lens of SARA's smartphone camera. Clearly, SARA had recorded the conversation between Wil and Marcus in the museum lobby. "Let me tell you how it's going to work," the televised, two-day-old version of Marcus James seemed to be saying. "You're going to complain for two years, and I'm going to keep sending you threatening letters and adding surcharges that you can't keep track of, until you lose interest in standing up to me."

"Turn it off!" bellowed the current-day version of Marcus. "For God's sake, somebody cut the feed!"

"I'll have my debt collectors take you to court," continued two-day-old Marcus. And I will own you, as I own all of my so-called customers."

"No! Somebody stop him! Please!"

"Because I make money the old-fashioned way: I steal it."

THERE WAS silence as Marcus James's face now froze on the screen, and the real-life, current-day Marcus slumped to the base of the glass. Silent sobs now emanated from his hunched shoulders.

"That was an epic fail of epic proportions," said Lucy, appreciatively. "Can we run that again?"

"*An exit strategy has now been determined, Wil Morgan and Lucy Price,*" said SARA. "*As an added bonus, we are now broadcasting to the entire Shopping Network from my inbuilt camera. You will have approximately fifteen seconds of live broadcast before shutdown occurs. Please break a leg. Thank you.*"

Lucy moved to the camera and began waving inanely at it. "Hi, everyone!" she said, happily. "Hi Mom! Hi Dad! Is this thing on?" She motioned off-camera for Wil to join her. Thinking quickly, he grabbed the bag of kit and caboodle and moved to the camera to rescue the good people of television land from any more of Lucy's dead space.

"That's it!" screamed Marcus James from outside the glass. "You've really done it now!"

Quite what "it" was, Wil couldn't be sure. Behind Marcus, the television studio was now completely empty. The producers had bolted. Wil moved in front of the smartphone camera, where Lucy was in full swing. Apparently this was an opportunity she'd been working toward for quite some time, and she had arrived with a fully conceived manifesto.

"Everyone out there in TV land! Be nice to each other!" Lucy happily burbled in the direction of SARA's camera. "Be nice to animals! Read books!"

Wil grabbed the camera as quickly as he could. A countdown at the bottom of the screen indicated there were five seconds remaining.

He quickly produced the wooden Sequitur from inside his plastic bag and dangled it in front of the camera. "You all need to look at things the right way!" he said, abruptly. "Don't believe everything that people tell you! Your eyes only see what your mind lets you believe!"

"Stay in school!" yelled Lucy.

And with that, the broadcast shut off. And Wil and Lucy were to be allowed less than one second to bask in their moment of triumph before the resentful universe outside the bulletproof glass began to blast its way in.

THE FIRST blast sounded like the kind of explosion one might hear in, say, a quartz mine after accidentally dropping a lit stick of dynamite in a shed marked DANGER: EXPLOSIVES. The sound was so incredibly loud—and packed such a concussive force—that Wil and Lucy staggered to stay upright.

Over at the bulletproof glass, Marcus James had taken a step or two backward. In his place, a simply enormous automaton armed with what appeared to be an industrial sledgehammer attacked the bulletproof glass with great gusto. Beyond, a second automaton approached, armed with a blowtorch. For the life of him, Wil could not understand why each of the massive machines wore what appeared to be headbands with some kind of sun symbol on them.

A few paces back from the door, Marcus James gloated. "You may think you have won this battle," he said in the manner of a nineteenth-century landlord building up to deliver his best cliché, "but I intend to win the war. Once my ninja-bots have pierced the outer glass casing, I am quite within my rights to have them rip you both to shreds."

Wil and Lucy looked at each other. "Ninja-bots," she said. "I told you so."

"What do you want, a prize?"

"Sure. What's on offer?"

"Well, if the ninja-bots get in here, not much, I'm afraid."

"Then I guess we'd better hurry up and find a way out."

Wil moved back to the computer screen, where SARA was wrapping up her evening festivities by transmitting embarrassing childhood photos of Marcus James that she'd found in a hidden folder. These photos were currently being uploaded to all of his social media accounts. "SARA!" he called to the smartphone. "Things are about to get a little heated in here!"

As if in response, the bulletproof glass suddenly cracked across its entire length, and one corner of it melted slightly as the blowtorch took effect.

"*I have calculated all parameters for an escape route,*" said SARA. "*Please follow all instructions exactly as directed. You will need to activate the device currently resting in your pocket.*"

Wil produced the Whatsit, which beeped on cue. "What does it do?" he asked. "Are there any instructions with this thing?"

"*The Whatsit is a theoretical device that reacts to the user's intuition and randomizes a solution to any problem. The user must not think directly of the solution. Instead, if the user acts intuitively, the Whatsit will take care of the rest.*"

"What the hell is that supposed to mean?"

"I think it means you're supposed to make a wish," said Lucy, taking an interest in proceedings. "But you're just not supposed to say it out loud. It's like a genie in a bottle, only in reverse."

"Okay, that's the most ridiculous thing I've heard all week. And it has been a week."

"*Lucy Price's summation is essentially accurate,*" said SARA. "*The user must silently intuit a solution to any problem. To do this, the user must concentrate hard to achieve a state of relaxation.*"

"But that's impossible. . . . Wait a minute." Wil placed the Whatsit on the floor, moved sharply to the rows of brand-new Air-Max 4000 golf clubs, and selected the one that looked most suited to his height. "That's it!" he yelled. "Concentrate on relaxing!"

"Leave those alone!" yelled Marcus from outside the melting and cracking glass. "Those are brand-new! They're not for the public!"

Ignoring Marcus James's cries of protest, Wil now settled in by the wall and began to whack imaginary golf balls, pretending he was hitting them high into the night sky over the adjacent rooftops. As long and straight as the pros.

"What are you doing?" shouted Lucy above the ever-increasing din.

"Ssh! I'm trying to concentrate!"

"Concentrate? By practicing your golf swing?"

"I don't have a golf swing! I need to concentrate on relaxing! You're not helping!"

"Oh! Sorry!"

Wil swished the club a few more times, feeling the shaft whipping around him. He tried to pretend he'd just split a nice, green fairway to the polite applause of an adoring public. A few days ago he'd had a dream of finishing second in a long drive competition. This time he would reset his expectations and finish first.

"*Wil Morgan,*" interrupted SARA. "*A structural breach will occur in approximately seventeen seconds.*"

Looking toward the glass, Wil could now see that a small legion of angry ninja-bot foot soldiers was gathering along the far wall. The two larger ninja-bots were making headway, and one side of the cracking wall was now almost completely melted. "Lucy!" he yelled. "Grab SARA and stand back!"

"What are you doing?"

"I have no idea!"

He moved toward the little Whatsit device, which continued to make plaintive beeps from its position in the center of the office floor. With the Air-Max 4000 in his right hand, he wet the index finger of his left hand and checked the imaginary wind direction. Satisfied, he lowered the golf club so that it rested against the Whatsit, and aimed in the direction of the glass wall.

Over at the office desk, Lucy removed SARA's charging cord from

Marcus James's laptop computer. Seeing Wil address the Whatsit with the driver, she squeaked with fear and took cover behind the desk.

Wil closed his eyes, and concentrated. He thought of Nikola Tesla and marshmallows, and Lucy's oh-so-cute ankle bracelet. And his mom. And the Perpetual Penny.

And he swung with all his might.

THE WHATSIT device seemed to freeze time at the very moment the head of the Air-Max 4000 made impact. In that split second, Wil imagined a lot of things. He imagined he could see the look of utter horror on Marcus James's face as the Whatsit came flying toward the bulletproof glass. He imagined his imaginary golf ball splitting the fairway, and landing at a distance roughly equal to the pros. He imagined himself kissing Lucy, and buying SARA a spiffy new carrying case. He imagined Mr. Dinsdale's beaming face as he presented the coveted electric bill that would prove the old man's ownership of the museum property, and Mary Gold's grudging look of admiration. He imagined his mother, in every atom around him. Living inside every electron. He imagined his dad ruffling his hair.

The Whatsit flew off the face of the golf club like a bat exiting the underworld. It had time to beep just once before it impacted with the surface of the bulletproof glass and turned it into a sheet of liquid. The Whatsit then took a quick left turn and clattered into the torch-wielding ninja-bot, turning the automaton into a small pile of plastic coat hangers and thereby rendering it completely ineffective as a weapon of mass destruction. Lucy chanced a peek over the top of the desk, and Wil opened one eye. The Whatsit caromed off the first ninja-bot and clattered to a stop in front of the second bot armed with the sledgehammer. There was a moment of silence. Wil closed his eyes again. And when he opened them, the ninja-bot's hammer had somehow turned into a banana, much to the surprise of the confused automaton.

With an impressive *whoosh*, the Whatsit suddenly let out a huge cloud of chalk dust, and then zipped out of existence. Wil felt a lump in his pocket, and found the Whatsit back where it had started the evening.

"So that's how it works," he muttered, genuinely impressed. He looked at the head of the Air-Max 4000, impressed. I'm keeping this, he thought.

Inside the broadcast area, Marcus James was having a pretty extraordinary coughing fit. "SARA!" shouted Lucy, urgently. "We have to get out of here! Which way do we go?"

"*Greetings*," said SARA, innocently pretending to be waking up from a nap. "*Would you like me to look up 'which way am I supposed to go' on the Internet?*"

"Yes!" yelled Lucy and Wil in unison.

"*It's about time*," said SARA. And with that, her entire screen lit up. "*Please proceed to the highlighted route. In ten yards, turn left.*"

"You can't be serious!" protested Lucy.

"Just do as she says," responded Wil. "I think we owe her that much!"

Blinded by chalk dust, Wil and Lucy raced forward, unable to see exactly where they were going. Wil was vaguely aware of the recovering smaller ninja-bots now converging on his and Lucy's position. After exactly ten yards, he turned left and found himself leading Lucy through a small corridor filled with red flashing lights and chalk dust.

"*At the next junction, turn left,*" instructed SARA. Wil and Lucy duly obliged, only to be met with a second wall of angry, buzzing ninja-bots, this time armed with smaller blowtorches. "*At the first opportunity, make a legal U-turn!*"

"Quick! Back the way we came!" yelled Lucy above the din as the wall of bots bore down.

"We can't go back! There's a hundred more of them following us!"

"Just go!"

Wil and Lucy doubled back, quickly. "*In three feet, jump abruptly to the right,*" said SARA in her metallic matter-of-fact manner. Wil and

Lucy immediately jumped to the right and found themselves inside an open storage closet just as the two converging legions of ninja-bots bore down on their position. In the resulting confusion, the two armies began to attack each other in the hallway, while Wil and Lucy looked on from their hidey-hole, confused beyond measure.

"At the earliest opportunity, please step out across the smoldering piles of slag in the hallway and move east," said SARA.

"Shouldn't we let them finish first?" said Wil.

"Time is of the essence," replied SARA. *"Please proceed to the high-lighted route."*

Wil checked the screen. The highlighted route would take he and Lucy up across the rooftops, down a drainpipe, and through a thirtieth-story window. It would culminate in a madcap dash across seventeen more floors before calling for them to squeeze through a series of air ducts while, presumably, taking a few bullets to the shoulder.

"Are you serious?" Wil cried. "We'll never make it that way!"

"Can't we use the elevator again?" asked Lucy.

"Recalculating . . . ," said SARA. On the screen of the smartphone, her navigation widget revolved for a few moments while she pondered the problem. And as the commotion in the hallway began to die down, she found a solution. *"Please proceed directly to the elevators, which have been rerouted. Do not initiate conversation, and try to avoid stepping on that green thing. Temporal paradox in T-minus seventy-three seconds."*

"Uh, okay. Are you sure?"

"Affirmative."

"What green thing? And for that matter, what temporal paradox?"

The screen of the smartphone simply glowed. SARA was no longer in the mood to be forthcoming.

"I think we might have overloaded her inputs," said Lucy. "She's gone completely off the deep end."

"I think we were already past that stage," replied Wil, grimly. "Come on."

Wil and Lucy stepped out into the hallway, where the remnants of a ninja-bot war smoldered. Farther along, a single ninja-bot groaned as it tried and failed to pull itself back to wherever some kind stranger might repair it. With their choices limited, Wil and Lucy began to pick their way through the debris and head toward the elevators.

"*Temporal paradox in T-minus twenty seconds,*" SARA reminded them, though she remained unclear on the nature of the approaching countdown.

"What on Earth is she talking about?" asked Lucy. "Is something going to happen?"

"Probably!" shouted Wil over the noise of the alarms. "She doesn't like to be specific!"

"Wait a second! I think I know what it is! Pass her to me!"

As they rushed toward a rapidly building clattering sound coming from the direction they were headed, Lucy examined the smartphone's screen to discover the telephone function had been activated. "SARA!" she cried, "Please call Mr. Dinsdale at the Curioddity Museum!"

"*Dialing . . . ,*" said SARA, knowingly. "*Paradox complete.*" At the other end of the line, Mr. Dinsdale's garbled voice could barely be heard over the sound of the chaos in the upper levels. "You have reached the Museum of Curioddity," said his recorded voice across the ether. "If you wish to leave a message . . . uhm . . . leave a message. Boop."

"Wil!" shouted Lucy in the direction of some point in the not-too-distant past. "We're inside Marcus James's offices! There's no time to explain! Whatever you do, make sure you bring SARA's charging cord so that you can plug her in. You'll understand this later." She cut off the call abruptly, and handed the phone back to Wil with a smug grin. "There you go. I think that about wraps that up." And with a wink, she jumped over the closest piece of debris and made her way toward the central lobby.

At the end of the hallway, they finally cleared the debris field. Wil looked out into a larger corridor to make sure the coast was clear. The blue lights now seemed to be dimming, and the batteries on the shrill alarm systems had weakened dramatically. The alarm now sounded more like a tired goat. Seeing no one in the corridor, Wil and

Lucy stepped out. Suddenly, a small, greenish individual rounded the far corner. Wil had to jump back to avoid stepping on the little creature. The alien raised a clipboard over its eyes and let out an unintelligible squeak before bolting in the direction of the accounting offices. Wil and Lucy watched the "camera operator" rush off with bemused looks on their faces.

"That must've been the green thing SARA was talking about," said Lucy. "Where d'you think it's going?"

"With any luck? Back where it came from."

"Attention!" came a voice from the weakening loudspeaker system. "All personnel: please attach trumpets bleating five nations!" Wil and Lucy glanced at each other. "Correction: all personnel, please abandon life markers plenty chop station!"

"I don't think English is their strong suit," said Wil.

"I kinda like it," replied Lucy. "Makes running away sound less formal."

LUCY KEPT her back to the wall and peered frequently behind them so that she could keep a lookout for errant ninja-bots. Despite the decreasingly frantic nature of the alarm systems, the upper levels were still in a state of chaos. On a large screen above the upper atrium, Marcus James's looped infomercial for rubberized gutter protectant was now playing for the third time in a row. The man himself was nowhere to be seen.

As Wil and Lucy rounded the corner to the elevator doors, they were surprised to find the secretary they'd met earlier standing at the elevator call buttons. With no apparent understanding of the situation, the secretary was simply waiting for the elevator to arrive, as opposed to finding an escape route or a panic room somewhere. To all intents and purposes, the girl simply seemed to feel that this was business as usual; in fact, she was more startled by Wil and Lucy's disheveled appearance than by the chaotic scenes unfolding in the building around her.

Lucy raised her eyebrows to acknowledge the girl, and together the three of them waited in uncomfortable silence for the elevators to arrive. Much to Wil's dismay, the elevator seemed to be stopping at every single floor on the way up. As they waited, trying to avoid making eye contact, a couple of the producers rushed by, making unintelligible noises. A single machine cog rolled past, covered with burning oil. Still no response from the secretary, who had found solace in her hairdressing magazine and was doing everything in her power not to make small talk. Despite the escalating danger, Lucy seemed to be encouraged by the comedic possibilities of the moment. Wil glared at her to be silent.

The girl finally looked up, annoyed that the elevator was taking so long. "So," said Lucy, gleefully. "Busy day?"

"Kinda," said the girl, not wishing to talk about it.

Lucy tried her best to let the moment die. Her best was not good enough. "Anything interesting happen at work today?" she asked, innocently.

"Nah," said the secretary, and returned to her magazine.

By now, the elevator was just a few floors down, and Wil had lost all semblance of control. "Come on . . . come on . . . ," he muttered, impatiently. "What's the holdup?"

"Where's Marcus?" hissed Lucy. "I don't like it. It's too quiet."

Wil was inclined to agree; surely, the little TV pitchman would not go this quietly, would he? On a whim, he retrieved the Civil War periscope that had been slung across his back, and extended it upward. The secretary tried and failed to contain her annoyance.

"What are you doing?" hissed Lucy again. "You're going to give us away."

"I think that particular ship has sailed," admitted Wil. "I'm just being careful." The periscope's weight caused him to stagger slightly.

"How careful can you be holding a hundred pounds of metal over your head in the middle of a penthouse lobby with a bunch of robots trying to kill you?"

"Not very! Just bear with me!"

Wil peered into the periscope to look at the floors below. Nothing doing but for a few frantic little gnome creatures piling into the back of a forklift truck, and the occasional errant ninja-bot rushing past in flames. Wil swiveled the periscope until it alighted on the elevator shaft. The elevator moved up to the floor directly below them. And standing in it was a very smug looking (not to mention nefarious) Marcus James. Next to him stood a heretofore-unseen ninja-bot armed with a military-grade machine-gun cannon. Wil gasped.

"What is it?"

"It's Marcus! He's in the elevator!" Wil tried not to look self-conscious as the secretary scowled at him. "He's in the elevator with another one of those robots, and this one doesn't look at all pleasant," he hissed.

"What do we do?"

"I don't know."

Just at that moment, the Whatsit beeped inside Wil's pocket.

❧

To say that Marcus James never knew what hit him as the elevator doors slowly opened was somewhat of an understatement. He was only briefly aware of the distinctive hollow *thwack* of an Air-Max 4000, and a short beeping sound flying directly toward his face. Moments later, his world (and legacy) would change in an incredibly dramatic fashion.

In those same moments, the weapons-grade ninja-bot would also endure a reorganization of its intended function. As it emerged from the elevator with its machine-gun cannons firing at full blast, its robotic sensors were rather confused to discover that instead of discharging hollow-point cannon shells capable of ripping human flesh to shreds, it had suddenly begun to shoot bright red tulips instead. The tulips seemed less of the "flesh shredding" variety and more of a benign and fragrant variety as they fell harmlessly to the floor, carpeting the place with vibrant color.

The ninja-bot looked around the upstairs lobby, confused, as three human flesh targets made their polite excuses and stepped past it into the elevator shaft. It tried valiantly to pepper them with heat-seeking thermo-grenades and was startled to find itself lobbing small orchids in their direction. As the doors to the elevator closed, the poor, confused machine set off down the hallway in search of someone who might be willing to reprogram it.

Had it looked up at one of the two huge HD screens dominating the lobby, it would have been perplexed to find its master key holder, Marcus James, standing completely naked in the middle of his broadcast studio amid a pile of discarded clipboards, with a single tulip in one hand, a small orchid in the other, and a very sheepish grin on his face indeed.

AND HAD Marcus been aware at that very moment that Wil and Lucy had made their way out of the Castle Towers and were now staring up at events unfolding above in the penthouse, flushed with success, his grin would have been of the upside-down variety.

CHAPTER FOURTEEN

DURING WHAT Lucy described as the "car ride" back to the museum (but which Wil would later describe as a "series of terror-filled near-accidents in the passenger seat of a rusted death trap driven by a crazy woman"), Wil allowed himself a brief moment of self-congratulation in between longer moments of sheer panic.

Genghis screeched away from the Castle Towers, leaving behind a pillar of rubberized smoke. Wil gripped the sides of his passenger seat with both hands, resolving never to go back to his former office building. This put him in a better mood than he might have expected. As he looked up into the night sky, he was astounded to see the upper levels of the building flashing intermittently with virtually every color of the rainbow. Wil could only imagine how many Air-Max 4000 golf clubs were being broken over someone's knee right at that very moment.

Next door to the Castle Towers, the Swiss clock was undergoing a transformation: the laser beam springing from the top of the building was growing in intensity, so much so that it had plowed a huge hole through the angry clouds above. The beam glowed with an unnatural blue light as red pulses upward flew along its length and into empty space above. No doubt, Marcus James's producers—acting in accordance with their kind—were rapidly deserting the failing production below. The pulses grew stronger and stronger until with a final flourish they lit up the night sky like an errant nuclear detonation . . . and then there was simply silence, and the black of the night sky. Wil listened intently for any concussive episode that might follow and was amused to hear instead the resonant (and satisfying) sound of the Swiss clock's KLONNG, as if the awful edifice were saying a final goodbye.

Suddenly, the top of the Castle Towers erupted in a flash of brilliant colors, ranging from a glowing magenta to a deep neon green. Orange fireworks seemed to blow out every window on the top floor, and a giant blue ball popped out of the roof and hurtled into the night sky. Despite his understandable terror, Wil couldn't help but be impressed by the pyrotechnics—this was just the sort of effect he'd always been going for when any of his childhood experiments had arbitrarily exploded.

His amazement was to be short-lived, however (though his terror would increase exponentially just to even things out). The giant blue ball described a huge, impressive arc against the pitch-black night and—despite Genghis the Pinto's own series of exotic maneuvers— began to grow bigger in size as it reached its apex and plummeted toward the ground.

"Lucy," said Wil, rather meekly. His fight-or-flight response mechanism was making a mental toss-up between interacting with his temporarily deranged girlfriend or the rapidly enlarging giant blue ball. "Lucy!" he repeated, a little more forcefully.

"What the hell is wrong with you?" yelled Lucy in response as her demonic possession took full hold. As if to emphasize her annoyance, she swerved across a sidewalk and dislodged a fire hydrant that had previously been minding its own business. "I'm trying to escape here!"

"Up in the sky! Imminent death! Step on it!" screamed Wil, pointing to the rapidly descending giant blue ball.

Seeing the instrument of her impending demise hurtling toward her at a very high rate of speed, Lucy let out a half gargle/half sneer and swerved to the right, scraping the side of an innocent parked car. "Hold tight!" she screamed, clearly unaware that Wil was already holding very tightly indeed. Lucy aimed Genghis for a pile of discarded dirt that some unfortunate street workers had handily left earlier, and with an engine roar that sounded roughly as powerful as, say, an electric screwdriver, the Ford Pinto caught four feet of air and slammed into the main drag of the one-way system. The massive blue ball missed them by inches. It crashed into the workers' pile of dirt and bounced a couple of times, sending a shower of impressive blue sparks in every direction. The strange mass careened into a parked truck, which exploded in a manner suitable for a Hollywood action flick, and then set off across the street like a silver pinball, where it made a beeline for an advertising billboard for Gleemodent toothpaste. Wil watched with great satisfaction as the huge ball crashed through Marcus James's impossibly white teeth and embedded itself in the side of a concrete wall behind the billboard.

Leaving only destruction in its wake, the mighty Genghis careened around the one-way system and off into the night, narrowly missing Pan's extended farewell on the driver's side of the Pinto. Wil was vaguely aware of a mass of flashing blue lights headed in the opposite direction, some of which now converged at the base of the Castle Towers and some of which headed toward the still-sparking blue ball, like worker ants rushing to the aid of their queen. Despite Wil's utter dread, he allowed himself a smile at the notion that the arriving police and emergency vehicles might have been better occupied following Genghis and his insane mistress, as opposed to bringing Marcus James to the minimal justice he would no doubt endure. The rusted Pinto barreled across three lanes and scraped the side of a barrier before righting itself and jetting off toward the Curioddity Museum in an attempt to set a world land speed record.

Time now seemed to slow down for Wil. Inside his left pocket, the Whatsit beeped in such a fashion that Wil took to mean it was either pleased with itself, or it wanted more action. In his other pocket, SARA glowed. He pulled her out for a moment or two and was amazed to discover a hitherto-undiscovered function playing across her screen: somehow, SARA had tapped into the Shopping Network and was able to replay the greatest moments from Marcus James's evening of shame, which seemed to be already making its way across the World Wide Web. Marcus James was about to discover that "going viral" was much like being attacked by a large fleet of pillaging Vikings. Wil had no doubt Marcus would be out on bail by Friday afternoon. But he'd wake in his opulent satin sheets come Saturday morning and feel as though he had been overrun by metaphorical Swedes with a penchant for foul-smelling clothing and violent drinking games.

"*Greetings, Wil Morgan,*" intoned SARA. "*You have eighty-seven incoming messages from Lahore, Pakistan. Would you like to respond?*"

"No thank you, SARA," replied Wil, happily. "Please just tell everyone over there I'll get back to them in a couple of years once the excitement has died down."

"*Affirmative.*"

"And SARA?"

"*Yes, Wil Morgan?*"

"I'm glad we finally understand each other. Thank you."

SARA SWITCHED off her screen and remained inert all the way back to Upside-Down Street—no mean feat considering the exotic set of maneuvers Lucy attempted to execute on the way there. At the museum, Genghis marauded across the recently replaced street sign and left his signature tire marks in the street outside the revolving door. Wil exited the vehicle quickly, and waited a few moments for the blood to rush out of Lucy's ears and back into her heart before attempting to make eye contact.

"Lucy," he said, breathless, "I want you to know that was the most amazing, terrifying, exhilarating experience I have ever had in my entire life."

"Really?" Lucy seemed both entranced at the notion and mildly concerned that he was referring only to her driving.

"Really. That was completely nuts."

"And also completely groovy."

"Exactly." Wil moved to Lucy's side of the car and took her half of the caboodle pile gently away from her. He set the items down on the sidewalk, held both of Lucy's hands, and looked deeply into her eyes. "I wouldn't have said it if it wasn't true. That was utterly ridiculous. Especially for a first date."

Lucy flashed the kind of smile that would sink ships, if she meant it to. "So does this mean you want to do it again?" she said, coyly.

"If it involves certain death, imminent danger, or just plain bubble tea, I'm your man."

"Except ninja-bots?"

"Especially ninja-bots."

"Groovy," she said. "And awkward. I think we just took out the last of them."

"Come on," said Wil with a grin spreading across his face. He grabbed as much of the pile as he could, checked his inner pocket to make sure the electricity bill was secure, and headed for the revolving door. "We need to get this stuff back to its rightful owner."

He had taken no more than two steps toward the revolving door before it whirled suddenly, and Mr. Dinsdale emerged with his hands in the air, looking for all the world like a psychotic evangelist.

"Wil!" yelled Mr. Dinsdale. "Lucy! Come quickly! Hurry!"

"Mr. Dinsdale! We got the piece of paper you were looking for!" cried Wil.

"Yes, yes! I know you did! SARA sent us an electronic copy from the cloud! Just hurry!"

As quickly as he had appeared, Dinsdale vaulted backward into the path of the revolving door and was whisked instantly inside. Wil and Lucy glanced at each other, impressed at the neatness by which he had managed the maneuver. They quickened their pace and, laden with a huge pile of unlikely items—all of which had proven unerringly useful in the evening's proceedings—they moved in on the revolving door and navigated it as easily as the Lord of the British Admiralty might navigate a bathtub.

❧

INSIDE THE museum lobby, Mr. Dinsdale clucked and fussed. "Ah! There you are!" he called as Wil and Lucy entered. "Upstairs! We don't have much time! Follow me!"

To one side, Mary Gold stood with her arms folded, smacking her gum loudly in an apparent attempt to set a world record at gum smacking. As Wil approached, she winked at him, and moved to the far side of the register to pretend she was annoyed about something. Wil resolved to keep this moment a secret between them.

Holding hands, he and Lucy followed Mr. Dinsdale toward the staircase. By the time they reached the base, he was standing at the top balcony and looking impatient. "Hurry!" he said again. "Both of you! Up here!"

"But Mr. Dinsdale—"

"Just hurry! They're going to be here within the hour!"

"Mr. Dinsdale!" yelled Wil at the top of his lungs. "We've just cracked a safe, been attacked by robots, attempted to communicate with a pair of no-legged conjoined twins from another dimension, and narrowly avoided being flattened by a giant globe that shot out of the top of the Castle Towers! So we've had a bit of a day!"

True to his arbitrary nature, Mr. Dinsdale completely ignored everything Wil had said and darted back into the hallway. As fast as their legs could carry them, Wil and Lucy barreled up the main stairs, where they found Mr. Dinsdale at the door to his office. "Quickly!" he called. "Everything's coming into focus! We have to marshal our forces!"

"What forces?"

"You'll see!" exclaimed Dinsdale before slipping through his office door. "Come on!"

Intrigued, Wil rushed to the door and followed Dinsdale through, where he abruptly stopped in his tracks. For the sight that awaited him was perhaps the very thing he had least expected to see. To one side of the table sat a strange man with unkempt hair who wore the kinds of clothes that would have made a fashionable accountant resplendent in the early nineteenth century. On the table in front of the man sat an ancient Egyptian abacus, and a printed piece of paper that looked exactly like the missing bill Wil and Lucy had recently retrieved. Wil intuitively knew this man to be Mr. Dinsdale's cousin, Engelbert. He knew it with a certainty that defied logic. But it was the identity of the person across the table from cousin Engelbert that really threw him for a loop.

"Hello, Wil," said Barry Morgan as he held up the Perpetual Penny. "I wanted to return this to you."

AND IN his eyes, Wil's father held the look of a man who had just rediscovered a magic he thought he had lost forever.

CHAPTER FIFTEEN

A NUMBER of possible questions flashed through Wil's mind at the very same time, like eager shoppers let loose inside an electronics store on a tax-free weekend.

These competing questions immediately ran into the bottleneck of his cerebral cortex, which had been dealing with a number of issues over the last few days and was in no mood to open itself up to more trampling. He opened his mouth, involuntarily, and made a couple of embarrassed gurgling sounds. This was exactly the opening the questions in his head had been looking for: within moments they had sorted themselves into an orderly line along one of his synapses, voted for an appropriate representative, and allowed said representative to the front of the line to make its case.

Wil settled upon the most predictable question possible, given the circumstances: "Dad," he blurted out in spite of himself, "what are you doing here?"

Barry Morgan blinked, evenly. "Well, I was hoping for something a little more welcoming, son," he said with a smile. "If I'm not mistaken, you invited me here. Or at least your mother did."

"What? How?"

Calmly, Barry balanced the Perpetual Penny on the table in front of him and set it spinning with a flick of his finger. He fixed his son with a gaze that seemed equal parts melancholy and accepting, never allowing his eyes to go back to the spinning penny.

"I'm not going to look down, Wil," said Barry, "because I don't want to believe in the rules anymore. I want to believe in something else."

"I don't understand."

"I want to believe that Mom has a hand in this—that if I don't look down, the old penny you two were always messing around with is going to keep on spinning forever. I haven't been letting myself think things like that since she died."

Like a man traversing a one-way system on a cold, foggy morning, Wil felt his heart emptying of all its joy. Tears welled up at the mention of his mother, and he felt years of longing and loneliness wash over him. Suddenly, he felt a hand on his: Lucy was falling in love with every inch of her antiboyfriend's great big sentimental heart.

"Dad," Wil said quietly, "I'm sorry I lied to you. I don't have any money and I'm not an accountant. I specialize in low-profile divorce surveillance—"

"And high-profile artifact retrieval!" interrupted Mr. Dinsdale, happily.

"—and high-profile artifact retrieval, yes—"

"Not to mention righting the wrongs of a hundred-year-old bogus electricity bill and bringing about at least half the downfall of a man who is himself the downfall of society!" continued Dinsdale, oblivious to the context of the moment.

"Along with his groovy assistant, minus her trained detective cat!" added Lucy with a flourish, as she tried to get into the spirit of things.

"Right," said Wil. He was determined not to lose his train of thought. "All of those things, yes. But honestly, Dad, only since Monday. Before that, I wasn't much of anything except a little morose and a lot caffeinated."

"I understand, Wil," said Barry. "And I think it's probably me who should be apologizing to you. It hasn't stopped spinning, has it?"

Wil looked down briefly toward the smooth tabletop, where the Perpetual Penny was still happily twirling in place. "Not yet."

"Good. Then I'm going to ask that you accept my apology for all of the pressure I must have put on you all these years. Not to mention all the times I threw aside your inventions, and your imagination in the process."

"He accepts!" exclaimed Lucy. Embarrassed by her involuntary outburst, she bit her bottom lip and scrunched her nose. "That is, if you're okay with it, Wil?"

There was a momentary shift in the direction of time, space, and the course of the conversation. Lucy winked at her new boyfriend in a delicious way, as if challenging Wil to extricate himself from this predicament.

"Dad, I'd like you to meet Lucy Price. I think she might be the best thing that's ever happened to me, even though I've only known her for a few days—*waitaminnit!*"

WIL SUDDENLY scowled at Mr. Dinsdale, who was watching the heartwarming family reunion from across the table, a look of eager anticipation on his face.

"What do you mean, 'They're going to be here any minute'?"

"Hmm?" mumbled the old curator with as much fake innocence as he could muster.

"Who's going to be here any minute? And for that matter, what forces are we marshaling? And what do you mean by 'half' of somebody's downfall?"

"Did I say that?"

"You said it when we were coming up the stairs! Hurry up, you said. They'll be here any minute. And I'm inclined to think, Mr. Dinsdale, that if this person who's going to be here any minute was of the friendly variety, we wouldn't be needing to marshal any forces, would we?"

"Yes. Right, well . . . I suppose when you put it like that, no."

"Yes or no?"

"No. No, we wouldn't. You are correct."

"Who's coming?"

Mr. Dinsdale pondered for a moment—it was the kind of moment where Wil had learned the old man was at his most arbitrary and dangerous.

"That giant globe you mentioned, Wil: the one that shot out the top of the Castle Towers—"

"What about it?"

"It wasn't red, was it? Please tell me it wasn't a giant, glowing red globe, for the sake of all humanity."

"No. It was blue."

"Well, that's a relief!" said Dinsdale, looking relieved. "Marcus James is a notoriously poor loser. If it had been red, the globe would have contained a twenty-megaton thermonuclear device."

"Well, what if it was blue?"

"That'd be his escape pod."

"What?" replied Wil with a level of disbelief entirely in keeping with the rest of his week so far.

"I tried to tell you the job is only half-completed. So that would be Marcus James, getting away scot-free, as usual. He'll be coming here, and probably with some reinforcements—"

"Whaa-aat!?"

"I said 'Marcus James! And probably with s—'"

"I know what you said! Why didn't you say it more forcefully?"

"I didn't want to spoil the moment! Family disentanglements are of the most monumental importance, Wil!"

"Not if all the family members are dead at the hands of a titanium-reinforced ninja-bot!"

"Really? Do they make them from titanium these days—?"

Wil shot Mr. Dinsdale a glare of the type that could neither be ignored nor misinterpreted—not even by a strange little museum curator dressed in a mustard-yellow jacket. "How long," he asked between gritted teeth, "before they get here?"

AT THIS moment, Mr. Dinsdale's diminutive cousin, Engelbert, decided to make his first foray into the conversation. "No more than ten or eleven minutes, tops! We've had one of our Roberts posted on surveillance just outside the Castle Towers, he spotted a couple of troop transporters rolling out past Pan's statue at high speed just after you left. If I know Marcus James, he's unleashed his army of lawyers on our assets, and he'll be slapping an injunction on the use of our evidence in court! We must hurry or all will be lost!"

The odd little lawyer had a voice like two breadfruit falling off the back of a rhinoceros. Wil was astonished both by the strangeness of the pint-sized attorney's vocal delivery and by the precise way in which he was able to liken it to two breadfruit falling off the back of a rhinoceros. For one thing, he had absolutely no idea what kind of noise a breadfruit might make if it fell. Whatever the case, he was not going to allow himself to be disoriented inside the museum by any more of Mr. Dinsdale's weird associations, relative or otherwise.

"What do we do?" Wil asked aloud, and to no one in particular. "I was just getting used to the idea we'd beaten Marcus James into submission."

"I'm afraid people like Marcus James don't submit very easily, Wil," replied Dinsdale. "I'm going to guess with his army of lawyers, he already has those injunctions in order. That escape pod of his is a fully functioning military exoskeleton. But we're not going to fret about that—not when we have Wil Morgan, Crack Detective, on the case!"

"What about the police? They were massing around his exits when we drove away!"

"Mmh. That sort of technology can easily avoid police radar. We're going to have to put Phase Two of our plan into action."

"Phase Two? We don't have a Phase Two!"

"Of course we do!"

"What's Phase Two?"

"You tell us. This was your idea, wasn't it?"

"It wasn't my idea! It was yours!"

"Oh dear."

WIL GULPED, realizing that all eyes were on him even though he hadn't asked for the attention, nor done anything remotely excellent enough to warrant it. His manic week had been a series of adventures and misadventures, to be sure—but he hardly felt like he had been in control of any of it. In fact, Wil felt more like a weekend rafter who'd inadvertently paddled down a class 5 series of rapids and was now headed backward at high speed, unable to turn to face his imminent demise at the hands of a rock.

He closed his eyes for a moment and imagined himself trudging. He was good at trudging. It calmed his thoughts. Wil imagined himself going along the city's one-way system. He thought of his mother, and his newly unestranged father. He thought of the beautiful girl holding his hand, and of the Curioddity Museum. He thought of all the things he had gained in a single week of doing everything he wasn't supposed to, and at that moment he realized what he now had to do. The worst that could happen had already happened; if he lived another thousand lifetimes he would never, ever go back and ride the

Rat Vomit Comet. So what would be the point of protecting what he'd already decided to throw away? Besides, the more he thought about it, he wasn't so much headed backward down some class 5 rapids as he was hurtling down a metaphorical Hill of Death on the back of a tea tray. And that just so happened to be one of the greatest memories of his life.

Wil opened his eyes to find the Perpetual Penny quietly whirling on the tabletop, and Barry Morgan looking slightly eager, and ever-so-slightly pained. He sighed, knowing he was going to do something irrational and ultimately life threatening, in spite of his better judgment.

"Tell you what, Dad," Wil whispered to his father. "We'll take this up when everything blows over. I'll deal with Marcus James. How about you take a look at that old electricity bill of Mr. Dinsdale's? Someone's going to have to recalculate a hundred and fifty years' worth of interest payments and overages. We could use a good accountant right about now."

"I thought you'd never ask, Wil," replied Barry. He cracked his knuckles for effect, and turned his attention to a digital copy of the ancient electricity bill displayed upon Engelbert's Lemon computer. "You buy me some time and I'll do the rest. Never fear: Barry Morgan is here!"

"And his trusty assistant, Engelbert!" said Engelbert with a very specific vocal inflection that sounded like sandpaper rubbing against the landing gear of a Westland Lysander Mk III reconnaissance plane.

With that, Barry and Engelbert turned their attention to the Lemon computer. Barry began to flip beads on the museum's ancient Egyptian abacus, while Engelbert busied himself perusing a copy of the long-lost original United States Constitution, complete with margin notes and ink blots, and a little doodle of a dinosaur drawn by Benjamin Franklin. Barry hardly turned a hair as a tiny will-o'-the-wisp floated past his head and collided with one of John Keely's antigravitic globes that was heading in the opposite direction—he had more pressing matters at hand.

Wil rolled his eyes. No matter the weight of the circumstance, it was virtually guaranteed his father would be able to embarrass him in front of his peers at a moment's notice.

Lucy squeezed his hand. "Now what?" she asked, innocently.

Wil thought for a second. "I have absolutely no idea," he replied.

MR. DINSDALE stood, abruptly, and moved toward the office door. "That's settled, then," he said, eschewing the customary common sense that accompanied such statements. "Come with me, please."

"Wait! Mr. *Dinsdale!*" yelled Wil in response as he and Lucy moved to follow the old man. He grabbed his bag of kit and caboodle and headed quickly toward the office door. "And don't you go halfway down the hall before I get there, you hear me?"

Outside, Wil and Lucy found Mr. Dinsdale halfway down the hall. He was staring at the room containing the temporal and spatial anomalies, and rubbing his furrowed chin.

"We must have a Phase Two, Wil," said Dinsdale as Wil and Lucy approached his position. "Engelbert and your father will need time to crunch those numbers and prove that I don't owe Marcus James's bank all that money. Every asset in this museum is at your disposal but you'd better come up with something quickly. Our surveillance system has just detected a giant blue space marble turning onto Upside-Down Street, accompanied by a military-grade automated escort."

"Your surveillance system?" said Wil, unable to contain his skepticism.

"Yes. That'll be Bob up on the roof. He sees everything that comes and goes around here. That means we have mere moments before everything hits the proverbial fan. The Roberts have battened down the hatches and locked the front door but they're too afraid to go near the revolving doors. So we're about to get a visit from one very unhappy television pitchman, and it's up to you to do something about it. After all, you're the one who just broke into his offices."

"Well, what am I supposed to do?" complained Wil, feebly.

"Oh, Wil! Haven't you learned anything in these last few days?" Dinsdale moved off, abruptly, toward the temporal and spatial anomalies exhibit. "In the space of a week, you've had magic come back into your life, reacquainted yourself with your estranged father, dated a very attractive girl, and completed a suicide mission without actually dying! And do you know how you managed all of this?"

"No! I'm so confused at this point I don't even know how to tie my own shoelaces anymore!"

"Then keep them untied. You managed it because you've re-learned how to un-look. So now it is up to you to finish the job you started. What do your instincts say?"

"I don't know! They're having trouble getting past my cerebral cortex—"

"Wait! Look!" cried Lucy, suddenly. Wil turned to find her pointing at one of the displays near the wall, which was making a familiar beeping sound. In one of his pockets, his Lemon phone began to buzz. In the other, the Sequitur began to beep. And on the wall, Albert Einstein's answering machine was flashing red.

Mr. Dinsdale approached the machine cautiously. "That's odd," he said. "It wasn't doing this when I got here moments ago. This must mean someone is going to leave another message."

"Aren't we going to listen to it?" asked Lucy.

Mr. Dinsdale pressed the Play function on the old device. Almost immediately, a familiar voice from the future came fluttering across the speakers, accompanied by the sounds of what appeared to be an electrical overload and some minor explosions. "Wil!" cried Barry Morgan from within a space that sounded suspiciously like a submarine. "If you can hear me, this is Dad! Uhm. Can you leave some of that blue clay on the counter at the front desk?" Another voice—garbled this time, and mostly unintelligible—yelled something from a distance. "Oh, and maybe loosen one of the gates?" continued Barry. Wil knew his father well enough to know that Barry Morgan was getting confused.

"Not gates," he heard Lucy cry from somewhere nearby, and in the not-too-distant future. "Crates!"

"Oh, right. Crates! Also, tell Mr. Dinsdale to duck—"

"Duck!!"

Now came a roaring, thunderous sound from the answering machine—it sounded almost as if a giant explosion of some kind had occurred wherever the message emanated from. The sheer decibel level coming through the speakers caused Wil, Lucy, and Dinsdale to blanch a little and glance at each other. Then, there was silence.

"*Greetings, Wil Morgan,*" came an all-too-familiar metallic voice through the temporal ether. "*Kindly turn your attention to the far end of the perpetual motion section of the museum—*"

The second, unintelligible voice yelled again from a distance. This was followed by some kind of crackling sound, like static. Finally, a distant sound of quiet sobbing could be heard.

"Oh, and make sure you bring the lightning catcher," said Barry, just as the chaotic message from the future ended abruptly. Wil, Lucy, and Dinsdale could only stare at each other, nonplussed.

"Well," said Dinsdale, reacting the quickest, "that was a bit random. But it seems we have our marching orders, wouldn't you say?"

THERE WAS a sudden, ominous shaking, emanating from the general area of the museum lobby, and the lights inside the entire museum flickered. Unless Wil missed his guess, that would be a legion of backup ninja-bots massing outside the front doors of the museum. If they managed to get inside, the unfortunate creatures were about to encounter a certain Miss Mary Gold, which would no doubt play havoc with their interpretive programming and buy everyone a little extra time. Wil had just moments to figure this out.

"Come on, Wil," said Mr. Dinsdale with an increasing urgency in his voice, "think!"

"I don't know what I'm supposed to think! I thought we'd already taken care of this!"

"Haven't you ever seen that eighties movie about the man fighting terrorists from the office tower air ducts? The bad guys always come back to life right at the end—it's a documented fact!"

"Hey, we were just talking about that film!" interjected Lucy.

"Yes, but it's not a documentary! So with all due respect, would the two of you please knock it off?" cried Wil. "I'm having a crisis here and it's not helping that we're about to go off on a tangent about some Hollywood movie! I need to concentrate!"

"You don't need to concentrate, Wil. That's the point," said Dinsdale. "You need to un-concentrate. Go with the flow. Say whatever random thing comes in your head."

"Why?"

"Because ninja-bots are very good at shooting things that behave in a predictable manner!"

"Hot chocolate!" blurted Wil, suddenly.

"What?"

"Hot chocolate! I don't know . . . it just came out, and I felt I needed to say it out loud. Hot chocolate. And also, I think we should lay down some paper clips on the floor inside the revolving door. Why? I have no idea. But let's do it anyway."

"That's it! That's the utterly random mental chaos I was looking for! No one's going to predict that response! Anything else?"

"Yes!" cried Wil as he warmed fully to the task. "Tell one of the Roberts to fetch that lightning-in-a-bottle exhibit and have it at the ready. Let's get Engelbert and my dad out here on the double . . . and somebody fetch me a crowbar!"

"I don't think violence is the answer, Wil," said Dinsdale. "I'd rather we tried diplomacy first. Even with someone as repugnant as Marcus James."

"I'm not going to hit anyone," replied Wil with a flourish worthy of a British secret agent. "I'm going to open one of those crates."

Mr. Dinsdale seemed spurred into sudden and decisive action—the old man was suddenly overcome with a demeanor of lucidity and competence—one that Wil had experienced before. Dinsdale was getting his way, and now he meant business.

"Lucy," said the curator, "please go down to the lobby and ask Mary to spread as many paper clips as possible by the revolving door. Then please fetch Wil's father and my cousin, Engelbert, as requested. Robert's on security duty inside the brown door at the back of the atrium; tell him to put on some hot chocolate and fetch the lightning catcher from its display shelf, and have him bring us a crowbar. Wil, do you still have the kit and caboodle?"

Wil fetched the remnants from his pocket: half of his original lump of blue clay, a bent paper clip, and the beeping Sequitur. Two of the items seemed utterly useless, in direct proportion to the immensity of the Sequitur's incredible powers. Nevertheless, if Wil had learned any lesson this week, it was that random and seemingly useless things always had the potential to do something amazing. Such as himself, for example.

One of the tiny will-o'-the-wisps floated by Wil's face. On a whim, he placed the slightly bent remnant of the paper clip inside it, and watched with amazement as the little creature floated away, clutching the small piece of metal within its plasma frame. He suspected this might be of later significance, simply because everything random that happened inside the museum was usually of some significance or other.

⚮

MOMENTS LATER, as Wil and Dinsdale moved back toward the atrium end of the upper hallway, Lucy came back into view ahead of Will's dad and Cousin Engelbert. Barry and Engelbert huffed and puffed as they lugged the old Lemon computer and a dozen file folders. Behind them, a squadron of John Keely's flying globes moved in formation, whereupon the flying machines formed into a line and took off in the direction of the Temporal Exhibit room. A couple of Roberts rushed by at the end of the hallway with a toolbox. Wil was astounded to notice a few of the empty wooden crates in the hallway shuffling out of the corner of his eye, as if with anticipation.

"Wil!" cried Lucy. "Marcus James's people have cordoned off the end of the street! There's a glowing blue light outside the museum entrance! What do we do?"

"Show my dad and Engelbert to the empty room that used to house the Levity box! It's the one connected to Lucy's Magic Locker! Hurry!"

"Where are we going?" asked Barry, who was looking like a pensioner who'd just been introduced into a massive online video game and was trying to work out how to use the controls.

"Don't worry, Dad!" called Wil in response. "Just stick with Cousin Engelbert and get us those accounting reports as soon as you can! I'll send you up some hot chocolate! We're relying on you!"

"Right-o!" yelled his dad as Lucy whisked him away toward the mostly empty room where Wil had previously seen her ghost. Looking rather pleased with this turn of events, odd little Cousin Engelbert set off in hot pursuit.

Mr. Dinsdale paused for a moment, put his index finger to his nose, and gave Wil a knowing chuckle. "I see where you're going with this, Wil. Bravo!"

"Do you?" replied Wil. "Because honestly, Mr. Dinsdale, if you know where I'm going, perhaps you'd be kind enough to give me directions!"

"It'll all be clear very soon!" said Dinsdale, cheerfully. "Now, let's see about those crates. I'll go and find our Robert in charge of maintenance."

As the curator set off down the hallway, the building shook in alarming fashion. Wil looked first toward Lucy, to make sure she had led his father and Engelbert to a position of relative safety. While Phase Two was in the nascent stages of planning it was also—by necessity—in the early stages of implementation. Wil paused for a second. May as well head down to the main lobby, he reasoned. He'd later conclude it was the Sequitur in one pocket and his mildly astonishing Lemon phone in his other pocket that gave him a false sense of security. And he'd blame them both equally for what happened next.

❦

At the bottom of the stairs, Wil was mildly amused to see Mary Gold standing calmly in her greeting booth watching with semidetachment as the two large goons Marcus had employed for his earlier visit to the museum struggled to extricate themselves from the revolving door. As instructed by future-Barry, Wil placed his remaining lump of blue clay on the end of Mary's counter before turning his attention to the scene unfolding at the museum's entrance. One of the goons seemed to have entered to the left of the door, while the second must have assumed it was an anticlockwise method of ingress. Either way, one of the two huge men had been wrong, and now they were both completely stuck. Outside, a giant blue light glowed and faded with a slow, dangerous pulse.

Mary smacked her gum, sending out waves of invisible disdain that threatened to derail the men's confidence entirely. Neither of these two massive specimens was taking her affront to their manhood very well at all.

"Let us out of here!" yelled one of the goons. "I'm warning you, lady! This is gonna go bad for you!"

"Badly," said Wil as he sidled toward the door with as much fake disinterest as he could muster.

"What?" replied the goon.

"Badly. It's not, 'gonna go bad.' It's 'gonna go badly.' Even though 'gonna' isn't really an acceptable contraction."

Wil had learned as a child that the best way to deal with goons—the more muscle-bound the better—was to confuse them. For while the human bicep was something anyone with a little patience could build up to an impressive size, the human brain was less a variable and more something a person was born with. Goons, in his experience, were rarely born with very large ones.

A quick peek through the glass panes revealed a couple of large tank-like vehicles waiting patiently for the chance to blow something up. To one side, a few annoyed ninja-bots zipped about from side to side, as if pacing up and down. And at the very center of the massed forces outside the museum sat Marcus James at the command of his giant blue escape pod, which had sprouted large cannons on either side. The entire area seemed to be charged with dangerous energy— every so often, a small electrical discharge would crackle out of Marcus's escape pod and flow across the attending ninja-bots, causing them to twitch and look even more agitated. As one of the bots passed by Genghis on the pavement outside, a small piece of metal from one of the Pinto's wiper blades suddenly flew off the car and stuck to the creature's side, as if drawn by a powerful magnetic force.

Despite his inner terror, Wil waved a friendly hand toward the TV pitchman and smiled as sweetly as he possibly could, just so he could display the effectiveness of his own, competing brand of toothpaste.

"Hiya, Marcus!" called Wil, sweetly. "We'll be with you in a minute! We just have to help your two goons over here! They've gotten themselves into a bit of a sticky wicket!"

Inside his giant blue globe, Marcus James glowered. Clearly, the pitchman was considering firing his cannons right there and then, and ending the conflict before it had really gotten under way. Luckily for everyone concerned, a couple of his assets were blocking a clear shot.

However, Wil was alarmed to notice the back of one of the tank devices open to reveal a detail of slightly smaller-than-normal bots, which promptly filed into a line to await their master's command.

"Not sure what you've got in mind out there," said Wil with as much artificial sweetener as his voice could muster, "but you might want to rethink whatever it is you're about to do."

By this time, Marcus James had given up any pretense of trying to keep up appearances; he had developed an unreasonable loathing for Wil that threatened to bubble out of his semiplastic skin and clog up the controls of his escape pod. "You think you've won, Mr. Morgan. But you haven't won anything at all. All you did was delay the inevitable, and cause me a slight headache on a Thursday evening."

"That's good to hear. I'd hate to think you have any lawsuits coming your way because you just bared your backside—I mean literally and figuratively—on national television."

"Oh, I'm sure you've caused a blip or two on the radar, nothing more. The stock market is going to experience a slight downturn, and by the time the bell rings on Monday morning my paid speculators will have turned this awkward event into a profit. They're good at what they do, and I pay them well for it."

"Also good to hear. What are you going to do about all those unsold golf clubs? Can I still have my upgrade?"

"I'll deliver it to you personally," said Marcus James from within gritted and impossibly white teeth. Clearly, he was ill prepared to combat sarcasm, no matter the size of his cannons.

The two goons were now so inextricably stuck inside the revolving door that it would take no less than a fire truck and the Jaws of Life to extricate them. Outside the museum entrance, confused ninja-bots wandered aimlessly. Wil felt slightly embarrassed for the poor automatons, as they seemed to be growing ever more morose by the second. Perhaps it was the effect of all the stray electrical discharge, he reasoned. If only his mother had been here to witness the chaos. This was exactly the kind of random and potentially explosive situation she would have loved.

Wil moved back into the atrium, chuckling. Someone was going to have to make a decision.

At the counter, Mary Gold was still busy smacking her gum. "Mary," said Wil, "would you please go up and tell Mr. Dinsdale we might be expecting visitors in a few minutes? I think we should make a stand in the Perpetual Exhibit." Mary smacked her gum in a manner intended to convey her disdain for menial tasks and floated off in the direction of the stairs. At the same time, one of the Roberts entered from a side door bearing a tray of hot chocolate. He carried a crowbar under one arm and the lightning catcher under the other.

"Mr. Dinsdale said you might be needing these," said the raspy-voiced Robert as Wil extracted the crowbar. "Is there anything else I can do for you?"

"Not unless you can see into the future," replied Wil. He removed the green glass bottle from underneath Robert's other arm, and took a cup of hot chocolate for good measure. "I can't be sure how all of this is going to shake down but whatever we decide to do, I think we'd better hurry. Can you take the rest of this hot chocolate up to my father and Cousin Engelbert, please? Dad always works better with hot chocolate."

Over at the door, the two goons had finally managed to extricate themselves from their predicament and had moved back into the street to face the music. A disturbingly coordinated sound of weaponry being armed echoed across the buildings outside. Wil guessed a tactical assault on the museum was about to go down in roughly the same manner—and at the same speed—as Marcus James's share prices.

"Afraid not," said the Robert. "We usually follow Mr. Dinsdale's lead in situations like this."

"Oh, this sort of thing happens a lot, does it?"

"A lot more than you'd think," said the Robert, enigmatically. And with that parting comment, the handyman headed off upstairs with the tray while Wil sipped at his cup of hot chocolate.

WITHIN MOMENTS, Robert had crested the stairs and headed off into the bowels of the museum. Wil was now alone in the atrium, save for a few of John Keely's wayward flying globes, and the little will-o'-the-wisps that seemed to delight in chasing them. Out of the corner of his eye, a couple of the wooden crates tried to grab his attention. Outside, a smaller ninja-bot armed with a blowtorch was rapidly dismantling the hinges on the revolving door. Wil smiled to himself. No doubt even the most vicious and bloodthirsty automated killing machine would think twice before attempting to navigate the museum's revolving door in the accepted, conventional manner. He could hardly blame Marcus James and his cronies for being cautious in that respect.

Wil grabbed the crowbar and moved toward one of the crates closest to the greeting desk. He dragged it over to one side and placed the crowbar inside one of its wooden slats. In his peripheral vision, the other crates seemed to shuffle in an agitated fashion. Wil paid them no mind. For unknown reasons, his future father (or someone close by) had instructed him to open one of these things, and this was no doubt as a response to whatever was inside, and its potential usefulness in defeating the maddened pitchman who was now moments from entering the museum. As Wil pushed down the crowbar with a slight grunt, a strange feeling began to nag at his mind. For some reason, he could smell mushrooms. He moved to a second slat, and loosened it slightly. All Wil now had to do was pull up the top of the crate to reveal its contents. He paused for a second, listening to his inner nagging feeling, which had been quite a helpful ally over the last few days. The growing smell of mushrooms threatened to overwhelm Wil's gag reflex. Intuitively, he closed his eyes and pulled the top off the crate. Then, with as much self-control as he could muster, he moved back toward the greeting counter without so much as casting a glance in the direction of the open crate. No, he decided; this little riddle would be left for someone else to decipher.

Wil positioned himself at the counter facing the main entrance, where the smaller ninja-bot had almost finished its task. Despite his curiosity regarding the open crate's contents, he was going to be damned before he looked first at the contents of the crate. He was immensely disturbed by the notion he could feel eyes boring into the left side of his head. Nearby crates rattled in a manner alarmingly similar to the rattle in his apartment pipes. But still he refused to look.

The Lemon phone buzzed insistently in his left pocket, while the Sequitur seemed to tremble softly in his other pocket. He fished the

Sequitur out of his pocket and placed it on the counter next to the lump of blue clay, just in case. He wasn't sure if it would even work now, since he'd left his stolen Air-Max 4000 in the back of Lucy's Ford Pinto. With a resigned sigh, he fished inside his pocket and produced the Lemon phone. SARA's interactive voice function was somehow activated. No doubt, the maniacal phone wished to discuss matters.

"*Greetings, Wil Morgan,*" SARA began as Wil tapped on her glass screen. "*Would you like me to look up 'what should I do now?' on the Internet?*"

"No thank you, SARA," replied Wil, cautiously. "Do you have anything relevant on ninja-bots or giant glass blue escape marbles?"

"*Ninja bots are theoretical weapons whose early prototype designs were abandoned by the Industricorp Corporation as a result of their instability under test conditions. They are impervious to fire, explosions, and attempts at reprogramming. Industricorp's other assets include a ninety percent global market share of skyscraper elevators and the chain of coffee shops known as Mug O' Joe's.*"

"Yes, I really should have seen that coming." Wil thought for a moment. "Why were they unstable under test conditions? Do they blow up if you overload their memory banks, or something?"

"*Negative, Wil Morgan. Ninja-bots are merely a theoretical design whose existence cannot be proven.*"

"That's good to know," Wil replied, wryly, as the main revolving door at the museum entrance clattered inward and four or five ninja-bots scuttled toward his position. As they came, hundreds of scattered paper clips began to fly across the atrium. The little pieces of metal caromed into the magnetized hulls of the ninja-bots, creating surreal miniexplosions every time they hit pay dirt. By the time the ninja-bots had arrived at the greeting desk, they were covered in paper clips. A strange blue glow began to illuminate the broken door from outside.

Wil surreptitiously placed SARA and the lightning catcher into his pockets. He began to reach for the Sequitur, whose remarkable— almost impossibly useful—properties had proven very handy in a pinch. But for some reason he couldn't fathom, he opted for the little lump of blue clay instead. Wil quickly grasped the lump of clay in his hand and lifted it above his head in a sign of unconditional surrender just as the bloodthirsty ninja-bots descended upon his position. He picked up his cup of hot chocolate with his free hand. If he was going to meet his end at the hands of a murderous automaton, he reasoned, at least he was going to meet it in comfort.

The blue glow now filled up the entire door fame. Moments later, Wil was astonished to see Marcus James enter wearing a bright-blue glowing exoskeleton. To his eye, Marcus looked like a refugee from a bad science fiction movie. As the TV pitchman stomped toward the counter, little waves of electrical energy sparked out of his exoskeleton with every heavy footstep. These drifting pockets of Tesla-like energy roamed across the waiting ninja-bots, causing the creatures to glitch, slightly. They seemed slightly embarrassed to be caught in such a degrading situation but resolutely stayed at attention.

"Hello, Marcus," Wil called, cheerily. "Did you come with my Air-Max 3000 upgrade?"

"No," Marcus James replied with the kind of sneer that a professional poker player would have been proud of. "I've come for a discussion. It's going to be a little one-sided, I'm afraid. Where's the old man?"

"Which one?"

"You know which one."

"I do? Well, that narrows it down."

Marcus James's eyes narrowed, dangerously. In terms of comedic articulation he knew he was wielding a slingshot against Wil's heavy cannons. In reality, however, the TV pitchman was wielding actual cannons and wasn't about to let himself get outgunned in a different sort of battle.

"I'm going to level with you, *Mr.* Morgan. This is not going to end well for you." Marcus's blue exoskeleton glowed, as if to affirm his murderous intent. "My people have already identified your accomplice, a certain Miss Lucy Price. Since she is a customer at one of my banks, steps have been taken to freeze her assets and bring about her eviction from her place of business. No more Lucy's Magic Locker, I'm afraid. I'm sure the world breathes a collective sigh of relief."

Wil sipped casually on his hot chocolate, and tried to ignore the ever-growing sense that a roughly four-feet-tall shadowy figure was now standing inside the opened wooden crate, just barely visible in his peripheral vision. "I'm sure it does. By the way, before we get into this, I just want to make it clear that you should under no circumstances look at that crate over to my left."

"Thank you so much for the advice. I will do my utmost."

"It's for the best," said Wil with a grin carefully calculated to infuriate. "Now what can I do you for, Mr. James?"

Marcus James's exoskeleton seemed to fold in on itself—small, revolving panels along both sides collapsed inward, revealing nasty-looking laser weapons built into the suit. "I would like," said the pitchman with just the right amount of carefully calculated menace, "to get my property back before there is any more damage, intended or otherwise."

"I'm sure you would. Now, just a couple of points of order before you shoot me, if you don't mind. I've had a phone call from my dad, which means if you were going to kill me, you would already have done it by now. I'm sure he wouldn't have bothered to call me if you were going to kill me anyway."

"What on Earth are you rambling about?"

"It's a bit of a temporally anomalous situation. I know I don't really understand it so I'm pretty sure you won't. Now about those paper clips: they're significant, as is this piece of clay I'm holding in my right hand and the cup of hot chocolate I'm holding in my left. I don't know exactly why but I'd say we're about to find out."

To the side of Wil's awareness, the strange black shadow inside the box seemed to be growing in size, so that it was less of a figure and more of a growing mass. Wil felt a shiver run up his spine. The smell of mushrooms was becoming overwhelming.

Marcus James raised his right arm to reveal yet another weapon protruding from below his wrist. "I'll give you one last chance: tell me

what you've done with my property or this hand cannon you're looking at will most definitely be discharged in your direction. Do I make
myself clear?"

"For once, yes." Wil gulped. It was now or never. In his peripheral
vision, the black mass was clearly moving toward them. Wil refused to
allow his eyes to wander from Marcus James's glare. "Incidentally," he
said with a level of saccharine equivalent to an American factory full
of soft drinks, "I meant what I said: don't look at that crate over there."

"I'm not falling for such an obvious diversionary tactic, you buf-
foon."

"Glad to hear it. That means you won't notice when it sneaks up on
you."

What—?"

To Wil, the next few moments seemed almost frozen, like they had
been written into a book and could be stopped or reversed with the
simple application of a bookmark. He'd carefully judged the measure
of his opponent's resolve, and knew that a man as greedy and weak
willed as Marcus James would always be the one to crack first under
duress. That is why it was to no one's surprise—not even Marcus James
himself—that the TV pitchman cracked first.

Marcus turned to look in the direction of the growing black mass,
which at this point simply could not be ignored. At the exact moment
it was being detected, the black mass suddenly folded in on itself and
vanished from Marcus James's awareness, leaving only a residual impression of something extremely nightmarish and unpleasant. Using
this momentary distraction to his advantage, Wil did the most arbitrary (and, frankly, pointless) thing he could think of: he threw his cup
of hot chocolate over Marcus's blue exoskeleton suit.

Absolutely nothing happened.

Wil blinked. That had not gone at all as planned, despite his absolute lack of preplanning. Slowly—in the incredulous manner of a lion

that has just been bitten by a small deer—Marcus blinked. He looked at Wil, astonished, and burst into as genuine a fit of giggles as a man of his minimal capacity for humor could be expected.

"Did you . . ." Marcus tried to gather himself. "Did you just throw coffee all over me?"

"It was hot chocolate."

"Ah, I see. So hot chocolate is more likely to short-circuit an Industricorp Hammerhead A27 military-grade exoskeleton?" Marcus was trying hard to contain his delight, which made him seem all the more obnoxious.

"I don't know," replied Wil, defiantly. He couldn't help but pout a little bit, given that his expectations of success had been so sorely dented. It had been a day full of triumphs, and this sudden setback was the last thing he might have thought would happen.

Marcus James's hand cannon began to whine as it came to a full charge. At that moment, the tiny will o'-the-wisp carrying Wil's paper clip floated in on the scene and fluttered toward Marcus's position.

"I'm going to have my evidence back," said Marcus with a villain's flourish. "But since my people have this museum on lockdown, I'm not entirely sure I'll need you to help me get it. Goodbye and good riddance, Mr. Morgan."

Marcus began to depress the built-in trigger for his hand cannon, which initiated yet another wave of sparking electricity that floated across the area, like rippling water. At that moment, the little globule of plasma moved to a position directly above Marcus, just as a small puddle of hot chocolate dripped down the exoskeleton's leg and made contact with a few of the remaining discarded paper clips.

With a resigned shrug, Wil flipped the small lump of clay he'd been holding. It narrowly missed the will-o'-the-wisp, causing the fairy-like creature to flutter a little and drop its precious cargo. Almost immediately, the discarded paper clip landed in the puddle of hot chocolate just as the wave of sparks flew over it, and from what Wil could tell as the resultant explosion threw him backward across the counter, it completed a full circuit that fried the operating systems of everything in the vicinity. By happy coincidence, the immediate vicinity happened to contain a large number of very surprised ninja-bots who until the moment of their demise had been programmed to believe they were invulnerable. The first of the bots exploded with a vigor normally reserved for a dynamited mine shaft, while the rest of the creatures took this opportunity to whirl about in frantic circles, blasting their cannons in whichever direction they happened to feel was worth obliterating. Outside, a number of presumably tank-fueled explosions rocked the front of the building. Marcus James screamed loudly as his exoskeleton went into full "armor" mode, locking up his faceplate and rendering him temporarily immobile as bullets spattered off his chest and limbs. Thinking quickly, Wil grabbed the Sequitur from the counter and made a beeline for the stairs, ducking underneath stray hollow-points as he made his escape. And to the forlorn sounds of Marcus's yells of anger, he made his way up the stairs and into the hallway leading back into the museum.

AT THE top of the stairs, Mr. Dinsdale and Mary Gold were moving quickly in Wil's direction. At the far end of the hall, Lucy and Barry were also making their way up from the temporal exhibit with little Engelbert in tow, clutching a bundle of important-looking papers.

"Wil!" called Lucy with a look of relief spreading across her face. "We heard those explosions! I thought—"

"It's okay! I'm okay!" interrupted Wil so that Lucy wouldn't have to complete her thought. "Everything's not okay, though: I think Marcus James will be up here any second now! He's a bit miffed at me!"

"What did you do?"

"I don't know but you would've liked it!"

The little museum curator made his way breathlessly to Wil's side, with Mary Gold gliding alongside him. "I'm glad to see you made it out alive, Wil! I never doubted you, of course!"

"Gee thanks!" yelled Wil in response as he took stock of the moment. "Where are we at with that electricity bill?"

"Wil, you're never going to believe this!" cried Barry Morgan as he, Engelbert, and Lucy made their way rapidly along the hall. "There was a discrepancy in the Edison Company's accounting! It's a miracle!"

"No! Dad, Lucy . . . we have to go back the other way!"

"What?" Barry didn't seem to "getting it" quite as quickly as Wil might have liked. And this would only lead him to "getting it" in a far less pleasant way within moments.

"Go back! Marcus James! Explosions! Ninja-bots!" yelled Wil, breathless. His protestations, however, did not seem to be having much effect. Luckily (at least for the point Wil was trying to make), the atrium below was rocked by a huge explosion, which sent strange blue flames shooting up the stairs and into the hallway.

Barry and Lucy slowed, so that Engelbert bumped into them from behind. Wil quickly turned to Mary and Dinsdale. "We've got to get to the perpetual motion machines! Hurry!"

"Why on Earth would we go in there?" asked Dinsdale with a look of genuine confusion. "Those machines are practically useless beyond just whirring about and violating the first law of thermodynamics."

"Because SARA told us to from the future!" called Wil as he set off toward the room full of pointless machines. "Come on! Hurry!"

Farther down the hall, Barry, Lucy, and Engelbert were now shuffling about and looking confused. Barry seemed to be taking the fact that Wil wasn't interested in his heroic accounting conclusions to heart. "Wil," he said, halfheartedly. "I did as you asked. We've made a major breakthrough."

"That's nice, Dad. Can we please go now?"

"Why? We have all the proof we need to end this thing once and for all."

"I have a feeling we might find something like heavy machine guns or bulletproof armor more useful, Dad!"

As if to help Wil make his point, the building was suddenly rocked by another tremendous explosion and all of the lights went out. A blue glow suddenly appeared at the far end of the hall in the direction of the atrium stairs. "That'll be imminent death," said Wil as he gently pushed his father in the direction of the perpetual exhibits. "He's not really all that interested in proof right now."

"I drew up a very nice legal agreement!" said Engelbert, hopefully. "We'll certainly be able to get this sorted out once both parties have reviewed and signed!"

"Again, wonderful," agreed Wil. "But I tend to think one of the parties isn't really going to be very accommodating right now." He gently shoved Cousin Engelbert through the near-darkness toward the perpetual motion exhibition room.

"Ah! I think I'm beginning to understand!" called Dinsdale as he and Mary now hustled in the direction Wil wanted everyone to go. "The perpetual motion machines . . . of course!"

"Oh yeah?" Wil was beginning to pick up a head of steam—partly fueled by his general sense of agitation but mostly fueled by a sense of self-preservation. "Would you mind explaining to the rest of us, Mr. Dinsdale?"

"The perpetual exhibits don't need electricity!" cried the old man. "They work just fine by themselves!"

"Doing what?"

"It doesn't matter! I'm sure you'll think of something!" And having satisfied his cryptic urges, Mr. Dinsdale forged toward the perpetual exhibition room just as the far end of the hallway caved in and a very testy blue monstrosity came through it, yelling profanities.

Not to lose the momentum he had so recently gained, Barry Morgan found Wil in the hallway as the group clattered toward the room with hollow-point bullets whizzing above their heads. "As it turns out, Wil, there was a clerical error!" he yelled above the noise of bullets clattering into the walls.

"What?"

"A clerical error! The old electricity bill was paid in full a century ago! Plus the thirteen-cent late fee!"

"That's nice, Dad! Can we please take this up later?"

"What?"

The conversation was getting out of hand in more ways than one. "I'd like to focus on survival, if you don't mind, Dad!" yelled Wil above the whine of Marcus James's laser weapons. "It's just that I've met a very nice girl who I think could be the one and I'd like to be around to find out if our second official date is as interesting as the first one!"

"Oh!"

Nearby, Lucy was enjoying herself thoroughly. "Is this still our first date?" she asked, impishly, as a nearby shelf carrying combine harvester parts from ancient Sumeria clattered to the floor by her feet. "Only I'm beginning to have second thoughts!"

WIL AND his group managed to round a corner into the perpetual exhibition room just as a final spattering of bullets went across the wall next to them. At the far end of the hall, the guns fell silent, and only an ominous blue glow now remained, which grew in intensity as the exoskeleton approached. Marcus was considering his options, which seemed limited to shooting hollow-point bullets or blasting people with his lasers.

A quick glance about the room revealed a disturbing scarcity of additional exits. But Wil already knew that escape was not an option—he was going to follow the random set of instructions about to be given to him by his future dad. Mary Gold glided her way to the back of the exhibits and stood next to a shelf, while Dinsdale and Engelbert chose the relative safety of a perpetual motion machine that looked like an egg and had supposedly been a gift to Sir Winston Churchill from a race of aliens from Sixty-one Cygni. Wil and Lucy set up shop across the room behind a device that looked like a pinball machine, which—upon further inspection—turned out to be a pinball machine.

"Now what?" asked Lucy, who in Wil's opinion was acting a little too wide-eyed and enthusiastic, considering the probabilities facing her.

"I don't know—*wait*!" Suddenly remembering the museum's logic, Wil fished the Lemon phone from his pocket.

"*Greetings, Wil Morgan*," said SARA cautiously. "*Would you like the latest stock market projections for Marcus James Industries, Incorporated?*"

"Not right now, SARA, but thank you anyway. I'm sure that'll be fun later. For the moment, please dial the Museum of Curioddity's main number."

"*Dialing . . .*"

SARA's rudimentary cell phone function—almost an afterthought to the Lemon phone's designers, it seemed—now sent out its request into the ether. Down the hallway in Mr. Dinsdale's office, a phone began to ring.

"What are you doing?" hissed Lucy, who was finally beginning to get a more accurate sense of her predicament as the bluish glow of Marcus's exoskeleton closed in on the entrance to her hiding spot.

"I'm not doing anything," whispered Wil through gritted teeth. "I think it's doing it all by itself. Whatever 'it' is! Dad! Here!"

Wil tossed the Lemon phone to his father across the room. Barry picked it up and listened as, presumably, Mr. Dinsdale's odd little message repeated itself once more.

"There's no one answering!" wailed Barry.

"Dad, that's not important right now! What's important is that you do exactly as I say, okay?"

"Okay!"

"And don't hang up!"

꩜

WIL PONDERED for a moment, for a moment was all he was going to get. Outside the room, the blue glow was increasing in intensity: this suggested not only that Marcus James was getting closer, but also that he was not going to be arriving in a very good mood at all.

Next to Wil, Lucy breathed heavily with anticipation. She either had a death wish, or a delusional belief that she and the group were going to come out of this unscathed, no matter the certainty that they were all going to die at the hands of an angry maniac.

The Sequitur beeped inside his pocket. Without his trusty Air-Max 4000, Wil wasn't sure he'd be able to concentrate on relaxing properly. He had a terrible feeling the strange device was about as useful to him right now as a screen door on a submarine.

All in all, things were not looking entirely positive. And yet despite all of this, Wil felt a sort of exhilaration, as if he were transported in time and headed down a snow-covered hill on the back of a tea tray. Across the room, his father seemed genuinely excited to be involved in something life threatening. Today was the first time Wil had seen his dad enthusiastic since he was seven years old and had accurately recited his nine-times table in front of some relatives at Thanksgiving.

If there was going to be a way out of this, Wil reasoned, it was going to require quite a stretch of the imagination. And if he wasn't going to trust his imagination after the week he'd experienced, exactly when would be the right time?

Wil steeled himself. For the first time in years, he felt completely in control of his destiny, simply by giving up any semblance of control and trusting to random chance. He rolled his English penny over and over in his pocket.

"Mom," Wil whispered quietly in the general direction of the ceiling, "I hope to God you know what you're doing."

Lucy leaned in and kissed his cheek. "That was from her," she said.

Comforted by this notion, Wil let go of the English penny and pulled out the lightning catcher, which he had been carrying in his other pocket. Quite a miniature storm had been building inside the green bottle since the last time he'd looked inside. And it was at this exact moment—as Wil stared into the heart of the storm—that the random connectivity of chance, imagination, and sheer, blind luck collided in his cerebral cortex, and he knew exactly what he was going to do.

Dad!" Wil cried from across the room, "I need you to leave a message for me! Don't ask questions because it's not going to make any sense! Just tell me to leave some of that blue clay I was carrying on the counter at the front desk! And Mr. Dinsdale, I need you to go and stand in the middle of the aisle, in plain sight! When I give the word, duck!"

"Righty ho! I remember your Dad leaving that message on the answering machine!" called Dinsdale, cheerfully, as he emerged from his hiding place and moved into the center of the room.

Wil grasped the lightning catcher firmly in his hand and positioned it like a grenade. The bottle trembled slightly. He crouched down below the level of the pinball table and positioned himself so that Mr. Dinsdale was not standing directly in the line of the doorway. Outside, the ominous blue glow was getting closer.

Dutifully—if a little hesitantly—Barry Morgan cradled the Lemon phone closely to his mouth and obliged. "Wil!" he cried into the receiver. "If you can hear me, this is Dad. Uhm." Barry was obviously beginning to feel a little self-conscious, considering the recipient of his message was hiding behind a pinball machine just a few feet away with a lightning grenade at the ready. Wil widened his eyes and gave his father an urgent look, hoping to spur Barry into action. "Can you leave some of that blue clay on the counter at the front desk?"

Outside, Marcus James had hastened his stomping and was making a beeline for the entrance to the perpetual exhibit, sensing his opponents had given the game away. "Dinsdale!" cried the maddened pitchman. "There's nowhere to hide, you old coot! Give me back my property!"

"Attaboy, Dad!" hissed Wil. "Now tell me to open one of the crates! And remind Mr. Dinsdale that when Marcus comes in he needs to duck!"

"Oh, and maybe loosen one of the gates?" called Barry into the Lemon phone.

"Not gates!" cried Lucy, exasperated. "Crates!"

"Oh, right. Crates! Also, tell Mr. Dinsdale to duck—"

WITH A crackle of electrical discharge, a blue glow skirted the corner of the door and became a rather angry individual with overly white teeth, dressed in an exoskeleton. Upon seeing Dinsdale standing before him, Marcus quickly leveled his hand cannon.

Wil tossed the lightning catcher directly at Dinsdale's head. "Duck!" he yelled as loudly as he could. Quickly, the little curator bent at the waist so that he could watch the proceedings from a very different angle, and the green bottle sailed over his head.

From Marcus James's perspective, Dinsdale suddenly disappeared from view, to be replaced by a rapidly approaching green glass bottle, which promptly smashed into the exoskeleton's chest plate and proceeded to do something most unusual. From within the bottle, a huge bolt of lightning shot out in all directions, fritzing half of the perpetual motion machines nearby, and most of Marcus James's onboard systems. With a shriek of pain, the overzealous pitchman staggered forward, clutching at his various armored body parts. He began to rapidly shed his protective headgear and gloves, while a very localized tempest raged all around him.

"He's short-circuiting!" Lucy yelled to Wil above the noise of the storm. "What are we going to do?"

"I don't know!" cried Wil. "I didn't get this far along in the planning phase!"

Another massive bolt of lightning suddenly shot out of the localized thunderstorm, causing Wil to dive for cover as it struck the pinball machine next to him. Lucy let out a small yelp of fear, and quickly backed away. Just as suddenly as it had arrived, the little storm folded in upon itself, leaving a man with slightly smoking hair in its wake, and a blue exoskeleton desperately trying to reboot its operating systems.

There was silence for a moment. A familiar metallic voice now made its presence known. *"Greetings, Wil Morgan,"* said SARA from the Lemon phone that Barry Morgan was still holding. *"Kindly turn your attention to the far end of the perpetual motion section of the museum."*

Marcus moaned slightly, like a golfer who'd just used his Air-Max 4000 to hit a hole in one only to realize there were no immediate witnesses. Wil turned his attention to the far end of the room, where Leonardo da Vinci's malfunctioning Perpetual Emotion machine purred happily along, throwing out a few sparks with which to entice its next victim. Before Wil could even fathom how events had handily unfolded in his favor—and before Marcus could recover and bring his vicious machinery back online—Wil suddenly grabbed the pitchman and shoved him roughly in the direction of the Perpetual Emotion machine. Marcus wobbled slightly, and with the weight of his exoskeleton's immobile legs rendering control virtually impossible, he clattered a few feet and toppled toward Leonardo's sparking monstrosity. With a yelp, Marcus raised his hand to prevent himself from falling into the machine's open orifice. But it was too late: his raised arm went all the way in to the shoulder, sending a huge shower of sparks across the immediate vicinity.

Wil, Lucy, and the others shielded their eyes as a mass of sparks flooded out of the diabolical machine, giving Marcus the appearance of a steel rod that had just been kissed by a welding torch. He immediately began to weep giant tears that came from the bottom of his cold, black heart—dredging up emotions he hadn't felt, presumably, since his first year of being the most unpleasant kid in the class at elementary school.

"It's not fair!" sobbed Marcus. "I don't know where it all went wrong!" Sparks were now playing across the remains of his defunct exoskeleton, which clearly knew when it was beaten and had mercifully switched itself off rather than endure an existential crisis of its own. "Why don't we ever know where we're going?" continued Marcus. "And what do we even find when we get there? It's all so pointless!"

WIL AND Mr. Dinsdale approached the machine cautiously as Barry and Engelbert gathered up fallen papers. Over at the pinball machine, Lucy and Mary had found each other intact and were trying to work out what to do next.

Barry seemed to realize that SARA was still in his possession, and still connected to a few hours ago. He stood up abruptly to close the connection. Before him, little shards of shattered green glass were spread across the room. "Oh, and make sure you bring the lightning catcher," said Barry into the receiver before closing the connection for good.

"Now what do we do?" said Wil as he and the curator watched Marcus James's existential overload with something akin to mild indifference. "Do we let him out?"

"Eventually, I'm sure," replied Dinsdale. "But let's have him stew in there for a while. He did try to fill us full of hollow-points, after all."

By now, Marcus had merely fallen into quiet sobs, accompanied by the occasional rhetorical question about the pointlessness of existence and the futility of trying to make anything of it. The sparks around him had dissipated somewhat but no one in their right mind was going to go anywhere near Leonardo's infernal Perpetual Emotion machine—not in a month of Sundays and for all the tea in China.

Lucy moved to Wil and put his arm around her waist. "We can't just leave him there. Eventually, we're going to have to call the police, aren't we?"

MR. DINSDALE allowed himself a smile. "Perhaps not," he said as his smile morphed from mirthful to a delicious, unrepentant wickedness in the blinking of an eye. "I think I might have a better idea."

CHAPTER SIXTEEN

———◆———

THE ONE thing Wil Morgan had concluded from his recent exploits was that a brand-new lease on life comes with substantially lower payments.

It was the end of a remarkable week, and the beginning of a new era. Though he hadn't slept all night, Wil Morgan was content to stand at the end of Upside-Down Street with one eye covered and watch the early-afternoon cars flying past on the city's one-way system. From this angle—bent at the waist as he was—the vehicles appeared to be zipping along on a gravity-defying monorail—much more satisfying, he thought, than simply looking at things the way he had always been taught.

Next to him, Lucy also stood bent at the waist and looked at the world with one eye closed and her mind and heart fully open. Together, they counted the red cars passing by.

"Fifty-four!" said Lucy. She had been concentrating on this task for the past ten minutes, and Wil was beginning to think the blood was rushing to her head.

"No, that's fifty-three," he countered.

"Nope. Fifty-four. You forgot that London bus full of circus clowns."

"Oh. Right." This way up, the world was far more interesting but it tended to induce headaches. Wil stood up straight and looked around him. "Do you really think this is it?" he asked.

"Sure it is," said Lucy as she also straightened and move in close to Wil. "Only better."

Despite the lack of sleep, Wil's unthinkable Thursday had given way to a fantastic Friday. All in all, things were looking up. Mr. Dinsdale had (quite rightly) hit upon a most unique solution to the bulk of the difficulties facing the museum.

With Marcus James trapped and sobbing inside the Perpetual Emotion machine—and therefore about as captive and willing an audience as has ever succumbed to blackmail of the highest order— Cousin Engelbert had hastily drawn up an agreement between the Curioddity Museum and Marcus James Enterprises, Incorporated. This agreement outlined Marcus James's obligations in a most delightful and satisfying manner in exchange for the dropping of all charges (and Marcus's release from his existential nightmare, natch). The pitchman would provide full reimbursement of all costs associated with the attack on the museum, and full ownership of his army of lawyers, without which he would be utterly powerless. Marcus also agreed to move his banking institutions to the far end of the city and also to return all of Mr. Dinsdale's original patents. But this was not to be the end of his extremely unsatisfying week.

As it turned out, there had indeed been a clerical error involving the old electricity bill, which had indeed been paid in full, as had the original thirteen-cent late fee and its two-cent surcharge. However, further research had uncovered a nominal discrepancy in the Edison Electric Company's calculation of the original bill: a two-cent overcharge that had never been refunded. Barry and Engelbert had calculated and recalculated, using standard addition of compound interest and market standards of late fees, even-later fees, and the dreaded so-late-it's-not-even-funny fees. By their calculation, Marcus James Enterprises, Incorporated—the lien holder for the original bill and therefore the debtor for the current, updated one—owed Mr. Dinsdale in excess of $133,386,703.12. All of which was due by late Saturday afternoon, failing which a surcharge of a further three cents would be tacked on. Cousin Engelbert had dutifully—enthusiastically, even—written a brand-new bill using his best quill and ink, which he had walked over to the bank next door and hand delivered to a very confused bank teller.

At the same time, one of the Roberts had delivered a whimpering Marcus James back to the lobby of the Castle Towers, where Mr. Whatley had made his boss a cup of hot chocolate in the janitor's closet and promptly sent him back up to the empty penthouse levels in the Rat Vomit Comet. Doubtless, he would be heard from again. But certainly not anytime soon.

MR. DINSDALE wandered down the museum steps and joined Wil and Lucy. "I've been thinking," he said by way of segueing. "How would you like a job here at the museum, Wil?"

"Doing what?" replied Wil. "And yes. Sure." If he had learned anything in the last few days, it was that Mr. Dinsdale responded well when things were at their most random.

"Good," replied Dinsdale, addressing Wil's second statement first. "I think we have an opening in the security, personnel, public relations, and acquisitions department. Plus, I need someone to keep an eye on the crates in the lobby. Mary doesn't trust them."

"Do I have to work directly with Mary?"

"I wouldn't advise it. She's not easy to get along with."

"Fair enough. I accept."

"Excellent. I took the liberty of paying your landlady, Mrs. Chappell, a year's rent. She gave you a glowing reference that she countersigned with neon ink."

"That sounds like her. She's a cat, you know."

"They live among us, Wil. They live among us."

Sensing a moment unfolding, Lucy wisely took a step toward Wil, kissed him on the forehead, and moved off in the direction of the museum. "I'm going to bond with your dad," she informed him. "D'you think he likes hot chocolate?"

Wil smiled. "I think he invented hot chocolate."

"Cool. I'll take him to Mug O' Joe's. See you in an hour?"

"Absolutely."

Lucy wandered off toward the entrance to the museum, and a date with the beginning of the rest of her life (or at least his father). Wil watched her go, admiring her curves through the flowing gypsy skirt, and her anklet, and wondering to himself if she'd actually been bare-foot all the way through the Castle Towers as she was now.

Mr. Dinsdale waited for Lucy to move through the revolving door. He looked along the length of Upside-Down Street, until his eyes rested on the old cinema.

"I have such memories of that theater, Wil," said the old man. "I've seen quite a bit of magic inside those four walls."

"It's everywhere, Mr. Dinsdale, or so I'm told. You just have to know where to un-look for it."

"Indeed it is, Mr. Wil Morgan. Indeed it is."

Wil looked into the old man's twinkling eyes. "I know that look, Mr. Dinsdale: it's the one you gave me just before I took the job to find the Levity box. What are you actually trying to say?"

Dinsdale stared into the distance, seeing things with his memories, not his eyes. This was the lucid Dinsdale, the one that could hide in plain sight and never let it be known that his world was full. "I knew you'd make it back, Wil," he said after a long pause. "It was only a matter of time."

"Back? From where?"

"From that extended period of your life you wasted being someone you are not. You have a beautiful girl who adores you, a steady job, and a brand-new lease on life. Your father—a brilliant accountant, I might add—is more proud of you than he has ever been. All of this in a single week—just imagine what you could do in a month. I'll warrant you haven't felt this way since the two hundred and seventh day of your tenth year of existence."

"Excuse me?"

Slowly—very quietly—Mr. Dinsdale reached inside his pocket and produced an old English penny. He ran it in and out of his fingers a few times, wondering how to begin, how to end, and how to say everything in between. "I wanted to tell you, Wil. But I wanted it to be the right time."

Wil felt an overwhelming emptiness, just as he always did—intensified beyond measure by the power of this revelation. "You knew my mom?" he asked, as the tears welled in his eyes and his heart began to slow.

"She came by every so often to drink coffee and consult on our Tesla exhibits. I used to enjoy her visits very much. And then one day she discovered you were living inside her. So then it became every single day, for almost nine months, come rain or shine. She'd walk the exhibits and sing lullabies. I once asked her why, and do you know what she told me? She told me you were going to grow up in a world of magic that was never going to end."

"But it ended."

"It just needed to be jump-started."

"But I *lost* her."

"No you didn't, Wil. Time doesn't work that way; neither does real magic. Your mother told me something once—one of the wisest things I ever heard a person say: your eyes only see what your mind lets you believe. Did you ever hear that saying before?"

"Once or twice." The tears were drifting across his cheeks now, like it or not. Wil couldn't be sure he wanted to hear any more, yet he wouldn't have avoided listening for all the tea in China.

"And what did you ever make of what it meant?"

"I don't know. I still don't."

"Then what you are going to have to decide, Wil Morgan, is what you are prepared to believe. The rest is up to you."

Mr. Dinsdale moved away toward the Curioddity Museum then, leaving Wil under the newly repaired street sign. He watched as the old man slowly made his way to the museum steps and through the revolving door.

He thought of the past and of the future, and he pictured the place where the roads meet in between.

AND HE dreamed of his mother all around him, in every atom. Endless.